PENGUIN

BILLY BUDD, SAILOR

AND OTHER STORIES

Harold Beaver is Professor of American Literature at the University of Amsterdam. He has also edited for the Penguin English Library Herman Melville's *Redburn* and *Moby-Dick*, as well as Edgar Allan Poe's *The Narrative of Arthur Gordon Pym of Nantucket* and *The Science Fiction of Edgar Allan Poe*.

HERMAN MELVILLE

Billy Budd, Sailor

AND OTHER STORIES

SELECTED AND EDITED
WITH AN INTRODUCTION BY
HAROLD BEAVER

PENGUIN BOOKS

Penguin Books Ltd, Harmondsworth, Middlesex, England
Viking Penguin Inc., 40 West 23rd Street, New York, New York 10010, U.S.A.
Penguin Books Australia Ltd, Ringwood, Victoria, Australia
Penguin Books Canada Limited, 2801 John Street, Markham, Ontario, Canada L3R 1B4
Penguin Books (N.Z.) Ltd, 182–190 Wairau Road, Auckland 10, New Zealand

—

This selection published in the Penguin English Library 1967
Reprinted (with minor revisions) 1970
Reprinted 1972, 1973, 1975, 1976, 1977, 1978, 1979,
1980, 1981, 1982, 1983
Reprinted in Penguin Classics 1985, 1986

—

—

BILLY BUDD, SAILOR *(An Inside Narrative)* is the Reading Text as edited from a
genetic study of the manuscript by Harrison Hayford and Merton M. Sealts, Jr,
here reprinted by kind permission of the University of Chicago Press (© 1962
University of Chicago).
DANIEL ORME is reprinted from *Melville's Billy Budd*, edited by F. Barron Freeman,
by kind permission of the Harvard University Press (© 1948 by the President and
Fellows of Harvard College).

—

Made and printed in Great Britain by
Hazell Watson & Viney Limited,
Member of the BPCC Group,
Aylesbury, Bucks
Set in Linotype Georgian

CONTENTS

HERMAN MELVILLE

A Biographical Note

HERMAN MELVILLE was born on 1 August 1819 in New York City, the son of a merchant. Only twelve when his father died bankrupt, young Herman tried work as a bank clerk, as a cabin-boy on a trip to Liverpool, as an elementary schoolteacher, before shipping in January 1841 on the whaler *Acushnet*, bound for the Pacific. Deserting ship the following year in the Marquesas, he made his way to Tahiti and Honolulu, returning as ordinary seaman on the frigate *United States* to Boston, where he was discharged in October 1844. Books based on these adventures won him immediate success. By 1850 he was married, had acquired a rural estate near Pittsfield, Massachusetts (the impetuous friend and neighbour of Nathaniel Hawthorne), and was hard at work on his masterpiece, *Moby-Dick*. Here the first five stories in this collection were written. But literary success faded as fast as it had blossomed. After a visit to the Holy Land in January 1857, he turned entirely from prose, publishing only poetry in small, privately subsidized editions. In 1863, during the Civil War, he moved back to New York City, where from 1866 to 1885 he was a deputy inspector in the Custom House, and where, on 28 September 1891, he died. A draft of a final prose work, *Billy Budd, Sailor,* was left unfinished and uncollated; packed tidily away by his widow, it was not rediscovered and published until 1924.

INTRODUCTION

SHORTLY before completing *Moby-Dick*, at the age of thirty-one, married, with a one-year-old son, Melville bought a house and an estate of a hundred and sixty acres in the Berkshire Hills, two miles from Pittsfield, Massachusetts. He renamed the house 'Arrowhead', and set up as farmer and author.

As farmer he was a tolerable success. The estate prospered, paying its way and financing the author. But as professional author, ambitious to live off his literary earnings, the next seven years proved Melville a failure. Each new venture was repeatedly and harassingly frustrated. Within six years the productive half of the farm had to be sold; five months later Melville left on an extended trip, financed by his father-in-law, to England (where he visited Hawthorne), the Mediterranean and the Holy Land. At the age of thirty-six the last prose work to be published in his lifetime was completed. After the age of thirty-seven, an uncaring public were to hear no more, verse apart, from this wayward writer, this haunted, restless poet and supreme artificer – now recognized as giant among American men of letters, equal in his own sphere to Dickens, Flaubert, Tolstoy, his European contemporaries.

But the legend of a fallen Titan living out the long aftermath of his years in the twilight of the New York Custom House – a Bannadonna maimed by his own absorbed, excessive imagination – is less than a half truth. *Moby-Dick* stands as his memorial, his masterpiece, his flawed Bell-Tower; but, while admitting to Hawthorne (as for life hereafter) that 'he had pretty much made up his mind to be annihilated', Melville was far from annihilated:

his restless genius searched to the end for new forms, new parables, new witness to the Armageddon of good and evil.

It is with the work of those vital years of his mid-thirties and with *Billy Budd*, the final flower of his old age – distant outcrop of those years – unfinished, unpublished until a generation after his death, that this collection is concerned. For even from beyond the grave his Ancient Mariner's eye transfixes us, the voice weaving its spell.

At Arrowhead, landlocked on his northerly veranda (or 'piazza', as it was called), surrounded by a growing family of sons and daughters, he joined that company of introspective ex-sailors, Merrymusk, John Marr, Daniel Orme – brooding, isolated men who haunt his tales. The years of youth and adventure were inevitably past; the resources of his art had been rapidly exploited. In the six years from 1846 to 1851 six novels had been published. Shipping as a nineteen-year-old merchant seaman to Liverpool had become *Redburn*; escapades on the Marquesas and beachcombing on Moorea, *Typee*, *Omoo* and (under dense veils of spiritual and political allegory) *Mardi*; the return home on a U.S. frigate from Honolulu, *White-Jacket*; and, of course, his original signing on to the whaler *Acushnet*, for her maiden voyage out of New Bedford to the South Seas in January 1841, had been transformed in widening circles of experience, gothic allegory and deep, speculative probing into *Moby-Dick*.

There had been moments of high joy and excitement in his new home. 'The Whale' had been driven through the press; Nathaniel Hawthorne discovered as close neighbour and hailed as fellow spirit. But the reception of *Moby-Dick* was disheartening; the Hawthornes moved after little more than a year; and with the catastrophic failure of *Pierre* in 1852 and the repeated failure of applications through his father-in-law, Chief Justice Lemuel Shaw, and his fellow ex-sailor, Richard Henry Dana Jr, for a consular post abroad, the circle of his fate seemed once more to narrow, his imagination increasingly to feed on historical sources and turn in upon itself.

Two years after the publication of *Moby-Dick*, he was still in debt to Harpers for 700 dollars' advance royalties. He had a wife and three children; other than the farm, his only income was royalties. His wife noted: 'We all felt anxious about the strain on his health in the spring of 1853.' He next decided to try his luck with magazine publication. In February 1853 Herman Melville was introduced by the new *Putnam's Monthly Magazine* as the first of 'Our Young Authors'; he was to be paid five dollars a page, the highest rate.

His first contribution, *Bartleby the Scrivener*, was published anonymously in the November and December issues of 1853, simultaneous with *Cock-A-Doodle-Doo!* in *Harper's New Monthly Magazine*. The same December Harpers paid Melville a 300 dollars advance for a new novel on '*Tortoises, or Tortoise Hunting*', which he hoped to complete by January. But failing to find a larger framework or story (except, perhaps, that of the Chola woman), he turned his Galapagos material into ten sketches and sold them for magazine publication to *Putnam's* (where they appeared in the issues of March, April and May, 1854, as *The Encantadas or Enchanted Isles* 'by Salvator R. Tarnmoor') – thus offending Harpers and losing their goodwill in what proved increasingly lean years; even worse, most of Harper's stock of his books had meanwhile been destroyed by fire.

Melville nevertheless managed to complete a historical novel, *Israel Potter*, published serially by *Putnam's*, and by March 1855 was proposing to them yet a further novel, *Benito Cereno*, begun the previous winter. Thus, even in these difficult years when on top of literary and financial worries he was physically crippled – 'helpless', in his wife's phrase, with 'severe rheumatism' – he achieved at least one novel and envisaged a further two. The inability to realize the proposal to Harpers lay with Melville but the inability to encourage the second proposal lay with Putnams. The magazine had recently changed hands and, after the failure of *Israel Potter*, *Putnam's* associate editor, G. W. Curtis, had advised the new publisher, J. A. Dix, 'to decline any novel from Melville which is not extremely good'. On reading *Benito Cereno* Curtis replied that it was 'very good' but complained 'it is a great pity he did not work it up as a connected tale instead of putting in the dreary documents at the end', adding he 'does everything too hurriedly now'. No wonder Melville once wrote despairingly: 'There are hardly five critics in America; and several of them are asleep.'

The Bell-Tower (that too Hawthorne-like creation) was published by *Putnam's* in August 1855, and *Benito Cereno*, as a long short story, eventually in October, November and December of the same year: both anonymously. That winter Melville completed *The Confidence-Man*, the last prose work to appear in his lifetime. On publication of *The Piazza Tales* Curtis wrote prophetically: 'He has lost his prestige, and I don't believe the Putnam stories will bring it up.' The publication of *The Confidence-Man* in 1857 was followed by the usual ironic coda: his latest publishers, Dix and Edwards, were dissolved the same year.

The astonishing creative outpouring of the first six literary years thus continued unabated for a second six: *Moby-Dick* marks not the end but the middle of Melville's miraculous span. Within the narrowed scope of his new fiction, his techniques sharpened, the interlockings of image and incident were used with surer and surer precision. But failure and isolation – even if upheld by an inflexible, withdrawn and inwardly consuming pride – were suffocating. 'I do not wonder', wrote Hawthorne in his Liverpool journal, 'that he found it necessary to take an airing through the world, after so many years of toilsome pen-labor and domestic life, following upon so wild and adventurous a youth as his was.' The walls had closed in on Ishmael.

Indeed *Bartleby* is a story of Wall Street, of a scrivener trapped between walls (one white, one black), long motionless in 'dead-wall reveries', till expiring behind 'walls of amazing thickness' – 'the dead-wall' of the Tombs. Was it himself Melville had in mind when ironically making the lawyer dismiss the scrivener as 'the victim of innate and incurable disorder'? Was he parodying some member of his own family by letting the lawyer soliloquize: 'It was his soul that suffered, and his soul I could not reach'? 'Look, there is the sky, and here is the grass', they might say. 'I know where I am', we hear the reply. 'You will have to find another job' or 'You will have to write a more popular book', his publishers might say. 'I would prefer not to', we hear the reply. 'At present I would prefer not to be a little reasonable.'

Is *Bartleby*, then, a parable of Melville the writer? Or perhaps of all writers? Myths in Melville's fiction, like a series of mirrors superimposed on each other – each at certain angles transparent – readily reflect the reader. There are as many readings of *Bartleby* as keys to the Wall Street chambers: one kept by the cleaning-woman, another by Turkey, a third by the elderly narrator, the fourth by 'I knew not who'. Yet Melville, it seems, intends some resolution. Though the 'combination of double-bowline-knot, treble-crown-knot, back-handed-well-knot, knot-in-and-out-knot, and jamming-knot' was too complex a token for Captain Delano, such intricacy can be untangled; the Deposition which concludes *Benito Cereno* proves 'the key to fit into the lock of the complications which precede it'. So in the entry to the Spouter-Inn hung a shadowed painting as clue to the entry of *Moby-Dick*. 'Padlock and key –' we are to echo the Captain, 'significant symbols, truly', even if Melville replies, as he replied once to Hawthorne: 'Why, ever since Adam, who has got to the meaning of this great allegory – the world? Then we pygmies must be content to have our paper allegories but ill comprehended.'

Ill comprehended, perhaps, because *Bartleby*, like so much of Melville's fiction, is deeply introspective. After his father's death young Herman had himself served as clerk, first in the New York State Bank in Albany, later assisting in his elder brother Gansevoort's cap and fur store. For a while, it seems, he was even a lawyer's clerk – or was he merely job-hunting? – in the desultory year before signing on to the *Acushnet*. So the knowing comedy of office life was fed from his own earliest experience, though visiting his younger brother Allan, now a lawyer in Wall Street, must have helped prompt the story. As to the scrivener, the neat, restrained, seemingly subservient Bartleby at first sight looks closely related to a near contemporary, his fellow-clerk Akaky Akakievich of Gogol's *The Overcoat*. But as his presence begins to weigh incubus-like on the narrator – as employer and employee, like public and private self, ego and superego are implacably entwined together – it is the world of Kafka's Joseph K. which most readily comes to mind. More than a self-portrait, then, *Bartleby* is already a clear-sighted projection of the future which threatened Melville: the literary conscience haunting and dominating the prospective Deputy Inspector of Customs, aloof, disdainful prisoner in the walled city, the writer who preferred not to, ex-clerk of the Dead Letter Office of Literature.

But, in a wider sense, it becomes a parable of all writers in a financial society who refuse to write on demand or to compromise, who say with Montaigne *Je m'abstiens* – Turkey and Nippers, on this analogy, being those middlebrow writers who have sold out to commerce 'and suffer from the occupational disease of the compromised artist in a commercial society – neurosis, alcoholism, and ulcers'; the lawyer himself is the writer as entrepreneur and business man, 'drawer-up of recondite documents of all sorts', and the Dead Letter Office, all modern literature, including the works of Melville, the once popular adventure-story writer – his own work now, and for the future, predestined to obscurity.

In its widest sense, in fact, it becomes a parable of all those who, like Melville to the Lightning-Rod Man, cry: 'In thunder as in sunshine, I stand at ease in the hands of my God. False negotiator, away!' or, in the concluding words of another essay of this period, 'for it is resolved between me and my chimney, that I and my chimney will never surrender'. As Melville wrote to Hawthorne, in a famous letter reviewing *The House of the Seven Gables*: 'There is the grand truth about Nathaniel Hawthorne. He says No! in thunder; but the Devil himself cannot make him say *yes*. For all men who say *yes*, lie; and all men who say *no* – why, they are in the happy condition of judicious, unincumbered travellers in Europe; they cross the frontiers into Eternity with nothing but a carpet-bag – that is to say, the Ego. Whereas those *yes*-gentry, they travel with heaps of baggage, and, damn them! they will never get through the Custom House.'

Clearly the narrator of *Bartleby* is one of 'those *yes*-gentry' whereas Bartleby like Hawthorne, says 'No!' – but not in thunder: his is the still, small voice of calm, 'but the Devil himself cannot make him say *yes*'. As the future Custom House inspector had noted in his New Testament long ago: 'In Life he appears as a true Philosopher – as a wise man in the highest sense. He stands *firm to his point*; he *goes on his way inflexibly....*' That philosopher was Christ.

For here yet another dimension of the story opens: point by point, as H. Bruce Franklin has shown, the narrator fulfils Christ's judgment on the righteous:

'For I was an hungred, and ye gave me meat: I was thirsty, and ye gave me drink: I was a stranger, and ye took me in:
Naked, and ye clothed me: I was sick, and ye visited me: I was in prison, and ye came unto me.' (Matthew xxv, 35–6)

The lawyer offers money for food and drink, offers Bartleby first his office, then his home, tries to minister to him in sickness and visits him in prison. Yet when he acts, he acts grudgingly – both dismissing him and evicting him, betraying him and escaping him, visiting him once in prison but finally deserting him – and always smugly: 'Here I can cheaply purchase a delicious self-approval. To befriend Bartleby; to humor him in his strange willfulness, will cost me little or nothing, while I lay up in my soul what will eventually prove a sweet morsel for my conscience.'

This 'rather elderly man' – this 'eminently *safe* man', in

fact, with his snug business and snug retreat – though calling himself 'a man of peace' believes only in prudence. With his 'profound conviction that the easiest way of life is the best' he had always behaved with singular permissiveness to his two scriveners. But in Bartleby the worldly passivity of this apostle of common sense, superstition and self-interest is confronted by the saintly passivity of an apostle of utter abnegation and step by step yields to his demands.

Compared to the inflexible single-mindedness of Bartleby, this lawyer, who so prides himself on 'method', seems merely impulsive and paradoxical. His every thought and action leads to its contrary. Far from 'a man of peace', he appears rather 'the victim' (to quote his own words) 'of innate and incurable disorder' – the ironic implication of the glass folding-doors behind which he sits no doubt being that such a person should not throw stones: at one moment filled with self-approval, the next with irritation; at one moment reconciled to Bartleby, the next falling into 'spasmodic passions'; now feeling pity, now repulsion; now uneasy on Bartleby's account, next minute giving him notice. Even when he recalls the 'new commandment ... that ye love one another', it remains in his eyes no more than 'a vastly wise and prudent principle', 'mere self-interest'; and, though he begins to perceive 'some mysterious purpose of an allwise Providence', gossip of fellow-attorneys and neighbours quickly hardens his heart. He moves, hardly able to tear himself from him he 'had so longed to be rid of', only like Peter to deny him thrice; and having denied him, to invite him home; and having been rejected, to flee – flee recognition, flee all responsibility. When he hears of Bartleby's arrest, he almost approves; yet on the same day visits him in prison, even tips the grub-man, only to ignore him again until it is too late.

At last, however, it seems he achieves something of an anagnorisis:

> 'Lives without dining,' said I, and closed the eyes.
> 'Eh! – He's asleep, ain't he?'
> 'With kings and counselors,' murmured I.

For Bartleby ('this forlornest of mankind', 'alone, absolutely alone in the universe') far more subtly than Billy Budd gathers a Christ-like vocabulary. 'Bartleby was one of those beings of whom nothing is ascertainable, except from the original sources, and, in his case, those are very small.' The increase in legal work takes place in a 'period just preceding the advent of Bartleby': it is on receiving the office of 'Master in Chancery' – 'the master's office' ('by the new Constitution' significantly defunct) – that the lawyer advertises for additional help and engages Bartleby. Tranquil in a room full of lawyers and witnesses, passively led to the Tombs, alone in the midst of murderers and thieves, Bartleby, whatever the lawyer's boast, is the true 'man of peace'.

Yet this saintly or 'passive resistance' – which Bartleby shares with Benito Cereno, even with Billy Budd – is only partially Christ-like. Christ, after all, was never a scrivener; let alone could he be conceived as a mechanical scrivener. Nor is Bartleby's abnegation (spreading from copy-reading to running errands, to answering queries, to copying itself, to resigning his employment, to quitting the premises) essentially Christian; nor his vegetarian diet, consisting of ginger-nuts and cheese. H. Bruce Franklin is surely right in arguing that there is more of a Hindu ascetic here than another Jesus. 'How can the prisoner reach outside except by thrusting through the wall?' Captain Ahab had boasted. Bartleby, gentle, firm, but utterly passive, allows the wall to crush him.

In a city of the dead – in Wall Street on Sunday, deserted as Petra – 'Bartleby makes his home'. Trinity Church remains unvisited: 'pardon for those who died despairing; hope for those who died unhoping; good tidings for those who died stifled by unrelieved calamities' – all are dead letters. The Evangelists, that is, the Epistles, the whole New Testament, including *Matthew* xxv, are consigned to the Dead Letter Office. For comedy in this story of office life plays not only on the surface but in its metaphysical depths. When the narrator asks Bartleby 'having nothing else earthly to do' to carry some letters to the post office, or concludes his dismissal, 'if, hereafter, in your new place of abode, I can be of any service to you, do not fail to advise me by letter', the ironies re-echo and sound – to the final sigh, 'Ah, Bartleby! Ah, humanity!'

Yet, whatever the literary or Christian implications, Bartleby can never be wholly interpreted as either writer or Christ-figure, artist or ascetic saint, nor is the story exhausted by such interpretations. At its roots lies a theme more compelling than both: of the *doppelgänger*, the shadow, the appointed 'other'. Bartleby appears from nowhere, without identity, only a copyist. He is the secret sharer (in Conrad's phrase) whom we cannot cast off, barter or pass by, and whom we alone recognize – the figure of death (cadaver, apparition, incubus, ghost) behind the green screen (of life). But if, as in Tolstoy's *The Death of Ivan Ilyich*, Bartleby is Death-in-Life, 'on errands of life, these letters speed to death': Bartleby is also Life-in-Death. As the symbolism is suggestive and imprecise, so finally the borderline between living and dead is blurred. John C. Colt, the murderer who intrudes into the tale, was married, while under death sentence in prison, to the mother of his child, shortly before committing suicide. Within the spectrum of white and black in which the drama is played – by the sallow Nippers, the sun of Turkey's countenance rising and setting, the green folding screen between – Bartleby's eyes alone are grey.

Poor Bartleby! Poor Colt! That is the final triumph of Melville's art, this blurring of the guide-lines, the landmarks of our normal perception, until groping in the nebulous landscape we can be sure of only one thing, that, like the blind men in the fable, we are roped one to another, conscious of only one law: that ye love one another. Sometimes his symbol is a ship's crew at sea; here it is a Wall Street lawyer's office; always it is a paradigm of Hell, with a glimpse of Heaven – between one black wall and one white, between the Pyramids or Petra and Trinity Church.

The cock-crow of Signor Beneventano, by contrast, 'so vast, mounting, swelling, soaring, as if spurted out from a golden throat, thrown far back', fairly throbs with an exultant and sexual joy; no pallid scrivener, he strides glittering 'like a Spanish grandee' in his blazon of red, white and gold. Yet this too is Melville, the humorist, spinning a yarn (an American 'tall story'); and here too the theme is ambivalent.

Merrymusk ('merry music'?), as parody makes clear, is a version of Wordsworth's Leech-Gatherer; *Cock-A-Doodle-Doo!*, a revision of two lines from *Resolution and Independence*:

> We Poets in our youth begin in gladness;
> But thereof come in the end despondency and madness.

For now gladness and madness are synchronized: there is both joy at the cock and terror at this 'overpowering angel in the Apocalypse'; the narrator's 'hypos' and the sawyer's intense calm are poised in balance; and the life of the one is enhanced in the end by the collapse of the other – the death of Merrymusk, his family, his cock.

Cock-crow ecstasy, in fact, is an ambivalent ecstasy; it heals and wounds, charges and destroys: joint symbol at once of artistic creation and neurotic self-mutilation. Poetic ecstasy, Melville answers Wordsworth, is by its very nature ambivalent: optimism, resolution, gladness, independence – COCK-A-DOODLE-DOO! – may, as here, triumph, but only if in the knowledge (a lesson also to be learnt from Bannadonna's fate in *The Bell-Tower*) that art not only creates, but also maims and kills. 'O death, where is thy sting?' is the epitaph (was it Bartleby's also?), the gravestone chiselled 'not with skull and cross-bones, but with a lusty cock in act of crowing'.

Whatever ultimate meaning Christian symbols held for Melville, this much is plain: the Trumpet call of faith – the paean and *laudamus 'Glory be to God in the highest!'* which alone makes life worth living – is a subjective, not objective, truth. 'By our own spirits are we deified', in Wordsworth's phrase; and this was applied by Melville equally to religion as to art.

But to skull and cross-bones he returned: literally, to the world of buccaneers; metaphorically, to the mortuary and infernal Galapagos. It was in the autumn of 1841 (six years after Darwin's more famous voyage on the sloop *Beagle*) that Melville had visited the islands. Following the Humboldt Current, in which great schools of whales attracted by the teeming squids and crustaceans move towards their calving-grounds off the Galapagos, the *Acushnet* cruised three months in that volcanic archipelago scattered over 23,000 square miles, 600 miles off the coast of Ecuador. Melville made only the single voyage and visited only a few of the thirteen major islands, but from this one experience, and from his subsequent reading in Captains Cowley, Colnett, Porter, Delano (the early voyagers of the South Seas), and, when all failed, from a free and abundant invention, Melville created *The Encantadas*. There are, inevitably, errors of fact: several islands are misplaced; rainfall, at least from January to April, is abundant; the higher zones are lush, it seems, with ferns and orchids; the herds of sea and land iguanas are curiously absent. But as the quotations from Spenser suggest, the intention was never wholly descriptive; it was allegorical.

The arid, eroded landscape in the equatorial heat, the flat basalt and lava on the shores of Albemarle, the active, sulphurous volcanoes, made even Darwin speak of 'infernal regions'. But to Darwin this crust of hell revealed a living paradise – a fool's paradise of the flightless cormorant and the booby bird – isolated, trusting, innocent. For Melville it remained hell, an image of evil 'glued into the very body of cadaverous death', its chief sound a hiss and, out of mist, 'screaming flights of unearthly birds'.

A spell-bound evil: these equatorial cinderheaps, without history, without seasons, surrounded by deceptive calms and currents, appear landscapes of enchantment; their giant tortoises, victims 'strangely self-condemned' of metempsychosis. As Hunilla's spell-bound eye – in a scene 'trance-like' in 'its mild pictorial effect' – watches husband and brother dashed to death on the distant reef, so this cadaverous imagery of corruption presents an 'air of spell-bound desertness'. Melville had not only been reading Spenser and Darwin, or Milton for that matter, but also Shakespeare's *The Tempest*. He is both guide (Prospero, the Enchanter himself) and innocent wonder (Miranda) to whose dreamy sailor's mind 'all things of the land wear a fabulous hue', even Sycorax's son sharing 'the dim investiture of wonder'.

What 'Cowley's Enchanted Isle' had been for that buccaneering cartographer among the Encantadas, these ten sketches ('spell-bound' at whose centre lies the U.S. frigate *Essex*) are among Melville's *Piazza Tales*: 'the spell within a spell'. The theme of spells – something dream-like which protects Amasa Delano sleep-walking on the *San Dominick*, which binds the Wall Street lawyer's office (till, consciously or unconsciously, all tongues are turned), which holds Billy Budd to his spell-bound role to the end – pervades all these tales. 'That Cowley linked his name', Melville adds, 'with this self-transforming and bemocking isle, suggests the possibility that it conveyed to him some meditative image of himself.' So with *The Encantadas*: that Melville linked his name with these self-transforming and bemocking islands suggests the possibility that the Galapagos conveyed some meditative image of himself. For it is not so much evil which is his theme, as the ambiguous nature of evil, even on these islands, even with civilization at its most degraded.

For here, too, there is one black wall, one white. 'The tortoise, dark and melancholy as it is upon the back, still possesses a bright side.' The 'dark craggy mass' of volcanic Narborough overtowers the calving-ground of the Sperm Whale; demons toil 'in that upper dark', while below sail the whales, 'a most harmonious concord of rushing keels'. Everything implies its opposite. Everything contains its opposite: the blacker the volcanic clouds by day, the brighter their blaze at night.

Far out to sea, Rock Rodondo – beset by 'the demoniac

din' of birds – stands whitewashed as a lighthouse. Isolated from the enchanted group, it rises like Dante's Purgatorio in shelf-like entablatures: on its lowest shelf, that anomaly, Nature's failure ('on land it stumps; afloat it sculls; in the air it flops'), the penguin; above, in ashy plumage, the pelican – pensive sea Friar 'of Orders Grey', 'penitential bird', 'tormented Job'; next, the grey albatross; till, higher and higher, above the gannets, haglets, jays, sea-hens, gulls – the whole aviary of bandit birds – floats 'a snow-white angelic thing', the 'Boatswain's Mate'. From black to white, in Melville's habitual spectrum, he modulates through grey.

The first glimpse of man is 'some tatterdemalion outlaw, staff in hand', descending the steep rocks of Massafuero. But the Encantadas, too, hide their outlaws. With *Sketch Fifth* as his enigmatic pivot, Melville turns from inanimate and animal nature to its human counterpart – on a mounting scale of evil: from 'plates of iron' to iron hearts; from volcanoes and reptiles to 'a volcanic creature', 'this Lord Anaconda'; from 'bandit birds, with long bills cruel as daggers' to the 'artificial claws and fangs' of his four slave murderers. The first five and last five sketches mirror each other and form their own mutual commentaries. Though 'the Encantadas refuse to harbor even the outcasts of the beasts', human runaways, castaways and solitaries abound. Man incarnates the landscape: alone among these reptiles he is malignant, 'beast-like', transformed by some Circe of the Enchanted Isles into a ranging Cow-Boy, lower and more degraded than any beast. This dissolution of *moral* nature is the worst, the utmost corruption. But even here, as the 'snow-white angelic' bird, the 'Boatswain's Mate', floats high above the Rock Rodondo, below, as if in answer, flutters the Chola widow's white handkerchief.

Which is the lesson of the 'dram of Peruvian pisco': good and evil are inextricably mixed. Those buccaneers on Barrington Isle (haven of water, trees, grass) may have lounged to their hearts' content in 'pure peacefulness and kindly fellowship with nature', but their rusty cutlasses and daggers prove them robbers and murderers. Nor does admitting a more truly meditative sage or rural poet help; the author of *Elegy Written in a Country Church-Yard*, lounging on his sofa, turns out merely to be titillating himself with something by Crébillon. The sophisticate, that is, who returns to 'kindly fellowship with nature', will introduce his own vices; and if Gray's book, by any chance, was Crébillon's most popular work, *Les Égarements du Cœur et de l'Esprit*, we should read the title perhaps in its moral (not Shandean) sense, as fitting epitaph for both buccaneers and all presidents of peace societies preaching a return to nature and virtue.

That 'often ill comes from the good' is the lesson of Charles's Isle, or the parable of the Creole dog-king (patriot hero of the Peruvian War of Liberation). The emigrants take ship for the promised land, but the capital they build with its 'walls of clinkers, and lava floors, nicely sanded with cinders' is a replica (now Melville turns to Milton) of Satan's Pandaemonium. Rebellion leads to retaliation; retaliation to a reign of terror, till only the king with his dog-regiment hounds the island. When autocracy at last is broken, the republic inaugurated soon degenerates into permanent *Riotocracy*, the deserters' ranks 'swelled by accessions of scamps from every ship which touched their shores'. Like a mad parody of the United States, Charles's Isle is 'proclaimed the asylum of the oppressed of all navies', becoming 'the unassailed lurking-place of all sorts of desperadoes, who in the name of liberty did just what they pleased'; its beacon-light, an ironic warning to all honest shipping. But anarchy – 'Do what thou wilt' – is not liberty: 'Fay ce que vouldras', the motto of Rabelais' Abbaye de Thélème, was meant only for those whom inborn virtue would keep from vice without rule, restriction or law.

If this is a partial lesson, the whole and complex truth is made explicit in the longest of these sketches, and their centrepiece, 'The Chola Widow'; but here, however subtly developed the theme, the rhetoric for once is overblown and ineffective. Is it because woman for once is the subject?

[23]

Most of Melville's fiction – all of it collected here – is, in Hemingway's phrase, of 'Men without Women': in this all-male cast, a half-breed Indian is the only heroine and her tragedy (of woman without men), the only tragedy of *The Encantadas*. Yet it remains a 'sham tragedy', a 'dumb show', with its unspeakable (sexual?) terrors. 'Humanity, thou strong thing,' Melville invokes her, 'I worship thee, not in the laureled victor, but in this vanquished one.' (What seems so strained, so falsely emotional, to us was of course precisely what his contemporaries most admired.)

The mystery is: why did the French captain leave the three tortoise-oil hunters (the half-breed Hunilla, Felipe, her Castilian husband, and Truxill, her Indian brother) marooned? Was it deliberate evil, worse in its treachery than any act of the Nimrod king? A kind of stepping-stone to that ultimate horror, the treacherous hermit? Of the whaling captain we know only one thing: he was 'a joyous man'; the last heard of his ship is 'the loud glee of the singing crew'. But so were Felipe and Truxill joyous men: it was through some 'natural negligence of joyfulness' that they perished on the reef, and they too by their gestures 'seemed singing at the time'. Then the French whaler, too, perhaps – far from double-crossing the trio – sank, like the catamaran, in carefree elation. 'Naught else abides on fickle earth but unkept promises of joy.' Mankind is fickle, as earth (where enigmatic ships emerge and, like a mirage, vanish) is fickle, and even heaven – who knows – may be 'faithless who created the faithful one'.

The imagery is ambiguous as good and evil are ambiguous. The dog-king had been a Creole; here married fidelity and Catholic faith (with its little brass crucifix 'worn featureless') is embodied in a half breed. The emblem, that is, of pure and passive virtue can neither be pure Castilian, nor pure Indian, but a cross between, embracing the ambiguity of light and dark ('the dark-damasked' waving a white handkerchief) whose mourning is constant as man's joy, despite himself, is fickle. Joyous Frenchmen, at the opening, maroon the trio: generous Americans, at the end, desert Hunilla's ringleted pets. As with the 'dram of Peruvian pisco', or the two sides of the tortoise, there is nothing straightforward either in life – or literature. (A lesson for readers not to 'ram themselves heroically against rocks' like tortoises 'and long abide there, nudging, wriggling, wedging, in order to displace them, and so hold on their inflexible path'.)

For carefree treachery, whatever its cause, remains treachery, and so fit prologue to deliberate, malignant treachery. But even here, where Melville reaches 'the central figure of a mongrel and assassin band', he does not forget his earlier advice: 'Neither should he, who cannot turn the tortoise from its natural position so as to hide the darker and expose his livelier aspect, like a great October pumpkin in the sun, for that cause declare the creature to be one total inky blot.'

Fatherless outcasts (from the runaway in *Typee*, to Ishmael in *Moby-Dick*, to 'the unblest foundling' Bannadonna, John Marr and Billy Budd) abound in Melville's fiction. The hermit is another; but from the accomplished and stylish letter, found pinned to his deserted hut, it is clear that 'Fatherless Oberlus' had enjoyed at least one advantage – education: 'not only did it evince a certain clerkliness, but was full of the strangest satiric effrontery'. His wilful choice of Sycorax for mother, then, far from turning him into Caliban, had turned him into – what is far worse – a perverted Calibanphile, a sophisticated degenerate playing at primitive savagery, 'more diabolical than ... any of the surrounding cannibals'. His only 'potency' is his blunderbuss; he is without sex or morality; aptly his slaves, 'rotted down from manhood', are turned (by an oxymoron) into 'Cow-Boys' and (by a pun) into 'cowards', animals and murderers.

Yet even this diabolically red-haired, volcanic creature has one redeeming touch. He is gifted with green fingers: 'the queer green-grocer' Melville calls him. He grows 'a sort of degenerate potatoes and pumpkins'. At last Melville's preoccupation with Syrian gourds, October pumpkins and pumpkin pie, reiterated throughout these sketches, becomes clear. The humble American pumpkin is the vegetative force which defies even these metallic, lava-barren islands, as it survives in Oberlus's wholly corrupted, degraded nature. The contrast is no longer of white and black, but of green and black, of life and death – the sullen market gardener with the 'black tarpaulin hat' coiled snake-like in his den of black lava and clinkers.

Civilization is at all times doubtful – not only among the buccaneers of Barrington Isle, the riotocrats of Charles's Isle or Oberlus's mongrel assassins: a reward of five pesos transforms Peruvian and Chilean Spaniards into man-hunters as readily as the advanced natives of Polynesia who 'have felt a civilizing influence'. Solitaries – voluntary exiles, tortoise-hunters, abandoned seamen – soon descend to the level of beasts, sucking the living blood out of their dying prey. 'Of comfort no man speak. . . .' As *Sketch Tenth* returns to *Sketch Fifth*, so, with perfect and deadly symmetry, in the end is Melville's beginning. He had opened with 'abandoned cemeteries': he closes with a 'Potter's Field'. It is neither the *Essex* nor her captain we find left their bones on the Encantadas but a twenty-one-year-old lieutenant 'attaining his majority in death'.

From the animate to the inanimate is but a step; from the bestial, Melville reverts (back through the chain of being) to the material: from 'hearts of iron' to 'plates of iron', from human assassins to a mechanical assassin, from cringing slaves 'of an inferior race' to the iron slave, who 'while serving' plots revenge. Bannadonna ('banish woman'?) is Oberlus transposed to Renaissance Italy: again father-less; again a 'cynic solitaire' glorying in self-esteem; again sole taskmaster of a subject creature of his contriving. Architect, bronze-caster, sculptor, clock-maker, engineer – a Leonardo of all talents, his creative intellect is in itself destructive. The 'practical materialist', that is, who sees men only in terms of semaphore, as puppets, whatever his pride in 'man', must be destructive. Not only destructive, but self-destructive. Oberlus, in jail, survives: Bannadonna – as violent, and a killer – is killed.

All Melville's work of these years is radically, self-consciously literary: a literature of literature. If *Bartleby* was (in part) a commentary on *Matthew* xxv, and *Cock-A-Doodle-Doo!* on Wordsworth's *The Leech-Gatherer*, and *The Encantadas* on various South Sea voyages (crossed by Shakespeare, Spenser, Milton), then *The Bell-Tower* is (in part) a variation on Hawthorne's *Ethan Brand*, composed in the master's own voice, crossed by imagery from *The Faerie Queene*, with widespread allusions to the Old Testament from *Genesis* to *Daniel*. Always there is this overlayering of ideas, images, meanings, references; and if the recipe here seems overelaborated, the language stilted, the allegorical intentions too explicit, this only points the absolute, the Shakespearian, fusion Melville achieves elsewhere. (Paradoxically, during the half century of Melville's eclipse, this was his only story, twice reissued, to remain in print.)

For the weakness of *The Bell-Tower* is not that the final paragraph reveals too much; it is rather that the precision of those five formulas is inadequate for its multiple and conflicting centre: Bannadonna the 'true artist' and Bannadonna 'the great mechanician'. The artist, killed in mid-artistry by his own creation, is a deeply felt – and personal – image: 'the great mechanician', killed by his own artifact at the feet of truth, is merely a symbol – for an age of science; and however private the core of experience, however mysterious the sexual echoes (when the tower, in the end, is 'groined' by the bell's fall), however obscure the Spenserian allusions, it is scorn we are meant to feel.

Increasingly, as the mid-century progressed, Melville fell foul of the triumphs of the new technology. 'Railroads and steamboats...', he snorted in *Cock-A-Doodle-Doo!*, 'Great improvements of the age! What! to call the facilitation of death and murder an improvement!' *The Bell-Tower* reveals, as it were, the metaphysics behind the loathing. The materialists of his age, Melville argued, 'stooped to conquer': for them 'machinery' was 'miracle', 'Prometheus, the

heroic name for machinist; man, the true God'. Instead
of rising, they sank through the scale of existence: which,
inevitably, means death. It is too casual to recognize here
only stage properties of gothic horror – of automata or the
Golem. Charles Babbage, after all, was a contemporary: the
digital computer, reality. From Frankenstein to Čapek's
Robots to the Androids of science fiction, the possibility of
controlling his environment by the spontaneous artifacts of
reason has fascinated man; beyond Haman (half man?)
Bannadonna envisaged 'an ulterior creature, a sort of elephantine Helot, adapted to further, in a degree scarcely to
be imagined, the universal conveniences and glories of
humanity; supplying nothing less than a supplement to the
Six Days' Work'. The more directly, that is, machines can
compete with men, the more pressing (Norbert Wiener,
founder of cybernetics, agreed) their religious implications.
An older humanism – of man 'infinite in faculty ... in
apprehension how like a god!' – is doomed if the machinist
is to be controlled by the machine. But this new 'humanism', Melville answered, is suicidal.

'Like negroes, these powers own man sullenly,' he headed
The Bell-Tower, 'mindful of their higher master....' For
throughout 1855 he was also at work on *Benito Cereno*. But
the roots of that story – again set off the coast of South
America, again hovering between death and enchantment
('tranced without wind') – reach back to *The Encantadas*;
and again voyaging in the South Seas, the buccaneer
Bachelor's Delight, turned honest, an American sealer now,
bridges both tales. For browsing through Delano's *A Narrative of Voyages and Travels*, perhaps on the look-out for
more Galapagos material, Melville had chanced on the
incident of 'the Capture of the Spanish Ship *Tryal*, at the
island of St Maria' and conceived *Benito Cereno*. But as
the idea lay incubating, awaiting its turn, he linked it, in
his usual manner, with other reading, in particular with a
popular history of the day, William Stirling's *The Cloister
Life of the Emperor Charles the Fifth*, until the *Tryal* fused
into 'a white-washed monastery', the captain's cuddy into

a monastic cell with missal, crucifix and friars' girdles, the sea into a mirage of parterres, terraces and formal alleys, a carved balustrade into 'the charred ruin of some summer-house'. 'Bisociation' Arthur Koestler has called mergers between two such disparate 'codes'; but whatever resonances and extra dimensions Melville gained, this graft on to Delano's *Narrative* remains somewhat wilful, somewhat intrusive.

For the theme once again, the drama, is played between the black and the white – literally between blacks and whites this time: Americans and Spaniards on one side, Negroes on the other. And as always the symbolism (of Black Friars in a whitewashed monastery, of a white noddy in the tops and a dark satyr on the stern, of black and white pawns, of the Nubian sculptor and his white statue-head) is resolved in an indeterminate grey – grey sky, grey fowl, leaden waves, the grey vapours of the opening. The stranger, at a distance, 'showed no colors': from the morning mists to the Spaniard's 'cloudy languor' to the greyness of dusk at noon, *Benito Cereno* revolves to moonlight and moonshadow, broken only, on close view, by one heraldic splash – a sailor's red breeches, a crimson curtain and, tucked under Cereno's chin, 'a closed castle in a blood-red field'. For now the spectrum has widened: between the sooty barber and the creamy lather – a streak of blood.

But in this middle ground of overwhelming grey, in the confusion of good and evil (which is the slaves' revolt), where does the American visitor stand? Is he innocence and benevolence incarnate, 'sound as an apple, practical and kindly, ... in the presence of evil ... uncomprehending', as many acclaim him, or does he too partake of the universal confusion? Is he perhaps its chief spokesman and protagonist? From *Bartleby* to *Billy Budd*, whenever one black wall confronts a white, it is not the problem of evil as much as the problem of innocence which ultimately beguiles Melville. Should we love our neighbour however eccentric, however clinging and intractable an incubus (as Bartleby)? Should we love our neighbour to a point of starry-eyed stupidity, alone, unarmed among slave-mutineers (as Delano)? Is this innocence or a form of immaturity? And if immaturity, is it innocence at all?

That Captain Delano is good-natured and compassionate, we know: we have his own word for it. That his goodness was too simple, too naïve to pierce such ambiguities was the gist of his own apology. But the whole of *Benito Cereno*, after all, is an elaborate exercise in irony; nothing is as it seems; a contrast of light and shade – moving from vaporous ambiguity into the sunlight of reality, from moonlit dream to a courtroom deposition – is itself the essence of its structure. As an eye-witness the sealer's captain, like the Wall Street lawyer, proves unsatisfactory. But if nothing is as it seems, must this not include the eye-witness also? If Delano was mistaken in his good-natured attitude to these particular Negroes, if he was blind to the Negroes' true role on this occasion, then perhaps his good-natured attitude to all Negroes on all other occasions may have been equally mistaken.

Captain Delano takes his stand, above all, on intellectual superiority. The whites, he considers, are by nature 'the shrewder race'; the blacks, blind to depravity, 'too stupid' even for intrigue. Theirs is a 'bland attachment' of 'indisputable inferiors', 'the unaspiring contentment of a limited mind'. Yet he himself conspicuously lacks (the irony is underlined from the start) even 'ordinary quickness and accuracy of intellectual perception'. When Babo's grin, for example, shifts from 'mere animal humor into an intelligent smile', Delano notes this; he even publicly recognizes the fact ('This is an uncommonly intelligent fellow of yours') over lunch to the Spaniard; but draw a conclusion, he cannot. Benito Cereno seems the somnambulist, but Amasa Delano is truly asleep, intellectually sleepwalking, a white noddy in the fullest dictionary sense (of 'fool', 'simpleton', 'noodle'), surveying the ship from stern to prow in 'dreamy inquietude'; 'trying to break one charm, he was but becharmed anew'. The intellectual is Babo: small and slight of frame, he 'was the plotter from first to last'; his 'brain, not body, had schemed and led the revolt'. *Benito Cereno* ends (a final irony to reflect the opening) with Babo's 'head, that hive of subtlety, fixed on a pole in the Plaza', meeting 'unabashed, the gaze of the whites'.

But why, when confronted with such high intelligence, does Delano still fail to recognize it? Why does he completely and consistently fail to draw the right conclusions? 'In fact, like most men of a good, blithe heart, Captain Delano took to negroes, not philanthropically, but genially, just as other men to Newfoundland dogs.' His first glance takes in the little Negro (a consummate actor, of course) as 'a shepherd's dog'. Delano is clearly fond of dogs. He sees his own boat as a 'good dog; a white bone in her mouth': back at home on the beach *Rover*, too, is a 'Newfoundland dog'. But what is peculiar to the American is his conceiving this relation in terms of friendship: 'Don Benito,' he proclaims, 'I envy you such a friend; slave I cannot call him.' For anyone, let alone a captain, even to consider a social contract as unequal as that between the half naked Negro and the finically elegant Spaniard as a basis for friendship is odd. But then, it appears, neither does the captain – in practice: one moment annoyed by Babo's 'conversational familiarities'; the next, kidding with an offer of 'fifty doubloons', cash down, to buy him. Whatever 'a devoted companion' may mean, whatever such 'republican impartiality' may imply, whatever those 'chatty and half-gamesome terms' with Negro sailors may suggest (and his playful remarks – gratifyingly – do 'not fail somewhat to tickle' the astute Babo), all Delano's attitudes are maintained from one firm and unqualified stand – white supremacy; and 'who ever heard of a white so far a renegade as to apostasize from his very species almost, by leaguing in against it with negroes?' The species are distinct and the white (*pace* the Barbadoes planter) must be superior: 'For it were strange, indeed, and not very creditable to us white-skins, if a little of our blood mixed with the African's, should, far from improving the latter's quality, have the sad effect of pouring vitriolic acid into black broth.'

On this rock of white supremacy Delano can afford to be smug – smug about the water ration (as long as 'the soft bread, sugar and bottled cider' are reserved for whites only), smug about his temper ('which was more than commonly pleasant' that morning), smug naturally ('Ah, this slavery breeds ugly passions....') about the slave trade itself. From his rock of intellectual and moral superiority, Delano can patronize the Negroes' aesthetic and humbler moral qualities: their 'affectionate zeal', their 'filial or fraternal acts', their 'good-humor' and 'easy cheerfulness'. He can sun himself in the pastoral qualities his imagination imposes on them: a Negress 'like a doe in the shade of a woodland rock'; her baby a fawn, 'its hands, like two paws, clambering upon her'. 'There's naked nature, now; pure tenderness and love, thought Captain Delano.' For in this pastoral of the mind (where leopardesses lie down with the doves, and foxes, pelicans, camels, bats and cawing crows are housed and jostle together) the Negro fills yet another role. The captain of the *Bachelor's Delight* is blinded not only by his racialism, or his Christian visions (confusing Cereno with 'some hypochondriac abbot', his servant with 'a begging friar of St Francis'), but because he is suffused with homoerotic fancies.

The American treats Babo, it seems, either as a kind of hound or as somehow feminine; and the two in his mind are oddly linked. That is, in a man's world he tends to think of the graceful, harmonious Negro as a faithful dog; in a womanless world he thinks of the same smooth-bodied, smiling Negro with all the favour of a wifely companion: both, ideally, are loyal, serviceable and affectionate. A pre-Freudian somnambulism, revealing such deep-seated neuroses, cries out for interpretation: for if to be 'Negro' is only to be a 'dog', or a 'wife', or even both at the same time, then clearly it can never mean a 'man'.

Already in *Robinson Crusoe* there is more than a hint of future seafaring and colonial sagas of men without women where the smiling native servant (the 'boy') assumes all the female attributes of 'wife'. The triple need of mastering the native, and in order to master his unknown savagery of emasculating his presence (for instance, by clothing him) and, having done so, of discovering in him, in a woman-less world, a soft and sweet substitute-wifely companion, is all inherent on Crusoe's island. Like Crusoe, Delano can admire the colossal form of Atufal as much as the mincing clownery of the mulatto Francesco; but it is Babo, specific-ally, who proves Friday's heir. Those swooning falls of the immaculately white and velvet clad, youthful Benito Cereno into the arms of his bare-chested Negro turn, in Delano's eyes, to embraces; a bleeding razor cut for razor cut is imperturbably acknowledged as 'but a sort of love-quarrel, after all'. Little Babo, it appears, is the exponent of a vision: 'the black upholding the white ... the beauty of that relationship which could present such a spectacle of fidelity on the one hand and confidence on the other'. In their complimentary roles, that is, the Negro – 'harmonious in every glance and gesture', 'the most pleasing body ser-vant in the world' – becomes the white man's natural valet and hairdresser. 'One readily perceives,' Delano adds, 'why those hypochondriacs, Johnson and Byron – it may be, something like the hypochondriac Benito Cereno – took to their hearts, almost to the exclusion of the entire white race, their serving men, the negroes, Barber and Fletcher.'

The vision, once in part Melville's own – the vision of the 'Siamese ligature' that tied Ishmael to the harpooner Queequeg 'in the most loving and affectionate manner' – is here destroyed. The American captain must wake not only to the truth of this one, particular slave-ship, the *San Dominick*, but from the whole tangled homoerotic vision of a complimentary, fraternal relationship between white master and Negro servitor – the marriage of aspiring, un-limited mind (the male part) to grace, tact and good-humoured, cheerful affection (the female part) 'singularly pleasing to behold, and still more so to be the manipulated subject of'. As slavery is slavery (not friendship), so war between black and white is real war (not a subtle version of the sex war, 'a sort of love-quarrel, after all').

This is the true awakening – the true anagnorisis implicit in *Benito Cereno*: that the 'fraternal unreserve' between two equals (the two captains on their final journey to Lima) has nothing in common with those 'filial or fraternal acts' of a menial for a master, which once seemed such a pleasing mark of affection. Don Benito, with his last leap, saved not only himself but Captain Delano from his own infatuation; saved him, too, as he admits, against his 'knowledge and will'. But if against his will, if 'to rush from darkness to light was the involuntary choice', the scales, surely, never dropped from his eyes. En route to Lima, genial as ever in the bright sunlight, he stands chatting of Providence, his pleasing temper that morning, his lucky *lack* (as it proved) of acuteness. Fanned by the warm trade winds, he can ask astonished: 'What has cast such a shadow upon you?' For his own temper, again, is 'more than commonly pleasant'; 'his conscience is clean'; drama apart, he has recognized nothing, he has experienced nothing and so has learnt nothing. His carefree and lightweight benevolence, neither wholly good nor wholly evil, but colourless in its effect – grey – continues to cruise with a white man's self-assured and (under God) providential innocence about the world.

'The embodiment of good in the pale Spanish captain and of evil in the mutinied African crew,' wrote F. O. Matthiessen, 'though pictorially and theatrically effective, was unfortunate in raising unanswered questions. Although the Negroes were savagely vindictive and drove a terror of blackness into Cereno's heart, the fact remains that they were slaves and that evil had thus originally been done to them. Melville's failure to reckon with this fact within the limits of his narrative makes its tragedy, for all its prolonged suspense, comparatively superficial.' But it is not Melville who is here superficial. It is precisely this fact – that the Negroes were slaves, that evil had 'originally been done to them': a traffic distorting both the white and the black man's vision, ossifying their mutual roles and destroying any simple formulation of good and evil – with which Melville so clearly reckons. Just as Benito Cereno wears 'white small-clothes' under his dark velvet jacket, so the habit of the Dominicans (or Black Friars), after all, is white, with a black mantle for preaching.

These affectionate, 'tractable', 'sleepy-looking' or cheerful Negroes are merely roles in a masque, played for the benefit of a white visitor, in which Don Benito acts the captain, Spanish sailors man the tiller or tar straps or splice cables, but the Negroes (the murderous José, Francesco, Atufal, Lecbe, Yan, Martiniqui) hold the whip-hand. They are the invisible men; and, like Ralph Ellison's 'Invisible Man', Babo could have turned on Delano in court, saying: '*He* bumped *me, he* insulted *me*. Shouldn't he, for his own personal safety, have recognized my hysteria, my "danger potential"? He was lost in a dream world.' For now the boot is on the other foot, the roles are reversed. Where Crusoe once, having clothed and converted and trained his Man Friday, could conclude, 'I began really to love the creature', it is now the Negro who controls the dream world. Black man is no longer 'whitey's' creature. Babo holds the razor to Don Benito's throat 'and pausing with an expression of subdued self-complacency, the servant surveyed his master, as, in toilet at least, the creature of his own tasteful hands'.

A 'creature' each 'species' remains, to the other an 'it'. Because for Negroes it is not Christopher Colon – a dreamer, an explorer – who can serve as figurehead, only a skeleton, the whitened skeleton of a white man at that. (In Negro hands the *San Dominick* had turned a skeleton ship – 'hearse-like', 'coffined'.) For them the vision of the New World was 'launched from Ezekiel's Valley of Dry Bones'. (Though Babo, their prophet, is no Ezekiel.) For them there is no Israel, no land of their own. (The way to Senegal remains for ever barred.)

> Thy friends are exultations, agonies,
> And love, and Man's unconquerable mind,

wrote Wordsworth to Toussaint L'Ouverture, Babo's contemporary. But Babo and Toussaint were both finally captured; Benito Cereno was broken and soon died from his
experience; Amasa Delano, white noddy in his pastoral
dream world, now calling trade winds his 'steadfast friends'
as readily as once Negroes, alone survives – and Babo's
heirs, still polishing their hatchets to an Ashantee refrain:

> (may a lost god damballah, rest or save us
> against the murders we intend
> against his lost white children
> black dada nihilismus

Benito Cereno, then, is essentially prophetic. All day
Delano wavers between two conjectures: 'innocent lunacy,
or wicked imposture'. A third deduction (innocent imposture) evades him. It evades him not, as the deposition main-
tains, because he is 'incapable of sounding such wickedness';
for it is not of evil that he is uncomprehending. He can
think of plenty of sinister examples and suspicious parallels,
from a Spanish ambuscade to Malay pirates: constantly
they flit through his head, knotting and entangling him.
It is of Negroes Delano is uncomprehending; when it
comes to Negroes, he is blind. Thus, far from being a tale
of Yankee innocence, or idealism, or even naïveté, this is
Melville's veiled but uncompromising attack on Yankee
gullibility due to corrosive double standards and a self-
deluding hypocrisy – an awful warning of the dangers of the
complacency, the ignorance, the sheer intellectual limita-
tions of gentlemen from Duxbury, Massachusetts, blankly
incomprehensive of a larger world beyond the grasp of
their patrician joviality with coloured seamen, valets and
barbers, whose ground may be 'mined into honey-combs'
under them.

The façade is ironic; the indictment, damning. For conceived in the mid-fifties, under threat of civil war, *Benito
Cereno* is also a profession of faith: Melville's personal
intervention in the great slavery debate to brand that New
England, northern superiority – which, with republican con-

descension, claimed to be above the battle, because blind to the issues involved – as racialist at heart, as racialist as the South. This includes the final assault on the slave-boat, spurred on by promise of plunder: like the impending war, it costs both white and Negro lives without solving one problem between them. (No wonder Melville altered the honest Puritan *Perseverance* to the buccaneer *Bachelor's Delight*: such provocation, he implies, was mere swash-buckling.)

But if trust in a God-given, benevolent dispensation for a white officer and gentleman hoodwinks Delano, faith in the Catholic mysteries of font, missal and crucifix destroys Cereno – as it destroyed Aranda, his friend, who also fol-lowed his leader and trusted the slaves. If at one level, then, the irony cuts at slavery, or rather the patronizing hypoc-risy inherent in all slave-societies, at a deeper level, where the shadow of the Negro merges into the black and brown habits of Dominican and Franciscan, it subverts the very foundations of Puritan and Catholic faith on which that institution and those attitudes ultimately rest. For Puritan and Catholic clasp hands 'across the black's body'. And as Amasa Delano's christian name (rooted in 'love') is seen in the end to be ironic, so Benito Cereno (suggesting 'blessed, serene') must die in the end on a Mount of Agony.

That Melville could attempt two such themes, linked within a single work, suggests the titanic hubris – piling Pelion on Ossa – of which he remained capable. Again and again in these years he attempted to storm to the centre of the confused, grey and conflicting world. 'It is strange how he persists,' wrote Hawthorne, '– and has persisted ever since I knew him, and probably long before – in wandering to-and-fro over these deserts, as dismal and monotonous as the sand hills amid which we were sitting. He can neither believe, nor be comfortable in his unbelief; and he is too honest and courageous not to try to do one or the other.'

The Confidence-Man was a last, supreme achievement; then he left on the trip which took him, via those Lanca-shire sand dunes, to Jerusalem. On his return he tried public lecturing for a while (the glamour of 'the man who had lived among cannibals' still held) and planned to sail round the world with his young brother Tom. But stuck in San Francisco – kept waiting – he hurried home by steamer. Then civil war broke out; he vainly tried for a commission in the navy; and in 1863 sold the rest of the Pittsfield property and moved back to New York. But not back to fiction. In the winter of 1866 Melville was at last offered public employment: a Deputy Inspectorship in the New York Custom House – outdoor work. 'Herman's position in the Custom House', wrote Elizabeth Melville in 1885, 'is in the Surveyor's Department – a *district inspector* – his work is all on the uptown piers nearly to Harlem....' Gauguin, that other victim of the South Seas, abandoned his Danish wife and children for the dream of Tahiti: Melville abandoned the dream and for almost twenty years trod the New York pavements daily cross-town to work.

'What I feel most moved to write, that is banned – it will not pay...', he had written to Hawthorne more than fifteen years earlier. But he never really abandoned his dreams; found glued to the inside of the desk on which he wrote *Billy Budd* was a tiny clipping: 'Keep true to the dreams of thy youth.' For the machine duplicates: the artist continually inaugurates (that was another lesson of *The Bell-Tower*); and machine and artist cannot coexist. True to himself, Melville remained an artist. Like John Marr (another inland sailor at his woodbench), Melville isolated himself in the big city. His past, too, 'was not the past of these pioneers'. Cut off from neighbours and old friends, linked by nothing except 'that mere work-a-day bond' to the wide world, he too was thrown 'more and more upon retrospective musings' – a man of fantasies, 'lit by that aureola circling over any object of the affections in the past, for reunion with which an imaginative heart passionately yearns'.

> Ye float around me, form and feature:
> Tattooings, ear-rings, love-locks curled;

Barbarians of man's simpler nature,
Unworldly servers of the world.

In twenty-five years, between 1866 and 1891, four volumes were quietly published: *Battle-Pieces and Aspects of the War* (1866), *Clarel: A Poem and Pilgrimage in the Holy Land* (1876), *John Marr and Other Sailors* (1888) and *Timoleon* (1891) – all poetry.

Many writers, beginning as poets, have matured into prose: fewer writers, like Melville or Hardy, beginning with prose, have refined into verse. While Melville's best prose (*Bartleby, Benito Cereno*) had long been serving a vision of something strangely static – rapt – with *Clarel*, paradoxically, he evolved what was almost a novel in verse. A new psychological interest, a new sense of dramatic conflict, took shape out of which (and out of other experiments, such as *John Marr*) a final prose tale was to spring. In December 1885, having inherited some money, Melville at last felt able to retire. 'After twenty years nearly, as an outdoor Custom House officer,' he wrote in 1889, 'I have latterly come into possession of unobstructed leisure, but only just as, in the course of nature, my vigor sensibly declines. What little of it is left I husband for certain matters as yet incomplete, and which indeed may never be completed –' That work, never to be completed, was *Billy Budd*.

Despite its posthumous popularity, *Billy Budd* cannot match the achievements of Melville's prime. He worked and reworked at the story, relating Druid mythology to 'The Great Mutiny' of 1797, Milton's *Paradise Lost* to Shakespeare's *Othello*, the '*Bellipotent* case' to the *Somers* case of 1842, till the narrative, overloaded with meanings and double-meanings, allegory and allusions, almost ground to a standstill. Technically, while intent on drama, his bias remained static, unable to resist interplay (on the page) at the expense of a forward propulsion (in time), imagery at the expense of plot. Admittedly *Billy Budd, Sailor* is unfinished, but as incident after incident became transformed, Melville's imaginative – purely aesthetic – grip no longer seemed to exercise the firm hold of thirty years earlier; at its very roots is something too conventionally gothic (those 'gelidly protruding' serpent eyes, that 'paralyzing lurch of the torpedo fish'), too predictably Victorian in setting yet another jet-curled Mephistopheles versus another blue-eyed Saxon innocent. Rightly Richard Chase called Billy Budd 'almost the first – first *crucial* – self-indulgence of a great intelligence'.

The background (as of all the stories here, except *Bartleby* and *Cock-A-Doodle-Doo!*) is historical, but this time the sources – Melville's study of William James's *Naval History of Great Britain* or Southey's *Life of Nelson* – only gradually influenced the design. For the final version amassed from a long process of interpolations. Beginning with a sketch of an older sailor, a mutineer soliloquizing as he faces death (in the style of *John Marr*), Melville next introduced the monstrous master-at-arms Iago/Claggart, or Satan/Claggart, only in the final phase, after November 1888, shifting the focus to Captain Vere, expanding and dramatizing his role until it overshadowed the rest. (The second Vere chapter – 7 in this text – and the Nelson digression were still in folders when Melville died on 28 September 1891: who knows how much further revision he had felt was necessary?)

The complexity of *Billy Budd*, then, lies in this triple confrontation of characters; there is little of the slow-dawning, complex reversals of value as in *Bartleby* or *Benito Cereno*. Here first impressions remain last impressions – except possibly of Captain Vere. It proves, in fact, not so much a story of Vere or of Budd or of Claggart as of an isosceles triangle 'nipped in the vice of fate', an infernal machine in which all three protagonists meet their death. The subtitle, 'An Inside Narrative', – no doubt to refute the official 'News from the Mediterranean' – holds out its promise: but what the psychological impulse ('the secret facts') behind Claggart's aberrant behaviour, or Vere's more frightening formalities, may be, is only hinted. For the three sides of the triangle are explored not for their psychological, but moral, contrasts – expressed within the familiar spectrum of white, black and grey.

Billy Budd, pink and white as his name – or the rosy cloud at his execution – is blond and blue-eyed as sunshine and water on that journey of 'fraternal unreserve' of the two sea captains to Lima. Illiterate, high-spirited, athletic, he is innocent utterly – which is not to say utterly perfect : physically, he has the impediment of his stutter, morally, his 'erring sense of uninstructed honor'. His is brute innocence. Imagery of dogs, horses, song-birds of all kinds gathers round him : at his execution 'a singing bird on the point of launching', he is buried to the 'croaked requiem' of sea-fowl. Both foundling and 'Handsome Sailor' of eighteenth-century ballads (in a revised, pointedly epicene, version), Apollo and 'childman' (before Christianity 'a sort of upright barbarian'), this adolescent, impressed from 'the happy family' of the *Rights-of-Man*, is Melville's last dream of the Noble Savage 'prior to Cain's city and citified man'. From the valley of the Typees to *Billy Budd* is but a single bound. Embodying a whole mythology according to Rousseau, Billy's very presence on a man-of-war is a potentially explosive threat to a civilization at war with itself.

For being a peacemaker on the *Bellipotent* – a fighting peacemaker – is as paradoxical as being a priest (to whom Captain Graveling had first compared Billy) serving the God of War. Theirs are the two polarities and, at the crisis of death, they meet in a kiss. But the sailor alone, at this historical juncture, must suffer. Claggart or no Claggart, such guilelessness is subversive : such childlike savagery is itself revolutionary. Though innocent, in a fallen world Billy Budd is guilty and must die. That, inevitably, is 'how it fared with the Handsome Sailor during the year of the Great Mutiny'.

Thus, too, the Christ imagery (of crucifixion, ascension and atonement) which he attracts. Not that Billy Budd *is* Christ obviously. Even if, like Jesus, he is illegitimate, an Ishmael in the world, he is too ignorant, too innocent of all temptation, too unconscious of evil, too untouched by

[41]

suffering or torment. 'The flaw of the stammer', W. H. Auden rightly remarks, 'will not quite do, for this is only an aesthetic weakness, not a deliberate abandonment of advantages.' Far from Satan's 'little card', it is the very expression of Billy's 'strong heart-feeling' – that of an Adam rather, 'young Adam before the fall'. For here also the metaphors are mixed.

The problem, again, is ultimately not that of evil. It is that of innocence: how is the world to deal with these simpletons – Bartleby, Delano, the Chola Widow, Budd? Should we, unlike Vere, spare the 'upright barbarian' because he did not mean to kill, because if he could have used his tongue, he would not have struck a blow? Once earlier, another innocent, another Adam in his 'white jacket' plunged from a mast overboard to a seeming wilful baptism of experience. But Billy Budd, like Bartleby, like the starry-eyed Captain Delano almost to the end, never wakens. 'A goldfinch popped into a cage', a nightingale into a mantrap, 'Billy made no demur'; 'he mechanically rose and, sleepily wondering what could be in the wind, betook himself to the designated place'. He walks in a trance, like a somnambulist, to his death.

Almost twice Billy's age, John Claggart (conflating 'clerk' plus 'haggard'?) is the pale, literate man, inhabitant of Cain's city. Black-curled, violet-eyed, he is evil utterly. 'Sinister dexterity', so wanting in Billy, is alive – with all the contortions of that punning paradox – in Claggart. Thus his serpentine, insinuating vocabulary: 'master-at-arms', his very title, seems 'somewhat equivocal'. Thus, too, the Satanic imagery which he attracts. Not that Claggart is Satan necessarily: merely one of the 'uncatalogued creatures of the deep,' merely one of 'the promiscuous lame ducks of morality' perhaps.

His head, like that of Milton's 'Arch Angel ruin'd', is shapely, his forehead intellectual and apt for circumlocution, masked by a bitter smile. His is a 'ferreting genius'. The temptation of Adam/Budd (a twinkle of coins at night: the language of mutiny) is carried out solely through underlings. He does nothing to insinuate himself personally with Budd. They have no intercourse: he burns secretly with 'a subterranean fire', watchful, melancholy, at a distance. 'Yes, and sometimes the melancholy expression would have in it a touch of soft yearning, as if Claggart could even have loved Billy but for fate and ban.'

'Evanescent as that tenderness was,' F. O. Matthiessen concluded, 'it shows that Claggart is not wholly diabolic.' *Pace* Matthiessen, Claggart remains wholly the monster. The ambivalent 'soft yearning', far from extenuating diabolic evil, is the very mark of Satan's first glimpse of Paradise; Milton's protagonist, too, could wonder, love, melt with pity while secretly spying man's naked innocence – the sole difference here being that this new Adam of the *Bellipotent*, the Handsome Sailor, is alone, without an Eve. Billy is 'strength and beauty'; it is this 'comeliness and power, always attractive in masculine conjunction', which proves so fatal an attraction to the serpent/Claggart.

When, through a glance of Claggart's eyes, we see 'belted Billy rolling along the upper gun deck', or through Captain Vere's, 'in the nude . . . posed for a statue of young Adam', a homosexual echo is inevitably sounded. It is deliberate:

'What too many seamen are when ashore is very well known,' Melville recorded in *White-Jacket*; 'but what some of them become when completely cut off from shore indulgences can hardly be imagined by landsmen. The sins for which the cities of the plain were overthrown still linger in some of these wooden-walled Gomorrahs of the deep. More than once complaints were made at the mast in the *Neversink*, from which the deck officer would turn away with loathing, refuse to hear them, and command the complainant out of his sight.'

'You have but noted his fair cheek. A mantrap may be under the ruddy-tipped daisies,' Claggart insinuates (though he, of course, is the mantrap!). His few words to Vere are as equivocal as his few words to Billy – as equivocal as the old Merlin's original merriment or the equivocal young afterguardsman with his equivocal 'word of good fellowship' in the evening promenade. As in a game of chess 'few moves are made in straightforwardness and ends are attained by indirection. . . .' 'Be direct, man', Captain Vere interrupts Claggart. But the master-at-arms had the cunning not to bring *that* complaint, openly at least, against Billy Budd. On the *Bellipotent*, as on the *Neversink*, the hearing would certainly have been refused.

Though on the *Neversink* certain youthful complainants, it seems, were not always turned away: a middle-aged sailor is 'flogged at the complaint of a midshipman . . . apt to indulge at times in undignified familiarities with some of the men, who, sooner or later, almost always suffered from his capricious preferences'. There informers, with conscious *double-entendre*, are referred to as 'white-mice' or 'fancy-men', just as here the young afterguardsman is equivocally chubby (with a rat's white lashes). On the *Rights-of-Man*, when Red Whiskers digs 'the sweet and pleasant young fellow' under the ribs, to show him 'just whence a sirloin steak was cut', the sexual innuendo is explicit: and Billy can openly prove he has 'the spirit of a gamecock'. By contrast the *Bellipotent*, where the Handsome Sailor is greeted with ambiguous smiles like 'a rustic beauty . . . brought into competition with the highborn dames of the court', seems a warren of male intrigue. How among such 'mantraps', ponders the Dansker, could innocence like Billy's survive.

But to speak (with Melville) 'by indirection': himself 'well molded', Claggart was somehow beyond 'a normal nature', 'rather queer at times', 'a nut not to be cracked by the tap of a lady's fan'; yet Billy's rare personal beauty (both Bull-God and English girl) aroused, it seems, that paradox – the yearning antipathy of the master-at-arms. In *Benito Cereno* the homosexual vision merely distorts: in *Billy Budd* it becomes wholly evil, actively bent on destruction. But even in the final ascent from the yard-arm, in that hanging which Claggart had so deviously inflicted on Billy, sexual spasm or ejaculation is absent. The erotic vision which feasts on executions is miraculously disarmed. The Handsome Sailor remains inviolate even in death.

Innocence alone lacks the subtlety to survive; but innocence in a fallen world inevitably involves others in its self-immolation. Between the illiterate Budd and the literate Claggart stands Captain the Honorable Edward Fairfax Vere, with equal knowledge of men and books. A reader of Montaigne, a humanist, he is both 'man' (*vir*, as his name suggests) and 'truth' (*veritas*), wholly sharing the ambivalences of the one and paradoxes of the other. Which makes him far from simple. His presentation alone veers, moving moon-like in and out of eclipse, from that of father to the most rigorous disciplinarian. He is all things at all times: discreet commander, barbarian Tsar, surrogate father. His is an instinctive, God-like understanding of both Claggart and Billy, yet his role shifts: if he condemns Billy by the letter of the law, he loves him like Abraham and Issac in the privacy of their last meeting, but executes him in public. Within the spectrum of white and black – between the black booms and white vapoury fleece where Billy's death is played – Vere is compounded of both: his eyes (like Bartleby's) are grey. 'Starry Vere' is his nickname, but he is not a star of the first magnitude – no Aldebaran in the constellation Taurus, no Nelson. His qualities are 'sterling', not 'brilliant'.

This is the place of civilization (as we know from *The Encantadas*) where good and evil merge: on the borderline of sanity and insanity where Vere imperceptibly moves; the grey world of suspicion and fear among another mutinied crew at the opening of *Benito Cereno*. Then it was on the traffic of slavery that civilization seemed to rest; here it is on a world at war with itself that Captain Vere knows the fate of 'forms, measured forms' to depend. So his way is the only civilized way – that is, the only possible way to prevent the disruption of civilization – the way of the world at war: the King's Law and the Naval Code. To this he holds 'rigid as a musket in the ship-armorer's rack'.

Melville, it seems, no more condemns Captain Vere with his 'music and religious rites subserving the discipline and purposes of war', than he condemned Captain Graveling for releasing Billy or the thirsty Lieutenant Ratcliffe for usurping him. The moral of the eighth sketch of the *The Encantadas* ('often ill comes from the good as good from the ill'), the ultimate moral of *Pierre, or the Ambiguities*, seems also the moral here. In life the line is blurred: 'speculatively regarded, it well might be referred to a jury of casuists', 'a matter for psychologic theologians to discuss'. But we must learn to accept the blur and live in the blur (though not to the point of accepting authorized publications which mistake the villain for the hero and the innocent for the villain). Like Billy with his last breath, we can only cry: 'God bless Captain Vere!'

For his is the agony. It is the living who must carry the stigmata of the dead. 'At the very moment when it seems to men that they are inflicting on one another the most terrible of all things,' wrote Tolstoy on the assassination of Alexander II, 'that terrible thing no longer exists for the victim, but recoils entirely upon those who inflict it.' That musket 'erectly rigid' after Billy's last cry suggests not only the firing-squad and martial law, but also the *rigor mortis* and even the sexual erection so miraculously absent in Billy – absent, perhaps, because already contracted by Vere. Grey-eyed, he lives in the twilit zone of the pelicans, those pensive 'sea Friars', and of 'tormented Job'. 'Billy Budd, Billy Budd' are his last murmured words. But not in the 'accents of remorse', for, like Job, Vere had nothing on his conscience – except the weight of his condition, which is the weight of the world. Another Benito Cereno, he soon dies, but this time at war – Gibraltar, his 'monastery on Mount Agonia'.

'Good-bye to you, too, old *Rights-of-Man*' – Billy's parting salute – is at the drama's core. It is good-bye to 'the happy family', to 'fiddler's green', to all 'exuberance of vitality' where are the songs of innocence. The warship – 'Cain's city' – by contrast is tarred and painted black. At

the very opening, Captain Graveling, 'honest soul', is set
by the side of Lieutenant Ratcliffe, tossing back tumblers
of grog: 'a ploughman' of troubled waters by the side of
'sensuous enjoyment'; pipe-smoking *gravitas* by a rat from
the 'rat-pit'. The whole weight of Graveling's despair is in
that opening pun. For Billy is cast in Graveling's mould :
his 'humane look' echoes his Captain's 'humanely intelligent' expression; his musical voice echoes Graveling's
'musical chime'. For all his youth, he is Graveling's spiritual
heir.

Captain Vere, Billy's lord and master (and old enough to
be his father), alone seems to rise above such commonplace
rural/urban contrasts. 'But do these buttons that we wear',
he asks rhetorically, 'attest that our allegiance is to Nature?
No, to the King. Though the ocean, which is inviolate
Nature primeval, though this be the element where we
move and have our being as sailors, yet as the King's
officers lies our duty in a sphere correspondingly natural?'
With such pedantic questions and crabbed logic the issues
of Nature versus civilization, country versus city, peace
versus war, life versus death, seem finally to be resolved.
'Forms' – the lyre of Orpheus – must spellbind 'the wild
denizens of the wood'.

But can this humourless, bookish bachelor (without any
of the dash, instinct, intelligence ultimately, of Nelson) be
trusted on such issues? His excited manner, his passionate
outburst, his 'desire for secrecy' all profoundly disturb the
surgeon. Abruptly, wilfully, he summons a drumhead court.
Once there, however, his tightly controlled, unobtrusive,
undemonstrative side again dominates. 'Let not warm
hearts', he warns, 'betray heads that should be cool.' 'That
is to say :' rings an echo, 'Toward the accomplishment of an
aim which in wantonness of atrocity would seem to partake of the insane, he will direct a cool judgment sagacious
and sound.' 'Was he unhinged?' the surgeon wonders.
'These men are madmen,' Melville had already answered,
'and of the most dangerous sort, for their lunacy is not continuous, but occasional, evoked by some special object; it

[47]

is protectively secretive, which is as much as to say it is self-contained. . . .'

The pivot of the action, once wholly within Claggart, now turns wholly on Vere. But Claggart himself, it seems, forms a commentary on Vere; Vere partly mirrors Claggart; and both share a common mania, a single 'depravity according to nature'. Only Vere, unlike Claggart, may finally 'have caught Billy to his heart' – may have melted back 'into what remains primeval in our formalized humanity', and expressed his passion – but whatever passed between Abraham and Isaac in that closeted interview, such dream fatherhood, so 'protectively secretive', so 'self-contained', was itself rooted lunacy. Between the master-at-arms and the Captain – both even-tempered, dry, discreetly proud intellectuals – Baby Budd was 'nipped in the vice': between a lover and a father – both madmen – he was destroyed.

As Milton's Satan, on entering Eden, is spied:

> Thrice chang'd with pale, ire, envy and despair,
> Which marr'd his borrow'd visage, and betray'd
> Him counterfeit . . .

so Claggart's 'distorting expression', after the accident of the spilled soup, strangely disconcerts the heedless drummer-boy; so Vere's expression of agony is a 'startling revelation' to the senior lieutenant meeting him after the closeted interview. Both linked in various ways – both 'queer' – are the victims of Billy Budd, as Billy, in his agony, is theirs. A machine so infernal implies ironic machinery. The whole narrative proves a mesh of tragic irony. It is Vere who sets up the 'mantrap' by preferring the privacy of his cabin to at once calling witnesses; it is Vere whose fatherly words prompt the moment of manslaughter, who acts as prosecutor (in secrecy) and executioner (in public) – to whose further discretion is due the report which acclaims Claggart the patriot and Budd the criminal.

Vere, Billy, Claggart – each, Melville claims, is 'exceptional', each, in fact or appearance, of 'noble descent' or of 'high quality'. Their drama, too, (with neoclassic scrupulousness) centres on a single place (the captain's cabin) within an unbroken span (of 'less than an hour and a half'). But who is its hero? The Handsome Sailor – an innocent, a scapegoat doomed by 'forms, measured forms'? Billy Agonistes, it is true, exists, but child-like, soon soothed in an embrace. Captain Vere Agonistes, then? His role, his 'inner nature', is equivocal – deeply, tragically flawed even, but hardly heroic. If 'tragedy' at all, as Melville insists, this would seem 'tragedy' without a tragic hero.

In the very perception, however, – that a modern tragedy has no need of tragic heroes; that agony and destruction are inherent in a man-of-war, madness in the floating hulk of our black civilization – the bitter seed of the tale lies buried. *Billy Budd* is neither Melville's 'testament of acceptance', as early readers claimed, nor of 'protest', as later critics replied, but his last parable of the human condition – his last signpost to forces which can drive the subterranean torrents of love to torment, or blessing, to destruction, or healing trust.

We are left with 'three brief chapters': Vere's truth (which preserves society, but kills), official lies (which is history) and sailor myth (in ballad and living faith). That, and the death of Nelson. For Nelson caps the tale, transcendent beyond 'forms', 'usage' or 'barbaric good humor', beyond prudence and imprudence. In him head and heart, reason and instinct are one. It is Nelson (the paradox of Copenhagen and Trafalgar: painstaking genius and impassioned lover of glory), not Christ, who is its touchstone and key. It is Nelson, adorning himself 'for the altar and the sacrifice', who becomes the archetype of all epic and tragic drama – the hero. He is both the humane Graveling and the sensuous Ratcliffe, both Vere and Budd, victor and victim, and thus a resolution of each and a compound beyond all: the ultimate Handsome Sailor, black or white.

Who in the rainbow can draw a line...? Between the black and the white the streak was no longer red, but rose, 'the full rose of the dawn'. After three violent deaths, one last, one quieter death: Daniel Orme,

[49]

> Like a Sea-beast crawled forth, that on a shelf
> Of rock or sand reposeth, there to sun itself . . .

on Easter Sunday, clay pipe cracked but smoked out to the last, open eyes still fixed on the 'hazy waters and the dim-seen sails coming and going or at anchor nearer by'.

So Melville, like the last of his hard, moody, solitary heroes, died – he too 'a sort of man forbid', part Christian, part pagan (or did the warrior scar cancel the heart-borne crucifix it crosses?), slipped into obscure moorings ashore, alone even in death among 'an obsolete battery of rusty guns' (his work long out of print or unpublished). With an Ancient Mariner's beady eye, he too had held to his course (clay pipe cracked but smoked out to the last). Through myth, despite allegory, past reefs of symbolism, he had kept true to the dreams of his youth. In prose *nouveau riche* in its verbal splendour, antiquarian in its delight, bible-echoed, allusive, elaborate, he had kept faith to the end – exactly, lyrically intent as a ship's prow cutting the waves, or a sea-gull dipping and diving in the wake of his questing and restless intellect.

HAROLD BEAVER

A NOTE ON THE TEXT

THE text of *Bartleby, The Encantadas, The Bell-Tower* and *Benito Cereno* is that of the first edition of *The Piazza Tales* (May 1856); both Melville and his publishers, Dix and Edwards, re-edited these stories from copies of *Putnam's Monthly Magazine* in which they had appeared between 1853 and 1855, though Melville was not entirely happy with the result. 'There seems to be a surprising profusion of commas in these proofs,' he wrote to Dix and Edwards. 'I have struck them out pretty much; but I hope that some one who understands punctuation better than I do, will give the final hand to it' (24 March 1856). Occasionally, with this for cue, I have deleted a comma, or even added one, as sense demanded.

Cock-A-Doodle-Doo!, which first appeared in *Harper's New Monthly Magazine*, November–December 1853, and the prose introduction to *John Marr* (from *John Marr and Other Sailors*, 1888), are here reprinted from the Standard Edition of Melville's works, Volumes 13 and 16, edited by Raymond Weaver (Constable, 1924).

This edition of *Billy Budd*, however, follows an exhaustive, and surely definitive, re-examination of the uncompleted manuscript, deposited in 1942 by Melville's grand-daughter, Eleanor Melville Metcalf, in the Harvard College Library. The pioneer transcription by Raymond Weaver (published in the Constable edition of 1924) and the more recent labours of F. Barron Freeman (published by Harvard University Press, 1948, with *Corrigenda* by Elizabeth Treeman, 1953) – both widely and frequently reprinted – are now finally superseded. Harrison Hayford and Merton M. Sealts, Jr in *Billy Budd, Sailor* (University of Chicago Press, 1962) presented two texts. 'In one,' they write, 'the Genetic Text, we give an exact transcription of what appeared in the *Billy Budd* manuscript as it stood at the time of Melville's death. . . . Since the manuscript itself, which Mrs Melville characterized as "unfinished", was never prepared for the printer, we give in the Reading Text the wording that in our judgment most closely approximates Melville's final intention had a new fair copy been made without his engaging in further expansion or revision.' It is this Reading Text which (with grateful acknowledgement) is here reprinted.

The text of *Daniel Orme*, once considered a related fragment of the *Billy Budd* manuscript, follows F. Barron Freeman's 'Version A: Revised Text' (*Melville's Billy Budd*, Harvard University Press, 1948), with some slight changes of punctuation. That both Weaver and Freeman, according to Hayford and Sealts, mistook Melville's notation on the folder which contains his last 'Manuscript Studies', transcribing as 'Daniel Orme/omitted of/ Billy Budd' what should read 'Daniel Orme/&/Omitted of Billy Budd', does not in this instance invalidate the text. But, freed from the status of a discarded footnote to an incomplete masterpiece, *Daniel Orme* can at last be recognized as a final and independent work in its own right.

Two titles also require comment: *Bartleby the Scrivener, A Story of Wall-Street* Melville himself had shortened to *Bartleby* for inclusion in *The Piazza Tales*; but that *Billy Budd, Sailor* is the correct and final heading for what had previously appeared as *Billy Budd, Foretopman* or *Baby Budd, Sailor* (and other such combinations) was first established by Hayford and Sealts. 'For the title of the story,' they write, 'two versions survive. One occurs in pencil draft on a slip attached to a separate leaf: "*Billy Budd/Foretopman*/What befell him/in the year of the/Great Mutiny/ &". The other occurs as a pencilled addition at the top of the first leaf of the story proper: "Billy Budd/Sailor/(An inside narrative.)". . . . That the second of these was in fact Melville's final intention for the title is made clear by all genetic evidence.' (*op. cit.* p. 19) It was Mrs Melville, apparently, sorting the manuscripts after her husband's death, who first mistook the cancelled title, retracing it carefully in pencil and possibly remounting the leaf, thus misleading both Weaver and Freeman, the subsequent editors.

To avoid burdening the text with superior numbers, the notes, under a separate heading for each story, are indicated by page references only.

BIBLIOGRAPHY

STUDENTS of *Billy Budd* will wish to turn to the definitive edition by Harrison Hayford and Merton M. Sealts, Jr, *Billy Budd, Sailor* (University of Chicago Press, 1962). Of editions of *The Piazza Tales*, that by Egbert S. Oliver (Farrar Straus, New York, 1948) remains the most reliable. For a collection of all Melville's shorter fiction, *The Complete Stories of Herman Melville*, edited by Jay Leyda (Random House, New York, 1949; Eyre & Spottiswoode, London, 1951), provides an authoritative text.

Among critical works dwelling at any length on Melville's shorter fiction, the following may be found valuable: Lewis Mumford, *Herman Melville, A Study of his Life and Vision* (Harcourt, Brace, New York, 1929; Jonathan Cape, London, 1929, reissued in a revised edition by Secker & Warburg, London, 1963); Richard Chase, *Herman Melville, A Critical Study* (Macmillan, New York, 1949) and Harry Levin, *The Power of Blackness* (Alfred A. Knopf, New York, 1958; Faber & Faber, London, 1958). H. Bruce Franklin's *The Wake of the Gods, Melville's Mythology* (Stanford University Press, 1963) throws an obliquely learned light on one aspect of Melville's genius.

For a variety of readings of *Billy Budd* – all pre-dating, however, the edition by Hayford and Sealts – the relevant pages from the following could be sampled: F. O. Matthiessen, *American Renaissance* (Oxford University Press, New York, 1941); F. Barron Freeman, *Melville's Billy Budd* (Harvard University Press, 1948); Newton Arvin, *Herman Melville* (William Sloane Associates, New York, 1950; Methuen, London, 1950; reprinted Viking Press, New York, 1957); W. H. Auden, *The Enchafèd Flood* (Random House,

New York, 1950; Faber & Faber, London, 1951); Ronald Mason, *The Spirit above the Dust* (John Lehmann, London, 1951); Milton R. Stern, *The Fine Hammered Steel of Herman Melville* (University of Illinois Press, 1957) and Merlin Bowen. *The Long Encounter: Self and Experience in the Writings of Herman Melville* (University of Chicago Press, 1960).

Leon Howard has written the standard life, *Herman Melville: A Biography* (University of California Press, 1951), while all documents relating to it have been garnered in *The Melville Log: A Documentary Life of Herman Melville, 1819–1891* (2 vols. Harcourt, Brace, New York, 1951) by Jay Leyda, which must remain the ultimate source-book. But the publication of the Melville family diaries and correspondence, with a connecting narrative, by Melville's oldest grandchild, Eleanor Melville Metcalf, *Herman Melville, Cycle and Epicycle* (Harvard University Press, 1953), is perhaps the most directly revealing introduction to the author as man.

BARTLEBY

I AM a rather elderly man. The nature of my avocations, for the last thirty years, has brought me into more than ordinary contact with what would seem an interesting and somewhat singular set of men, of whom, as yet, nothing, that I know of, has ever been written – I mean, the law-copyists, or scriveners. I have known very many of them, professionally and privately, and, if I pleased, could relate divers histories, at which good-natured gentlemen might smile, and sentimental souls might weep. But I waive the biographies of all other scriveners, for a few passages in the life of Bartleby, who was a scrivener, the strangest I ever saw, or heard of. While, of other law-copyists, I might write the complete life, of Bartleby nothing of that sort can be done. I believe that no materials exist, for a full and satisfactory biography of this man. It is an irreparable loss to literature. Bartleby was one of those beings of whom nothing is ascertainable, except from the original sources, and, in his case, those are very small. What my own astonished eyes saw of Bartleby, *that* is all I know of him, except, indeed, one vague report, which will appear in the sequel.

Ere introducing the scrivener, as he first appeared to me, it is fit I make some mention of myself, my *employés*, my business, my chambers, and general surroundings; because some such description is indispensable to an adequate understanding of the chief character about to be presented. Imprimis: I am a man who, from his youth upwards, has been filled with a profound conviction that the easiest way of life is the best. Hence, though I belong to a profession proverbially energetic and nervous, even to turbulence, at times, yet nothing of that sort have I ever suffered to invade my peace. I am one of those unambitious lawyers who never addresses a jury, or in any way draws down public applause; but, in the cool tranquillity of a snug retreat, do a snug business among rich men's bonds, and mortgages, and title-deeds. All who know me, consider me an eminently *safe* man. The late John Jacob Astor, a personage little given to poetic enthusiasm, had no hesitation in pronouncing my first grand point to be prudence; my next, method. I do not speak it in vanity, but simply record the fact, that I was not unemployed in my profession by the late John Jacob Astor; a name which, I admit, I love to repeat; for it hath a rounded and orbicular sound to it, and rings like unto bullion. I will freely add, that I was not insensible to the late John Jacob Astor's good opinion.

Some time prior to the period at which this little history begins, my avocations had been largely increased. The good old office, now extinct in the State of New York, of a Master in Chancery, had been conferred upon me. It was not a very arduous office, but very pleasantly remunerative. I seldom lose my temper; much more seldom indulge in dangerous indignation at wrongs and outrages; but, I must be permitted to be rash here, and declare, that I consider the sudden and violent abrogation of the office of Master in Chancery, by the new Constitution, as a —— premature act; inasmuch as I had counted upon a life-lease of the profits, whereas I only received those of a few short years. But this is by the way.

My chambers were up stairs, at No. —— Wall Street. At one end, they looked upon the white wall of the interior of a spacious sky-light shaft, penetrating the building from top to bottom.

This view might have been considered rather tame than otherwise, deficient in what landscape painters call 'life'. But, if so, the view from the other end of my chambers offered, at least, a contrast, if nothing more. In that direction, my windows commanded an unobstructed view of a lofty brick wall, black by age and everlasting shade; which wall required no spy-glass to bring out its lurking beauties, but, for the benefit of all near-sighted spectators, was pushed up to within ten feet of my window panes. Owing to the great height of the surrounding buildings, and my chambers being on the second floor, the interval between this wall and mine not a little resembled a huge square cistern.

At the period just preceding the advent of Bartleby, I had two persons as copyists in my employment, and a promising lad as an office-boy. First, Turkey; second, Nippers; third, Ginger Nut. These may seem names, the like of which are not usually found in the Directory. In truth, they were nicknames, mutually conferred upon each other by my three clerks, and were deemed expressive of their respective persons or characters. Turkey was a short, pursy Englishman, of about my own age – that is, somewhere not far from sixty. In the morning, one might say, his face was of a fine florid hue, but after twelve o'clock, meridian – his dinner hour – it blazed like a grate full of Christmas coals; and continued blazing – but, as it were, with a gradual wane – till six o'clock, P.M., or thereabouts; after which, I saw no more of the proprietor of the face, which, gaining its meridian with the sun, seemed to set with it, to rise, culminate, and decline the following day, with the like regularity and undiminished glory. There are many singular coincidences I have known in the course of my life, not the least among which was the fact, that, exactly when Turkey displayed his fullest beams from his red and radiant countenance, just then, too, at that critical moment, began the daily period when I considered his business capacities as seriously disturbed for the remainder of the twenty-four hours. Not that he was absolutely idle, or averse to business, then; far from it. The difficulty was, he was apt to be altogether too energetic. There was a strange, inflamed, flurried, flighty recklessness of activity about him. He would be incautious in dipping his pen into his inkstand. All his blots upon my documents were dropped there after twelve o'clock, meridian. Indeed, not only would he be reckless, and sadly given to making blots in the afternoon, but, some days, he went further, and was rather noisy. At such times, too, his face flamed with augmented blazonry, as if cannel coal had been heaped on anthracite. He made an unpleasant racket with his chair; spilled his sand-box; in mending his pens, impatiently split them all to pieces, and threw them on the floor in a sudden passion; stood up, and leaned over his table, boxing his papers about in a most indecorous manner, very sad to behold in an elderly man like him. Nevertheless, as he was in many ways a most valuable person to me, and all the time before twelve o'clock, meridian, was the quickest, steadiest creature, too, accomplishing a great deal of work in a style not easily to be matched – for these reasons, I was willing to overlook his eccentricities, though, indeed, occasionally, I remonstrated with him. I did this very gently, however, because, though the civilest, nay, the blandest and most reverential of men in the morning, yet, in the afternoon, he was disposed, upon provocation, to be slightly rash with his tongue – in fact insolent. Now, valuing his morning services as I did, and resolved not to lose them – yet, at the same time, made uncomfortable by his inflamed ways after twelve o'clock – and being a man of peace, unwilling by my admonitions to call forth unseemly retorts from him, I took upon me, one Saturday noon (he was always worse on Saturdays) to hint to him, very kindly, that, perhaps, now that he was growing old, it might be well to abridge his labors; in short, he need not come to my chambers after twelve o'clock, but, dinner over, had best go home to his lodgings, and rest himself till tea-time. But no; he insisted upon his afternoon devotions. His countenance became intolerably fervid, as he oratorically assured me – gesticulating with a long ruler at the other end of the room – that if his services in the morning were useful, how indispensable, then, in the afternoon?

'With submission, sir,' said Turkey, on this occasion, 'I consider myself your right-hand man. In the morning I but marshal and deploy my columns; but in the afternoon I

put myself at their head, and gallantly charge the foe, thus'
– and he made a violent thrust with the ruler.

'But the blots, Turkey,' intimated I.

'True; but, with submission, sir, behold these hairs! I am
getting old. Surely, sir, a blot or two of a warm afternoon is
not to be severely urged against gray hairs. Old age – even
if it blot the page – is honorable. With submission, sir, we
both are getting old.'

This appeal to my fellow-feeling was hardly to be resisted.
At all events, I saw that go he would not. So, I made up
my mind to let him stay, resolving, nevertheless, to see to
it that, during the afternoon, he had to do with my less
important papers.

Nippers, the second on my list, was a whiskered, sallow,
and, upon the whole, rather piratical-looking young man,
of about five and twenty. I always deemed him the victim
of two evil powers – ambition and indigestion. The ambition was evinced by a certain impatience of the duties of
a mere copyist, an unwarrantable usurpation of strictly professional affairs, such as the original drawing up of legal
documents. The indigestion seemed betokened in an occasional nervous testiness and grinning irritability, causing
the teeth to audibly grind together over mistakes committed in copying; unnecessary maledictions, hissed, rather
than spoken, in the heat of business; and especially by a
continual discontent with the height of the table where he
worked. Though of a very ingenious mechanical turn,
Nippers could never get this table to suit him. He put chips
under it, blocks of various sorts, bits of pasteboard, and at
last went so far as to attempt an exquisite adjustment, by
final pieces of folded blotting-paper. But no invention
would answer. If, for the sake of easing his back, he brought
the table lid at a sharp angle well up towards his chin, and
wrote there like a man using the steep roof of a Dutch
house for his desk, then he declared that it stopped the
circulation in his arms. If now he lowered the table to his
waistbands, and stooped over it in writing, then there was
a sore aching in his back. In short, the truth of the matter

was, Nippers knew not what he wanted. Or, if he wanted anything, it was to be rid of a scrivener's table altogether. Among the manifestations of his diseased ambition was a fondness he had for receiving visits from certain ambiguous-looking fellows in seedy coats, whom he called his clients. Indeed, I was aware that not only was he, at times, considerable of a ward-politician, but he occasionally did a little business at the Justices' courts, and was not unknown on the steps of the Tombs. I have good reason to believe, however, that one individual who called upon him at my chambers, and who, with a grand air, he insisted was his client, was no other than a dun, and the alleged title-deed, a bill. But, with all his failings, and the annoyances he caused me, Nippers, like his compatriot Turkey, was a very useful man to me; wrote a neat, swift hand; and, when he chose, was not deficient in a gentlemanly sort of deportment. Added to this, he always dressed in a gentlemanly sort of way; and so, incidentally, reflected credit upon my chambers. Whereas, with respect to Turkey, I had much ado to keep him from being a reproach to me. His clothes were apt to look oily, and smell of eating-houses. He wore his pantaloons very loose and baggy in summer. His coats were execrable; his hat not to be handled. But while the hat was a thing of indifference to me, inasmuch as his natural civility and deference, as a dependent Englishman, always led him to doff it the moment he entered the room, yet his coat was another matter. Concerning his coats, I reasoned with him; but with no effect. The truth was, I suppose, that a man with so small an income could not afford to sport such a lustrous face and a lustrous coat at one and the same time. As Nippers once observed, Turkey's money went chiefly for red ink. One winter day, I presented Turkey with a highly respectable-looking coat of my own – a padded gray coat, of a most comfortable warmth, and which buttoned straight up from the knee to the neck. I thought Turkey would appreciate the favor, and abate his rashness and obstreperousness of afternoons. But no; I verily believe that buttoning himself up in so downy and blanket-like a coat had a pernicious effect upon him – upon the same principle that too much oats are bad for horses. In fact, precisely as a rash, restive horse is said to feel his oats, so Turkey felt his coat. It made him insolent. He was a man whom prosperity harmed.

Though, concerning the self-indulgent habits of Turkey, I had my own private surmises, yet, touching Nippers, I was well persuaded that, whatever might be his faults in other respects, he was, at least, a temperate young man. But, indeed nature herself seemed to have been his vintner, and, at his birth, charged him so thoroughly with an irritable, brandy-like disposition, that all subsequent potations were needless. When I consider how, amid the stillness of my chambers, Nippers would sometimes impatiently rise from his seat, and stooping over his table, spread his arms wide apart, seize the whole desk, and move it, and jerk it, with a grim, grinding motion on the floor, as if the table were a perverse voluntary agent, intent on thwarting and vexing him, I plainly perceive that, for Nippers, brandy-and-water were altogether superfluous.

It was fortunate for me that, owing to its peculiar cause – indigestion – the irritability and consequent nervousness of Nippers were mainly observable in the morning, while in the afternoon he was comparatively mild. So that, Turkey's paroxysms only coming on about twelve o'clock, I never had to do with their eccentricities at one time. Their fits relieved each other, like guards. When Nippers's was on, Turkey's was off; and *vice versa*. This was a good natural arrangement, under the circumstances.

Ginger Nut, the third on my list, was a lad, some twelve years old. His father was a car-man, ambitious of seeing his son on the bench instead of a cart, before he died. So he sent him to my office, as student at law, errand-boy, cleaner and sweeper, at the rate of one dollar a week. He had a little desk to himself, but he did not use it much. Upon inspection, the drawer exhibited a great array of the shells of various sorts of nuts. Indeed, to this quick-witted youth, the whole noble science of the law was contained in a nutshell. Not the least among the employments of Ginger Nut, as well as one which he discharged with the most alacrity, was his duty as cake and apple purveyor for Turkey and Nippers. Copying law-papers being proverbially a dry, husky sort of business, my two scriveners were fain to moisten their mouths very often with Spitzenbergs, to be had at the numerous stalls nigh the Custom House and Post Office. Also, they sent Ginger Nut very frequently for that peculiar cake – small, flat, round, and very spicy – after which he had been named by them. Of a cold morning, when business was but dull, Turkey would gobble up scores of these cakes, as if they were mere wafers – indeed, they sell them at the rate of six or eight for a penny – the scrape of his pen blending with the crunching of the crisp particles in his mouth. Of all the fiery afternoon blunders and flurried rashnesses of Turkey, was his once moistening a ginger-cake between his lips, and clapping it on to a mortgage, for a seal. I came within an ace of dismissing him then. But he mollified me by making an oriental bow, and saying –

'With submission, sir, it was generous of me to find you in stationery on my own account.'

Now my original business – that of a conveyancer and title hunter, and drawer-up of recondite documents of all sorts – was considerably increased by receiving the master's office. There was now great work for scriveners. Not only must I push the clerks already with me, but I must have additional help.

In answer to my advertisement, a motionless young man one morning stood upon my office threshold, the door being open, for it was summer. I can see that figure now – pallidly neat, pitiably respectable, incurably forlorn! It was Bartleby.

After a few words touching his qualifications, I engaged him, glad to have among my corps of copyists a man of so singularly sedate an aspect, which I thought might operate beneficially upon the flighty temper of Turkey, and the fiery one of Nippers.

I should have stated before that ground glass folding-doors divided my premises into two parts, one of which was occupied by my scriveners, the other by myself. According to my humor, I threw open these doors, or closed them. I resolved to assign Bartleby a corner by the folding-doors, but on my side of them, so as to have this quiet man within easy call, in case any trifling thing was to be done. I placed his desk close up to a small side-window in that part of the room, a window which originally had afforded a lateral view of certain grimy back-yards and bricks, but which, owing to subsequent erections, commanded at present no view at all, though it gave some light. Within three feet of the panes was a wall, and the light came down from far above, between two lofty buildings, as from a very small opening in a dome. Still further to a satisfactory arrangement, I procured a high green folding screen, which might entirely isolate Bartleby from my sight, though not remove him from my voice. And thus, in a manner, privacy and society were conjoined.

At first, Bartleby did an extraordinary quantity of writing. As if long famishing for something to copy, he seemed to gorge himself on my documents. There was no pause for digestion. He ran a day and night line, copying by sun-light and by candle-light. I should have been quite delighted with his application, had he been cheerfully industrious. But he wrote on silently, palely, mechanically.

It is, of course, an indispensable part of a scrivener's business to verify the accuracy of his copy, word by word. Where there are two or more scriveners in an office, they assist each other in this examination, one reading from the copy, the other holding the original. It is a very dull, wearisome, and lethargic affair. I can readily imagine that, to some sanguine temperaments, it would be altogether intolerable. For example, I cannot credit that the mettlesome poet, Byron, would have contentedly sat down with Bartleby to examine a law document of, say five hundred pages, closely written in a crimpy hand.

Now and then, in the haste of business, it had been my

habit to assist in comparing some brief document myself, calling Turkey or Nippers for this purpose. One object I had, in placing Bartleby so handy to me behind the screen, was, to avail myself of his services on such trivial occasions. It was on the third day, I think, of his being with me, and before any necessity had arisen for having his own writing examined, that, being much hurried to complete a small affair I had in hand, I abruptly called to Bartleby. In my haste and natural expectancy of instant compliance, I sat with my head bent over the original on my desk, and my right hand sideways, and somewhat nervously extended with the copy, so that, immediately upon emerging from his retreat, Bartleby might snatch it and proceed to business without the least delay.

In this very attitude did I sit when I called to him, rapidly stating what it was I wanted him to do – namely, to examine a small paper with me. Imagine my surprise, nay, my consternation, when, without moving from his privacy, Bartleby, in a singularly mild, firm voice, replied, 'I would prefer not to.'

I sat awhile in perfect silence, rallying my stunned faculties. Immediately it occurred to me that my ears had deceived me, or Bartleby had entirely misunderstood my meaning. I repeated my request in the clearest tone I could assume; but in quite as clear a one came the previous reply, 'I would prefer not to.'

'Prefer not to,' echoed I, rising in high excitement, and crossing the room with a stride. 'What do you mean? Are you moon-struck? I want you to help me compare this sheet here – take it,' and I thrust it towards him.

'I would prefer not to,' said he.

I looked at him steadfastly. His face was leanly composed; his gray eye dimly calm. Not a wrinkle of agitation rippled him. Had there been the least uneasiness, anger, impatience or impertinence in his manner; in other words, had there been any thing ordinarily human about him, doubtless I should have violently dismissed him from the premises. But as it was, I should have as soon thought of turning my pale plaster-of-paris bust of Cicero out of doors. I stood gazing at him awhile, as he went on with his own writing, and then reseated myself at my desk. This is very strange, thought I. What had one best do? But my business hurried me: I concluded to forget the matter for the present, reserving it for my future leisure. So calling Nippers from the other room, the paper was speedily examined.

A few days after this, Bartleby concluded four lengthy documents, being quadruplicates of a week's testimony taken before me in my High Court of Chancery. It became necessary to examine them. It was an important suit, and great accuracy was imperative. Having all things arranged, I called Turkey, Nippers, and Ginger Nut, from the next room, meaning to place the four copies in the hands of my four clerks, while I should read from the original. Accordingly, Turkey, Nippers, and Ginger Nut had taken their seats in a row, each with his document in his hand, when I called to Bartleby to join this interesting group.

'Bartleby! quick, I am waiting.'

I heard a slow scrape of his chair legs on the uncarpeted floor, and soon he appeared standing at the entrance of his hermitage.

'What is wanted?' said he, mildly.

'The copies, the copies,' said I hurriedly. 'We are going to examine them. There' – and I held towards him the fourth quadruplicate.

'I would prefer not to,' he said, and gently disappeared behind the screen.

For a few moments I was turned into a pillar of salt, standing at the head of my seated column of clerks. Recovering myself, I advanced towards the screen, and demanded the reason for such extraordinary conduct.

'*Why* do you refuse?'

'I would prefer not to.'

With any other man I should have flown outright into a dreadful passion, scorned all further words, and thrust him ignominiously from my presence. But there was something about Bartleby that not only strangely disarmed me, but, in a wonderful manner, touched and disconcerted me. I began to reason with him.

'These are your own copies we are about to examine. It is labor saving to you, because one examination will answer for your four papers. It is common usage. Every copyist is bound to help examine his copy. Is it not so? Will you not speak? Answer!'

'I prefer not to,' he replied in a flutelike tone. It seemed to me that, while I had been addressing him, he carefully revolved every statement that I made; fully comprehended the meaning; could not gainsay the irresistible conclusion; but, at the same time, some paramount consideration prevailed with him to reply as he did.

'You are decided, then, not to comply with my request – a request made according to common usage and common sense?'

He briefly gave me to understand, that on that point my judgment was sound. Yes: his decision was irreversible.

It is not seldom the case that, when a man is browbeaten in some unprecedented and violently unreasonable way, he begins to stagger in his own plainest faith. He begins, as it were, vaguely to surmise that, wonderful as it may be, all the justice and all the reason is on the other side. Accordingly, if any disinterested persons are present, he turns to them for some reinforcement of his own faltering mind.

'Turkey,' said I, 'what do you think of this? Am I not right?'

'With submission, sir,' said Turkey, in his blandest tone, 'I think that you are.'

'Nippers,' said I, 'what do *you* think of it?'

'I think I should kick him out of the office.'

(The reader, of nice perceptions, will here perceive that, it being morning, Turkey's answer is couched in polite and tranquil terms, but Nippers replies in ill-tempered ones. Or, to repeat a previous sentence, Nippers's ugly mood was on duty, and Turkey's off.)

'Ginger Nut,' said I, willing to enlist the smallest suffrage in my behalf, 'what do *you* think of it?'

'I think, sir, he's a little *luny*,' replied Ginger Nut, with a grin.

'You hear what they say,' said I, turning towards the screen, 'come forth and do your duty.'

But he vouchsafed no reply. I pondered a moment in sore perplexity. But once more business hurried me. I determined again to postpone the consideration of this dilemma to my future leisure. With a little trouble we made out to examine the papers without Bartleby, though at every page or two Turkey deferentially dropped his opinion, that this proceeding was quite out of the common; while Nippers, twitching in his chair with a dyspeptic nervousness, ground out, between his set teeth, occasional hissing maledictions against the stubborn oaf behind the screen. And for his (Nippers's) part, this was the first and the last time he would do another man's business without pay.

Meanwhile Bartleby sat in his hermitage, oblivious to everything but his own peculiar business there.

Some days passed, the scrivener being employed upon another lengthy work. His late remarkable conduct led me to regard his ways narrowly. I observed that he never went to dinner; indeed, that he never went anywhere. As yet I had never, of my personal knowledge, known him to be outside of my office. He was a perpetual sentry in the corner. At about eleven o'clock though, in the morning, I noticed that Ginger Nut would advance towards the opening in Bartleby's screen, as if silently beckoned thither by a gesture invisible to me where I sat. The boy would then leave the office, jingling a few pence, and reappear with a handful of ginger-nuts, which he delivered in the hermitage, receiving two of the cakes for his trouble.

He lives, then, on ginger-nuts, thought I; never eats a dinner, properly speaking; he must be a vegetarian, then; but no; he never eats even vegetables, he eats nothing but ginger-nuts. My mind then ran on in reveries concerning the probable effects upon the human constitution of living entirely on ginger-nuts. Ginger-nuts are so called, because they contain ginger as one of their peculiar constituents, and the final flavoring one. Now, what was ginger? A hot, spicy thing. Was Bartleby hot and spicy? Not at all. Ginger, then, had no effect upon Bartleby. Probably he preferred it should have none.

Nothing so aggravates an earnest person as a passive resistance. If the individual so resisted be of a not inhumane temper, and the resisting one perfectly harmless in his passivity, then, in the better moods of the former, he will endeavor charitably to construe to his imagination what proves impossible to be solved by his judgment. Even so, for the most part, I regarded Bartleby and his ways. Poor fellow! thought I, he means no mischief; it is plain he intends no insolence; his aspect sufficiently evinces that his eccentricities are involuntary. He is useful to me. I can get along with him. If I turn him away, the chances are he will fall in with some less-indulgent employer, and then he will be rudely treated, and perhaps driven forth miserably to starve. Yes. Here I can cheaply purchase a delicious self-approval. To befriend Bartleby; to humor him in his strange willfulness, will cost me little or nothing, while I lay up in my soul what will eventually prove a sweet morsel for my conscience. But this mood was not invariable with me. The passiveness of Bartleby sometimes irritated me. I felt strangely goaded on to encounter him in new opposition – to elicit some angry spark from him answerable to my own. But, indeed, I might as well have essayed to strike fire with my knuckles against a bit of Windsor soap. But one afternoon the evil impulse in me mastered me, and the following little scene ensued:

'Bartleby,' said I, 'when those papers are all copied, I will compare them with you.'

'I would prefer not to.'

'How? Surely you do not mean to persist in that mulish vagary?'

No answer.

I threw open the folding-doors near by, and, turning upon Turkey and Nippers, exclaimed:

'Bartleby a second time says, he won't examine his papers. What do you think of it, Turkey?'

It was afternoon, be it remembered. Turkey sat glowing like a brass boiler; his bald head steaming; his hands reeling among his blotted papers.

'Think of it?' roared Turkey; 'I think I'll just step behind his screen, and black his eyes for him!'

So saying, Turkey rose to his feet and threw his arms into a pugilistic position. He was hurrying away to make good his promise, when I detained him, alarmed at the effect of incautiously rousing Turkey's combativeness after dinner.

'Sit down, Turkey,' said I, 'and hear what Nippers has to say. What do you think of it, Nippers? Would I not be justified in immediately dismissing Bartleby?'

'Excuse me, that is for you to decide, sir. I think his conduct quite unusual, and, indeed, unjust, as regards Turkey and myself. But it may only be a passing whim.'

'Ah,' exclaimed I, 'you have strangely changed your mind, then – you speak very gently of him now.'

'All beer,' cried Turkey; 'gentleness is effects of beer – Nippers and I dined together to-day. You see how gentle *I* am, sir. Shall I go and black his eyes?'

'You refer to Bartleby, I suppose. No, not to-day, Turkey,' I replied; 'pray, put up your fists.'

I closed the doors, and again advanced towards Bartleby. I felt additional incentives tempting me to my fate. I burned to be rebelled against again. I remembered that Bartleby never left the office.

'Bartleby,' said I, 'Ginger Nut is away; just step around to the Post Office, won't you? (it was but a three minutes' walk), and see if there is anything for me.'

'I would prefer not to.'

'You *will* not?'

'I *prefer* not.'

I staggered to my desk, and sat there in a deep study. My blind inveteracy returned. Was there any other thing in which I could procure myself to be ignominiously repulsed by this lean, penniless wight? – my hired clerk? What added thing is there, perfectly reasonable, that he will be sure to refuse to do?

'Bartleby!'

No answer.

'Bartleby,' in a louder tone.

No answer.

'Bartleby,' I roared.

Like a very ghost, agreeably to the laws of magical invocation, at the third summons, he appeared at the entrance of his hermitage.

'Go to the next room, and tell Nippers to come to me.'

'I prefer not to,' he respectfully and slowly said, and mildly disappeared.

'Very good, Bartleby,' said I, in a quiet sort of serenely-severe self-possessed tone, intimating the unalterable purpose of some terrible retribution very close at hand. At the moment I half intended something of the kind. But upon the whole, as it was drawing towards my dinner-hour, I thought it best to put on my hat and walk home for the day, suffering much from perplexity and distress of mind.

Shall I acknowledge it? The conclusion of this whole business was, that it soon became a fixed fact of my chambers, that a pale young scrivener, by the name of Bartleby, had a desk there; that he copied for me at the usual rate of four cents a folio (one hundred words); but he was permanently exempt from examining the work done by him, that duty being transferred to Turkey and Nippers, out of compliment, doubtless, to their superior acuteness; moreover, said Bartleby was never, on any account, to be dispatched on the most trivial errand of any sort; and that even if entreated to take upon him such a matter, it was generally understood that he would 'prefer not to' – in other words, that he would refuse point-blank.

As days passed on, I became considerably reconciled to Bartleby. His steadiness, his freedom from all dissipation, his incessant industry (except when he chose to throw himself into a standing revery behind his screen), his great stillness, his unalterableness of demeanor under all circumstances, made him a valuable acquisition. One prime thing was this – *he was always there* – first in the morning, continually through the day, and the last at night. I had a singular confidence in his honesty. I felt my most precious papers perfectly safe in his hands. Sometimes, to be sure, I could not, for the very soul of me, avoid falling into sudden spasmodic passions with him. For it was exceeding difficult to bear in mind all the time those strange peculiarities, privileges, and unheard of exemptions, forming the tacit stipulations on Bartleby's part under which he remained in my office. Now and then, in the eagerness of dispatching pressing business, I would inadvertently summon Bartleby, in a short, rapid tone, to put his finger, say, on the incipient tie of a bit of red tape with which I was about compressing some papers. Of course, from behind the screen the usual answer, 'I prefer not to,' was sure to come; and then, how could a human creature, with the common infirmities of our nature, refrain from bitterly exclaiming upon such perverseness – such unreasonableness. However, every added repulse of this sort which I received only tended to lessen the probability of my repeating the inadvertence.

Here it must be said, that according to the custom of most legal gentlemen occupying chambers in densely-populated law buildings, there were several keys to my door. One was kept by a woman residing in the attic, which person weekly scrubbed and daily swept and dusted my apartments. Another was kept by Turkey for convenience sake. The third I sometimes carried in my own pocket. The fourth I knew not who had.

Now, one Sunday morning I happened to go to Trinity Church, to hear a celebrated preacher, and finding myself rather early on the ground I thought I would walk around to my chambers for a while. Luckily I had my key with me; but upon applying it to the lock, I found it resisted by something inserted from the inside. Quite surprised, I called out; when to my consternation a key was turned from within; and thrusting his lean visage at me, and holding the door ajar, the apparition of Bartleby appeared, in his shirt sleeves, and otherwise in a strangely tattered deshabille, saying quietly that he was sorry, but he was deeply engaged just then, and – preferred not admitting me at present. In a brief word or two, he moreover added, that perhaps I had better walk around the block two or three times, and by that time he would probably have concluded his affairs.

Now, the utterly unsurmised appearance of Bartleby, tenanting my law-chambers of a Sunday morning, with his cadaverously gentlemanly *nonchalance*, yet withal firm and self-possessed, had such a strange effect upon me, that incontinently I slunk away from my own door, and did as desired. But not without sundry twinges of impotent rebellion against the mild effrontery of this unaccountable scrivener. Indeed, it was his wonderful mildness chiefly, which not only disarmed me, but unmanned me as it were. For I consider that one, for the time, is a sort of unmanned when he tranquilly permits his hired clerk to dictate to him, and order him away from his own premises. Furthermore, I was full of uneasiness as to what Bartleby could possibly be doing in my office in his shirt sleeves, and in an otherwise dismantled condition of a Sunday morning. Was anything amiss going on? Nay, that was out of the question. It was not to be thought of for a moment that Bartleby was an immoral person. But what could he be doing there? – copying? Nay again, whatever might be his eccentricities, Bartleby was an eminently decorous person. He would be the last man to sit down to his desk in any state approaching to nudity. Besides, it was Sunday; and there was someing about Bartleby that forbade the supposition that he would by any secular occupation violate the proprieties of the day.

Nevertheless, my mind was not pacified; and full of a restless curiosity, at last I returned to the door. Without hindrance I inserted my key, opened it, and entered. Bartleby was not to be seen. I looked round anxiously, peeped behind his screen; but it was very plain that he was gone. Upon more closely examining the place, I surmised that for an indefinite period Bartleby must have ate, dressed, and slept in my office, and that, too without plate, mirror, or bed. The cushioned seat of a ricketty old sofa in one corner bore the faint impress of a lean, reclining form. Rolled away under his desk, I found a blanket; under the empty grate, a blacking box and brush; on a chair, a tin basin, with soap and a ragged towel; in a newspaper a few crumbs of ginger-nuts and a morsel of cheese. Yes, thought I, it is evident enough that Bartleby has been making his home here, keeping bachelor's hall all by himself. Immediately then the thought came sweeping across me, what miserable friendliness and loneliness are here revealed! His poverty is great; but his solitude, how horrible! Think of it. Of a Sunday, Wall Street is deserted as Petra; and every night of every day it is an emptiness. This building, too, which of week-days hums with industry and life, at nightfall echoes with sheer vacancy, and all through Sunday is forlorn. And here Bartleby makes his home; sole spectator of a solitude which he has seen all populous – a sort of innocent and transformed Marius brooding among the ruins of Carthage!

For the first time in my life a feeling of over-powering stinging melancholy seized me. Before, I had never experienced aught but a not unpleasing sadness. The bond of a common humanity now drew me irresistibly to gloom. A fraternal melancholy! For both I and Bartleby were sons of Adam. I remembered the bright silks and sparkling faces I had seen that day, in gala trim, swan-like sailing down the Mississippi of Broadway; and I contrasted them with the pallid copyist, and thought to myself, Ah, happiness courts the light, so we deem the world is gay; but misery hides aloof, so we deem that misery there is none. These sad fancyings – chimeras, doubtless, of a sick and silly brain – led on to other and more special thoughts, concerning the eccentricities of Bartleby. Presentiments of strange discoveries hovered round me. The scrivener's pale form appeared to me laid out, among uncaring strangers, in its shivering winding sheet.

Suddenly I was attracted by Bartleby's closed desk, the key in open sight left in the lock.

I mean no mischief, seek the gratification of no heartless curiosity, thought I; besides, the desk is mine, and its contents, too, so I will make bold to look within. Everything was methodically arranged, the papers smoothly placed. The pigeon holes were deep, and removing the files of documents, I groped into their recesses. Presently I felt something there, and dragged it out. It was an old bandanna handkerchief, heavy and knotted. I opened it, and saw it was a saving's bank.

I now recalled all the quiet mysteries which I had noted in the man. I remembered that he never spoke but to answer; that, though at intervals he had considerable time to himself, yet I had never seen him reading – no, not even a newspaper; that for long periods he would stand looking out, at his pale window behind the screen, upon the dead brick wall; I was quite sure he never visited any refectory or eating house; while his pale face clearly indicated that he never drank beer like Turkey, or tea and coffee even, like other men; that he never went anywhere in particular that I could learn; never went out for a walk, unless, indeed, that was the case at present; that he had declined telling who he was, or whence he came, or whether he had any relatives in the world; that though so thin and pale, he never complained of ill health. And more than all, I remembered a certain unconscious air of pallid – how shall I call it? – of pallid haughtiness, say, or rather an austere reserve about him, which had positively awed me into my tame compliance with his eccentricities, when I had feared to ask him to do the slightest incidental thing for me, even though I might know, from his long-continued motionlessness, that behind his screen he must be standing in one of those dead-wall reveries of his.

Revolving all these things, and coupling them with the recently discovered fact, that he made my office his constant abiding place and home, and not forgetful of his morbid moodiness; revolving all these things, a prudential feeling began to steal over me. My first emotions had been those of pure melancholy and sincerest pity; but just in proportion as the forlornness of Bartleby grew and grew to my imagination, did that same melancholy merge into fear, that pity into repulsion. So true it is, and so terrible, too, that up to a certain point the thought or sight of misery enlists our best affections; but, in certain special cases, beyond that point it does not. They err who would assert that invariably this is owing to the inherent selfishness of the human heart. It rather proceeds from a certain hopelessness of remedying excessive and organic ill. To a sensitive being, pity is not seldom pain. And when at last it is perceived that such pity cannot lead to effectual succor, common sense bids the soul be rid of it. What I saw that morning persuaded me that the scrivener was the victim of innate and incurable disorder. I might give alms to his body; but his body did not pain him; it was his soul that suffered, and his soul I could not reach.

I did not accomplish the purpose of going to Trinity Church that morning. Somehow, the things I had seen disqualified me for the time from church-going. I walked homeward, thinking what I would do with Bartleby. Finally, I resolved upon this – I would put certain calm questions to him the next morning, touching his history, etc., and if he declined to answer them openly and unreservedly (and I supposed he would prefer not), then to give him a twenty dollar bill over and above whatever I might owe him, and tell him his services were no longer required; but that if in any other way I could assist him, I would be happy to do so, especially if he desired to return to his native place, wherever that might be, I would willingly help to defray the expenses. Moreover, if, after reaching home, he found himself at any time in want of aid, a letter from him would be sure of a reply.

The next morning came.

'Bartleby,' said I, gently calling to him behind his screen.

No reply.

'Bartleby,' said I, in a still gentler tone, 'come here; I am not going to ask you to do anything you would prefer not to do – I simply wish to speak to you.'

Upon this he noiselessly slid into view.

'Will you tell me, Bartleby, where you were born?'

'I would prefer not to.'

'Will you tell me *anything* about yourself?'

'I would prefer not to.'

'But what reasonable objection can you have to speak to me? I feel friendly towards you.'

He did not look at me while I spoke, but kept his glance fixed upon my bust of Cicero, which, as I then sat, was directly behind me, some six inches above my head.

'What is your answer, Bartleby,' said I, after waiting a considerable time for a reply, during which his countenance remained immovable, only there was the faintest conceivable tremor of the white attenuated mouth.

'At present I prefer to give no answer,' he said, and retired into his hermitage.

It was rather weak in me I confess, but his manner, on this occasion, nettled me. Not only did there seem to lurk in it a certain calm disdain, but his perverseness seemed ungrateful, considering the undeniable good usage and indulgence he had received from me.

Again I sat ruminating what I should do. Mortified as I was at his behavior, and resolved as I had been to dismiss him when I entered my office, nevertheless I strangely felt something superstitious knocking at my heart, and forbidding me to carry out my purpose, and denouncing me for a villain if I dared to breathe one bitter word against this forlornest of mankind. At last, familiarly drawing my chair behind his screen, I sat down and said: 'Bartleby, never mind, then, about revealing your history; but let me entreat you, as a friend, to comply as far as may be with the usages of this office. Say now, you will help to examine papers tomorrow or next day: in short, say now, that in a day or two you will begin to be a little reasonable: – say so, Bartleby.'

'At present I would prefer not to be a little reasonable,' was his mildly cadaverous reply.

Just then the folding doors opened, and Nippers approached. He seemed suffering from an unusually bad night's rest, induced by severer indigestion than common. He overheard those final words of Bartleby.

'*Prefer not*, eh?' gritted Nippers – 'I'd *prefer* him, if I were you, sir,' addressing me – 'I'd *prefer* him; I'd give him preferences, the stubborn mule! What is it, sir, pray, that he *prefers* not to do now?'

Bartleby moved not a limb.

'Mr Nippers,' said I, 'I'd prefer that you would withdraw for the present.'

Somehow, of late, I had got into the way of involuntarily using the word 'prefer' upon all sorts of not exactly suitable occasions. And I trembled to think that my contact with the scrivener had already and seriously affected me in a mental way. And what further and deeper aberration might it not yet produce? This apprehension had not been without efficacy in determining me to summary measures.

As Nippers, looking very sour and sulky, was departing, Turkey blandly and deferentially approached.

'With submission, sir,' said he, 'yesterday I was thinking about Bartleby here, and I think that if he would but prefer to take a quart of good ale every day, it would do much towards mending him, and enabling him to assist in examining his papers.'

'So you have got the word, too,' said I, slightly excited.

'With submission, what word, sir,' asked Turkey, respectfully crowding himself into the contracted space behind the screen, and by so doing, making me jostle the scrivener. 'What word, sir?'

'I would prefer to be left alone here,' said Bartleby, as if offended at being mobbed in his privacy.

'*That's* the word, Turkey,' said I – '*that's* it.'

'Oh, *prefer*? oh yes – queer word. I never use it myself. But, sir, as I was saying, if he would but prefer –'

'Turkey,' interrupted I, 'you will please withdraw.'

'Oh, certainly, sir, if you prefer that I should.'

As he opened the folding-door to retire, Nippers at his desk caught a glimpse of me, and asked whether I would prefer to have a certain paper copied on blue paper or white. He did not in the least roguishly accent the word prefer. It was plain that it involuntarily rolled from his tongue. I thought to myself, surely I must get rid of a demented man, who already has in some degree turned the tongues, if not the heads of myself and clerks. But I thought it prudent not to break the dismission at once.

The next day I noticed that Bartleby did nothing but stand at his window in his dead-wall revery. Upon asking him why he did not write, he said that he had decided upon doing no more writing.

'Why, how now? what next?' exclaimed I, 'do no more writing?'

'No more.'

'And what is the reason?'

'Do you not see the reason for yourself?' he indifferently replied.

I looked steadfastly at him, and perceived that his eyes looked dull and glazed. Instantly it occurred to me, that his unexampled diligence in copying by his dim window for the first few weeks of his stay with me might have temporarily impaired his vision.

I was touched. I said something in condolence with him. I hinted that of course he did wisely in abstaining from writing for a while; and urged him to embrace that opportunity of taking wholesome exercise in the open air. This, however, he did not do. A few days after this, my other clerks being absent, and being in a great hurry to dispatch certain letters by the mail, I thought that, having nothing else earthly to do, Bartleby would surely be less inflexible than usual, and carry these letters to the post-office. But he blankly declined. So, much to my inconvenience, I went myself.

Still added days went by. Whether Bartleby's eyes improved or not, I could not say. To all appearance, I thought they did. But when I asked him if they did, he vouchsafed no answer. At all events, he would do no copying. At last, in reply to my urgings, he informed me that he had permanently given up copying.

'What!' exclaimed I; 'suppose your eyes should get entirely well – better than ever before – would you not copy then?'

'I have given up copying,' he answered, and slid aside.

He remained as ever, a fixture in my chamber. Nay – if that were possible – he became still more of a fixture than before. What was to be done? He would do nothing in the office; why should he stay there? In plain fact, he had now become a millstone to me, not only useless as a necklace, but afflictive to bear. Yet I was sorry for him. I speak less than the truth when I say that, on his own account, he occasioned me uneasiness. If he would but have named a single relative or friend, I would instantly have written, and urged their taking the poor fellow away to some convenient retreat. But he seemed alone, absolutely alone in the universe. A bit of wreck in the mid Atlantic. At length, necessities connected with my business tyrannized over all other considerations. Decently as I could, I told Bartleby that in six days time he must unconditionally leave the office. I warned him to take measures, in the interval, for procuring some other abode. I offered to assist him in this endeavor, if he himself would but take the first step towards a removal. 'And when you finally quit me, Bartleby,' added I, 'I shall see that you go not away entirely unprovided. Six days from this hour, remember.'

At the expiration of that period, I peeped behind the screen, and lo! Bartleby was there.

I buttoned up my coat, balanced myself; advanced slowly towards him, touched his shoulder, and said, 'The time has come; you must quit this place; I am sorry for you; here is money; but you must go.'

'I would prefer not,' he replied, with his back still towards me.

'You *must*.'

He remained silent.

Now I had an unbounded confidence in this man's common honesty. He had frequently restored to me sixpences and shillings carelessly dropped upon the floor, for I am apt to be very reckless in such shirt-button affairs. The proceeding, then, which followed will not be deemed extraordinary.

'Bartleby,' said I, 'I owe you twelve dollars on account; here are thirty-two; the odd twenty are yours – Will you take it?' and I handed the bills towards him.

But he made no motion.

'I will leave them here, then,' putting them under a weight on the table. Then taking my hat and cane and going to the door, I tranquilly turned and added – 'After you have removed your things from these offices, Bartleby, you will of course lock the door – since every one is now gone for the day but you – and if you please, slip your key underneath the mat, so that I may have it in the morning. I shall not see you again; so good-by to you. If, hereafter, in your new place of abode, I can be of any service to you, do not fail to advise me by letter. Good-by, Bartleby, and fare you well.'

But he answered not a word; like the last column of some ruined temple, he remained standing mute and solitary in the middle of the otherwise deserted room.

As I walked home in a pensive mood, my vanity got the better of my pity. I could not but highly plume myself on my masterly management in getting rid of Bartleby. Masterly I call it, and such it must appear to any dispassionate thinker. The beauty of my procedure seemed to consist in its perfect quietness. There was no vulgar bullying, no bravado of any sort, no choleric hectoring, and striding to and fro across the apartment, jerking out vehement commands for Bartleby to bundle himself off with his beggarly traps. Nothing of the kind. Without loudly bidding Bartleby depart – as an inferior genius might have done – I *assumed* the ground that depart he must; and upon that assumption built all I had to say. The more I thought over my procedure, the more I was charmed with it. Nevertheless, next morning, upon awakening, I had my doubts – I had somehow slept off the fumes of vanity. One of the coolest and wisest hours a man has, is just after he awakes in the morning. My procedure seemed as sagacious as ever – but only in theory. How it would prove in practice – there was the rub. It was truly a beautiful thought to have assumed Bartleby's departure; but, after all, that assumption was simply my own, and none of Bartleby's. The great point was, not whether I had assumed that he would quit me, but whether he would prefer so to do. He was more a man of preferences than assumptions.

After breakfast, I walked down town, arguing the probabilities *pro* and *con*. One moment I thought it would prove a miserable failure, and Bartleby would be found all alive at my office as usual; the next moment it seemed certain that I should find his chair empty. And so I kept veering about. At the corner of Broadway and Canal Street, I saw quite an excited group of people standing in earnest conversation.

'I'll take odds he doesn't,' said a voice as I passed.

'Doesn't go? – done!' said I, 'put up your money.'

I was instinctively putting my hand in my pocket to produce my own, when I remembered that this was an election day. The words I had overheard bore no reference to Bartleby, but to the success or non-success of some candidate for the mayoralty. In my intent frame of mind, I had, as it were, imagined that all Broadway shared in my excitement, and were debating the same question with me. I passed on, very thankful that the uproar of the street screened my momentary absent-mindedness.

As I had intended, I was earlier than usual at my office door. I stood listening for a moment. All was still. He must be gone. I tried the knob. The door was locked. Yes, my procedure had worked to a charm; he indeed must be vanished. Yet a certain melancholy mixed with this: I was almost sorry for my brilliant success. I was fumbling under the door mat for the key, which Bartleby was to have left there for me, when accidentally my knee knocked against a panel, producing a summoning sound, and in response a voice came to me from within – 'Not yet; I am occupied.'

It was Bartleby.

I was thunderstruck. For an instant I stood like the man who, pipe in mouth, was killed one cloudless afternoon long ago in Virginia, by summer lightning; at his own warm open window he was killed, and remained leaning out there upon the dreamy afternoon, till some one touched him, when he fell.

'Not gone!' I murmured at last. But again obeying that wondrous ascendancy which the inscrutable scrivener had over me, and from which ascendancy, for all my chafing, I could not completely escape, I slowly went down stairs and out into the street, and while walking round the block, considered what I should next do in this unheard-of perplexity. Turn the man out by an actual thrusting I could not; to drive him away by calling him hard names would not do; calling in the police was an unpleasant idea; and yet, permit him to enjoy his cadaverous triumph over me – this, too, I could not think of. What was to be done? or, if nothing could be done, was there anything further that I could *assume* in the matter? Yes, as before I had prospectively assumed that Bartleby would depart, so now I might retrospectively assume that departed he was. In the legitimate carrying out of this assumption, I might enter my office in a great hurry, and pretending not to see Bartleby at all, walk straight against him as if he were air. Such a proceeding would in a singular degree have the appearance of a home-thrust. It was hardly possible that Bartleby could withstand such an application of the doctrine of assumptions. But upon second thoughts the success of the plan seemed rather dubious. I resolved to argue the matter over with him again.

'Bartleby,' said I, entering the office, with a quietly severe expression, 'I am seriously displeased. I am pained, Bartleby. I had thought better of you. I had imagined you of such a gentlemanly organization, that in any delicate dilemma a slight hint would suffice – in short, an assumption. But it appears I am deceived. Why,' I added, unaffectedly starting, 'you have not even touched that money yet,' pointing to it, just where I had left it the evening previous.

He answered nothing.

'Will you, or will you not, quit me?' I now demanded in a sudden passion, advancing close to him.

'I would prefer *not* to quit you,' he replied, gently emphasizing the *not*.

'What earthly right have you to stay here? Do you pay any rent? Do you pay my taxes? Or is this property yours?'

He answered nothing.

'Are you ready to go on and write now? Are your eyes recovered? Could you copy a small paper for me this morning? or help examine a few lines? or step round to the post-office? In a word, will you do anything at all, to give a coloring to your refusal to depart the premises?'

He silently retired into his hermitage.

I was now in such a state of nervous resentment that I thought it but prudent to check myself at present from further demonstrations. Bartleby and I were alone. I remembered the tragedy of the unfortunate Adams and the still more unfortunate Colt in the solitary office of the latter; and how poor Colt, being dreadfully incensed by Adams, and imprudently permitting himself to get wildly excited, was at unawares hurried into his fatal act – an act which certainly no man could possibly deplore more than the actor himself. Often it had occurred to me in my ponderings upon the subject, that had that altercation taken place in the public street, or at a private residence, it would not have terminated as it did. It was the circumstance of being alone in a solitary office, up stairs, of a building entirely unhallowed by humanizing domestic associations –

an uncarpeted office, doubtless, of a dusty, haggard sort of appearance – this it must have been, which greatly helped to enhance the irritable desperation of the hapless Colt.

But when this old Adam of resentment rose in me and tempted me concerning Bartleby, I grappled him and threw him. How? Why, simply by recalling the divine injunction: 'A new commandment give I unto you, that ye love one another.' Yes, this it was that saved me. Aside from higher considerations, charity often operates as a vastly wise and prudent principle – a great safeguard to its possessor. Men have committed murder for jealousy's sake, and anger's sake, and hatred's sake, and selfishness' sake, and spiritual pride's sake; but no man, that ever I heard of, ever committed a diabolical murder for sweet charity's sake. Mere self-interest, then, if no better motive can be enlisted, should, especially with high-tempered men, prompt all beings to charity and philanthropy. At any rate, upon the occasion in question, I strove to drown my exasperated feelings towards the scrivener by benevolently construing his conduct. Poor fellow, poor fellow! thought I, he don't mean anything; and besides, he has seen hard times, and ought to be indulged.

I endeavored, also, immediately to occupy myself, and at the same time to comfort my despondency. I tried to fancy, that in the course of the morning, at such time as might prove agreeable to him, Bartleby, of his own free accord, would emerge from his hermitage and take up some decided line of march in the direction of the door. But no. Half-past twelve o'clock came; Turkey began to glow in the face, overturn his inkstand, and become generally obstreperous; Nippers abated down into quietude and courtesy; Ginger Nut munched his noon apple; and Bartleby remained standing at his window in one of his profoundest dead-wall reveries. Will it be credited? Ought I to acknowledge it? That afternoon I left the office without saying one further word to him.

Some days now passed, during which, at leisure intervals I looked a little into 'Edwards on the Will,' and 'Priestley on Necessity.' Under the circumstances, those books induced a salutary feeling. Gradually I slid into the persuasion that these troubles of mine, touching the scrivener, had been all predestinated from eternity, and Bartleby was billeted upon me for some mysterious purpose of an allwise Providence, which it was not for a mere mortal like me to fathom. Yes, Bartleby, stay there behind your screen, thought I; I shall persecute you no more; you are harmless and noiseless as any of these old chairs; in short, I never feel so private as when I know you are here. At last I see it, I feel it; I penetrate to the predestinated purpose of my life. I am content. Others may have loftier parts to enact; but my mission in this world, Bartleby, is to furnish you with office-room for such period as you may see fit to remain.

I believe that this wise and blessed frame of mind would have continued with me, had it not been for the unsolicited and uncharitable remarks obtruded upon me by my professional friends who visited the rooms. But thus it often is, that the constant friction of illiberal minds wears out at last the best resolves of the more generous. Though to be sure, when I reflected upon it, it was not strange that people entering my office should be struck by the peculiar aspect of the unaccountable Bartleby, and so be tempted to throw out some sinister observations concerning him. Sometimes an attorney, having business with me, and calling at my office, and finding no one but the scrivener there, would undertake to obtain some sort of precise information from him touching my whereabouts; but without heeding his idle talk, Bartleby would remain standing immovable in the middle of the room. So after contemplating him in that position for a time, the attorney would depart, no wiser than he came.

Also, when a reference was going on, and the room full of lawyers and witnesses, and business driving fast, some deeply-occupied legal gentleman present, seeing Bartleby wholly unemployed, would request him to run round to his (the legal gentleman's) office and fetch some papers for him. Thereupon, Bartleby would tranquilly decline, and yet remain idle as before. Then the lawyer would give a great stare, and turn to me. And what could I say? At last I was made aware that all through the circle of my professional acquaintance, a whisper of wonder was running round, having reference to the strange creature I kept at my office. This worried me very much. And as the idea came upon me of his possibly turning out a long-lived man, and keep occupying my chambers, and denying my authority; and perplexing my visitors; and scandalizing my professional reputation; and casting a general gloom over the premises; keeping soul and body together to the last upon his savings (for doubtless he spent but half a dime a day), and in the end perhaps outlive me, and claim possession of my office by right of his perpetual occupancy: as all these dark anticipations crowded upon me more and more, and my friends continually intruded their relentless remarks upon the apparition in my room; a great change was wrought in me. I resolved to gather all my faculties together, and forever rid me of this intolerable incubus.

Ere revolving any complicated project, however, adapted to this end, I first simply suggested to Bartleby the propriety of his permanent departure. In a calm and serious tone, I commended the idea to his careful and mature consideration. But, having taken three days to meditate upon it, he apprised me, that his original determination remained the same; in short, that he still preferred to abide with me.

What shall I do? I now said to myself, buttoning up my coat to the last button. What shall I do? what ought I to do? what does conscience say I *should* do with this man, or, rather, ghost. Rid myself of him, I must; go, he shall. But how? You will not thrust him, the poor, pale, passive mortal – you will not thrust such a helpless creature out of your door? you will not dishonor yourself by such cruelty? No, I will not, I cannot do that. Rather would I let him live and die here, and then mason up his remains in the wall. What, then, will you do? For all your coaxing, he will not budge. Bribes he leaves under your own paper-weight on your table; in short, it is quite plain that he prefers to cling to you.

Then something severe, something unusual must be done. What! surely you will not have him collared by a constable, and commit his innocent pallor to the common jail? And upon what ground could you procure such a thing to be done? – a vagrant, is he? What! he a vagrant, a wanderer, who refuses to budge? It is because he will *not* be a vagrant, then, that you seek to count him *as* a vagrant. That is too absurd. No visible means of support: there I have him. Wrong again: for indubitably he *does* support himself, and that is the only unanswerable proof that any man can show of his possessing the means so to do. No more, then. Since he will not quit me, I must quit him. I will change my offices; I will move elsewhere, and give him fair notice, that if I find him on my new premises I will then proceed against him as a common trespasser.

Acting accordingly, next day I thus addressed him: 'I find these chambers too far from the City Hall; the air is unwholesome. In a word, I propose to remove my offices next week, and shall no longer require your services. I tell you this now, in order that you may seek another place.'

He made no reply, and nothing more was said.

On the appointed day I engaged carts and men, proceeded to my chambers, and, having but little furniture, everything was removed in a few hours. Throughout, the scrivener remained standing behind the screen, which I directed to be removed the last thing. It was withdrawn; and, being folded up like a huge folio, left him the motionless occupant of a naked room. I stood in the entry watching him a moment, while something from within me upbraided me.

I re-entered, with my hand in my pocket – and – and my heart in my mouth.

'Good-by, Bartleby; I am going – good-by, and God some way bless you; and take that,' slipping something in his hand. But it dropped upon the floor, and then – strange to say – I tore myself from him whom I had so longed to be rid of.

Established in my new quarters, for a day or two I kept the door locked, and started at every footfall in the passages. When I returned to my rooms, after any little absence, I would pause at the threshold for an instant, and attentively listen, ere applying my key. But these fears were needless. Bartleby never came nigh me.

I thought all was going well, when a perturbed-looking stranger visited me, inquiring whether I was the person who had recently occupied rooms at No. — Wall Street.

Full of forebodings, I replied that I was.

'Then, sir,' said the stranger, who proved a lawyer, 'you are responsible for the man you left there. He refuses to do any copying; he refuses to do anything; he says he prefers not to; and he refuses to quit the premises.'

'I am very sorry, sir,' said I, with assumed tranquillity, but an inward tremor, 'but, really, the man you allude to is nothing to me – he is no relation or apprentice of mine, that you should hold me responsible for him.'

'In mercy's name, who is he?'

'I certainly cannot inform you. I know nothing about him. Formerly I employed him as a copyist; but he has done nothing for me now for some time past.'

'I shall settle him, then – good morning, sir.'

Several days passed, and I heard nothing more; and, though I often felt a charitable prompting to call at the place and see poor Bartleby, yet a certain squeamishness, of I know not what, withheld me.

All is over with him, by this time, thought I, at last, when, through another week, no further intelligence reached me. But, coming to my room the day after, I found several persons waiting at my door in a high state of nervous excitement.

'That's the man – here he comes,' cried the foremost one, whom I recognized as the lawyer who had previously called upon me alone.

'You must take him away, sir, at once,' cried a portly

person among them, advancing upon me, and whom I knew to be the landlord of No. — Wall Street. 'These gentlemen, my tenants, cannot stand it any longer; Mr B——,' pointing to the lawyer, 'has turned him out of his room, and he now persists in haunting the building generally, sitting upon the banisters of the stairs by day, and sleeping in the entry by night. Everybody is concerned; clients are leaving the offices; some fears are entertained of a mob; something you must do, and that without delay.'

Aghast at this torrent, I fell back before it, and would fain have locked myself in my new quarters. In vain I persisted that Bartleby was nothing to me – no more than to any one else. In vain – I was the last person known to have anything to do with him, and they held me to the terrible account. Fearful, then, of being exposed in the papers (as one person present obscurely threatened), I considered the matter, and, at length, said, that if the lawyer would give me a confidential interview with the scrivener, in his (the lawyer's) own room, I would, that afternoon, strive my best to rid them of the nuisance they complained of.

Going up stairs to my old haunt, there was Bartleby silently sitting upon the banister at the landing.

'What are you doing here, Bartleby?' said I.

'Sitting upon the banister,' he mildly replied.

I motioned him into the lawyer's room, who then left us.

'Bartleby,' said I, 'are you aware that you are the cause of great tribulation to me, by persisting in occupying the entry after being dismissed from the office?'

No answer.

'Now one of two things must take place. Either you must do something, or something must be done to you. Now what sort of business would you like to engage in? Would you like to re-engage in copying for some one?'

'No; I would prefer not to make any change.'

'Would you like a clerkship in a dry-goods store?'

'There is too much confinement about that. No, I would not like a clerkship; but I am not particular.'

'Too much confinement,' I cried, 'why you keep yourself confined all the time!'

'I would prefer not to take a clerkship,' he rejoined, as if to settle that little item at once.

'How would a bar-tender's business suit you? There is no trying of the eye-sight in that.'

'I would not like it at all; though, as I said before, I am not particular.'

His unwonted wordiness inspirited me. I returned to the charge.

'Well, then, would you like to travel through the country collecting bills for the merchants? That would improve your health.'

'No, I would prefer to be doing something else.'

'How, then, would going as a companion to Europe, to entertain some young gentleman with your conversation – how would that suit you?'

'Not at all. It does not strike me that there is anything definite about that. I like to be stationary. But I am not particular.'

'Stationary you shall be, then,' I cried, now losing all patience, and, for the first time in all my exasperating connection with him, fairly flying into a passion. 'If you do not go away from these premises before night, I shall feel bound – indeed, I *am* bound – to – to – to quit the premises myself!' I rather absurdly concluded, knowing not with what possible threat to try to frighten his immobility into compliance. Despairing of all further efforts, I was precipitately leaving him, when a final thought occurred to me – one which had not been wholly unindulged before.

'Bartleby,' said I, in the kindest tone I could assume under such exciting circumstances, 'will you go home with me now – not to my office, but my dwelling – and remain there till we can conclude upon some convenient arrangement for you at our leisure? Come, let us start now, right away.'

'No: at present I would prefer not to make any change at all.'

I answered nothing; but, effectually dodging every one by the suddenness and rapidity of my flight, rushed from the building, ran up Wall Street towards Broadway, and, jumping into the first omnibus, was soon removed from pursuit. As soon as tranquillity returned, I distinctly perceived that I had now done all that I possibly could, both in respect to the demands of the landlord and his tenants, and with regard to my own desire and sense of duty, to benefit Bartleby, and shield him from rude persecution. I now strove to be entirely care-free and quiescent; and my conscience justified me in the attempt; though, indeed, it was not so successful as I could have wished. So fearful was I of being again hunted out by the incensed landlord and his exasperated tenants, that, surrendering my business to Nippers, for a few days, I drove about the upper part of the town and through the suburbs, in my rockaway; crossed over to Jersey City and Hoboken, and paid fugitive visits to Manhattanville and Astoria. In fact, I almost lived in my rockaway for the time.

When again I entered my office, lo, a note from the landlord lay upon the desk. I opened it with trembling hands. It informed me that the writer had sent to the police, and had Bartleby removed to the Tombs as a vagrant. Moreover, since I knew more about him than any one else, he wished me to appear at that place, and make a suitable statement of the facts. These tidings had a conflicting effect upon me. At first I was indignant; but, at last, almost approved. The landlord's energetic, summary disposition, had led him to adopt a procedure which I do not think I would have decided upon myself; and yet, as a last resort, under such peculiar circumstances, it seemed the only plan.

As I afterwards learned, the poor scrivener, when told that he must be conducted to the Tombs, offered not the slightest obstacle, but, in his pale, unmoving way, silently acquiesced.

Some of the compassionate and curious bystanders joined the party; and headed by one of the constables arm in arm with Bartleby, the silent procession filed its way through all the noise, and heat, and joy of the roaring thorough-fares at noon.

The same day I received the note, I went to the Tombs, or, to speak more properly, the Halls of Justice. Seeking the right officer, I stated the purpose of my call, and was informed that the individual I described was, indeed, within. I then assured the functionary that Bartleby was a perfectly honest man, and greatly to be compassionated, however unaccountably eccentric. I narrated all I knew, and closed by suggesting the idea of letting him remain in as indulgent confinement as possible, till something less harsh might be done – though, indeed, I hardly knew what. At all events, if nothing else could be decided upon, the alms-house must receive him. I then begged to have an interview.

Being under no disgraceful charge, and quite serene and harmless in all his ways, they had permitted him freely to wander about the prison, and, especially, in the inclosed grass-platted yards thereof. And so I found him there, standing all alone in the quietest of the yards, his face to-wards a high wall, while all around, from the narrow slits of the jail windows, I thought I saw peering out upon him the eyes of murderers and thieves.

'Bartleby!'

'I know you,' he said, without looking round – 'and I want nothing to say to you.'

'It was not I that brought you here, Bartleby,' said I, keenly pained at his implied suspicion. 'And to you, this should not be so vile a place. Nothing reproachful attaches to you by being here. And see, it is not so sad a place as one might think. Look, there is the sky, and here is the grass.'

'I know where I am,' he replied, but would say nothing more, and so I left him.

As I entered the corridor again, a broad meat-like man, in an apron, accosted me, and, jerking his thumb over his shoulder, said – 'Is that your friend?'

'Yes.'

'Does he want to starve? If he does, let him live on the prison fare, that's all.'

'Who are you?' asked I, not knowing what to make of such an unofficially speaking person in such a place.

'I am the grub-man. Such gentlemen as have friends here, hire me to provide them with something good to eat.'

'Is this so?' said I, turning to the turnkey.

He said it was.

'Well, then,' said I, slipping some silver into the grub-man's hands (for so they called him), 'I want you to give particular attention to my friend there; let him have the best dinner you can get. And you must be as polite to him as possible.'

'Introduce me, will you?' said the grub-man, looking at me with an expression which seemed to say he was all impatience for an opportunity to give a specimen of his breeding.

Thinking it would prove of benefit to the scrivener, I acquiesced; and, asking the grub-man his name, went up with him to Bartleby.

'Bartleby, this is a friend; you will find him very useful to you.'

'Your sarvant, sir, your sarvant,' said the grub-man, making a low salutation behind his apron. 'Hope you find it pleasant here, sir; nice grounds – cool apartments – hope you'll stay with us sometime – try to make it agreeable. What will you have for dinner to-day?'

'I prefer not to dine to-day,' said Bartleby, turning away. 'It would disagree with me; I am unused to dinners.' So saying, he slowly moved to the other side of the inclosure, and took up a position fronting the dead-wall.

'How's this?' said the grub-man, addressing me with a stare of astonishment. 'He's odd, ain't he?'

'I think he is a little deranged,' said I, sadly.

'Deranged? deranged is it? Well, now, upon my word, I thought that friend of yourn was a gentleman forger; they are always pale and genteel-like, them forgers. I can't help pity 'em – can't help it, sir. Did you know Monroe Edwards?' he added, touchingly, and paused. Then, laying his hand piteously on my shoulder, sighed, 'he died of consumption at Sing-Sing. So you weren't acquainted with Monroe?'

'No, I was never socially acquainted with any forgers. But I cannot stop longer. Look to my friend yonder. You will not lose by it. I will see you again.'

Some few days after this, I again obtained admission to the Tombs, and went through the corridors in quest of Bartleby; but without finding him.

'I saw him coming from his cell not long ago,' said a turnkey, 'may be he's gone to loiter in the yards.'

So I went in that direction.

'Are you looking for the silent man?' said another turnkey, passing me. 'Yonder he lies – sleeping in the yard there. 'Tis not twenty minutes since I saw him lie down.'

The yard was entirely quiet. It was not accessible to the common prisoners. The surrounding walls, of amazing thickness, kept off all sounds behind them. The Egyptian character of the masonry weighed upon me with its gloom. But a soft imprisoned turf grew under foot. The heart of the eternal pyramids, it seemed, wherein, by some strange magic, through the clefts, grass-seed, dropped by birds, had sprung.

Strangely huddled at the base of the wall, his knees drawn up, and lying on his side, his head touching the cold stones, I saw the wasted Bartleby. But nothing stirred. I paused; then went close up to him; stooped over, and saw that his dim eyes were open; otherwise he seemed profoundly sleeping. Something prompted me to touch him. I felt his hand, when a tingling shiver ran up my arm and down my spine to my feet.

The round face of the grub-man peered upon me now. 'His dinner is ready. Won't he dine today, either? Or does he live without dining?'

'Lives without dining,' said I, and closed the eyes.

'Eh! – He's asleep, ain't he?'
'With kings and counselors,' murmured I.

*

There would seem little need for proceeding further in this history. Imagination will readily supply the meagre recital of poor Bartleby's interment. But, ere parting with the reader, let me say, that if this little narrative has sufficiently interested him, to awaken curiosity as to who Bartleby was, and what manner of life he led prior to the present narrator's making his acquaintance, I can only reply, that in such curiosity I fully share, but am wholly unable to gratify it. Yet here I hardly know whether I should divulge one little item of rumor, which came to my ear a few months after the scrivener's decease. Upon what basis it rested, I could never ascertain; and hence, how true it is I cannot now tell. But, inasmuch as this vague report has not been without a certain suggestive interest to me, however said, it may prove the same with some others; and so I will briefly mention it. The report was this: that Bartleby had been a subordinate clerk in the Dead Letter Office at Washington, from which he had been suddenly removed by a change in the administration. When I think over this rumor, hardly can I express the emotions which seize me. Dead letters! does it not sound like dead men? Conceive a man by nature and misfortune prone to a pallid hopelessness, can any business seem more fitted to heighten it than that of continually handling these dead letters, and assorting them for the flames? For by the cart-load they are annually burned. Sometimes from out the folded paper the pale clerk takes a ring – the finger it was meant for, perhaps, moulders in the grave; a bank-note sent in swiftest charity – he whom it would relieve, nor eats nor hungers any more; pardon for those who died despairing; hope for those who died unhoping; good tidings for those who died stifled by unrelieved calamities. On errands of life, these letters speed to death.

Ah, Bartleby! Ah, humanity!

COCK-A-DOODLE-DOO!

OR THE CROWING
OF THE NOBLE COCK
BENEVENTANO

IN all parts of the world many high-spirited revolts from rascally despotisms had of late been knocked on the head; many dreadful casualties, by locomotive and steamer, had likewise knocked hundreds of high-spirited travellers on the head (I lost a dear friend in one of them); my own private affairs were also full of despotisms, casualties, and knockings on the head, when early one morning in Spring, being too full of hypos to sleep, I sallied out to walk on my hill-side pasture.

It was a cool and misty, damp, disagreeable air. The country looked underdone, its raw juices squirting out all round. I buttoned out this squitchy air as well as I could with my lean, double-breasted dress-coat – my overcoat being so long-skirted I only used it in my wagon – and spitefully thrusting my crab-stick into the oozy sod, bent my blue form to the steep ascent of the hill. This toiling posture brought my head pretty well earthward, as if I were in the act of butting it against the world. I marked the fact, but only grinned at it with a ghastly grin.

All round me were tokens of a divided empire. The old grass and the new grass were striving together. In the low wet swales the verdure peeped out in vivid green; beyond, on the mountains, lay light patches of snow, strangely relieved against their russet sides; all the humped hills looked like brindled kine in the shivers. The woods were strewn with dry dead boughs, snapped off by the riotous winds of March, while the young trees skirting the woods were just beginning to show the first yellowish tinge of the nascent spray.

I sat down for a moment on a great rotting log nigh the

top of the hill, my back to a heavy grove, my face presented toward a wide, sweeping circuit of mountains enclosing a rolling, diversified country. Along the base of one long range of heights ran a lagging, fever-and-agueish river, over which was a duplicate stream of dripping mist, exactly corresponding in every meander with its parent water below. Low down, here and there, shreds of vapor listlessly wandered in the air, like abandoned or helmless nations or ships – or very soaky towels hung on criss-cross clothes-lines to dry. Afar, over a distant village lying in a bay of the plain formed by the mountains, there rested a great flat canopy of haze, like a pall. It was the condensed smoke of the chimneys, with the condensed, exhaled breath of the villagers, prevented from dispersion by the imprisoning hills. It was too heavy and lifeless to mount of itself; so there it lay, between the village and the sky, doubtless hiding many a man with the mumps, and many a queasy child.

My eye ranged over the capacious rolling country, and over the mountains, and over the village, and over a farm-house here and there, and over woods, groves, streams, rocks, fells – and I thought to myself, what a slight mark, after all, does man make on this huge great earth. Yet the earth makes a mark on him. What a horrid accident was that on the Ohio, where my good friend and thirty other good fellows were sloped into eternity at the bidding of a thick-headed engineer, who knew not a valve from a flue. And that crash on the railroad just over yon mountains there, where two infatuate trains ran pell-mell into each other, and climbed and clawed each other's backs; and one locomotive was found fairly shelled, like a chick, inside of a passenger car in the antagonist train; and near a score of noble hearts, a bride and her groom, and an innocent little infant, were all disembarked into the grim hulk of Charon, who ferried them over, all baggageless, to some clinkered iron-foundry country or other. Yet what's the use of complaining? What justice of the peace will right this matter? Yea, what's the use of bothering the very heavens about it?

Don't the heavens themselves ordain these things – else they could not happen?

A miserable world! Who would take the trouble to make a fortune in it, when he knows not how long he can keep it, for the thousand villains and asses who have the management of railroads and steamboats, and innumerable other vital things in the world. If they would make me Dictator in North America a while, I'd string them up, and hang, draw, and quarter; fry, roast, and boil; stew, grill, and devil them, like so many turkey-legs – the rascally numskulls of stokers; I'd set them to stokering in Tartarus – I would!

Great improvements of the age! What! to call the facilitation of death and murder an improvement! Who wants to travel so fast? My grandfather did not, and he was no fool. Hark! here comes that old dragon again – that gigantic gad-fly of a Moloch – snort! puff! scream! – here he comes straight-bent through these vernal woods, like the Asiatic cholera cantering on a camel. Stand aside! here he comes, the chartered murderer! the death monopoliser! judge, jury, and hangman all together, whose victims die always without benefit of clergy. For two hundred and fifty miles that iron fiend goes yelling through the land, crying 'More! more! more!' Would that fifty conspiring mountains would fall atop of him! And, while they were about it, would they also fall atop of that smaller dunning fiend, my creditor, who frightens the life out of me more than any locomotive – a lantern-jawed rascal, who seems to run on a railroad track, too, and duns me even on Sunday, all the way to church and back, and comes and sits in the same pew with me, and pretending to be polite and hand me the prayer-book opened at the proper place, pokes his pesky bill under my nose in the very midst of my devotions, and so shoves himself between me and salvation; for how can one keep his temper on such occasions?

I can't pay this horrid man; and yet they say money was never so plentiful – a drug in the market; but blame me if I can get any of the drug, though there never was a sick man more in need of that particular sort of medicine. It's a lie; money ain't plenty – feel of my pocket. Ha! here's a powder I was going to send to the sick baby in yonder hovel, where the Irish ditcher lives. That baby has the scarlet fever. They say the measles are rife in the country, too, and the varioloid, and the chicken-pox, and it's bad for teething children. And after all, I suppose many of the poor little ones, after going through all this trouble, snap off short; and so they had the measles, mumps, croup, scarlet fever, chicken pox, cholera-morbus, summer-complaint, and all else, in vain! Ah! there's that twinge of the rheumatics in my right shoulder. I got it one night on the North River, when, in a crowded boat, I gave up my berth to a sick lady, and stayed on deck till morning in drizzling weather. There's the thanks one gets for charity! Twinge! Shoot away, ye rheumatics! Ye couldn't lay on worse if I were some villain who had murdered the lady instead of befriending her. Dyspepsia, too – I am troubled with that.

Hallo! here come the calves, the two-year-olds, just turned out of the barn into the pasture, after six months of cold victuals. What a miserable-looking set, to be sure! A breaking up of a hard winter, that's certain: sharp bones sticking out like elbows; all quilted with a strange stuff dried on their flanks like layers of pancakes. Hair worn quite off too, here and there; and where it ain't pancaked, or worn off, looks like the rubbed sides of mangy old hair-trunks. In fact, they are not six two-year-olds, but six abominable old hair-trunks wandering about here in this pasture.

Hark! By Jove, what's that? See! the very hair-trunks prick their ears at it, and stand and gaze away down into the rolling country yonder. Hark again! How clear! how musical! how prolonged! What a triumphant thanksgiving of a cock-crow! *'Glory be to God in the highest!'* It says those very words as plain as ever cock did in this world. Why, why, I begin to feel a little in sorts again. It ain't so very misty, after all. The sun yonder is beginning to show himself: I feel warmer.

Hark! There again! Did ever such a blessed cock-crow so ring out over the earth before! Clear, shrill, full of pluck, full of fire, full of fun, full of glee. It plainly says – '*Never say die!*' My friends, it is extraordinary, is it not?

Unwittingly, I found that I had been addressing the two-year-olds – the calves – in my enthusiasm; which shows how one's true nature will betray itself at times in the most unconscious way. For what a very two-year-old, and calf, I had been to fall into the sulks, on a hill-top too, when a cock down in the lowlands there, without discourse of reason, and quite penniless in the world, and with death hanging over him at any moment from his hungry master, sends up a cry like a very laureate celebrating the glorious victory of New Orleans.

Hark! there it goes again! My friends, that must be a Shanghai; no domestic-born cock could crow in such prodigious exulting strains. Plainly, my friends, a Shanghai of the Emperor of China's breed.

But my friends the hair-trunks, fairly alarmed at last by such clamorously-victorious tones, were now scampering off, with their tails flirting in the air, and capering with their legs in clumsy enough sort of style, sufficiently evincing that they had not freely flourished them for the six months last past.

Hark! there again! Whose cock is that? Who in this region can afford to buy such an extraordinary Shanghai? Bless me – it makes my blood bound – I feel wild. What? jumping on this rotten old log here, to flap my elbows and crow too? And just now in the doleful dumps. And all this from the simple crow of a cock. Marvellous cock! But soft – this fellow now crows most lustily; but it's only morning; let's see how he'll crow about noon, and toward nightfall. Come to think of it, cocks crow mostly in the beginning of the day. Their pluck ain't lasting, after all. Yes, yes; even cocks have to succumb to the universal spell of tribulation: jubilant in the beginning, but down in the mouth at the end.

> . . . 'Of fine mornings,
> We fine lusty cocks begin our crows in gladness;
> But when eve does come we don't crow quite so much,
> For then cometh despondency and madness.'

The poet had this very Shanghai in his mind when he wrote that. But stop. There he rings out again, ten times richer, fuller, longer, more obstreperously exulting than before! Why, this is equal to hearing the great bell of St Paul's rung at a coronation! In fact, that bell ought to be taken down, and this Shanghai put in its place. Such a crow would jollify all London, from Mile-End (which is no end) to Primrose Hill (where there ain't any primroses), and scatter the fog.

Well, I have an appetite for my breakfast this morning, if I have not had it for a week before. I meant to have only tea and toast; but I'll have coffee and eggs – no, brown stout and a beefsteak. I want something hearty. Ah, here comes the down train; white cars, flashing through the trees like a vein of silver. How cheerfully the steam-pipe chirps! Gay are the passengers. There waves a handkerchief – going down to the city to eat oysters, and see their friends, and drop in at the circus. Look at the mist yonder; what soft curls and undulations round the hills, and the sun weaving his rays among them. See the azure smoke of the village, like the azure tester over a bridal-bed. How bright the country looks there where the river overflowed the meadows. The old grass has to knock under to the new. Well, I feel the better for this walk. Home now, and walk into that steak, and crack that bottle of brown stout; and by the time that's drunk – a quart of stout – by that time, I shall feel about as stout as Samson. Come to think of it, that dun may call, though. I'll just visit the woods and cut a club. I'll club him, by Jove, if he duns me this day.

Hark! there goes Shanghai again. Shanghai says, 'Bravo!' Shanghai says 'Club him!'

Oh, brave cock!

I felt in rare spirits the whole morning. The dun called about eleven. I had the boy Jake send the dun up. I was reading *Tristram Shandy,* and could not go down under the circumstances. The lean rascal (a lean farmer, too – think of that!) entered, and found me seated in an arm-chair, with my feet on the table, and the second bottle of brown stout handy, and the book under eye.

'Sit down,' said I; 'I'll finish this chapter, and then attend to you. Fine morning. Ha! Ha! – this is a fine joke about my Uncle Toby and the Widow Wadman! Ha! ha! ha! let me read this to you.'

'I have no time; I've got my noon *chores* to do.'

'To the deuce with your *chores!*' said I. 'Don't drop your old tobacco about here, or I'll turn you out.'

'Sir!'

'Let me read you this about the Widow Wadman. Said the Widow Wadman –'

'There's my bill sir.'

'Very good. Just twist it up, will you; it's about my smoking-time; and hand a coal, will you, from the hearth yonder!'

'My bill, sir!' said the rascal, turning pale with rage and amazement at my unwonted air (formerly I had always dodged him with a pale face), but too prudent as yet to betray the extremity of his astonishment. 'My bill, sir!' – and he stiffly poked it at me.

'My friend,' said I, 'what a charming morning! How sweet the country looks! Pray, did you hear that extra-ordinary cock-crow this morning? Take a glass of my stout!'

'*Yours?* First pay your debts before you offer folks *your* stout!'

'You think, then, that, properly speaking, I have no *stout,*' said I, deliberately rising. 'I'll undeceive you. I'll show you stout of a superior brand to Barclay and Perkins.'

Without more ado, I seized that insolent dun by the slack of his coat – (and, being a lean, shad-bellied wretch, there was plenty of slack to it) – I seized him that way, tied him with a sailor-knot, and thrusting his bill between his teeth, introduced him to the open country lying round about my place of abode.

'Jake,' said I, 'you'll find a sack of blue-nosed potatoes lying under the shed. Drag it here, and pelt this pauper away; he's been begging pence of me, and I know he can work, but he's lazy. Pelt him away, Jake!'

Bless my stars, what a crow! Shanghai sent up such a perfect pæan and *laudamus* – such a trumpet-blast of triumph, that my soul fairly snorted in me. Duns! – I could have fought an army of them! Plainly, Shanghai was of the opinion that duns only came into the world to be kicked, hanged, bruised, battered, choked, walloped, hammered, drowned, clubbed!

Returning indoors, when the exultation of my victory over the dun had a little subsided, I fell to musing over the mysterious Shanghai. I had no idea I would hear him so nigh my house. I wondered from what rich gentleman's yard he crowed. Nor had he cut short his crows so easily as I supposed he would. This Shanghai crowed till midday, at least. Would he keep a-crowing all day? I resolved to learn. Again I ascended the hill. The whole country was now bathed in a rejoicing sunlight. The warm verdure was bursting all round me. Teams were afield. Birds, newly arrived from the south, were blithely singing in the air. Even the crows cawed with a certain unction, and seemed a shade or two less black than usual.

Hark! there goes the cock! How shall I describe the crow of the Shanghai at noontide? His sunrise crow was a whisper to it. It was the loudest, longest, and most strangely musical crow that ever amazed mortal man. I had heard plenty of cock-crows before, and many fine ones; but this one! so smooth and flute-like in its very clamour; so self-possessed in its very rapture of exultation; so vast, mounting, swelling, soaring, as if spurted out from a golden throat, thrown far back. Nor did it sound like the foolish, vain-glorious crow of some young sophomorean cock, who knew not the world, and was beginning life in audacious gay spirits, because in wretched ignorance of what might

be to come. It was the crow of a cock who crowed not without advice; the crow of a cock who knew a thing or two;
the crow of a cock who had fought the world and got the
better of it, and was now resolved to crow, though the
earth should heave and the heavens should fall. It was a
wise crow; an invincible crow; a philosophic crow; a crow
of all crows.

I returned home once more full of reinvigorated spirits,
with a dauntless sort of feeling. I thought over my debts
and other troubles, and over the unlucky risings of the poor
oppressed *peoples* abroad, and over the railroad and steam-
boat accidents, and over even the loss of my dear friend,
with a calm, good-natured rapture of defiance, which
astounded myself. I felt as though I could meet Death, and
invite him to dinner, and toast the Catacombs with him, in
pure overflow of self-reliance and a sense of universal
security.

Toward evening I went up to the hill once more to find
whether, indeed, the glorious cock would prove game even
from the rising of the sun unto the going down thereof. Talk
of Vespers or Curfew! – the evening crow of the cock went
out of his mighty throat all over the land and inhabited it,
like Xerxes from the East with his double-winged host. It
was miraculous. Bless me, what a crow! The cock went
game to roost that night, depend upon it, victorious over
the entire day, and bequeathing the echoes of his thousand
crows to night.

After an unwontedly sound, refreshing sleep I rose early,
feeling like a carriage-spring – light, elliptical, airy, buoyant
as sturgeon-nose – and, like a football, bounded up the hill.
Hark! Shanghai was up before me. The early bird that
caught the worm – crowing like a bugle worked by an
engine – lusty, loud, all jubilation. From the scattered
farm-houses a multitude of other cocks were crowing, and
replying to each other's crows. But they were as flageolets
to a trombone. Shanghai would suddenly break in, and
overwhelm all their crows with his one domineering blast.
He seemed to have nothing to do with any other concern.

He replied to no other crow, but crowed solely by himself, on his own account, in solitary scorn and independence.

Oh, brave cock! – oh, noble Shanghai! – oh, bird rightly offered up by the invincible Socrates, in testimony of his final victory over life.

As I live, thought I, this blessed day will I go and seek out the Shanghai, and buy him, if I have to clap another mortgage on my land.

I listened attentively now, striving to mark from what direction the crow came. But it so charged and replenished, and made bountiful and overflowing all the air, that it was impossible to say from what precise point the exultation came. All that I could decide upon was this: the crow came from out of the east, and not from out of the west. I then considered with myself how far a cock-crow might be heard. In this still country, shut in, too, by mountains, sounds were audible at great distances. Besides, the undulations of the land, the abuttings of the mountains into the rolling hill and valley below, produced strange echoes, and reverberations, and multiplications, and accumulations of resonance, very remarkable to hear, and very puzzling to think of. Where lurked this valiant Shanghai – this bird of cheerful Socrates – the game-fowl Greek who died unappalled? Where lurked he? Oh, noble cock, where are you? Crow once more, my Bantam! my princely, my imperial Shanghai! my bird of the Emperor of China! Brother of the Sun! Cousin of great Jove! where are you? – one crow more, and tell me your number!

Hark! like a full orchestra of the cocks of all nations, forth burst the crow. But where from? There it is; but where? There was no telling, further than it came from out the east.

After breakfast I took my stick and sallied down the road. There were many gentlemen's seats dotting the neighbouring country, and I made no doubt that some of these opulent gentlemen had invested a hundred-dollar bill in some royal Shanghai recently imported in the ship *Trade Wind*, or the ship *White Squall*, or the ship *Sovereign of the Seas*;

for it must needs have been a brave ship with a brave name which bore the fortunes of so brave a cock. I resolved to to walk the entire country, and find this noble foreigner out; but thought it would not be amiss to inquire on the way at the humblest homesteads, whether, peradventure, they had heard of a lately-imported Shanghai belonging to any of the gentlemen settlers from the city; for it was plain that no poor farmer, no poor man of any sort, could own such an oriental trophy, such a Great Bell of St Paul's swung in a cock's throat.

I met an old man, ploughing, in a field nigh the road-side fence.

'My friend, have you heard an extraordinary cock-crow of late?'

'Well, well,' he drawled, 'I don't know – the Widow Crowfoot has a cock – and Squire Squaretoes has a cock – and I have a cock, and they all crow. But I don't know of any on 'em with 'strordinary crows.'

'Good morning to you,' said I, shortly; 'it's plain that you have not heard the crow of the Emperor of China's chanticleer.'

Presently I met another old man mending a tumbledown old rail-fence. The rails were rotten, and at every move of the old man's hand they crumbled into yellow ochre. He had much better let the fence alone, or else get him new rails. And here I must say, that one cause of the sad fact why idiocy more prevails among farmers than any other class of people, is owing to their undertaking the mending of rotten rail-fences in warm, relaxing spring weather. The enterprise is a hopeless one. It is a laborious one; it is a bootless one. It is an enterprise to make the heart break. Vast pains squandered upon a vanity. For how can one make rotten rail-fences stand up on their rotten pins? By what magic put pith into sticks which have lain freezing and baking through sixty consecutive winters and summers? This it is, this wretched endeavour to mend rotten rail-fences with their own rotten rails, which drives many farmers into the asylum.

[113]

On the face of the old man in question incipient idiocy was plainly marked. For, about sixty rods before him extended one of the most unhappy and desponding brokenhearted Virginia rail-fences I ever saw in my life. While in a field behind, were a set of young steers, possessed as by devils, continually butting at this forlorn old fence, and breaking through it here and there, causing the old man to drop his work and chase them back within bounds. He would chase them with a piece of rail huge as Goliath's beam, but as light as cork. At the first flourish, it crumbled into powder.

'My friend,' said I, addressing this woeful mortal, 'have you heard an extraordinary cock-crow of late?'

I might as well have asked him if he had heard the deathtick. He stared at me with a long, bewildered, doleful, and unutterable stare, and without reply resumed his unhappy labours.

What a fool, thought I, to have asked such an uncheerful and uncheerable creature about a cheerful cock!

I walked on. I had now descended the high land where my house stood, and being in a low tract could not hear the crow of the Shanghai, which doubtless overshot me there. Besides, the Shanghai might be at lunch of corn and oats, or taking a nap, and so interrupted his jubilations for a while.

At length I encountered riding along the road, a portly gentleman – nay, a *pursy* one – of great wealth, who had recently purchased him some noble acres, and built him a noble mansion, with a goodly fowl-house attached, the fame whereof spread through all that country. Thought I, Here now is the owner of the Shanghai.

'Sir,' said I, 'excuse me, but I am a countryman of yours, and would ask, if so be you own any Shanghais?'

'Oh, yes; I have ten Shanghais.'

'Ten!' exclaimed I in wonder; 'and do they all crow?'

'Most lustily; every soul of them; I wouldn't own a cock that wouldn't crow.'

'Will you turn back, and show me those Shanghais?'

'With pleasure: I am proud of them. They cost me, in the lump, six hundred dollars.'

As I walked by the side of his horse, I was thinking to myself whether possibly I had not mistaken the harmoniously combined crowings of ten Shanghais in a squad, for the supernatural crow of a single Shanghai by himself.

'Sir,' said I, 'is there one of your Shanghais which far exceeds all the others in the lustiness, musicalness, and inspiring effects of his crow?'

'They crow pretty much alike, I believe,' he courteously replied; 'I really don't know that I could tell their crow apart.'

I began to think that after all my noble chanticleer might not be in the possession of this wealthy gentleman. However, we went into his fowl-yard, and I saw his Shanghais. Let me say that hitherto I had never clapped eye on this species of imported fowl. I had heard what enormous prices were paid for them, and also that they were of an enormous size, and had somehow fancied they must be of a beauty and brilliancy proportioned both to size and price. What was my surprise, then, to see ten carrot-coloured monsters, without the smallest pretension to effulgence of plumage. Immediately I determined that my royal cock was neither among these, nor could possibly be a Shanghai at all; if these gigantic gallows-bird fowl were fair specimens of the true Shanghai.

I walked all day, dining and resting at a farm-house, inspecting various fowl-yards, interrogating various owners of fowls, hearkening to various crows, but discovered not the mysterious chanticleer. Indeed, I had wandered so far and deviously, that I could not hear his crow. I began to suspect that this cock was a mere visitor in the country, who had taken his departure by the eleven o'clock train from the south, and was now crowing and jubilating somewhere on the verdant banks of Long Island Sound.

But next morning, again I heard the inspiring blast, again felt my blood bound in me, again felt superior to all the ills of life, again felt like turning my dun out of doors. But displeased with the reception given him at his last visit, the dun stayed away, doubtless being in a huff. Silly fellow that he was, to take a harmless joke in earnest.

Several days passed, during which I made sundry excursions in the regions round about, but in vain sought the cock. Still, I heard him from the hill, and sometimes from the house, and sometimes in the stillness of the night. If at times I would relapse into my doleful dumps, straightway at the sound of the exultant and defiant crow, my soul, too, would turn chanticleer, and clap her wings, and throw back her throat, and breathe forth a cheerful challenge to all the world of woes.

At last, after some weeks I was necessitated to clap another mortgage on my estate in order to pay certain debts, and among others the one I owed the dun, who of late had commenced a civil-process against me. The way the process was served was a most insulting one. In a private room I had been enjoying myself in the village tavern over a bottle of Philadelphia porter, and some Herkimer cheese, and a roll, and having apprised the landlord, who was a friend of mine, that I would settle with him when I received my next remittances, stepped to the peg where I had hung my hat in the bar-room, to get a choice cigar I had left in the hall, when lo! I found the civil-process enveloping the cigar. When I unrolled the cigar, I unrolled the civil-process, and the constable standing by rolled out, with a thick tongue, 'Take notice!' and added, in a whisper, 'Put that in your pipe and smoke it!'

I turned short round upon the gentlemen then and there present in that bar-room. Said I, 'Gentlemen, is this an honourable – nay, is this a lawful way of serving a civil-process? Behold!'

One and all they were of opinion that it was a highly inelegant act in the constable to take advantage of a gentleman's lunching on cheese and porter, to be so uncivil as to slip a civil-process into his hat. It was ungenerous; it was cruel; for the sudden shock of the thing coming *instanter* upon the lunch would impair the proper digestion of the cheese, which is proverbially not so easy of digestion as blanc-mange.

Arrived home, I read the process, and felt a twinge of melancholy. Hard world! hard world! Here I am, as good a fellow as ever lived – hospitable – open-hearted – generous to a fault: and the Fates forbid that I should possess the fortune to bless the country with my bounteousness. Nay, while many a stingy curmudgeon rolls in idle gold, I, heart of nobleness as I am, I have civil-processes served on me! I bowed my head, and felt forlorn – unjustly used – abused – unappreciated – in short, miserable.

Hark! like a clarion! yea, like a jolly bolt of thunder with bells to it – came the all-glorious and defiant crow! Ye gods, how it set me up again! Right on my pins! Yea, verily on stilts!

Oh, noble cock!

Plain as cock could speak, it said: 'Let the world and all aboard of it go to pot. Do you be jolly, and never say die. What's the world compared to you? What is it anyhow but a lump of loam? Do you be jolly!'

Oh, noble cock!

'But my dear and glorious cock,' mused I, upon second thought, 'one can't so easily send this world to pot; one can't so easily be jolly with civil-processes in his hat or hand.'

Hark! the crow again. Plain as cock could speak, it said: 'Hang the process, and hang the fellow that sent it! If you have not land or cash, go and thrash the fellow, and tell him you never mean to pay him. Be jolly!'

Now this was the way – through the imperative intimations of the cock – that I came to clap the added mortgage on my estate; paid all my debts by fusing them into this one added bond and mortgage. Thus made at ease again, I renewed my search for the noble cock. But in vain, though I heard him every day. I began to think there was some sort of deception in this mysterious thing: some wonderful ventriloquist prowled around my barns, or in my cellar, or on my roof, and was minded to be gaily mischievous. But no – what ventriloquist could so crow with such an heroic and celestial crow?

At last, one morning there came to me a certain singular man, who had sawed and split my wood in March – some five-and-thirty cords of it – and now he came for his pay. He was a singular man, I say. He was tall and spare, with a long, saddish face, yet somehow a latently joyous eye, which offered the strangest contrast. His air seemed staid, but undepressed. He wore a long, gray, shabby coat, and a big battered hat. This man had sawed my wood at so much a cord. He would stand and saw all day long in a driving snowstorm, and never wink at it. He never spoke unless spoken to. He only sawed. Saw, saw, saw – snow, snow, snow. The saw and the snow went together like two natural things. The first day this man came, he brought his dinner with him, and volunteered to eat it sitting on his buck in the snowstorm. From my window, where I was reading Burton's *Anatomy of Melancholy*, I saw him in the act. I burst out of doors bare-headed. 'Good heavens!' cried I; 'what are you doing? Come in. *This* your dinner!'

He had a hunk of stale bread and another hunk of salt beef, wrapped in a wet newspaper, and washed his morsels down by melting a handful of fresh snow in his mouth. I took this rash man indoors, planted him by the fire, gave him a dish of hot pork and beans, and a mug of cider.

'Now,' said I, 'don't you bring any of your damp dinners here. You work by the job, to be sure, but I'll dine you for all that.'

He expressed his acknowledgments in a calm, proud, but not ungrateful way, and dispatched his meal with satisfaction to himself, and me also. It afforded me pleasure to perceive that he quaffed down his mug of cider like a man. I honoured him. When I addressed him in the way of business at his buck, I did so in a guardedly respectful and deferential manner. Interested in his singular aspect, struck by his wondrous intensity of application at his saw – a most wearisome and disgustful occupation to most people – I often sought to gather from him who he was, what sort of a life he led, where he was born, and so on. But he was mum. He came to saw my wood, and eat my dinners – if I chose to offer them – but not to gabble. At first I somewhat resented his sullen silence under the circumstances. But better considering it, I honoured him the more. I increased the respectfulness and deferentialness of my address toward him. I concluded within myself that this man had experienced hard times; that he had had many sore rubs in the world; that he was of a solemn disposition; that he was of the mind of Solomon; that he lived calmly, decorously, temperately; and though a very poor man, was, nevertheless, a highly respectable one. At times I imagined that he might even be an elder or deacon of some small country church. I thought it would not be a bad plan to run this excellent man for President of the United States. He would prove a great reformer of abuses.

His name was Merrymusk. I had often thought how jolly a name for so unjolly a wight. I inquired of people whether they knew Merrymusk. But it was some time before I learned much about him. He was by birth a Marylander, it appeared, who had long lived in the country round about; a wandering man; until within some ten years ago, a thriftless man, though perfectly innocent of crime; a man who would work hard a month with surprising soberness, and then spend all his wages in one riotous night. In youth he had been a sailor, and run away from his ship at Batavia, where he caught the fever, and came nigh dying. But he rallied, reshipped, landed home, found all his friends dead, and struck for the Northern interior, where he had since tarried. Nine years back he had married a wife, and now had four children. His wife was become a perfect invalid; one child had the white-swelling, and the rest were rickety. He and his family lived in a shanty on a lonely barren patch nigh the railroad-track, where it passed close to the base of a mountain. He had bought a fine cow to have plenty of wholesome milk for his children; but the cow died during an accouchement, and he could not afford to buy another.

Still, his family never suffered for lack of food. He worked hard and brought it to them.

Now, as I said before, having long previously sawed my wood, this Merrymusk came for his pay.

'My friend,' said I, 'do you know of any gentleman hereabouts who owns an extraordinary cock?'

The twinkle glittered quite plain in the wood-sawyer's eye.

'I know of no *gentleman*,' he replied, 'who has what might well be called an extraordinary cock.'

Oh, thought I, this Merrymusk is not the man to enlighten me. I am afraid I shall never discover this extraordinary cock.

Not having the full change to pay Merrymusk, I gave him his due, as nigh as I could make it, and told him that in a day or two I would take a walk and visit his place, and hand him the remainder. Accordingly one fine morning I sallied forth upon the errand. I had much ado finding the best road to the shanty. No one seemed to know where it was exactly. It lay in a very lonely part of the country, a densely-wooded mountain on one side (which I call October Mountain, on account of its bannered aspect in that month), and a thicketed swamp on the other, the railroad cutting the swamp. Straight as a die the railroad cut it; many times a day tantalising the wretched shanty with the sight of all the beauty, rank, fashion, health, trunks, silver and gold, dry-goods and groceries, brides and grooms, happy wives and husbands, flying by the lonely door – no time to stop – flash! here they are – and there they go! – out of sight at both ends – as if that part of the world were only made to fly over, and not to settle upon. And this was about all the shanty saw of what people call 'life.'

Though puzzled somewhat, yet I knew the general direction where the shanty lay, and on I trudged. As I advanced, I was surprised to hear the mysterious cock crow with more and more distinctness. Is it possible, thought I, that any gentleman owning a Shanghai can dwell in such a lonesome, dreary region? Louder and louder, nigher and nigher, sounded the glorious and defiant clarion. Though somehow I may be out of the track to my wood-sawyer's, I said to myself, yet, thank Heaven, I seem to be on the way toward that extraordinary cock. I was delighted with this auspicious accident. On I journeyed; while at intervals the crow sounded most invitingly, and jocundly, and superbly; and the last crow was ever nigher than the former one. At last, emerging from a thicket of elders, straight before me I saw the most resplendent creature that ever blessed the sight of man.

A cock, more like a golden eagle than a cock. A cock, more like a field-marshal than a cock. A cock, more like Nelson with all his glittering arms on, standing on the *Vanguard's* quarter-deck going into battle, than a cock. A cock, more like the Emperor Charlemagne in his robes at Aix-la-Chapelle, than a cock.

Such a cock!

He was of a haughty size, stood haughtily on his haughty legs. His colours were red, gold, and white. The red was on his crest alone, which was a mighty and symmetric crest, like unto Hector's helmet, as delineated on antique shields. His plumage was snowy, traced with gold. He walked in front of the shanty, like a peer of the realm; his crest lifted, his chest heaved out, his embroidered trappings flashing in the light. His pace was wonderful. He looked like some noble foreigner. He looked like some Oriental king in some magnificent Italian opera.

Merrymusk advanced from the door.

'Pray, is not that the Signor Beneventano?'

'Sir!'

'That's the cock,' said I, a little embarrassed. The truth was, my enthusiasm had betrayed me into a rather silly inadvertence. I had made a somewhat learned sort of allusion in the presence of an unlearned man. Consequently, upon discovering it by his honest stare, I felt foolish; but carried it off by declaring that *this was the cock*.

Now, during the preceding autumn I had been to the city, and had chanced to be present at a performance of the

Italian Opera. In that opera figured in some royal character a certain Signor Beneventano – a man of a tall, imposing person, clad in rich raiment, like to plumage, and with a most remarkable, majestic, scornful stride. The Signor Beneventano seemed on the point of tumbling over backward with exceeding haughtiness. And, for all the world, the proud pace of the cock seemed the very stage-pace of the Signor Beneventano.

Hark! Suddenly the cock paused, lifted his head still higher, ruffled his plumes, seemed inspired, and sent forth a lusty crow. October Mountain echoed it; other mountains sent it back; still others rebounded it; it overran the country round. Now I plainly perceived how it was I had chanced to hear the gladdening sound on my distant hill.

'Good heavens! do you own the cock? Is that cock yours?'

'Is it my cock!' said Merrymusk, looking slyly gleeful out of the corner of his long, solemn face.

'Where did you get it?'

'It chipped the shell here. I raised it.'

'You?'

Hark! Another crow. It might have raised the ghosts of all the pines and hemlocks ever cut down in that country. Marvellous cock! Having crowed, he strode on again, surrounded by a bevy of admiring hens.

'What will you take for Signor Beneventano?'

'Sir?'

'That magic cock! – what will you take for him?'

'I won't sell him.'

'I will give you fifty dollars.'

'Pooh!'

'One hundred!'

'Pish!'

'Five hundred!'

'Bah!'

'And you a poor man?'

'No; don't I own that cock, and haven't I refused five hundred dollars for him?'

'True,' said I, in profound thought; 'that's a fact. You won't sell him, then?'

'No.'

'Will you give him?'

'No.'

'Will you *keep* him, then!' I shouted, in a rage.

'Yes.'

I stood a while admiring the cock, and wondering at the man. At last I felt a redoubled admiration of the one, and a redoubled deference for the other.

'Won't you step in?' said Merrymusk.

'But won't the cock be prevailed upon to join us?' said I.

'Yes. Trumpet! hither, boy! hither!'

The cock turned round, and strode up to Merrymusk.

'Come!'

The cock followed us into the shanty.

'Crow!'

The roof jarred.

Oh, noble cock!

I turned in silence upon my entertainer. There he sat on an old battered chest, in his old tattered gray coat, with patches at his knees and elbows, and a deplorably bunged hat. I glanced round the room. Bare rafters overhead, but solid junks of jerked beef hanging from them. Earth floor, but a heap of potatoes in one corner, and a sack of Indian meal in another. A blanket was strung across the apartment at the farther end, from which came a woman's ailing voice and the voices of ailing children. But somehow in the ailing of these voices there seemed no complaint.

'Mrs Merrymusk and children?'

'Yes.'

I looked at the cock. There he stood majestically in the middle of the room. He looked like a Spanish grandee caught in a shower, and standing under some peasant's shed. There was a strange supernatural look of contrast about him. He irradiated the shanty; he glorified its meanness. He glorified the battered chest, and tattered gray coat,

[123]

and the bunged hat. He glorified the very voices which came in ailing tones from behind the screen.

'Oh, father,' cried a little sickly voice, 'let Trumpet sound again.'

'Crow,' cried Merrymusk.

The cock threw himself into a posture.

The roof jarred.

'Does not this disturb Mrs Merrymusk and the sick children?'

'Crow again, Trumpet.'

The roof jarred.

'It does not disturb them, then?'

'Didn't you hear 'em *ask* for it?'

'How is it, that your sick family like this crowing?' said I. 'The cock is a glorious cock, with a glorious voice, but not exactly the sort of thing for a sick-chamber, one would suppose. Do they really like it?'

'Don't *you* like it? Don't it do *you* good? Ain't it inspiring? Don't it impart pluck? give stuff against despair?'

'All true,' said I, removing my hat with profound humility before the brave spirit disguised in the base coat.

'But then,' said I, still with some misgivings, 'so loud, so wonderfully clamorous a crow, methinks might be amiss to invalids, and retard their convalescence.'

'Crow your best now, Trumpet!'

I leaped from my chair. The cock frightened me, like some overpowering angel in the Apocalypse. He seemed crowing over the fall of wicked Babylon, or crowing over the triumph of righteous Joshua in the vale of Askalon. When I regained my composure somewhat, an inquisitive thought occurred to me. I resolved to gratify it.

'Merrymusk, will you present me to your wife and children?'

'Yes. Wife, the gentleman wants to step in.'

'He is very welcome,' replied a weak voice.

Going behind the curtain, there lay a wasted, but strangely cheerful human face; and that was pretty much all; the body, hid by the counterpane and an old coat, seemed too shrunken to reveal itself through such impediments. At the bedside sat a pale girl, ministering. In another bed lay three children, side by side: three more pale faces.

'Oh, father, we don't mislike the gentleman, but let us see Trumpet too.'

At a word, the cock strode behind the screen, and perched himself on the children's bed. All their wasted eyes gazed at him with a wild and spiritual delight. They seemed to sun themselves in the radiant plumage of the cock.

'Better than a 'pothecary, eh?' said Merrymusk. 'This is Dr Cock himself.'

We retired from the sick ones, and I reseated myself again, lost in thought over this strange household.

'You seem a glorious independent fellow!' said I.

'And I don't think you a fool, and never did. Sir, you are a trump.'

'Is there any hope of your wife's recovery?' said I, modestly seeking to turn the conversation.

'Not the least.'

'The children?'

'Very little.'

'It must be a doleful life, then, for all concerned. This lonely solitude – this shanty – hard work – hard times.'

'Haven't I Trumpet? He's the cheerer. He crows through all; crows at the darkest: Glory to God in the highest! Continually he crows it.'

'Just the import I first ascribed to his crow, Merrymusk, when first I heard it from my hill. I thought some rich nabob owned some costly Shanghai; little weening any such poor man as you owned this lusty cock of a domestic breed.'

'*Poor* man like *me*? Why call *me* poor? Don't the cock *I* own glorify this otherwise inglorious, lean, lantern-jawed land? Didn't *my* cock encourage *you*? And *I* give you all this glorification away gratis. I am a great philanthropist. I am a rich man – a very rich man, and a very happy one. Crow, Trumpet.'

The roof jarred.

I returned home in a deep mood. I was not wholly at rest

concerning the soundness of Merrymusk's views of things, though full of admiration for him. I was thinking on the matter before my door, when I heard the cock crow again. Enough. Merrymusk is right.

Oh, noble cock! oh, noble man!

I did not see Merrymusk for some weeks after this; but hearing the glorious and rejoicing crow, I supposed that all went as usual with him. My own frame of mind remained a rejoicing one. The cock still inspired me. I saw another mortgage piled on my plantation; but only bought another dozen of stout, and a dozen-dozen of Philadelphia porter. Some of my relatives died; I wore no mourning, but for three days drank stout in preference to porter, stout being of the darker colour. I heard the cock crow the instant I received the unwelcome tidings.

'Your health in this stout, oh, noble cock!'

I thought I would call on Merrymusk again, not having seen or heard of him for some time now. Approaching the place, there were no signs of motion about the shanty. I felt a strange misgiving. But the cock crew from within doors, and the boding vanished. I knocked at the door. A feeble voice bade me enter. The curtain was no longer drawn; the whole house was a hospital now. Merrymusk lay on a heap of old clothes; wife and children were all in their beds. The cock was perched on an old hogshead hoop, swung from the ridge-pole in the middle of the shanty.

'You are sick, Merrymusk,' said I, mournfully.

'No, I am well,' he feebly answered. 'Crow, Trumpet.'

I shrunk. The strong soul in the feeble body appalled me. But the cock crew.

The roof jarred.

'How is Mrs Merrymusk?'

'Well.'

'And the children?'

'Well. All well.'

The last two words he shouted forth in a kind of wild ecstasy of triumph over ill. It was too much. His head fell

[126]

back. A white napkin seemed dropped upon his face. Merry-musk was dead.

An awful fear seized me.

But the cock crew.

The cock shook his plumage as if each feather were a banner. The cock hung from the shanty roof as erewhile the trophied flags from the dome of St Paul's. The cock terrified me with exceeding wonder.

I drew nigh the bedsides of the woman and children. They marked my look of strange affright; they knew what had happened.

'My good man is just dead,' breathed the woman lowly. 'Tell me true?'

'Dead,' said I.

The cock crew.

She fell back, without a sigh, and through long-loving sympathy was dead.

The cock crew.

The cock shook sparkles from his golden plumage. The cock seemed in a rapture of benevolent delight. Leaping from the hoop, he strode up majestically to the pile of old clothes, where the wood-sawyer lay, and planted himself, like an armorial supporter, at his side. Then raised one long, musical, triumphant, and final sort of crow, with throat heaved far back, as if he meant the blast to waft the wood-sawyer's soul sheer up to the seventh heaven. Then he strode, king-like, to the woman's bed. Another upturned and exultant crow, mated to the former.

The pallor of the children was changed to radiance. Their faces shone celestially through grime and dirt. They seemed children of emperors and kings, disguised. The cock sprang upon their bed, shook himself, and crowed, and crowed again, and still and still again. He seemed bent upon crowing the souls of the children out of their wasted bodies. He seemed bent upon rejoining *instanter* this whole family in the upper air. The children seemed to second his endeavours. Far, deep, intense longings for release transfigured them into spirits before my eyes. I saw angels where they lay.

They were dead.

The cock shook his plumage over them. The cock crew. It was now like a Bravo! like a Hurrah! like a Three-times-three! hip! hip! He strode out of the shanty. I followed. He flew upon the apex of the dwelling, spread wide his wings, sounded one supernatural note, and dropped at my feet.

The cock was dead.

If now you visit that hilly region, you will see, nigh the railroad track, just beneath October Mountain, on the other side of the swamp – there you will see a gravestone, not with skull and cross-bones, but with a lusty cock in act of crowing, chiselled on it, with the words beneath: —

> 'O death, where is thy sting?
> O grave, where is thy victory?'

The wood-sawyer and his family, with the Signor Beneventano, lie in that spot; and I buried them, and planted the stone, which was a stone made to order; and never since then have I felt the doleful dumps, but under all circumstances crow late and early with a continual crow.

Cock-a-doodle-doo! – oo! – oo! – oo! – oo!

THE ENCANTADAS

OR
ENCHANTED ISLES

SKETCH FIRST

THE ISLES AT LARGE

—'That may not be, said then the Ferryman
Least we unweeting hap to be fordonne:
For those same Islands, seeming now and than,
Are not firme lande, nor any certein wonne,
But straggling plots, which to and fro do ronne
In the wide waters: therefore are they hight
The wandring Islands. Therefore doe them shonne;
For they have oft drawne many a wandring wight
Into most deadly daunger and distressed plight;
For whosoever once hath fastened
His foot thereon, may never it recure,
But wandreth ever more uncertain and unsure.'

*

'Darke, dolefull, drearie, like a greedie grave,
That still for carrion carcases doth crave:
On top whereof aye dwelt the ghastly Owle,
Shrieking his balefull note, which ever drave
Farre from that haunt all other chearefull fowle;
And all about it wandring ghostes did waile and howle.'

TAKE five-and-twenty heaps of cinders dumped here and there in an outside city lot; imagine some of them magnified into mountains, and the vacant lot the sea; and you will have a fit idea of the general aspect of the Encantadas, or Enchanted Isles. A group rather of extinct volcanoes than of isles; looking much as the world at large might, after a penal conflagration.

It is to be doubted whether any spot of earth can, in desolateness, furnish a parallel to this group. Abandoned cemeteries of long ago, old cities by piecemeal tumbling to their ruin, these are melancholy enough; but, like all else which has but once been associated with humanity, they still awaken in us some thoughts of sympathy, however sad. Hence, even the Dead Sea, along with whatever other emotions it may at times inspire, does not fail to touch in the pilgrim some of his less unpleasurable feelings.

And as for solitariness; the great forests of the north, the expanses of unnavigated waters, the Greenland ice-fields, are the profoundest of solitudes to a human observer; still the magic of their changeable tides and seasons mitigates their terror; because, though unvisited by men, those forests are visited by the May; the remotest seas reflect familiar stars even as Lake Erie does; and, in the clear air of a fine Polar day, the irradiated, azure ice shows beautifully as malachite.

But the special curse, as one may call it, of the Encantadas, that which exalts them in desolation above Idumea and the Pole, is, that to them change never comes; neither the change of seasons nor of sorrows. Cut by the Equator, they know not autumn, and they know not spring; while already reduced to the lees of fire, ruin itself can work little more upon them. The showers refresh the deserts; but in these isles, rain never falls. Like split Syrian gourds left withering in the sun, they are cracked by an everlasting drought beneath a torrid sky. 'Have mercy upon me,' the wailing spirit of the Encantadas seems to cry, 'and send Lazarus that he may dip the tip of his finger in water and cool my tongue, for I am tormented in this flame.'

Another feature in these isles is their emphatic uninhabitableness. It is deemed a fit type of all-forsaken overthrow, that the jackal should den in the wastes of weedy Babylon; but the Encantadas refuse to harbor even the outcasts of the beasts. Man and wolf alike disown them. Little but reptile life is here found: tortoises, lizards, immense spiders, snakes, and that strangest anomaly of outlandish nature, the *aguano*. No voice, no low, no howl is heard; the chief sound of life here is a hiss.

On most of the isles where vegetation is found at all, it is more ungrateful than the blankness of Aracama. Tangled thickets of wiry bushes, without fruit and without a name, springing up among deep fissures of calcined rock, and treacherously masking them; or a parched growth of distorted cactus trees.

In many places the coast is rock-bound, or, more properly, clinker-bound; tumbled masses of blackish or greenish stuff like the dross of an iron-furnace, forming dark clefts and caves here and there, into which a ceaseless sea pours a fury of foam; overhanging them with a swirl of gray, haggard mist, amidst which sail screaming flights of unearthly birds heightening the dismal din. However calm the sea without, there is no rest for these swells and those rocks; they lash and are lashed, even when the outer ocean is most at peace with itself. On the oppressive, clouded days, such as are peculiar to this part of the watery Equator, the dark, vitrified masses, many of which raise themselves among white whirlpools and breakers in detached and perilous places off the shore, present a most Plutonian sight. In no world but a fallen one could such lands exist.

Those parts of the strand free from the marks of fire, stretch away in wide level beaches of multitudinous dead shells, with here and there decayed bits of sugar-cane, bamboos, and cocoanuts, washed upon this other and darker world from the charming palm isles to the westward and southward; all the way from Paradise to Tartarus; while mixed with the relics of distant beauty you will sometimes see fragments of charred wood and mouldering ribs of wrecks. Neither will any one be surprised at meeting these last, after observing the conflicting currents which eddy throughout nearly all the wide channels of the entire group. The capriciousness of the tides of air sympathizes with those of the sea. Nowhere is the wind so light, baffling, and every way unreliable, and so given to perplexing calms, as at the Encantadas. Nigh a month has been spent by a ship going from one isle to another, though but ninety miles between; for owing to the force of the current, the boats employed to tow barely suffice to keep the craft from sweeping upon the cliffs, but do nothing towards accelerating her voyage. Sometimes it is impossible for a vessel from afar to fetch up with the group itself, unless large allowances for prospective lee-way have been made ere its coming in sight. And yet, at other times, there is a mysterious indraft, which irresistibly draws a passing vessel among the isles, though not bound to them.

True, at one period, as to some extent at the present day, large fleets of whalemen cruised for spermaceti upon what some seamen call the Enchanted Ground. But this, as in due place will be described, was off the great outer isle of Albemarle, away from the intricacies of the smaller isles, where there is plenty of sea-room; and hence, to that vicinity, the above remarks do not altogether apply; though even there the current runs at times with singular force, shifting, too, with as singular a caprice.

Indeed, there are seasons when currents quite unaccountable prevail for a great distance round about the total group, and are so strong and irregular as to change a vessel's course against the helm, though sailing at the rate of four or five miles the hour. The difference in the reckonings of navigators, produced by these causes, along with the light and variable winds, long nourished a persuasion, that there existed two distinct clusters of isles in the parallel of the Encantadas, about a hundred leagues apart. Such was the idea of their earlier visitors, the Buccaneers; and as late as 1750, the charts of that part of the Pacific accorded with the strange delusion. And this apparent fleetingness and unreality of the locality of the isles was most probably one reason for the Spaniards calling them the Encantada, or Enchanted Group.

But not uninfluenced by their character, as they now confessedly exist, the modern voyager will be inclined to fancy that the bestowal of this name might have in part originated in that air of spell-bound desertness which so significantly invests the isles. Nothing can better suggest the aspect of once living things malignly crumbled from ruddiness into ashes. Apples of Sodom, after touching, seem these isles.

However wavering their place may seem by reason of the currents, they themselves, at least to one upon the shore, appear invariably the same: fixed, cast, glued into the very body of cadaverous death.

Nor would the appellation, enchanted, seem misapplied in still another sense. For concerning the peculiar reptile inhabitant of these wilds – whose presence gives the group its second Spanish name, Gallipagos – concerning the tortoises found here, most mariners have long cherished a superstition, not more frightful than grotesque. They earnestly believe that all wicked sea-officers, more especially commodores and captains, are at death (and, in some cases, before death) transformed into tortoises; thenceforth dwelling upon these hot aridities, sole solitary lords of Asphaltum.

Doubtless, so quaintly dolorous a thought was originally inspired by the woe-begone landscape itself; but more particularly, perhaps, by the tortoises. For, apart from their strictly physical features, there is something strangely self-condemned in the appearance of these creatures. Lasting sorrow and penal hopelessness are in no animal form so suppliantly expressed as in theirs; while the thought of their wonderful longevity does not fail to enhance the impression.

Nor even at the risk of meriting the charge of absurdly believing in enchantments, can I restrain the admission that sometimes, even now, when leaving the crowded city to wander out July and August among the Adirondack Mountains, far from the influences of towns and proportionally nigh to the mysterious ones of nature; when at such times I sit me down in the mossy head of some deep-wooded gorge, surrounded by prostrate trunks of blasted pines and recall, as in a dream, my other and far-distant rovings in the baked heart of the charmed isles: and remember the sudden glimpses of dusky shells, and long languid necks protruded from the leafless thickets; and again have beheld the vitreous inland rocks worn down and grooved into deep ruts by ages and ages of the slow draggings of tortoises in quest of pools of scanty water; I can hardly resist the feeling that in my time I have indeed slept upon evilly enchanted ground.

Nay, such is the vividness of my memory, or the magic of my fancy, that I know not whether I am not the occasional victim of optical delusion concerning the Gallipagos. For, often in scenes of social merriment, and especially at revels held by candle-light in old-fashioned mansions, so that shadows are thrown into the further recesses of an angular and spacious room, making them put on a look of haunted undergrowth of lonely woods, I have drawn the attention of my comrades by my fixed gaze and sudden change of air, as I have seemed to see, slowly emerging from those imagined solitudes, and heavily crawling along the floor, the ghost of a gigantic tortoise, with 'Memento * * * * *' burning in live letters upon his back.

SKETCH SECOND

TWO SIDES TO A TORTOISE

> 'Most ugly shapes, and horrible aspects,
> Such as Dame Nature selfe mote feare to see,
> Or shame, that ever should so fowle defects
> From her most cunning hand escaped bee;
> All dreadfull pourtraicts of deformitee.
> Ne wonder, if these do a man appall;
> For all that here at home we dreadfull hold,
> Be but as bugs to fearen babes withall,
> Compared to the creatures in these isles' entrall.

*

> Feare nought, (then said the Palmer well aviz'd;)
> For these same Monsters are not there in deed,
> But are into these fearfull shapes disguiz'd.

*

> And lifting up his vertuous staffe on hye,
> Then all that dreadfull Armie fast gan flye
> Into great Tethys bosome, where they hidden lye.'

In view of the description given, may one be gay upon the Encantadas? Yes: that is, find one the gayety, and he will be gay. And indeed, sackcloth and ashes as they are, the isles are not perhaps unmitigated gloom. For while no spectator can deny their claims to a most solemn and superstitious consideration, no more than my firmest resolutions can decline to behold the spectre-tortoise when emerging from its shadowy recess; yet even the tortoise, dark and melancholy as it is upon the back, still possesses a bright side; its calipee or breast-plate being sometimes of a faint yellowish or golden tinge. Moreover, every one knows that tortoises as well as turtles are of such a make, that if you but put them on their backs you thereby expose their bright sides without the possibility of their recovering themselves, and turning into view the other. But after you have done this, and because you have done this, you should not swear that the tortoise has no dark side. Enjoy the bright, keep it turned up perpetually if you can, but be honest, and don't deny the black. Neither should he, who cannot turn the tortoise from its natural position so as to hide the darker and expose his livelier aspect, like a great October pumpkin in the sun, for that cause declare the creature to be one total inky blot. The tortoise is both black and bright. But let us to particulars.

Some months before my first stepping ashore upon the group, my ship was cruising in its close vicinity. One noon we found ourselves off the South Head of Albemarle, and not very far from the land. Partly by way of freak, and partly by way of spying out so strange a country, a boat's crew was sent ashore, with orders to see all they could, and besides, bring back whatever tortoises they could conveniently transport.

It was after sunset, when the adventurers returned. I looked down over the ship's high side as if looking down over the curb of a well, and dimly saw the damp boat deep in the sea with some unwonted weight. Ropes were dropt over, and presently three huge antediluvian-looking tortoises, after much straining, were landed on deck. They seemed hardly of the seed of earth. We had been broad upon the waters for five long months, a period amply sufficient to make all things of the land wear a fabulous hue to the dreamy mind. Had three Spanish custom-house officers boarded us then, it is not unlikely that I should have curiously stared at them, felt of them, and stroked them much as savages serve civilized guests. But instead of three custom-house officers, behold these really wondrous tortoises – none of your schoolboy mud-turtles – but black as widower's weeds, heavy as chests of plate, with vast shells medallioned and orbed like shields, and dented and blistered like shields that have breasted a battle, shaggy, too, here and there, with dark green moss, and slimy with the spray of the sea. These mystic creatures, suddenly translated by night from unutterable solitudes to our peopled deck, affected me in a manner not easy to unfold. They seemed newly crawled forth from beneath the foundations of the world. Yea, they seemed the identical tortoises whereon the Hindoo plants this total sphere. With a lantern I inspected them more closely. Such worshipful venerableness of aspect! Such furry greenness mantling the rude peelings and healing the fissures of their shattered shells. I no more saw three tortoises. They expanded – became transfigured. I seemed to see three Roman Coliseums in magnificent decay.

Ye oldest inhabitants of this, or any other isle, said I, pray, give me the freedom of your three-walled towns.

The great feeling inspired by these creatures was that of age: – dateless, indefinite endurance. And in fact that any other creature can live and breathe as long as the tortoise of the Encantadas, I will not readily believe. Not to hint of their known capacity of sustaining life, while going without food for an entire year, consider that impregnable armor of their living mail. What other bodily being possesses such a citadel wherein to resist the assaults of Time?

As, lantern in hand, I scraped among the moss and beheld the ancient scars of bruises received in many a sullen fall among the marly mountains of the isle – scars strangely widened, swollen, half obliterate, and yet distorted like those sometimes found in the bark of very hoary trees, I seemed an antiquary of a geologist, studying the bird-tracks and ciphers upon the exhumed slates trod by incredible creatures whose very ghosts are now defunct.

As I lay in my hammock that night, overhead I heard the slow weary draggings of the three ponderous strangers along the encumbered deck. Their stupidity or their resolution was so great, that they never went aside for any impediment. One ceased his movements altogether just before the mid-watch. At sunrise I found him butted like a battering-ram against the immovable foot of the foremast, and still striving, tooth and nail, to force the impossible passage. That these tortoises are the victims of a penal, or malignant,

or perhaps a downright diabolical enchanter, seems in nothing more likely than in that strange infatuation of hopeless
toil which so often possesses them. I have known them in
their journeyings ram themselves heroically against rocks,
and long abide there, nudging, wriggling, wedging, in order
to displace them, and so hold on their inflexible path.
Their crowning curse is their drudging impulse to straightforwardness in a belittered world.

Meeting with no such hinderance as their companion did,
the other tortoises merely fell foul of small stumbling-
blocks – buckets, blocks, and coils of rigging – and at times
in the act of crawling over them would slip with an
astounding rattle to the deck. Listening to these draggings
and concussions, I thought me of the haunt from which
they came; an isle full of metallic ravines and gulches, sunk
bottomlessly into the hearts of splintered mountains, and
covered for many miles with inextricable thickets. I then
pictured these three straightforward monsters, century
after century, writhing through the shades, grim as black-
smiths; crawling so slowly and ponderously, that not only
did toad-stools and all fungus things grow beneath their
feet, but a sooty moss sprouted upon their backs. With
them I lost myself in volcanic mazes; brushed away endless
boughs of rotting thickets; till finally in a dream I found
myself sitting crosslegged upon the foremost, a Brahmin
similarly mounted upon either side, forming a tripod of
foreheads which upheld the universal cope.

Such was the wild nightmare begot by my first impression of the Encantadas tortoise. But next evening, strange
to say, I sat down with my shipmates, and made a merry
repast from tortoise steaks and tortoise stews; and supper
over, out knife, and helped convert the three mighty con-
cave shells into three fanciful soup-tureens, and polished
the three flat yellowish calipees into three gorgeous salvers.

SKETCH THIRD

ROCK RODONDO

'For they this hight The Rocke of vile Reproch,
A daungerous and dreadful place,
To which nor fish nor fowle did once approch,
But yelling Meawes, with Seagulles hoarse and bace,
And Cormoyrants, with birds of ravenous race,
Which still sate waiting on that dreadful clift.'

*

'With that the rolling sea resounding soft,
In his big base them fitly answered,
And on the rocke the waves breaking aloft,
A solemne Meane unto them measured.'

*

'Then he the boateman bad row easily,
And let him heare some part of that rare melody.'

*

'Suddeinly an innumerable flight
Of harmefull fowles about them fluttering, cride,
And with their wicked wings them oft did smight,
And sore annoyed, groping in that griesly night.'

*

'Even all the nation of unfortunate
And fatall birds about them flocked were.'

To go up into a high stone tower is not only a very fine
thing in itself, but the very best mode of gaining a comprehensive view of the region round about. It is all the
better if this tower stand solitary and alone, like that mysterious Newport one, or else be sole survivor of some
perished castle.

[141]

Now, with reference to the Enchanted Isles, we are fortunately supplied with just such a noble point of observation in a remarkable rock, from its peculiar figure called of old by the Spaniards, Rock Rodondo, or Round Rock. Some two hundred and fifty feet high, rising straight from the sea ten miles from land, with the whole mountainous group to the south and east, Rock Rodondo occupies, on a large scale, very much the position which the famous Campanile or detached Bell Tower of St Mark does with respect to the tangled group of hoary edifices around it.

Ere ascending, however, to gaze abroad upon the Encantadas, this sea-tower itself claims attention. It is visible at the distance of thirty miles; and, fully participating in that enchantment which pervades the group, when first seen afar invariably is mistaken for a sail. Four leagues away, of a golden, hazy noon, it seems some Spanish Admiral's ship, stacked up with glittering canvas. Sail ho! Sail ho! Sail ho! from all three masts. But coming nigh, the enchanted frigate is transformed apace into a craggy keep.

My first visit to the spot was made in the gray of the morning. With a view of fishing, we had lowered three boats, and pulling some two miles from our vessel, found ourselves just before dawn of day close under the moon-shadow of Rodondo. Its aspect was heightened, and yet softened, by the strange double twilight of the hour. The great full moon burnt in the low west like a half-spent beacon, casting a soft mellow tinge upon the sea like that cast by a waning fire of embers upon a midnight hearth; while along the entire east the invisible sun sent pallid intimations of his coming. The wind was light; the waves languid; the stars twinkled with a faint effulgence; all nature seemed supine with the long night watch, and half-suspended in jaded expectation of the sun. This was the critical hour to catch Rodondo in his perfect mood. The twilight was just enough to reveal every striking point, without tearing away the dim investiture of wonder.

From a broken stair-like base, washed, as the steps of a water-palace, by the waves, the tower rose in entablatures of strata to a shaven summit. These uniform layers, which compose the mass, form its most peculiar feature. For at their lines of junction they project flatly into encircling shelves, from top to bottom, rising one above another in graduated series. And as the eaves of any old barn or abbey are alive with swallows, so were all these rocky ledges with unnumbered sea-fowl. Eaves upon eaves, and nests upon nests. Here and there were long birdlime streaks of a ghostly white staining the tower from sea to air, readily accounting for its sail-like look afar. All would have been bewitchingly quiescent, were it not for the demoniac din created by the birds. Not only were the eaves rustling with them, but they flew densely overhead, spreading themselves into a winged and continually shifting canopy. The tower is the resort of aquatic birds for hundreds of leagues around. To the north, to the east, to the west, stretches nothing but eternal ocean; so that the man-of-war hawk coming from the coasts of North America, Polynesia, or Peru, makes his first land at Rodondo. And yet though Rodondo be terra-firma, no land-bird ever lighted on it. Fancy a red-robin or a canary there! What a falling into the hands of the Philistines, when the poor warbler should be surrounded by such locust-flights of strong bandit birds, with long bills cruel as daggers.

I know not where one can better study the Natural History of strange sea-fowl than at Rodondo. It is the aviary of Ocean. Birds light here which never touched mast or tree; hermit-birds, which ever fly alone; cloud-birds, familiar with unpierced zones of air.

Let us first glance low down to the lowermost shelf of all, which is the widest, too, and but a little space from high-water mark. What outlandish beings are these? Erect as men, but hardly as symmetrical, they stand all round the rock like sculptured caryatides, supporting the next range of eaves above. Their bodies are grotesquely mis-shapen; their bills short; their feet seemingly legless; while the members at their sides are neither fin, wing, nor arm. And truly neither fish, flesh, nor fowl is the penguin; as an edible, pertaining neither to Carnival nor Lent; without exception the most ambiguous and least lovely creature yet discovered by man. Though dabbling in all three elements, and indeed possessing some rudimental claims to all, the penguin is at home in none. On land it stumps; afloat it sculls; in the air it flops. As if ashamed of her failure, Nature keeps this ungainly child hidden away at the ends of the earth, in the Straits of Magellan, and on the abased sea-story of Rodondo.

But look, what are yon wobegone regiments drawn up on the next shelf above? what rank and file of large strange fowl? what sea Friars of Orders Gray? Pelicans. Their elongated bills, and heavy leathern pouches suspended thereto, give them the most lugubrious expression. A pensive race, they stand for hours together without motion. Their dull, ashy plumage imparts an aspect as if they had been powdered over with cinders. A penitential bird, indeed, fitly haunting the shores of the clinkered Encantadas, whereon tormented Job himself might have well sat down and scraped himself with potsherds.

Higher up now we mark the gony, or gray albatross, anomalously so called, an unsightly, unpoetic bird, unlike its storied kinsman, which is the snow-white ghost of the haunted Capes of Hope and Horn.

As we still ascend from shelf to shelf, we find the tenants of the tower serially disposed in order of their magnitude: – gannets, black and speckled haglets, jays, sea-hens, sperm-whale-birds, gulls of all varieties: – thrones, princedoms, powers, dominating one above another in senatorial array; while, sprinkled over all, like an ever-repeated fly in a great piece of broidery, the stormy petrel or Mother Cary's chicken sounds his continual challenge and alarm. That this mysterious humming-bird of ocean – which, had it but brilliancy of hue, might, from its evanescent liveliness, be almost called its butterfly, yet whose chirrup under the stern is ominous to mariners as to the peasant the death-tick sounding from behind the chimney jamb – should have its special haunt at the Encantadas, contributes, in the seaman's mind, not a little to their dreary spell.

As day advances the dissonant din augments. With ear-splitting cries the wild birds celebrate their matins. Each moment, flights push from the tower, and join the aerial choir hovering overhead, while their places below are supplied by darting myriads. But down through all this discord of commotion, I hear clear, silver, bugle-like notes unbrokenly falling, like oblique lines of swift-slanting rain in a cascading shower. I gaze far up, and behold a snow-white angelic thing, with one long, lance-like feather thrust out behind. It is the bright, inspiriting chanticleer of ocean, the beauteous bird, from its bestirring whistle of musical invocation, fitly styled the 'Boatswain's Mate.'

The winged, life-clouding Rodondo had its full counterpart in the finny hosts which peopled the waters at its base. Below the water-line, the rock seemed one honey-comb of grottoes, affording labyrinthine lurking-places for swarms of fairy fish. All were strange; many exceedingly beautiful; and would have well graced the costliest glass globes in which gold-fish are kept for a show. Nothing was more striking than the complete novelty of many individuals of this multitude. Here hues were seen as yet unpainted, and figures which are unengraved.

To show the multitude, avidity, and nameless fearlessness and tameness of these fish, let me say, that often, marking through clear spaces of water – temporarily made so by the concentric dartings of the fish above the surface – certain larger and less unwary wights, which swam slow and deep; our anglers would cautiously essay to drop their lines down to these last. But in vain; there was no passing the uppermost zone. No sooner did the hook touch the sea, than a hundred infatuates contended for the honor of capture. Poor fish of Rodondo! in your victimized confidence, you are of the number of those who inconsiderately trust, while they do not understand, human nature.

But the dawn is now fairly day. Band after band, the

sea-fowl sail away to forage the deep for their food. The tower is left solitary, save the fish-caves at its base. Its bird-lime gleams in the golden rays like the whitewash of a tall light-house, or the lofty sails of a cruiser. This moment, doubtless, while we know it to be a dead desert rock, other voyagers are taking oaths it is a glad populous ship.

But ropes now, and let us ascend. Yet soft, this is not so easy.

SKETCH FOURTH

A PISGAH VIEW FROM THE ROCK

'That done, he leads him to the highest Mount,
From whence, far off he unto him did shew . . .'

IF you seek to ascend Rock Rodondo, take the following prescription. Go three voyages round the world as a main-royal-man of the tallest frigate that floats; then serve a year or two apprenticeship to the guides who conduct strangers up the Peak of Teneriffe; and as many more respectively to a rope-dancer, an Indian juggler, and a chamois. This done, come and be rewarded by the view from our tower. How we get there, we alone know. If we sought to tell others, what the wiser were they? Suffice it, that here at the summit you and I stand. Does any balloonist, does the outlooking man in the moon, take a broader view of space? Much thus, one fancies, looks the universe from Milton's celestial battlements. A boundless watery Kentucky. Here Daniel Boone would have dwelt content.

Never heed for the present yonder Burnt District of the Enchanted Isles. Look edgeways, as it were, past them, to the south. You see nothing; but permit me to point out the direction, if not the place, of certain interesting objects in the vast sea, which, kissing this tower's base, we behold un-scrolling itself towards the Antarctic Pole.

We stand now ten miles from the Equator. Yonder, to the East, some six hundred miles, lies the continent; this Rock being just about on the parallel of Quito.

Observe another thing here. We are at one of three un-inhabited clusters, which, at pretty nearly uniform distances from the main, sentinel, at long intervals from each other, the entire coast of South America. In a peculiar manner, also, they terminate the South American character of coun-try. Of the unnumbered Polynesian chains to the westward,

not one partakes of the qualities of the Encantadas or Gallipagos, the isles of St Felix and St Ambrose, the isles Juan
Fernandez and Massafuero. Of the first, it needs not here to
speak. The second lie a little above the Southern Tropic;
lofty, inhospitable, and uninhabitable rocks, one of which,
presenting two round hummocks connected by a low reef,
exactly resembles a huge double-headed shot. The last lie
in the latitude of 33°; high, wild and cloven. Juan Fernandez is sufficiently famous without further description.
Massafuero is a Spanish name, expressive of the fact, that
the isle so called lies *more without*, that is further off the
main than its neighbor Juan. This isle Massafuero has a
very imposing aspect at a distance of eight or ten miles.
Approached in one direction, in cloudy weather, its great
overhanging height and rugged contour, and more especially a peculiar slope of its broad summits, give it much
the air of a vast iceberg drifting in tremendous poise. Its
sides are split with dark cavernous recesses, as an old
cathedral with its gloomy lateral chapels. Drawing nigh one
of these gorges from sea, after a long voyage, and beholding
some tatterdemalion outlaw, staff in hand, descending its
steep rocks toward you, conveys a very queer emotion to a
lover of the picturesque.

On fishing parties from ships, at various times, I have
chanced to visit each of these groups. The impression they
give to the stranger pulling close up in his boat under their
grim cliffs is, that surely he must be their first discoverer,
such, for the most part, is the unimpaired . . . . . silence and
solitude. And here, by the way, the mode in which these
isles were really first lighted upon by Europeans is not
unworthy of mention, especially as what is about to be
said, likewise applies to the original discovery of our Encantadas.

Prior to the year 1563, the voyages made by Spanish ships
from Peru to Chili, were full of difficulty. Along this coast,
the winds from the South most generally prevail; and it had
been an invariable custom to keep close in with the land,

from a superstitious conceit on the part of the Spaniards, that were they to lose sight of it, the eternal trade-wind would waft them into unending waters, from whence would be no return. Here, involved among tortuous capes and headlands, shoals and reefs, beating, too, against a continual head wind, often light, and sometimes for days and weeks sunk into utter calm, the provincial vessels, in many cases, suffered the extremest hardships, in passages, which at the present day seem to have been incredibly protracted. There is on record in some collections of nautical disasters, an account of one of these ships, which, starting on a voyage whose duration was estimated at ten days, spent four months at sea, and indeed never again entered harbor, for in the end she was cast away. Singular to tell, this craft never encountered a gale, but was the vexed sport of malicious calms and currents. Thrice, out of provisions, she put back to an intermediate port, and started afresh, but only yet again to return. Frequent fogs enveloped her; so that no observation could be had of her place, and once, when all hands were joyously anticipating sight of their destination, lo! the vapors lifted and disclosed the mountains from which they had taken their first departure. In the like deceptive vapors she at last struck upon a reef, whence ensued a long series of calamities too sad to detail.

It was the famous pilot, Juan Fernandez, immortalized by the island named after him, who put an end to these coasting tribulations, by boldly venturing the experiment – as De Gama did before him with respect to Europe – of standing broad out from land. Here he found the winds favorable for getting to the South, and by running westward till beyond the influences of the trades, he regained the coast without difficulty; making the passage which, though in a high degree circuitous, proved far more expeditious than the nominally direct one. Now it was upon these new tracks, and about the year 1670, or thereabouts, that the Enchanted Isles, and the rest of the sentinel groups, as they may be called, were discovered. Though I know of no account as to whether any of them were found inhabited or no, it may be reasonably concluded that they have been immemorial solitudes. But let us return to Rodondo.

Southwest from our tower lies all Polynesia, hundreds of leagues away; but straight west, on the precise line of his parallel, no land rises till your keel is beached upon the Kingsmills, a nice little sail of, say 5000 miles.

Having thus by such distant references – with Rodondo the only possible ones – settled our relative place on the sea, let us consider objects not quite so remote. Behold the grim and charred Enchanted Isles. This nearest crater-shaped headland is part of Albemarle, the largest of the group, being some sixty miles or more long, and fifteen broad. Did you ever lay eye on the real genuine Equator? Have you ever, in the largest sense, toed the Line? Well, that identical crater-shaped headland there, all yellow lava, is cut by the Equator exactly as a knife cuts straight through the centre of a pumpkin pie. If you could only see so far, just to one side of that same headland, across yon low dikey ground, you would catch sight of the isle of Narborough, the loftiest land of the cluster; no soil whatever; one seamed clinker from top to bottom; abounding in black caves like smithies; its metallic shore ringing under foot like plates of iron; its central volcanoes standing grouped like a gigantic chimney-stack.

Narborough and Albemarle are neighbors after a quite curious fashion. A familiar diagram will illustrate this strange neighborhood:

E

Cut a channel at the above letter joint, and the middle transverse limb is Narborough, and all the rest is Albemarle. Volcanic Narborough lies in the black jaws of Albemarle like a wolf's red tongue in his open mouth.

If now you desire the population of Albemarle, I will give you, in round numbers, the statistics, according to the most reliable estimates made upon the spot:

Men,	none
Ant-eaters,	unknown
Man-haters,	unknown
Lizards,	500,000
Snakes,	500,000
Spiders,	10,000,000
Salamanders,	unknown
Devils,	do.
Making a clean total of	11,000,000

exclusive of an incomputable host of fiends, ant-eaters, man-haters, and salamanders.

Albemarle opens his mouth towards the setting sun. His distended jaws form a great bay, which Narborough, his tongue, divides into halves, one whereof is called Weather Bay, the other Lee Bay; while the volcanic promontories, terminating his coasts, are styled South Head and North Head. I note this, because these bays are famous in the annals of the Sperm Whale Fishery. The whales come here at certain seasons to calve. When ships first cruised here-abouts, I am told, they used to blockade the entrance of Lee Bay, when their boats going round by Weather Bay, passed through Narborough channel, and so had the Levi-athans very neatly in a pen.

The day after we took fish at the base of this Round Tower, we had a fine wind, and shooting round the north headland, suddenly descried a fleet of full thirty sail, all beating to windward like a squadron in line. A brave sight as ever man saw. A most harmonious concord of rushing keels. Their thirty kelsons hummed like thirty harp-strings, and looked as straight whilst they left their parallel traces on the sea. But there proved too many hunters for the game. The fleet broke up, and went their separate ways out of sight, leaving my own ship and two trim gentlemen of Lon-don. These last, finding no luck either, likewise vanished; and Lee Bay, with all its appurtenances, and without a rival, devolved to us.

The way of cruising here is this. You keep hovering about

the entrance of the bay, in one beat and out the next. But at times – not always, as in other parts of the group – a race-horse of a current sweeps right across its mouth. So, with all sails set, you carefully ply your tacks. How often, standing at the foremast head at sunrise, with our patient prow pointed in between these isles, did I gaze upon that land, not of cakes, but of clinkers, not of streams of sparkling water, but arrested torrents of tormented lava.

As the ship runs in from the open sea, Narborough presents its side in one dark craggy mass, soaring up some five or six thousand feet, at which point it hoods itself in heavy clouds, whose lowest level fold is as clearly defined against the rocks as the snow-line against the Andes. There is dire mischief going on in that upper dark. There toil the demons of fire, who, at intervals, irradiate the nights with a strange spectral illumination for miles and miles around, but un-accompanied by any further demonstration; or else, sud-denly announce themselves by terrific concussions, and the full drama of a volcanic eruption. The blacker that cloud by day, the more may you look for light by night. Often whalemen have found themselves crusing nigh that burn-ing mountain when all aglow with a ball-room blaze. Or, rather, glass-works, you may call this same vitreous isle of Narborough, with its tall chimney-stacks.

Where we still stand, here on Rodondo, we cannot see all the other isles, but it is a good place from which to point out where they lie. Yonder, though, to the E.N.E., I mark a distant dusky ridge. It is Abington Isle, one of the most northerly of the group; so solitary, remote, and blank, it looks like No-Man's Land seen off our northern shore. I doubt whether two human beings ever touched upon that spot. So far as yon Abington Isle is concerned, Adam and his billions of posterity remain uncreated.

Ranging south of Abington, and quite out of sight behind the long spine of Albemarle, lies James's Isle, so called by the early Buccaneers after the luckless Stuart, Duke of York. Observe here, by the way, that, excepting the isles particu-larized in comparatively recent times, and which mostly received the names of famous Admirals, the Encantadas were first christened by the Spaniards; but these Spanish names were generally effaced on English charts by the subsequent christenings of the Buccaneers, who, in the middle of the seventeenth century, called them after English noblemen and kings. Of these loyal freebooters and the things which associate their name with the Encantadas, we shall hear anon. Nay, for one little item, immediately; for between James's Isle and Albemarle, lies a fantastic islet, strangely known as 'Cowley's Enchanted Isle.' But, as all the group is deemed enchanted, the reason must be given for the spell within a spell involved by this particular designation. The name was bestowed by that excellent Buccaneer himself, on his first visit here. Speaking in his published voyages of this spot, he says – 'My fancy led me to call it Cowley's Enchanted Island, for we having had a sight of it upon several points of the compass, it appeared always in as many different forms; sometimes like a ruined fortification; upon another point like a great city, etc.' No wonder though, that among the Encantadas all sorts of ocular deceptions and mirages should be met.

That Cowley linked his name with this self-transforming and bemocking isle, suggests the possibility that it conveyed to him some meditative image of himself. At least, as is not impossible, if he were any relative of the mildly-thoughtful and self-upbraiding poet Cowley, who lived about his time, the conceit might seem not unwarranted; for that sort of thing evinced in the naming of this isle runs in the blood, and may be seen in pirates as in poets.

Still south of James's Isle lie Jervis Isle, Duncan Isle, Crossman's Isle, Brattle Isle, Wood's Isle, Chatham Isle, and various lesser isles, for the most part an archipelago of aridities, without inhabitant, history, or hope of either in all time to come. But not far from these are rather notable isles – Barrington, Charles's, Norfolk, and Hood's. Succeeding chapters will reveal some ground for their notability.

SKETCH FIFTH

THE FRIGATE, AND SHIP FLYAWAY

> '*Looking far foorth into the Ocean wide,*
> *A goodly ship with banners bravely dight,*
> *And flag in her top-gallant I espide,*
> *Through the maine sea making her merry flight.*'

ERE quitting Rodondo, it must not be omitted that here, in 1813, the U.S. frigate *Essex*, Captain David Porter, came near leaving her bones. Lying becalmed one morning with a strong current setting her rapidly towards the rock, a strange sail was descried, which – not out of keeping with alleged enchantments of the neighborhood – seemed to be staggering under a violent wind, while the frigate lay lifeless as if spell-bound. But a light air springing up, all sail was made by the frigate in chase of the enemy, as supposed – he being deemed an English whale-ship – but the rapidity of the current was so great, that soon all sight was lost of him; and, at meridian, the *Essex*, spite of her drags, was driven so close under the foam-lashed cliffs of Rodondo that, for a time, all hands gave her up. A smart breeze, however, at last helped her off, though the escape was so critical as to seem almost miraculous.

Thus saved from destruction herself, she now made use of that salvation to destroy the other vessel, if possible. Renewing the chase in the direction in which the stranger had disappeared, sight was caught of him the following morning. Upon being descried he hoisted American colors and stood away from the *Essex*. A calm ensued; when, still confident that the stranger was an Englishman, Porter dispatched a cutter, not to board the enemy, but drive back his boats engaged in towing him. The cutter succeeded. Cutters were subsequently sent to capture him; the stranger now showing English colors in place of American. But, when the frigate's boats were within a short distance of their hoped-for prize, another sudden breeze sprang up; the stranger, under all sail, bore off to the westward, and, ere night, was hull down ahead of the *Essex*, which, all this time, lay perfectly becalmed.

This enigmatic craft – American in the morning, and English in the evening – her sails full of wind in a calm – was never again beheld. An enchanted ship no doubt. So, at least, the sailors swore.

This cruise of the *Essex* in the Pacific during the war of 1812, is, perhaps, the strangest and most stirring to be found in the history of the American navy. She captured the furthest wandering vessels; visited the remotest seas and isles; long hovered in the charmed vicinity of the enchanted group; and, finally, valiantly gave up the ghost fighting two English frigates in the harbor of Valparaiso. Mention is made of her here for the same reason that the Buccaneers will likewise receive record; because, like them, by long cruising among the isles, tortoise-hunting upon their shores, and generally exploring them; for these and other reasons, the *Essex* is peculiarly associated with the Encantadas.

Here be it said that you have but three eye-witness authorities worth mentioning touching the Enchanted Isles: — Cowley, the Buccaneer (1684); Colnet, the whaling-ground explorer (1798); Porter, the post captain (1813). Other than these you have but barren, bootless allusions from some few passing voyagers or compilers.

SKETCH SIXTH

BARRINGTON ISLE AND THE BUCCANEERS

'Let us all servile base subiection scorne;
And as we bee sonnes of the earth so wide,
Let us our fathers heritage divide,
And chalenge to our selves our portions dew
Of all the patrimonie, which a few
Now hold in hugger mugger in their hand.'

*

'Lords of the world, and so will wander free
Where so us listeth, uncontrol'd of anie.'

*

'How bravely now we live, how jocund, how near the first
inheritance, without fear, how free from little troubles!'

NEAR two centuries ago Barrington Isle was the resort of that famous wing of the West Indian Buccaneers, which, upon their repulse from the Cuban waters, crossing the Isthmus of Darien, ravaged the Pacific side of the Spanish colonies, and, with the regularity and timing of a modern mail, waylaid the royal treasure-ships plying between Manilla and Acapulco. After the toils of piratic war, here they came to say their prayers, enjoy their free-and-easies, count their crackers from the cask, their doubloons from the keg, and measure their silks of Asia with long Toledos for their yard-sticks.

As a secure retreat, an undiscoverable hiding-place, no spot in those days could have been better fitted. In the centre of a vast and silent sea, but very little traversed – surrounded by islands, whose inhospitable aspect might well drive away the chance navigator – and yet within a few days' sail of the opulent countries which they made their prey – the unmolested Buccaneers found here that tranquillity which they fiercely denied to every civilized harbor in that part of the world. Here, after stress of weather, or a temporary drubbing at the hands of their vindictive foes, or in swift flight with golden booty, those old marauders came, and lay snugly out of all harm's reach. But not only was the place a harbor of safety, and a bower of ease, but for utility in other things it was most admirable.

Barrington Isle is, in many respects, singularly adapted to careening, refitting, refreshing, and other seamen's purposes. Not only has it good water, and good anchorage, well sheltered from all winds by the high land of Albemarle, but it is the least unproductive isle of the group. Tortoises good for food, trees good for fuel, and long grass good for bedding, abound here, and there are pretty natural walks, and several landscapes to be seen. Indeed, though in its locality belonging to the Enchanted group, Barrington Isle is so unlike most of its neighbors, that it would hardly seem of kin to them.

'I once landed on its western side,' says a sentimental voyager long ago, 'where it faces the black buttress of Albemarle. I walked beneath groves of trees – not very lofty, and not palm trees, or orange trees, or peach trees, to be sure – but, for all that, after long sea-faring, very beautiful to walk under, even though they supplied no fruit. And here, in calm spaces at the heads of glades, and on the shaded tops of slopes commanding the most quiet scenery – what do you think I saw? Seats which might have served Brahmins and presidents of peace societies. Fine old ruins of what had once been symmetric lounges of stone and turf, they bore every mark both of artificialness and age, and were, undoubtedly, made by the Buccaneers. One had been a long sofa, with back and arms, just such a sofa as the poet Gray might have loved to throw himself upon, his Crébillon in hand.

'Though they sometimes tarried here for months at a time, and used the spot for a storing-place for spare spars, sails, and casks; yet it is highly improbable that the Buccaneers ever erected dwelling-houses upon the isle. They never were here except their ships remained, and they would most likely have slept on board. I mention this, because I cannot avoid the thought, that it is hard to impute the construction of these romantic seats to any other motive than one of pure peacefulness and kindly fellowship with nature. That the Buccaneers perpetrated the greatest outrages is very true – that some of them were mere cut-throats is not to be denied; but we know that here and there among their host was a Dampier, a Wafer, and a Cowley, and likewise other men, whose worst reproach was their desperate fortunes – whom persecution, or adversity, or secret and unavengeable wrongs, had driven from Christian society to seek the melancholy solitude or the guilty adventures of the sea. At any rate, long as those ruins of seats on Barrington remain, the most singular monuments are furnished to the fact, that all of the Buccaneers were not unmitigated monsters.

'But during my ramble on the isle I was not long in discovering other tokens, of things quite in accordance with those wild traits, popularly, and no doubt truly enough, imputed to the freebooters at large. Had I picked up old sails and rusty hoops I would only have thought of the ship's carpenter and cooper. But I found old cutlasses and daggers reduced to mere threads of rust, which, doubtless, had stuck between Spanish ribs ere now. These were signs of the murderer and robber; the reveler likewise had left his trace. Mixed with shells, fragments of broken jars were lying here and there, high up upon the beach. They were precisely like the jars now used upon the Spanish coast for the wine and Pisco spirits of that country.

'With a rusty dagger-fragment in one hand, and a bit of a wine-jar in another, I sat me down on the ruinous green sofa I have spoken of, and bethought me long and deeply of these same Buccaneers. Could it be possible, that they robbed and murdered one day, reveled the next, and rested themselves by turning meditative philosophers, rural poets, and seat-builders on the third? Not very improbable, after all. For consider the vacillations of a man. Still, strange as it may seem, I must also abide by the more charitable thought; namely, that among these adventurers were some gentlemanly, companionable souls, capable of genuine tranquillity and virtue.'

SKETCH SEVENTH

CHARLES'S ISLE AND THE DOG-KING

'Loe with outragious cry
A thousand villeins round about him swarmd
Out of the rockes and caves adjoining nye,
Vile caytive wretches, ragged, rude, deformd,
All threatning death, all in straunge manner armd,
Some with unweldy clubs, some with long speares,
Some rusty knives, some staves in fire warmd.'

*

'We will not be of anie occupation,
Let such vile vassalls, borne to base vocation
Drudge in the world, and for their living droyle
Which have no wit to live withouten toyle.'

SOUTHWEST of Barrington lies Charles's Isle. And hereby hangs a history which I gathered long ago from a shipmate learned in all the lore of outlandish life.

During the successful revolt of the Spanish provinces from Old Spain, there fought on behalf of Peru a certain Creole adventurer from Cuba, who, by his bravery and good fortune, at length advanced himself to high rank in the patriot army. The war being ended, Peru found itself like many valorous gentlemen, free and independent enough, but with few shot in the locker. In other words, Peru had not wherewithal to pay off its troops. But the Creole – I forget his name – volunteered to take his pay in lands. So they told him he might have his pick of the Enchanted Isles, which were then, as they still remain, the nominal appanage of Peru. The soldier straightaway embarks thither, explores the group, returns to Callao, and says he will take a deed of Charles's Isle. Moreover, this deed must stipulate that henceforth Charles's Isle is not only the sole property of the Creole, but is for ever free of Peru, even as

Peru of Spain. To be short, this adventurer procures himself to be made in effect Supreme Lord of the Island, one of the princes of the powers of the earth.*

He now sends forth a proclamation inviting subjects to his as yet unpopulated kingdom. Some eighty souls, men and women, respond; and being provided by their leader with necessaries, and tools of various sorts, together with a few cattle and goats, take ship for the promised land; the last arrival on board, prior to sailing, being the Creole himself, accompanied, strange to say, by a disciplined cavalry company of large grim dogs. These, it was observed on the passage, refusing to consort with the emigrants, remained aristocratically grouped around their master on the elevated quarter-deck, casting disdainful glances forward upon the inferior rabble there; much as, from the ramparts, the soldiers of a garrison, thrown into a conquered town, eye the inglorious citizen-mob over which they are set to watch.

Now Charles's Isle not only resembles Barrington Isle in being much more inhabitable than other parts of the group, but it is double the size of Barrington, say forty or fifty miles in circuit.

Safely debarked at last, the company, under direction of their lord and patron, forthwith proceeded to build their capital city. They make considerable advance in the way of walls of clinkers, and lava floors, nicely sanded with cinders. On the least barren hills they pasture their cattle, while the goats, adventurers by nature, explore the far inland solitudes for a scanty livelihood of lofty herbage. Meantime, abundance of fish and tortoises supply their other wants.

The disorders incident to settling all primitive regions,

---

*The American Spaniards have long been in the habit of making presents of islands to deserving individuals. The pilot Juan Fernandez procured a deed of the isle named after him, and for some years resided there before Selkirk came. It is supposed, however, that he eventually contracted the blues upon his princely property, for after a time he returned to the main, and as report goes, became a very garrulous barber in the city of Lima.

in the present case were heightened by the peculiarly un-
toward character of many of the pilgrims. His Majesty was
forced at last to proclaim martial law, and actually hunted
and shot with his own hand several of his rebellious subjects, who, with most questionable intentions, had clan-
destinely encamped in the interior, whence they stole by
night, to prowl barefooted on tiptoe round the precincts
of the lava-palace. It is to be remarked, however, that prior
to such stern proceedings, the more reliable men had been
judiciously picked out for an infantry body-guard, subordinate to the cavalry body-guard of dogs. But the stage
of politics in this unhappy nation may be somewhat imagined, from the circumstances that all who were not of the
body-guard were downright plotters and malignant traitors.
At length the death penalty was tacitly abolished, owing to
the timely thought, that were strict sportsman's justice to be
dispensed among such subjects, ere long the Nimrod King
would have little or no remaining game to shoot. The
human part of the life-guard was now disbanded, and set
to work cultivating the soil, and raising potatoes; the regular army now solely consisting of the dog-regiment. These,
as I have heard, were of a singularly ferocious character,
though by severe training rendered docile to their master.
Armed to the teeth, the Creole now goes in state, surrounded
by his canine janizaries, whose terrific bayings prove quite
as serviceable as bayonets in keeping down the surgings of
revolt.

But the census of the isle, sadly lessened by the dispensation of justice, and not materially recruited by matrimony,
began to fill his mind with sad mistrust. Some way the
population must be increased. Now, from its possessing a
little water, and its comparative pleasantness of aspect,
Charles's Isle at this period was occasionally visited by
foreign whalers. These His Majesty had always levied upon
for port charges, thereby contributing to his revenue. But
now he had additional designs. By insidious arts he, from
time to time, cajoles certain sailors to desert their ships, and
enlist beneath his banner. Soon as missed, their captains

crave permission to go and hunt them up. Whereupon His Majesty first hides them very carefully away, and then freely permits the search. In consequence, the delinquents are never found, and the ships retire without them.

Thus, by a two-edged policy of this crafty monarch, foreign nations were crippled in the number of their subjects, and his own were greatly multiplied. He particularly petted these renegado strangers. But alas for the deep-laid schemes of ambitious princes, and alas for the vanity of glory. As the foreign-born Pretorians, unwisely introduced into the Roman state, and still more unwisely made favorites of the Emperors, at last insulted and overturned the throne, even so these lawless mariners, with all the rest of the body-guard and all the populace, broke out into a terrible mutiny, and defied their master. He marched against them with all his dogs. A deadly battle ensued upon the beach. It raged for three hours, the dogs fighting with determined valor, and the sailors reckless of everything but victory. Three men and thirteen dogs were left dead upon the field, many on both sides were wounded, and the king was forced to fly with the remainder of his canine regiment. The enemy pursued, stoning the dogs with their master into the wilderness of the interior. Discontinuing the pursuit, the victors returned to the village on the shore, stove the spirit casks, and proclaimed a Republic. The dead men were interred with the honors of war, and the dead dogs ignominiously thrown into the sea. At last, forced by stress of suffering, the fugitive Creole came down from the hills and offered to treat for peace. But the rebels refused it on any other terms than his unconditional banishment. Accordingly, the next ship that arrived carried away the ex-king to Peru.

The history of the king of Charles's Island furnishes another illustration of the difficulty of colonizing barren islands with unprincipled pilgrims.

Doubtless for a long time the exiled monarch, pensively ruralizing in Peru, which afforded him a safe asylum in his calamity, watched every arrival from the Encantadas, to hear news of the failure of the Republic, the consequent

penitence of the rebels, and his own recall to royalty. Doubtless he deemed the Republic but a miserable experiment
which would soon explode. But no, the insurgents had con-
federated themselves into a democracy neither Grecian,
Roman, nor American. Nay, it was no democracy at all, but
a permanent *Riotocracy*, which gloried in having no law
but lawlessness. Great inducements being offered to deserters, their ranks were swelled by accessions of scamps
from every ship which touched their shores. Charles's
Island was proclaimed the asylum of the oppressed of all
navies. Each runaway tar was hailed as a martyr in the cause
of freedom, and became immediately installed a ragged
citizen of this universal nation. In vain the captains of
absconding seamen strove to regain them. Their new com-
patriots were ready to give any number of ornamental eyes
in their behalf. They had few cannon, but their fists were
not to be trifled with. So at last it came to pass that no
vessels acquainted with the character of that country durst
touch there, however sorely in want of refreshment. It became Anathema – a sea Alsatia – the unassailed lurking-
place of all sorts of desperadoes, who in the name of liberty
did just what they pleased. They continually fluctuated in
their numbers. Sailors, deserting ships at other islands, or
in boats at sea anywhere in that vicinity, steered for
Charles's Isle, as to their sure home of refuge; while, sated
with the life of the isle, numbers from time to time crossed
the water to the neighboring ones, and there presenting
themselves to strange captains as shipwrecked seamen, often
succeeded in getting on board vessels bound to the Spanish
coast, and having a compassionate purse made up for them
on landing there.

One warm night during my first visit to the group, our
ship was floating along in languid stillness, when some one
on the forecastle shouted 'Light ho!' We looked and saw
a beacon burning on some obscure land off the beam. Our
third mate was not intimate with this part of the world.
Going to the captain he said, 'Sir, shall I put off in a boat?
These must be shipwrecked men.'

The captain laughed rather grimly, as, shaking his fist towards the beacon, he rapped out an oath, and said – 'No, no, you precious rascals, you don't juggle one of my boats ashore this blessed night. You do well, you thieves – you do benevolently to hoist a light yonder as on a dangerous shoal. It tempts no wise man to pull off and see what's the matter, but bids him steer small and keep off shore – that is Charles's Island; brace up, Mr Mate, and keep the light astern.'

SKETCH EIGHTH

NORFOLK ISLE AND THE CHOLA WIDOW

'At last they in an Island did espy
A seemely woman, sitting by the shore,
That with great sorrow and sad agony
Seemed some great misfortune to deplore,
And loud to them for succour called evermore.'

'Blacke hys eye as the midnyghte sky,
Whyte hys neck as the driven snowe,
Redde hys cheek as the mornynge lyghte,
Cold he lys ynne the ground belowe;
  Mie love ys dedde,
  Gon to hys deathe-bedde,
  All under the cactus tree.'

'Each lonely scene shall thee restore,
For thee the tear be duly shed;
Belov'd till life can charm no more,
And mourn'd till Pity's self be dead.'

FAR to the northeast of Charles's Isle, sequestered from the rest, lies Norfolk Isle; and, however insignificant to most voyagers, to me, through sympathy, that lone island has become a spot made sacred by the strangest trials of humanity.

It was my first visit to the Encantadas. Two days had been spent ashore in hunting tortoises. There was not time to capture many; so on the third afternoon we loosed our sails. We were just in the act of getting under way, the uprooted anchor yet suspended and invisibly swaying beneath the wave, as the good ship gradually turned her heel to leave the isle behind, when the seaman who heaved with me at the windlass paused suddenly, and directed my attention to something moving on the land, not along the beach, but somewhat back, fluttering from a height.

In view of the sequel of this little story, be it here narrated how it came to pass, that an object which partly from its being so small was quite lost to every other man on board, still caught the eye of my handspike companion. The rest of the crew, myself included, merely stood up to our spikes in heaving, whereas, unwontedly exhilarated, at every turn of the ponderous windlass, my belted comrade leaped atop of it, with might and main giving a downward, thewey, perpendicular heave, his raised eye bent in cheery animation upon the slowly receding shore. Being high lifted above all others was the reason he perceived the object, otherwise unperceivable; and this elevation of his eye was owing to the elevation of his spirits; and this again – for truth must out – to a dram of Peruvian pisco, in guerdon for some kindness done, secretly administered to him that morning by our mulatto steward. Now, certainly, pisco does a deal of michief in the world; yet seeing that, in the present case, it was the means, though indirect, of rescuing a human being from the most dreadful fate, must we not also needs admit that sometimes pisco does a deal of good?

Glancing across the water in the direction pointed out, I saw some white thing hanging from an inland rock, perhaps half a mile from the sea.

'It is a bird; a white-winged bird; perhaps a – no; it is – it is a handkerchief!'

'Ay, a handkerchief!' echoed my comrade, and with a louder shout apprised the captain.

Quickly now – like the running out and training of a great gun – the long cabin spy-glass was thrust through the mizzen rigging from the high platform of the poop; whereupon a human figure was plainly seen upon the inland rock, eagerly waving towards us what seemed to be the handkerchief.

Our captain was a prompt, good fellow. Dropping the glass, he lustily ran forward, ordering the anchor to be dropped again; hands to stand by a boat, and lower away.

In a half-hour's time the swift boat returned. It went

with six and came with seven; and the seventh was a woman.

It is not artistic heartlessness, but I wish I could but draw in crayons; for this woman was a most touching sight; and crayons, tracing softly melancholy lines, would best depict the mournful image of the dark-damasked Chola widow.

Her story was soon told, and though given in her own strange language was as quickly understood; for our captain, from long trading on the Chilean coast, was well versed in the Spanish. A Cholo, or half-breed Indian woman of Payta in Peru, three years gone by, with her young new-wedded husband Felipe, of pure Castilian blood, and her one only Indian brother, Truxill, Hunilla had taken passage on the main in a French whaler, commanded by a joyous man; which vessel, bound to the cruising grounds beyond the Enchanted Isles, proposed passing close by their vicinity. The object of the little party was to procure tortoise oil, a fluid which for its great purity and delicacy is held in high estimation wherever known; and it is well known all along this part of the Pacific coast. With a chest of clothes, tools, cooking utensils, a rude apparatus for trying out the oil, some casks of biscuit, and other things, not omitting two favorite dogs, of which faithful animal all the Cholos are very fond, Hunilla and her companions were safely landed at their chosen place; the Frenchman, according to the contract made ere sailing, engaged to take them off upon returning from a four months' cruise in the westward seas; which interval the three adventurers deemed quite sufficient for their purposes.

On the isle's lone beach they paid him in silver for their passage out, the stranger having declined to carry them at all except upon that condition; though willing to take every means to insure the due fulfillment of his promise. Felipe had striven hard to have this payment put off to the period of the ship's return. But in vain. Still they thought they had, in another way, ample pledge of the good faith of the Frenchman. It was arranged that the expenses of the passage home should not be payable in silver, but in tortoises;

one hundred tortoises ready captured to the returning captain's hand. These the Cholos meant to secure after their own work was done, against the probable time of the Frenchman's coming back; and no doubt in prospect already felt, that in those hundred tortoises – now somewhere ranging the isle's interior – they possessed one hundred hostages. Enough: the vessel sailed; the gazing three on shore answered the loud glee of the singing crew; and ere evening, the French craft was hull down in the distant sea, its masts three faintest lines which quickly faded from Hunilla's eye.

The stranger had given a blithesome promise, and anchored it with oaths; but oaths and anchors equally will drag; naught else abides on fickle earth but unkept promises of joy. Contrary winds from out unstable skies, or contrary moods of his more varying mind, or shipwreck and sudden death in solitary waves; whatever was the cause, the blithe stranger never was seen again.

Yet, however dire a calamity was here in store, misgivings of it ere due time never disturbed the Cholos' busy mind, now all intent upon the toilsome matter which had brought them hither. Nay, by swift doom coming like the thief at night, ere seven weeks went by, two of the little party were removed from all anxieties of land or sea. No more they sought to gaze with feverish fear, or still more feverish hope, beyond the present's horizon line; but into the furthest future their own silent spirits sailed. By persevering labor beneath that burning sun, Felipe and Truxill had brought down to their hut many scores of tortoises and tried out the oil, when, elated with their good success, and to reward themselves for such hard work, they, too hastily, made a catamaran, or Indian raft, much used on the Spanish main, and merrily started on a fishing trip, just without a long reef with many jagged gaps, running parallel with the shore, about half a mile from it. By some bad tide or hap, or natural negligence of joyfulness (for though they could not be heard, yet by their gestures they seemed singing at the time) forced in deep water against that iron bar, the ill-made catamaran was overset, and came all to pieces; when dashed by broad chested swells between their broken logs and the sharp teeth of the reef, both adventurers perished before Hunilla's eyes.

Before Hunilla's eyes they sank. The real woe of this event passed before her sight as some sham tragedy on the stage. She was seated on a rude bower among the withered thickets, crowning a lofty cliff, a little back from the beach. The thickets were so disposed, that in looking upon the sea at large she peered out from among the branches as from the lattice of a high balcony. But upon the day we speak of here, the better to watch the adventure of those two hearts she loved, Hunilla had withdrawn the branches to one side, and held them so. They formed an oval frame, through which the bluely boundless sea rolled like a painted one. And there, the invisible painter painted to her view the wave-tossed and disjointed raft, its once level logs slantingly upheaved, as raking masts, and the four struggling arms undistinguishable among them; and then all subsided into smooth-flowing creamy waters, slowly drifting the splintered wreck; while first and last, no sound of any sort was heard. Death in a silent picture; a dream of the eye; such vanishing shapes as the mirage shows.

So instant was the scene, so trance-like its mild pictorial effect, so distant from her blasted bower and her common sense of things, that Hunilla gazed and gazed, nor raised a finger or a wail. But as good to sit thus dumb, in stupor staring at that dumb show, for all that otherwise might be done. With half a mile of sea between, how could her two enchanted arms aid those four fated ones? The distance long, the time one sand. After the lightning is beheld, what fool shall stay the thunder-bolt? Felipe's body was washed ashore, but Truxill's never came; only his gay, braided hat of golden straw – that same sunflower thing he waved to her, pushing from the strand – and now, to the last gallant, it still saluted her. But Felipe's body floated to the marge, with one arm encirclingly outstretched. Lock-jawed in grim death, the lover-husband softly clasped his bride, true to her even in death's dream. Ah, heaven, when man thus keeps his faith, wilt thou be faithless who created the faithful one? But they cannot break faith who never plighted it.

It needs not to be said what nameless misery now wrapped the lonely widow. In telling her own story she passed this almost entirely over, simply recounting the event. Construe the comment of her features as you might, from her mere words little would you have weened that Hunilla was herself the heroine of her tale. But not thus did she defraud us of our tears. All hearts bled that grief could be so brave.

She but showed us her soul's lid, and the strange ciphers thereon engraved; all within, with pride's timidity, was withheld. Yet was there one exception. Holding out her small olive hand before her captain, she said in mild and slowest Spanish, 'Señor, I buried him;' then paused, struggled as against the writhed coilings of a snake, and cringing suddenly, leaped up, repeating in impassioned pain, 'I buried him, my life, my soul!'

Doubtless, it was by half-unconscious, automatic motions of her hands, that this heavy-hearted one performed the final office for Felipe, and planted a rude cross of withered sticks – no green ones might be had – at the head of that lonely grave, where rested now in lasting uncomplaint and quiet haven he whom untranquil seas had overthrown.

But some dull sense of another body that should be interred, of another cross that should hallow another grave – unmade as yet – some dull anxiety and pain touching her undiscovered brother, now haunted the oppressed Hunilla. Her hands fresh from the burial earth, she slowly went back to the beach, with unshaped purposes wandering there, her spell-bound eye bent upon the incessant waves. But they bore nothing to her but a dirge, which maddened her to think that murderers should mourn. As time went by, and these things came less dreamingly to her mind, the strong persuasions of her Romish faith, which sets peculiar store by consecrated urns, prompted her to resume in waking earnest that pious search which had but been begun as in somnambulism. Day after day, week after week, she trod the cindery beach, till at length a double motive edged every eager glance. With equal longing she now looked for the living and the dead; the brother and the captain; alike vanished, never to return. Little accurate note of time had Hunilla taken under such emotions as were hers, and little, outside herself, served for calendar or dial. As to poor Crusoe in the self-same sea, no saint's bell pealed forth the lapse of week or month; each day went by unchallenged; no chanticleer announced those sultry dawns, no lowing herds those poisonous nights. All wonted and steadily recurring sounds, human, or humanized by sweet fellowship with man, but one stirred that torrid trance – the cry of dogs; save which naught but the rolling sea invaded it, an all-pervading monotone; and to the widow that was the least loved voice she could have heard.

No wonder, that as her thoughts now wandered to the unreturning ship, and were beaten back again, the hope against hope so struggled in her soul, that at length she desperately said, 'Not yet, not yet; my foolish heart runs on too fast.' So she forced patience for some further weeks. But to those whom earth's sure indraft draws, patience or impatience is still the same.

Hunilla now sought to settle precisely in her mind, to an hour, how long it was since the ship had sailed; and then, with the same precision, how long a space remained to pass. But this proved impossible. What present day or month it was she could not say. Time was her labyrinth, in which Hunilla was entirely lost.

And now follows –

Against my own purposes a pause descends upon me here. One knows not whether nature doth not impose some secrecy upon him who has been privy to certain things. At least, it is to be doubted whether it be good to blazon such. If some books are deemed most baneful and their sale forbid, how, then, with deadlier facts, not dreams of doting men? Those whom books will hurt will not be proof against events. Events, not books, should be forbid. But in all things

[172]

man sows upon the wind, which bloweth just there whither it listeth; for ill or good, man cannot know. Often ill comes from the good, as good from ill.

When Hunilla –

Dire sight it is to see some silken beast long dally with a golden lizard ere she devour. More terrible, to see how feline Fate will sometimes dally with a human soul, and by a nameless magic make it repulse a sane despair with a hope which is but mad. Unwittingly I imp this cat-like thing, sporting with the heart of him who reads; for if he feel not he reads in vain.

– 'The ship sails this day, today,' at last said Hunilla to herself; 'this gives me certain time to stand on; without certainty I go mad. In loose ignorance I have hoped and hoped; now in firm knowledge I will but wait. Now I live and no longer perish in bewilderings. Holy Virgin, aid me! Thou wilt waft back the ship. Oh, past length of weary weeks – all to be dragged over – to buy the certainty of to-day, I freely give ye, though I tear ye from me!'

As mariners, tost in tempest on some desolate ledge, patch them a boat out of the remnants of their vessel's wreck, and launch it in the self-same waves, see here Hunilla, this lone shipwrecked soul, out of treachery invoking trust. Humanity, thou strong thing, I worship thee, not in the laureled victor, but in this vanquished one.

Truly Hunilla leaned upon a reed, a real one; no metaphor; a real Eastern reed. A piece of hollow cane, drifted from unknown isles, and found upon the beach, its once jagged ends rubbed smoothly even as by sand-paper; its golden glazing gone. Long ground between the sea and land, upper and nether stone, the unvarnished substance was filed bare, and wore another polish now, one with itself, the polish of its agony. Circular lines at intervals cut all round this surface, divided it into six panels of unequal length. In the first were scored the days, each tenth one marked by a longer and deeper notch; the second was scored for the number of sea-fowl eggs for sustenance, picked out from the rocky nests; the third, how many fish had been caught from the shore; the fourth, how many small tortoises found inland; the fifth, how many days of sun; the sixth, of clouds; which last, of the two, was the greater one. Long night of busy numbering, misery's mathematics, to weary her too-wakeful soul to sleep; yet sleep for that was none.

The panel of the days was deeply worn – the long tenth notches half effaced, as alphabets of the blind. Ten thousand times the longing widow had traced her finger over the bamboo – dull flute, which played on, gave no sound – as if counting birds flown by in air would hasten tortoises creeping through the woods.

After the one hundred and eightieth day no further mark was seen; that last one was the faintest, as the first the deepest.

'There were more days,' said our Captain; 'many, many more; why did you not go on and notch them, too, Hunilla?'

'Señor, ask me not.'

'And meantime, did no other vessel pass the isle?'

'Nay, Señor; – but –'

'You do not speak; but *what*, Hunilla?'

'Ask me not, Señor.'

'You saw ships pass, far away; you waved to them; they passed on; – was that it, Hunilla?'

'Señor, be it as you say.'

Braced against her woe, Hunilla would not, durst not trust the weakness of her tongue. Then when our Captain asked whether any whale-boats had –

But no, I will not file this thing complete for scoffing souls to quote, and call it firm proof upon their side. The half shall here remain untold. Those two unnamed events which befell Hunilla on this isle, let them abide between her and her God. In nature, as in law, it may be libelous to speak some truths.

Still, how it was that, although our vessel had lain three days anchored nigh the isle, its one human tenant should not have discovered us till just upon the point of sailing, never to revisit so lone and far a spot, this needs explaining ere the sequel come.

The place where the French captain had landed the little party was on the further and opposite end of the isle. There, too, it was that they had afterwards built their hut. Nor did the widow in her solitude desert the spot where her loved ones had dwelt with her, and where the dearest of the twain now slept his last long sleep, and all her plaints awaked him not, and he of husbands the most faithful during life.

Now, high broken land rises between the opposite extremities of the isle. A ship anchored at one side is invisible from the other. Neither is the isle so small, but a considerable company might wander for days through the wilderness of one side, and never be seen, or their halloos heard, by any stranger holding aloof on the other. Hence Hunilla, who naturally associated the possible coming of ships with her own part of the isle, might to the end have remained quite ignorant of the presence of our vessel, were it not for a mysterious presentiment, borne to her, so our mariners averred, by this isle's enchanted air. Nor did the widow's answer undo the thought.

'How did you come to cross the isle this morning, then, Hunilla?' said our Captain.

'Señor, something came flitting by me. It touched my cheek, my heart, Señor.'

'What do you say, Hunilla?'

'I have said, Señor, something came through the air.'

It was a narrow chance. For when in crossing the isle Hunilla gained the high land in the centre, she must then for the first have perceived our masts, and also marked that their sails were being loosed, perhaps even heard the echoing chorus of the windlass song. The strange ship was about to sail, and she behind. With all haste she now descends the height on the hither side, but soon loses sight of the ship among the sunken jungles at the mountain's base. She struggles on through the withered branches, which seek at every step to bar her path, till she comes to the isolated rock, still some way from the water. This she climbs, to reassure herself. The ship is still in plainest sight. But now, worn out with over-tension, Hunilla all but faints; she fears to step down from her giddy perch; she is fain to pause, there where she is, and as a last resort catches the turban from her head, unfurls and waves it over the jungles towards us.

During the telling of her story the mariners formed a voiceless circle round Hunilla and the Captain; and when at length the word was given to man the fastest boat, and pull round to the isle's thither side, to bring away Hunilla's chest and the tortoise-oil, such alacrity of both cheery and sad obedience seldom before was seen. Little ado was made. Already the anchor had been recommitted to the bottom, and the ship swung calmly to it.

But Hunilla insisted upon accompanying the boat as indispensable pilot to her hidden hut. So being refreshed with the best the steward could supply, she started with us. Nor did ever any wife of the most famous admiral, in her husband's barge, receive more silent reverence of respect than poor Hunilla from this boat's crew.

Rounding many a vitreous cape and bluff, in two hours' time we shot inside the fatal reef; wound into a secret cove, looked up along a green many-gabled lava wall, and saw the island's solitary dwelling.

It hung upon an impending cliff, sheltered on two sides by tangled thickets, and half-screened from view in front by juttings of the rude stairway, which climbed the precipice from the sea. Built of canes, it was thatched with long, mildewed grass. It seemed an abandoned hay-rick, whose haymakers were now no more. The roof inclined but one way; the eaves coming to within two feet of the ground. And here was a simple apparatus to collect the dews, or rather doubly-distilled and finest winnowed rains, which, in mercy or in mockery, the night-skies sometimes drop upon these blighted Encantadas. All along beneath the eaves, a spotted sheet, quite weather-stained, was spread, pinned to short, upright stakes, set in the shallow sand. A small clinker, thrown into the cloth, weighed its middle down, thereby straining all moisture into a calabash placed below. This vessel supplied each drop of water ever drunk upon the isle by the Cholos. Hunilla told us the calabash would sometimes, but not often, be half filled overnight. It held six quarts, perhaps. 'But,' she said, 'we were used to thirst. At sandy Payta, where I live, no shower from heaven ever fell; all the water there is brought on mules from the inland vales.'

Tied among the thickets were some twenty moaning tortoises, supplying Hunilla's lonely larder; while hundreds of vast tableted black bucklers, like displaced, shattered tombstones of dark slate, were also scattered round. These were the skeleton backs of those great tortoises from which Felipe and Truxill had made their precious oil. Several large calabashes and two goodly kegs were filled with it. In a pot near by were the caked crusts of a quantity which had been permitted to evaporate. 'They meant to have strained it off the next day,' said Hunilla, as she turned aside.

I forgot to mention the most singular sight of all, though the first that greeted us after landing.

Some ten small, soft-haired, ringleted dogs, of a beautiful breed, peculiar to Peru, set up a concert of glad welcomings when we gained the beach, which was responded to by Hunilla. Some of these dogs had, since her widowhood, been born upon the isle, the progeny of the two brought from Payta. Owing to the jagged steeps and pitfalls, tortuous thickets, sunken clefts and perilous intricacies of all sorts in the interior, Hunilla, admonished by the loss of one favorite among them, never allowed these delicate creatures to follow her in her occasional birds'-nests climbs and other wanderings; so that, through long habituation, they offered not to follow, when that morning she crossed the land, and her own soul was then too full of other things to heed their lingering behind. Yet, all along she had so clung to them, that, besides what moisture they lapped up at early daybreak from the small scoop-holes among the adjacent rocks, she had shared the dew of her calabash among them; never laying by any considerable store against those prolonged and utter droughts which, in some disastrous seasons, warp these isles.

Having pointed out, at our desire, what few things she would like transported to the ship – her chest, the oil, not omitting the live tortoises which she intended for a grateful present to our Captain – we immediately set to work, carrying them to the boat down the long, sloping stair of deeply-shadowed rock. While my comrades were thus employed, I looked and Hunilla had disappeared.

It was not curiosity alone, but, it seems to me, something different mingled with it, which prompted me to drop my tortoise, and once more gaze slowly around. I remembered the husband buried by Hunilla's hands. A narrow pathway led into a dense part of the thickets. Following it through many mazes, I came out upon a small, round, open space, deeply chambered there.

The mound rose in the middle; a bare heap of finest sand, like that unverdured heap found at the bottom of an hourglass run out. At its head stood the cross of withered sticks; the dry, peeled bark still fraying from it; its transverse limb tied up with rope, and forlornly adroop in the silent air.

Hunilla was partly prostrate upon the grave; her dark head bowed, and lost in her long, loosened Indian hair; her hands extended to the cross-foot, with a little brass crucifix clasped between; a crucifix worn featureless, like an ancient graven knocker long plied in vain. She did not see me, and I made no noise, but slid aside, and left the spot.

A few moments ere all was ready for our going, she reappeared among us. I looked into her eyes, but saw no tear. There was something which seemed strangely haughty in her air, and yet it was the air of woe. A Spanish and an Indian grief, which would not visibly lament. Pride's height in vain abased to proneness on the rack; nature's pride subduing nature's torture.

Like pages the small and silken dogs surrounded her, as

she slowly descended towards the beach. She caught the two most eager creatures in her arms: – 'Mia Teeta! Mia Tomoteeta!' and fondling them, inquired how many could we take on board.

The mate commanded the boat's crew; not a hard-hearted man, but his way of life had been such that in most things, even in the smallest, simple utility was his leading motive.

'We cannot take them all, Hunilla; our supplies are short; the winds are unreliable; we may be a good many days going to Tombez. So take those you have, Hunilla; but no more.'

She was in the boat; the oarsmen, too, were seated; all save one, who stood ready to push off and then spring himself. With the sagacity of their race, the dogs now seemed aware that they were in the very instant of being deserted upon a barren strand. The gunwales of the boat were high; its prow – presented inland – was lifted; so owing to the water, which they seem instinctively to shun, the dogs could not well leap into the little craft. But their busy paws hard scraped the prow, as it had been some farmer's door shutting them out from shelter in a winter storm. A clamorous agony of alarm. They did not howl, or whine; they all but spoke.

'Push off! Give way!' cried the mate. The boat gave one heavy drag and lurch, and next moment shot swiftly from the beach, turned on her heel, and sped. The dogs ran howling along the water's marge; now pausing to gaze at the flying boat, then motioning as if to leap in chase, but mysteriously withheld themselves; and again ran howling along the beach. Had they been human beings, hardly would they have more vividly inspired the sense of desolation. The oars were plied as confederate feathers of two wings. No one spoke. I looked back upon the beach, and then upon Hunilla, but her face was set in a stern dusky calm. The dogs crouching in her lap vainly licked her rigid hands. She never looked behind her; but sat motionless, till we turned a promontory of the coast and lost all sights and sounds astern. She seemed as one who, having experienced the sharpest of mortal pangs, was henceforth content to have all lesser heartstrings riven, one by one. To Hunilla, pain seemed so necessary, that pain in other beings, though by love and sympathy made her own, was unrepiningly to be borne. A heart of yearning in a frame of steel. A heart of earthly yearning, frozen by the frost which falleth from the sky.

The sequel is soon told. After a long passage, vexed by calms and baffling winds, we made the little port of Tombez in Peru, there to recruit the ship. Payta was not very distant. Our captain sold the tortoise oil to a Tombez merchant; and adding to the silver a contribution from all hands, gave it to our silent passenger, who knew not what the mariners had done.

The last seen of lone Hunilla she was passing into Payta town, riding upon a small gray ass; and before her on the ass's shoulders, she eyed the jointed workings of the beast's armorial cross.

SKETCH NINTH

HOOD'S ISLE AND THE HERMIT OBERLUS

> 'That darkesome glen they enter, where they find
> That cursed man, low sitting on the ground,
> Musing full sadly in his sullein mind;
> His griesly lockes long growen and unbound,
> Disordred hong about his shoulders round,
> And hid his face; through which his hollow eyne
> Lookt deadly dull, and stared as astound;
> His raw-bone cheekes, through penurie and pine,
> Were shronke into his jawes, as he did never dine.
> His garment nought but many ragged clouts,
> With thornes together pind and patched reads,
> The which his naked sides he wrapt abouts.'

SOUTHEAST of Crossman's Isle lies Hood's Isle, or McCain's Beclouded Isle; and upon its south side is a vitreous cove with a wide strand of dark pounded black lava, called Black Beach, or Oberlus's Landing. It might fitly have been styled Charon's.

It received its name from a wild white creature who spent many years here; in the person of a European bringing into this savage region qualities more diabolical than are to be found among any of the surrounding cannibals.

About half a century ago, Oberlus deserted at the above-named island, then, as now, a solitude. He built himself a den of lava and clinkers, about a mile from the Landing, subsequently called after him, in a vale, or expanded gulch, containing here and there among the rocks about two acres of soil capable of rude cultivation; the only place on the isle not too blasted for that purpose. Here he succeeded in raising a sort of degenerate potatoes and pumpkins, which from time to time he exchanged with needy whalemen passing, for spirits or dollars.

His appearance, from all accounts, was that of the victim

of some malignant sorceress; he seemed to have drunk of Circe's cup; beast-like; rags insufficient to hide his nakedness; his befreckled skin blistered by continual exposure to the sun; nose flat; countenance contorted, heavy, earthy; hair and beard unshorn, profuse, and of fiery red. He struck strangers much as if he were a volcanic creature thrown up by the same convulsion which exploded into sight the isle. All bepatched and coiled asleep in his lonely lava den among the mountains, he looked, they say, as a heaped drift of withered leaves, torn from autumn trees, and so left in some hidden nook by the whirling halt for an instant of a fierce night-wind, which then ruthlessly sweeps on, somewhere else to repeat the capricious act. It is also reported to have been the strangest sight, this same Oberlus, of a sultry, cloudy morning, hidden under his shocking old black tarpaulin hat, hoeing potatoes among the lava. So warped and crooked was his strange nature, that the very handle of his hoe seemed gradually to have shrunk and twisted in his grasp, being a wretched bent stick, elbowed more like a savage's war-sickle than a civilized hoe-handle. It was his mysterious custom upon a first encounter with a stranger ever to present his back; possibly, because that was his better side, since it revealed the least. If the encounter chanced in his garden, as it sometimes did – the new-landed strangers going from the sea-side straight through the gorge, to hunt up the queer green-grocer reported doing business here – Oberlus for a time hoed on, unmindful of all greeting, jovial or bland; as the curious stranger would turn to face him, the recluse, hoe in hand, as diligently would avert himself; bowed over, and sullenly revolving round his murphy hill. Thus far for hoeing. When planting, his whole aspect and all his gestures were so malevolently and uselessly sinister and secret, that he seemed rather in act of dropping poison into wells than potatoes into soil. But among his lesser and more harmless marvels was an idea he had, that his visitors came equally as well led by longings to behold the mighty hermit Oberlus in his royal state of solitude, as simply to obtain potatoes, or find whatever company might be upon a barren isle. It seems incredible that such a being should possess such vanity; a misanthrope be conceited; but he really had his notion; and upon the strength of it, often gave himself amusing airs to captains. But after all, this is somewhat of a piece with the well-known eccentricity of some convicts, proud of that very hatefulness which makes them notorious. At other times, another unaccountable whim would seize him, and he would long dodge advancing strangers round the clinkered corners of his hut; sometimes like a stealthy bear, he would slink through the withered thickets up the mountains, and refuse to see the human face.

Except his occasional visitors from the sea, for a long period, the only companions of Oberlus were the crawling tortoises; and he seemed more than degraded to their level, having no desires for a time beyond theirs, unless it were for the stupor brought on by drunkenness. But sufficiently debased as he appeared, there yet lurked in him, only awaiting occasion for discovery, a still further proneness. Indeed, the sole superiority of Oberlus over the tortoises was his possession of a larger capacity of degradation; and along with that, something like an intelligent will to it. Moreover, what is about to be revealed, perhaps will show, that selfish ambition, or the love of rule for its own sake, far from being the peculiar infirmity of noble minds is shared by beings which have no mind at all. No creatures are so selfishly tyrannical as some brutes; as any one who has observed the tenants of the pasture must occasionally have observed.

'This island's mine by Sycorax my mother,' said Oberlus to himself, glaring round upon his haggard solitude. By some means, barter or theft – for in those days ships at intervals still kept touching at his Landing – he obtained an old musket, with a few charges of powder and ball. Possessed of arms, he was stimulated to enterprise, as a tiger that first feels the coming of its claws. The long habit of sole dominion over every object round him, his almost unbroken solitude, his never encountering humanity except on terms of misanthropic independence, or mercantile craftiness, and even such encounters being comparatively but rare; all this must have gradually nourished in him a vast idea of his own importance, together with a pure animal sort of scorn for all the rest of the universe.

The unfortunate Creole, who enjoyed his brief term of royalty at Charles's Isle was perhaps in some degree influenced by not unworthy motives; such as prompt other adventurous spirits to lead colonists into distant regions and assume political preëminence over them. His summary execution of many of his Peruvians is quite pardonable, considering the desperate characters he had to deal with; while his offering canine battle to the banded rebels seems under the circumstances altogether just. But for this King Oberlus and what shortly follows, no shade of palliation can be given. He acted out of mere delight in tyranny and cruelty, by virtue of a quality in him inherited from Sycorax his mother. Armed now with that shocking blunderbuss, strong in the thought of being master of that horrid isle, he panted for a chance to prove his potency upon the first specimen of humanity which should fall unbefriended into his hands.

Nor was he long without it. One day he spied a boat upon the beach, with one man, a negro, standing by it. Some distance off was a ship, and Oberlus immediately knew how matters stood. The vessel had put in for wood, and the boat's crew had gone into the thickets for it. From a convenient spot he kept watch of the boat, till presently a straggling company appeared loaded with billets. Throwing these on the beach, they again went into the thickets, while the negro proceeded to load the boat.

Oberlus now makes all haste and accosts the negro, who, aghast at seeing any living being inhabiting such a solitude, and especially so horrific a one, immediately falls into a panic, not at all lessened by the ursine suavity of Oberlus, who begs the favor of assisting him in his labors. The negro stands with several billets on his shoulder, in act of shouldering others; and Oberlus, with a short cord concealed in his bosom, kindly proceeds to lift those other billets to their place. In so doing, he persists in keeping behind the negro, who, rightly suspicious of this, in vain dodges about to gain the front of Oberlus; but Oberlus dodges also; till at last, weary of this bootless attempt at treachery, or fearful of being surprised by the remainder of the party, Oberlus runs off a little space to a bush, and fetching his blunderbuss, savagely commands the negro to desist work and follow him. He refuses. Whereupon, presenting his piece, Oberlus snaps at him. Luckily the blunderbuss misses fire; but by this time, frightened out of his wits, the negro, upon a second intrepid summons, drops his billets, surrenders at discretion, and follows on. By a narrow defile familiar to him, Oberlus speedily removes out of sight of the water.

On their way up the mountains, he exultingly informs the negro, that henceforth he is to work for him, and be his slave, and that his treatment would entirely depend on his future conduct. But Oberlus, deceived by the first impulsive cowardice of the black, in an evil moment slackens his vigilance. Passing through a narrow way and perceiving his leader quite off his guard, the negro, a powerful fellow, suddenly grasps him in his arms, throws him down, wrests his musketoon from him, ties his hands with the monster's own cord, shoulders him, and returns with him down to the boat. When the rest of the party arrive, Oberlus is carried on board the ship. This proved an Englishman, and a smuggler; a sort of craft not apt to be over-charitable. Oberlus is severely whipped, then handcuffed, taken ashore, and compelled to make known his habitation and produce his property. His potatoes, pumpkins, and tortoises, with a pile of dollars he had hoarded from his mercantile operations were secured on the spot. But while the too vindictive smugglers were busy destroying his hut and garden, Oberlus makes his escape into the mountains, and conceals himself there in impenetrable recesses, only known to himself, till the ship sails, when he ventures back, and by means of an old file which he sticks into a tree, contrives to free himself from his handcuffs.

Brooding among the ruins of his hut, and the desolate clinkers and extinct volcanoes of this outcast isle, the insulted misanthrope now meditates a signal revenge upon humanity, but conceals his purposes. Vessels still touch the Landing at times; and by-and-by Oberlus is enabled to supply them with some vegetables.

Warned by his former failure in kidnapping strangers, he now pursues a quite different plan. When seamen come ashore, he makes up to them like a free-and-easy comrade, invites them to his hut, and with whatever affability his red-haired grimness may assume, entreats them to drink his liquor and be merry. But his guests need little pressing; and so, soon as rendered insensible, are tied hand and foot, and pitched among the clinkers, are there concealed till the ship departs, when, finding themselves entirely dependent upon Oberlus, alarmed at his changed demeanor, his savage threats, and above all, that shocking blunderbuss, they willingly enlist under him, becoming his humble slaves, and Oberlus the most incredible of tyrants. So much so, that two or three perish beneath his initiating process. He sets the remainder – four of them – to breaking the caked soil; transporting upon their backs loads of loamy earth, scooped up in moist clefts among the mountains; keeps them on the roughest fare; presents his piece at the slightest hint of insurrection; and in all respects converts them into reptiles at his feet – plebeian garter-snakes to this Lord Anaconda.

At last, Oberlus contrives to stock his arsenal with four rusty cutlasses, and an added supply of powder and ball intended for his blunderbuss. Remitting in good part the labor of his slaves, he now approves himself a man, or rather devil, of great abilities in the way of cajoling or coercing others into acquiescence with his own ulterior designs, however at first abhorrent to them. But indeed, prepared for almost any eventual evil by their previous lawless life, as a sort of ranging Cow-Boys of the sea, which had dissolved within them the whole moral man, so that they were ready to concrete in the first offered mould of baseness now; rotted down from manhood by their hopeless misery on the isle; wonted to cringe in all things to their lord, himself the worst of slaves; these wretches were now become wholly corrupted to his hands. He used them as creatures of an inferior race; in short, he gaffles his four animals, and makes murderers of them; out of cowards fitly manufacturing bravos.

Now, sword or dagger, human arms are but artificial claws and fangs, tied on like false spurs to the fighting cock. So, we repeat, Oberlus, czar of the isle, gaffles his four subjects; that is, with intent of glory, puts four rusty cutlasses into their hands. Like any other autocrat, he had a noble army now.

It might be thought a servile war would hereupon ensue. Arms in the hands of trodden slaves? how indiscreet of Emperor Oberlus! Nay, they had but cutlasses – sad old scythes enough – he a blunderbuss, which by its blind scatterings of all sort of boulders, clinkers, and other scoria would annihilate all four mutineers, like four pigeons at one shot. Besides, at first he did not sleep in his accustomed hut; every lurid sunset, for a time, he might have been seen wending his way among the riven mountains, there to secrete himself till dawn in some sulphurous pitfall, undiscoverable to his gang; but finding this at last too troublesome, he now each evening tied his slaves hand and foot, hid the cutlasses, and thrusting them into his barracks, shut to the door, and lying down before it, beneath a rude shed lately added, slept out the night, blunderbuss in hand.

It is supposed that not content with daily parading over a cindery solitude at the head of his fine army, Oberlus now meditated the most active mischief; his probable object being to surprise some passing ship touching at his dominions, massacre the crew, and run away with her to parts unknown. While these plans were simmering in his head, two ships touch in company at the isle, on the opposite side to his; when his designs undergo a sudden change.

The ships are in want of vegetables, which Oberlus promises in great abundance, provided they send their boats round to his landing, so that the crews may bring the vegetables from his garden; informing the two captains, at the same time, that his rascals – slaves and soldiers – had become so abominably lazy and good-for-nothing of late, that he could not make them work by ordinary inducements, and did not have the heart to be severe with them.

The arrangement was agreed to, and the boats were sent and hauled upon the beach. The crews went to the lava hut; but to their surprise nobody was there. After waiting till their patience was exhausted, they returned to the shore, when lo, some stranger – not the Good Samaritan either – seems to have very recently passed that way. Three of the boats were broken in a thousand pieces, and the fourth was missing. By hard toil over the mountains and through the clinkers, some of the strangers succeeded in returning to that side of the isle where the ships lay, when fresh boats are sent to the relief of the rest of the hapless party.

However amazed at the treachery of Oberlus, the two captains, afraid of new and still more mysterious atrocities – and indeed, half imputing such strange events to the enchantments associated with these isles – perceive no security but in instant flight; leaving Oberlus and his army in quiet possession of the stolen boat.

On the eve of sailing they put a letter in a keg, giving the Pacific Ocean intelligence of the affair, and moored the keg in the bay. Some time subsequent, the keg was opened by another captain chancing to anchor there, but not until after he had dispatched a boat round to Oberlus's Landing. As may be readily surmised, he felt no little inquietude till the boat's return; when another letter was handed him, giving Oberlus's version of the affair. This precious document had been found pinned half-mildewed to the clinker wall of the sulphurous and deserted hut. It ran as follows: showing that Oberlus was at least an accomplished writer, and no mere boor; and what is more, was capable of the most tristful eloquence.

'Sir: I am the most unfortunate ill-treated gentleman that lives. I am a patriot, exiled from my country by the cruel hand of tyranny.

'Banished to these Enchanted Isles, I have again and again besought captains of ships to sell me a boat, but always have been refused, though I offered the handsomest prices in Mexican dollars. At length an opportunity presented of possessing myself of one, and I did not let it slip.

'I have been long endeavoring, by hard labor and much solitary suffering, to accumulate something to make myself comfortable in a virtuous though unhappy old age; but at various times have been robbed and beaten by men professing to be Christians.

'To-day I sail from the Enchanted group in the good boat *Charity* bound to the Feejee Isles.

'FATHERLESS OBERLUS.

'P.S.—Behind the clinkers, nigh the oven, you will find the old fowl. Do not kill it; be patient; I leave it setting; if it shall have any chicks, I hereby bequeath them to you, whoever you may be. But don't count your chicks before they are hatched.'

The fowl proved a starveling rooster, reduced to a sitting posture by sheer debility.

Oberlus declares that he was bound to the Feejee Isles; but this was only to throw pursuers on a false scent. For, after a long time, he arrived, alone in his open boat, at Guayaquil. As his miscreants were never again beheld on Hood's Isle, it is supposed, either that they perished for want of water on the passage to Guayaquil, or, what is quite as probable, were thrown overboard by Oberlus, when he found the water growing scarce.

From Guayaquil Oberlus proceeded to Payta; and there, with that nameless witchery peculiar to some of the ugliest animals, wound himself into the affections of a tawny damsel; prevailing upon her to accompany him back to his Enchanted Isle; which doubtless he painted as a Paradise of flowers, not a Tartarus of clinkers.

But unfortunately for the colonization of Hood's Isle with a choice variety of animated nature, the extraordinary and devilish aspect of Oberlus made him to be regarded in Payta as a highly suspicious character. So that being found concealed one night, with matches in his pocket, under the hull of a small vessel just ready to be launched, he was seized and thrown into jail.

The jails in most South American towns are generally of the least wholesome sort. Built of huge cakes of sun-burnt brick, and containing but one room, without windows or yard, and but one door heavily grated with wooden bars, they present both within and without the grimmest aspect. As public edifices they conspicuously stand upon the hot and dusty Plaza, offering to view, through the gratings, their villainous and hopeless inmates, burrowing in all sorts of tragic squalor. And here, for a long time, Oberlus was seen, the central figure of a mongrel and assassin band; a creature whom it is religion to detest, since it is philanthropy to hate a misanthrope.

Note. – They who may be disposed to question the possibility of the character above depicted, are referred to the 2d vol. of Porter's Voyage into the Pacific, where they will recognize many sentences, for expedition's sake derived verbatim from thence, and incorporated here; the main difference – save a few passing reflections – between the two accounts being, that the present writer has added to Porter's facts accessory ones picked up in the Pacific from reliable sources; and where facts conflict, has naturally preferred his own authorities to Porter's. As, for instance, *his* authorities place Oberlus on Hood's Isle : Porter's, on Charles's Isle. The letter found in the hut is also somewhat different; for while at the Encantadas he was informed that, not only did it evince a certain clerkliness, but was full of the strangest satiric effrontery which does not adequately appear in Porter's version. I accordingly altered it to suit the general character of its author.

SKETCH TENTH

RUNAWAYS, CASTAWAYS, SOLITARIES,
GRAVE-STONES, ETC.

'And all about old stockes and stubs of trees,
Whereon nor fruit, nor leafe was ever seene,
Did hang upon the ragged knotty knees,
On which had many wretches hanged beene.'

SOME relics of the hut of Oberlus partially remain to this
day at the head of the clinkered valley. Nor does the
stranger, wandering among other of the Enchanted Isles,
fail to stumble upon still other solitary abodes, long abandoned to the tortoise and the lizard. Probably few parts of
earth have, in modern times, sheltered so many solitaries.
The reason is, that these isles are situated in a distant sea,
and the vessels which occasionally visit them are mostly all
whalers, or ships bound on dreary and protracted voyages,
exempting them in a good degree from both the oversight
and the memory of human law. Such is the character of
some commanders and some seamen, that under these un-
toward circumstances, it is quite impossible but that scenes
of unpleasantness and discord should occur between them.
A sullen hatred of the tyrannic ship will seize the sailor,
and he gladly exchanges it for isles, which, though blighted
as by a continual sirocco and burning breeze, still offer
him, in their labyrinthine interior, a retreat beyond the
possibility of capture. To flee the ship in any Peruvian or
Chilian port, even the smallest and most rustical, is not un-
attended with great risk of apprehension, not to speak
of jaguars. A reward of five pesos sends fifty dastardly
Spaniards into the wood, who, with long knives, scour them
day and night in eager hopes of securing their prey. Neither
is it, in general, much easier to escape pursuit at the isles
of Polynesia. Those of them which have felt a civilizing

influence present the same difficulty to the runaway with the Peruvian ports, the advanced natives being quite as mercenary and keen of knife and scent as the retrograde Spaniards; while, owing to the bad odor in which all Europeans lie, in the minds of aboriginal savages who have chanced to hear aught of them, to desert the ship among primitive Polynesians, is, in most cases, a hope not unforlorn. Hence the Enchanted Isles become the voluntary tarrying places of all sorts of refugees; some of whom too sadly experience the fact, that flight from tyranny does not of itself insure a safe asylum, far less a happy home.

Moreover, it has not seldom happened that hermits have been made upon the isles by the accidents incident to tortoise-hunting. The interior of most of them is tangled and difficult of passage beyond description; the air is sultry and stifling; an intolerable thirst is provoked, for which no running stream offers its kind relief. In a few hours, under an equatorial sun, reduced by these causes to entire exhaustion, woe betide the straggler at the Enchanted Isles! Their extent is such as to forbid an adequate search, unless weeks are devoted to it. The impatient ship waits a day or two; when, the missing man remaining undiscovered, up goes a stake on the beach, with a letter of regret, and a keg of crackers and another of water tied to it, and away sails the craft.

Nor have there been wanting instances where the inhumanity of some captains has led them to wreak a secure revenge upon seamen who have given their caprice or pride some singular offense. Thrust ashore upon the scorching marl, such mariners are abandoned to perish outright, unless by solitary labors they succeed in discovering some precious dribblets of moisture oozing from a rock or stagnant in a mountain pool.

I was well acquainted with a man, who, lost upon the Isle of Narborough, was brought to such extremes by thirst, that at last he only saved his life by taking that of another being. A large hair-seal came upon the beach. He rushed upon it, stabbed it in the neck, and then throwing himself upon the panting body quaffed at the living wound; the palpitations of the creature's dying heart injected life into the drinker.

Another seaman, thrust ashore in a boat upon an isle at which no ship ever touched, owing to its peculiar sterility and the shoals about it, and from which all other parts of the group were hidden – this man, feeling that it was sure death to remain there, and that nothing worse than death menaced him in quitting it, killed two seals, and inflating their skins, made a float, upon which he transported himself to Charles's Island, and joined the republic there.

But men, not endowed with courage equal to such desperate attempts, find their only resource in forthwith seeking some watering-place, however precarious or scanty; building a hut; catching tortoises and birds; and in all respects preparing for a hermit life, till tide or time, or a passing ship arrives to float them off.

At the foot of precipices on many of the isles, small rude basins in the rocks are found, partly filled with rotted rubbish or vegetable decay, or overgrown with thickets, and sometimes a little moist; which, upon examination, reveal plain tokens of artificial instruments employed in hollowing them out, by some poor castaway or still more miserable runaway. These basins are made in places where it was supposed some scanty drops of dew might exude into them from the upper crevices.

The relics of hermitages and stone basins are not the only signs of vanishing humanity to be found upon the isles. And, curious to say, that spot which of all others in settled communities is most animated, at the Enchanted Isles presents the most dreary of aspects. And though it may seem very strange to talk of post-offices in this barren region, yet post-offices are occasionally to be found there. They consist of a stake and a bottle. The letters being not only sealed, but corked. They are generally deposited by captains of Nantucketers for the benefit of passing fishermen, and contain statements as to what luck they had in whaling or tortoise-hunting. Frequently, however, long months and months, whole years glide by and no applicant appears. The stake rots and falls, presenting no very exhilarating object.

If now it be added that grave-stones, or rather grave-boards, are also discovered upon some of the isles, the picture will be complete.

Upon the beach of James's Isle, for many years, was to be seen a rude finger-post, pointing inland. And, perhaps, taking it for some signal of possible hospitality in this otherwise desolate spot – some good hermit living there with his maple dish – the stranger would follow on in the path thus indicated, till at last he would come out in a noiseless nook, and find his only welcome, a dead man – his sole greeting the inscription over a grave. Here, in 1813, fell, in a day-break duel, a lieutenant of the U.S. frigate *Essex*, aged twenty-one: attaining his majority in death.

It is but fit that, like those old monastic institutions of Europe, whose inmates go not out of their own walls to be inurned, but are entombed there where they die, the Encantadas, too, should bury their own dead, even as the great general monastery of earth does hers.

It is known that burial in the ocean is a pure necessity of sea-faring life, and that it is only done when land is far astern, and not clearly visible from the bow. Hence, to vessels cruising in the vicinity of the Enchanted Isles, they afford a convenient Potter's Field. The interment over, some good-natured forecastle poet and artist seizes his paint-brush, and inscribes a doggerel epitaph. When, after a long lapse of time, other good-natured seamen chance to come upon the spot, they usually make a table of the mound, and quaff a friendly can to the poor soul's repose.

As a specimen of these epitaphs, take the following, found in a bleak gorge of Chatham Isle:—

> '*Oh, Brother Jack, as you pass by,*
> *As you are now, so once was I.*
> *Just so game, and just so gay,*
> *But now, alack, they've stopped my pay.*
> *No more I peep out of my blinkers,*
> *Here I be – tucked in with clinkers!*'

THE BELL-TOWER

*'Like negroes, these powers own man sul-
lenly; mindful of their higher master; while
serving, plot revenge.'*

*'The world is apoplectic with high-living of
ambition; and apoplexy has its fall.'*

*'Seeking to conquer a larger liberty, man but
extends the empire of necessity.'*

From a Private MS.

IN the south of Europe, nigh a once frescoed capital, now with dank mould cankering its bloom, central in a plain, stands what, at distance, seems the black mossed stump of some immeasurable pine, fallen, in forgotten days, with Anak and the Titan.

As all along where the pine tree falls, its dissolution leaves a mossy mound – last-flung shadow of the perished trunk; never lengthening, never lessening; unsubject to the fleet falsities of the sun; shade immutable, and true gauge which cometh by prostration – so westward from what seems the stump, one steadfast spear of lichened ruin veins the plain.

From that tree-top, what birded chimes of silver throats had rung. A stone pine; a metallic aviary in its crown: the Bell-Tower, built by the great mechanician, the unblest foundling, Bannadonna.

Like Babel's, its base was laid in a high hour of renovated earth, following the second deluge, when the waters of the Dark Ages had dried up, and once more the green appeared. No wonder that, after so long and deep submersion, the jubilant expectation of the race should, as with Noah's sons, soar into Shinar aspiration.

In firm resolve, no man in Europe at that period went beyond Bannadonna. Enriched through commerce with the Levant, the state in which he lived voted to have the noblest Bell-Tower in Italy. His repute assigned him to be architect.

Stone by stone, month by month, the tower rose. Higher, higher; snail-like in pace, but torch or rocket in its pride.

After the masons would depart, the builder, standing alone upon its ever-ascending summit, at close of every day, saw that he overtopped still higher walls and trees. He would tarry till a late hour there, wrapped in schemes of other and still loftier piles. Those who of saints' days thronged the spot – hanging to the rude poles of scaffolding, like sailors on yards, or bees on boughs, unmindful of lime and dust, and falling chips of stone – their homage not the less inspirited him to self-esteem.

At length the holiday of the Tower came. To the sound of viols, the climax-stone slowly rose in air, and, amid the firing of ordnance, was laid by Bannadonna's hands upon the final course. Then mounting it, he stood erect, alone, with folded arms, gazing upon the white summits of blue inland Alps, and whiter crests of bluer Alps off-shore – sights invisible from the plain. Invisible, too, from thence was that eye he turned below, when, like the cannon booms, came up to him the people's combustions of applause.

That which stirred them so was, seeing with what serenity the builder stood three hundred feet in air, upon an unrailed perch. This none but he durst do. But his periodic standing upon the pile, in each stage of its growth – such discipline had its last result.

Little remained now but the bells. These, in all respects, must correspond with their receptacle.

The minor ones were prosperously cast. A highly enriched one followed, of a singular make, intended for suspension in a manner before unknown. The purpose of this bell, its rotary motion, and connection with the clock-work, also executed at the time, will, in the sequel, receive mention.

In the one erection, bell-tower and clock-tower were united, though, before that period, such structures had commonly been built distinct; as the Campanile and Torre del 'Orologio of St Mark to this day attest.

But it was upon the great state-bell that the founder lavished his more daring skill. In vain did some of the less elated magistrates here caution him; saying that though truly the tower was Titanic, yet limit should be set to the dependent weight of its swaying masses. But undeterred, he prepared his mammoth mould, dented with mythological devices; kindled his fires of balsamic firs; melted his tin and copper, and, throwing in much plate, contributed by the public spirit of the nobles, let loose the tide.

The unleashed metals bayed like hounds. The workmen shrunk. Through their fright, fatal harm to the bell was dreaded. Fearless as Shadrach, Bannadonna, rushing through the glow, smote the chief culprit with his ponderous ladle. From the smitten part, a splinter was dashed into the seething mass, and at once was melted in.

Next day a portion of the work was heedfully uncovered. All seemed right. Upon the third morning, with equal satisfaction, it was bared still lower. At length, like some old Theban king, the whole cooled casting was disinterred. All was fair except in one strange spot. But as he suffered no one to attend him in these inspections, he concealed the blemish by some preparation which none knew better to devise.

The casting of such a mass was deemed no small triumph for the caster; one, too, in which the state might not scorn to share. The homicide was overlooked. By the charitable that deed was but imputed to sudden transports of esthetic passion, not to any flagitious quality. A kick from an Arabian charger; not sign of vice, but blood.

His felony remitted by the judge, absolution given him by the priest, what more could even a sickly conscience have desired.

Honoring the tower and its builder with another holiday, the republic witnessed the hoisting of the bells and clockwork amid shows and pomps superior to the former.

Some months of more than usual solitude on Bannadonna's part ensued. It was not unknown that he was engaged upon something for the belfry, intended to complete it, and surpass all that had gone before. Most people imagined that the design would involve a casting like the bells. But those who thought they had some further insight, would shake their heads, with hints, that not for nothing did the mechanician keep so secret. Meantime, his seclusion failed not to invest his work with more or less of that sort of mystery pertaining to the forbidden.

Ere long he had a heavy object hoisted to the belfry, wrapped in a dark sack or cloak – a procedure sometimes had in the case of an elaborate piece of sculpture, or statue, which, being intended to grace the front of a new edifice, the architect does not desire exposed to critical eyes, till set up, finished, in its appointed place. Such was the impression now. But, as the object rose, a statuary present observed, or thought he did, that it was not entirely rigid, but was, in a manner, pliant. At last, when the hidden thing had attained its final height, and, obscurely seen from below, seemed almost of itself to step into the belfry, as if with little assistance from the crane, a shrewd old blacksmith present ventured the suspicion that it was but a living man. This surmise was thought a foolish one, while the general interest failed not to augment.

Not without demur from Bannadonna, the chief-magistrate of the town, with an associate – both elderly men – followed what seemed the image up the tower. But, arrived at the belfry, they had little recompense. Plausibly entrenching himself behind the conceded mysteries of his art, the mechanician withheld present explanation. The magistrates glanced toward the cloaked object, which, to their surprise, seemed now to have changed its attitude, or else had before been more perplexingly concealed by the violent muffling action of the wind without. It seemed now seated upon some sort of frame, or chair, contained within the domino. They observed that nigh the top, in a sort of square, the web of the cloth, either from accident or design, had its warp partly withdrawn, and the cross threads plucked out here and there, so as to form a sort of woven grating. Whether it were the low wind or no, stealing through the stone lattice-work, or only their own perturbed imaginations, is uncertain, but they thought they discerned a slight sort of fitful, spring-like motion, in the domino. Nothing, however incidental or insignificant, escaped their uneasy eyes. Among other things, they pried out, in a corner, an earthen cup, partly corroded and partly encrusted, and one whispered to the other, that this cup was just such a one as might, in mockery, be offered to the lips of some brazen statue, or, perhaps, still worse.

But, being questioned, the mechanician said, that the cup was simply used in his founder's business, and described the purpose; in short, a cup to test the condition of metals in fusion. He added, that it had got into the belfry by the merest chance.

Again, and again, they gazed at the domino, as at some suspicious incognito at a Venetian mask. All sorts of vague apprehensions stirred them. They even dreaded lest, when they should descend, the mechanician, though without a flesh and blood companion, for all that, would not be left alone.

Affecting some merriment at their disquietude, he begged to relieve them, by extending a coarse sheet of workman's canvas between them and the object.

Meantime he sought to interest them in his other work; nor, now that the domino was out of sight, did they long remain insensible to the artistic wonders lying round them; wonders hitherto beheld but in their unfinished state; because, since hoisting the bells, none but the caster had entered within the belfry. It was one trait of his, that, even in details, he would not let another do what he could, without too great loss of time, accomplish for himself. So, for several preceding weeks, whatever hours were unemployed in his secret design, had been devoted to elaborating the figures on the bells.

The clock-bell, in particular, now drew attention. Under a patient chisel, the latent beauty of its enrichments, before obscured by the cloudings incident to casting, that beauty in its shyest grace, was now revealed. Round and round the bell, twelve figures of gay girls, garlanded, hand-in-hand, danced in a choral ring – the embodied hours.

'Bannadonna,' said the chief, 'this bell excels all else. No added touch could here improve. Hark!' hearing a sound, 'was that the wind?'

'The wind, Excellenza,' was the light response. 'But the figures, they are not yet without their faults. They need some touches yet. When those are given, and the – block yonder,' pointing towards the canvas screen, 'when Haman there, as I merrily call him, – him? *it*, I mean – when Haman is fixed on this, his lofty tree, then, gentlemen, will I be most happy to receive you here again.'

The equivocal reference to the object caused some return of restlessness. However, on their part, the visitors forbore further allusion to it, unwilling, perhaps, to let the foundling see how easily it lay within his plebeian art to stir the placid dignity of nobles.

'Well, Bannadonna,' said the chief, 'how long ere you are ready to set the clock going, so that the hour shall be sounded? Our interest in you, not less than in the work itself, makes us anxious to be assured of your success. The people, too, – why, they are shouting now. Say the exact hour when you will be ready.'

'To-morrow, Excellenza, if you listen for it, – or should you not, all the same – strange music will be heard. The stroke of one shall be the first from yonder bell,' pointing to the bell adorned with girls and garlands, 'that stroke shall fall there, where the hand of Una clasps Dua's. The stroke of one shall sever that loved clasp. To-morrow, then, at one o'clock, as struck here, precisely here,' advancing and placing his finger upon the clasp, 'the poor mechanic will be most happy once more to give you liege audience, in this his littered shop. Farewell till then, illustrious magnificoes, and hark ye for your vassal's stroke.'

His still, Vulcanic face hiding its burning brightness like a forge, he moved with ostentatious deference towards the scuttle, as if so far to escort their exit. But the junior magistrate, a kind-hearted man, troubled at what seemed to him a certain sardonical disdain, lurking beneath the foundling's humble mien, and in Christian sympathy more distressed at it on his account than on his own, dimly surmising what might be the final fate of such a cynic solitaire, not perhaps uninfluenced by the general strangeness of surrounding things, this good magistrate had glanced sadly, sideways from the speaker, and thereupon his foreboding eye had started at the expression of the unchanging face of the Hour Una.

'How is this, Bannadonna?' he lowly asked, 'Una looks unlike her sisters.'

'In Christ's name, Bannadonna,' impulsively broke in the chief, his attention for the first attracted to the figure, by his associate's remark, 'Una's face looks just like that of Deborah, the prophetess, as painted by the Florentine, Del Fonca.'

'Surely, Bannadonna,' lowly resumed the milder magistrate, 'you meant the twelve should wear the same jocundly abandoned air. But see, the smile of Una seems but a fatal one. 'Tis different.'

While his mild associate was speaking, the chief glanced, inquiringly, from him to the caster, as if anxious to mark how the discrepancy would be accounted for. As the chief stood, his advanced foot was on the scuttle's curb.

Bannadonna spoke:

'Excellenza, now that, following your keener eye, I glance upon the face of Una, I do, indeed perceive some little variance. But look all round the bell, and you will find no two faces entirely correspond. Because there is a law in art – but the cold wind is rising more; these lattices are but a poor defense. Suffer me, magnificoes, to conduct you, at least, partly on your way. Those in whose well-being there is a public stake, should be heedfully attended.'

'Touching the look of Una, you were saying, Bannadonna, that there was a certain law in art,' observed the chief, as the three now descended the stone shaft, 'pray, tell me, then –.'

'Pardon; another time, Excellenza; – the tower is damp.'

'Nay, I must rest, and hear it now. Here, – here is a wide landing, and through this leeward slit, no wind, but ample light. Tell us of your law; and at large.'

'Since, Excellenza, you insist, know that there is a law in art, which bars the possibility of duplicates. Some years ago, you may remember, I graved a small seal for your republic, bearing, for its chief device, the head of your own ancestor, its illustrious founder. It becoming necessary, for the customs' use, to have innumerable impressions for bales and boxes, I graved an entire plate, containing one hundred of the seals. Now, though, indeed, my object was to have those hundred heads identical, and though, I dare say, people think them so, yet, upon closely scanning an uncut impression from the plate, no two of those five-score faces, side by side, will be found alike. Gravity is the air of all; but, diversified in all. In some, benevolent; in some, ambiguous; in two or three, to a close scrutiny, all but incipiently malign, the variation of less than a hair's breadth in the linear shadings round the mouth sufficing to all this. Now, Excellenza, transmute that general gravity into joyousness, and subject it to twelve of those variations I have described, and tell me, will you not have my hours here, and Una one of them? But I like –.'

'Hark! is that – a footfall above?'

'Mortar, Excellenza; sometimes it drops to the belfry-floor from the arch where the stone-work was left undressed. I must have it seen to. As I was about to say: for one, I like this law forbidding duplicates. It evokes fine personalities. Yes, Excellenza, that strange, and – to you – uncertain smile, and those fore-looking eyes of Una, suit Bannadonna very well.'

'Hark! – sure we left no soul above?'

'No soul, Excellenza; rest assured, no *soul*. – Again the mortar.'

'It fell not while we were there.'

'Ah, in your presence, it better knew its place, Excellenza,' blandly bowed Bannadonna.

'But, Una,' said the milder magistrate, 'she seemed intently gazing on you; one would have almost sworn that she picked you out from among us three.'

'If she did, possibly, it might have been her finer apprehension, Excellenza.'

'How, Bannadonna? I do not understand you.'

'No consequence, no consequence, Excellenza – but the shifted wind is blowing through the slit. Suffer me to escort you on; and then, pardon, but the toiler must to his tools.'

'It may be foolish, Signor,' said the milder magistrate, as, from the third landing, the two now went down unescorted, 'but, somehow, our great mechanician moves me strangely. Why, just now, when he so superciliously replied, his walk seemed Sisera's, God's vain foe, in Del Fonca's painting. And that young, sculptured Deborah, too. Ay, and that –.'

'Tush, tush, Signor!' returned the chief. 'A passing whim. Deborah? – Where's Jael, pray?'

'Ah,' said the other, as they now stepped upon the sod, 'Ah, Signor, I see you leave your fears behind you with the chill and gloom; but mine, even in this sunny air, remain. Hark!'

It was a sound from just within the tower door, whence they had emerged. Turning, they saw it closed.

'He has slipped down and barred us out,' smiled the chief; 'but it is his custom.'

Proclamation was now made, that the next day, at one hour after meridian, the clock would strike, and – thanks to the mechanician's powerful art – with unusual accompaniments. But what those should be, none as yet could say. The announcement was received with cheers.

By the looser sort, who encamped about the tower all night, lights were seen gleaming through the topmost blind-work, only disappearing with the morning sun. Strange sounds, too, were heard, or were thought to be, by those whom anxious watching might not have left mentally undisturbed – sounds, not only of some ringing implement, but also – so they said – half-suppressed screams and plainings, such as might have issued from some ghostly engine, over-plied.

Slowly the day drew on; part of the concourse chasing the weary time with songs and games, till, at last, the great blurred sun rolled, like a football, against the plain.

At noon, the nobility and principal citizens came from the town in cavalcade, a guard of soldiers, also, with music, the more to honor the occasion.

Only one hour more. Impatience grew. Watches were

held in hands of feverish men, who stood, now scrutinizing their small dial-plates, and then, with neck thrown back, gazing toward the belfry, as if the eye might foretell that which could only be made sensible to the ear; for, as yet, there was no dial to the tower-clock.

The hour hands of a thousand watches now verged within a hair's breadth of the figure 1. A silence, as of the expectation of some Shiloh, pervaded the swarming plain. Suddenly a dull, mangled sound – naught ringing in it; scarcely audible, indeed, to the outer circles of the people – that dull sound dropped heavily from the belfry. At the same moment, each man stared at his neighbor blankly. All watches were upheld. All hour-hands were at – had passed – the figure 1. No bell-stroke from the tower. The multitude became tumultuous.

Waiting a few moments, the chief magistrate, commanding silence, hailed the belfry, to know what thing unforeseen had happened there.

No response.

He hailed again and yet again.

All continued hushed.

By his order, the soldiers burst in the tower-door; when, stationing guards to defend it from the now surging mob, the chief, accompanied by his former associate, climbed the winding stairs. Half-way up, they stopped to listen. No sound. Mounting faster, they reached the belfry; but, at the threshold, started at the spectacle disclosed. A spaniel, which, unbeknown to them, had followed them thus far, stood shivering as before some unknown monster in a brake: or rather, as if it snuffed footsteps leading to some other world.

Bannadonna lay, prostrate and bleeding, at the base of the bell which was adorned with girls and garlands. He lay at the feet of the hour Una; his head coinciding, in a vertical line, with her left hand, clasped by the hour Dua. With downcast face impending over him, like Jael over nailed Sisera in the tent, was the domino; now no more becloaked.

It had limbs, and seemed clad in a scaly mail, lustrous as a dragon-beetle's. It was manacled, and its clubbed arms were uplifted, as if, with its manacles, once more to smite its already smitten victim. One advanced foot of it was inserted beneath the dead body, as if in the act of spurning it.

Uncertainty falls on what now followed.

It were but natural to suppose that the magistrates would, at first, shrink from immediate personal contact with what they saw. At the least, for a time, they would stand in involuntary doubt; it may be, in more or less of horrified alarm. Certain it is, that an arquebus was called for from below. And some add, that its report, followed by a fierce whiz, as of the sudden snapping of a main-spring, with a steely din, as if a stack of sword-blades should be dashed upon a pavement, these blended sounds came ringing to the plain, attracting every eye far upward to the belfry, whence, through the lattice-work, thin wreaths of smoke were curling.

Some averred that it was the spaniel, gone mad by fear, which was shot. This, others denied. True it was, the spaniel never more was seen; and, probably, for some unknown reason, it shared the burial now to be related of the domino. For, whatever the preceding circumstances may have been, the first instinctive panic over, or else all ground of reasonable fear removed, the two magistrates, by themselves, quickly rehooded the figure in the drooped cloak wherein it had been hoisted. The same night, it was secretly lowered to the ground, smuggled to the beach, pulled far out to sea, and sunk. Nor to any after urgency, even in free convivial hours, would the twain ever disclose the full secrets of the belfry.

From the mystery unavoidably investing it, the popular solution of the foundling's fate involved more or less of supernatural agency. But some few less unscientific minds pretended to find little difficulty in otherwise accounting for it. In the chain of circumstantial inferences drawn, there may, or may not, have been some absent or defective links.

But, as the explanation in question is the only one which tradition has explicitly preserved, in dearth of better, it will here be given. But, in the first place, it is requisite to present the supposition entertained as to the entire motive and mode, with their origin, of the secret design of Bannadonna; the minds above-mentioned assuming to penetrate as well into his soul as into the event. The disclosure will indirectly involve reference to peculiar matters, none of the clearest, beyond the immediate subject.

At that period, no large bell was made to sound otherwise than as at present, by agitation of a tongue within, by means of ropes, or percussion from without, either from cumbrous machinery, or stalwart watchmen, armed with heavy hammers, stationed in the belfry, or in sentry-boxes on the open roof, according as the bell was sheltered or exposed.

It was from observing these exposed bells, with their watchmen, that the foundling, as was opined, derived the first suggestion of his scheme. Perched on a great mast or spire, the human figure, viewed from below, undergoes such a reduction in its apparent size, as to obliterate its intelligent features. It evinces no personality. Instead of bespeaking volition, its gestures rather resemble the automatic ones of the arms of a telegraph.

Musing, therefore, upon the purely Punchinello aspect of the human figure thus beheld, it had indirectly occurred to Bannadonna to devise some metallic agent, which should strike the hour with its mechanic hand, with even greater precision than the vital one. And, moreover, as the vital watchman on the roof, sallying from his retreat at the given periods, walked to the bell with uplifted mace, to smite it, Bannadonna had resolved that his invention should likewise possess the power of locomotion, and, along with that, the appearance, at least, of intelligence and will.

If the conjectures of those who claimed acquaintance with the intent of Bannadonna be thus far correct, no unenterprising spirit could have been his. But they stopped not here; intimating that though, indeed, his design had, in the first place, been prompted by the sight of the watch-man, and confined to the devising of a subtle substitute for him: yet, as is not seldom the case with projectors, by insensible gradations, proceeding from comparatively pig-my aims to Titanic ones, the original scheme had, in its anticipated eventualities, at last, attained to an unheard of degree of daring. He still bent his efforts upon the loco-motive figure for the belfry, but only as a partial type of an ulterior creature, a sort of elephantine Helot, adapted to further, in a degree scarcely to be imagined, the universal conveniences and glories of humanity; supplying nothing less than a supplement to the Six Days' Work; stocking the earth with a new serf, more useful than the ox, swifter than the dolphin, stronger than the lion, more cunning than the ape, for industry an ant, more fiery than serpents, and yet, in patience, another ass. All excellences of all God-made creatures, which served man, were here to receive advance-ment, and then to be combined in one. Talus was to have been the all-accomplished Helot's name. Talus, iron slave to Bannadonna, and, through him, to man.

Here, it might well be thought that, were these last con-jectures as to the foundling's secrets not erroneous, then must he have been hopelessly infected with the craziest chimeras of his age; far outgoing Albert Magus and Cor-nelius Agrippa. But the contrary was averred. However marvelous his design, however apparently transcending not alone the bounds of human invention, but those of divine creation, yet the proposed means to be employed were alleged to have been confined within the sober forms of sober reason. It was affirmed that, to a degree of more than skeptic scorn, Bannadonna had been without sympathy for any of the vain-glorious irrationalities of his time. For example, he had not concluded, with the visionaries among the metaphysicians, that between the finer mechanic forces and the ruder animal vitality some germ of correspondence might prove discoverable. As little did his scheme partake of the enthusiasm of some natural philosophers, who hoped, by physiological and chemical inductions, to arrive at a knowledge of the source of life, and so qualify themselves to manufacture and improve upon it. Much less had he aught in common with the tribe of alchemists, who sought, by a species of incantations, to evoke some surprising vitality from the laboratory. Neither had he imagined, with certain sanguine theosophists, that, by faithful adoration of the Highest, unheard-of powers would be vouchsafed to man. A practical materialist, what Bannadonna had aimed at was to have been reached, not by logic, not by crucible, not by altars; but by plain vice-bench and hammer. In short, to solve nature, to steal into her, to intrigue beyond her, to procure some one else to bind her to his hand; – these, one and all, had not been his objects; but, asking no favors from any element or any being, of himself, to rival her, outstrip her, and rule her. He stooped to conquer. With him, common sense was theurgy; machinery, miracle; Prometheus, the heroic name for machinist; man, the true God.

Nevertheless, in his initial step, so far as the experimental automaton for the belfry was concerned, he allowed fancy some little play; or, perhaps, what seemed his fancifulness was but his utilitarian ambition collaterally extended. In figure, the creature for the belfry should not be likened after the human pattern, nor any animal one, nor after the ideals, however wild, of ancient fable, but equally in aspect as in organism be an original production; the more terrible to behold, the better.

Such, then, were the suppositions as to the present scheme, and the reserved intent. How, at the very threshold, so unlooked for a catastrophe overturned all, or rather, what was the conjecture here, is now to be set forth.

It was thought that on the day preceding the fatality, his visitors having left him, Bannadonna had unpacked the belfry image, adjusted it, and placed it in the retreat provided – a sort of sentry-box in one corner of the belfry; in short, throughout the night, and for some part of the ensuing morning, he had been engaged in arranging everything connected with the domino; the issuing from the sentry-box each sixty minutes; sliding along a grooved way, like a railway; advancing to the clock-bell, with up-lifted manacles; striking it at one of the twelve junctions of the four-and-twenty hands; then wheeling, circling the bell, and retiring to its post, there to bide for another sixty minutes, when the same process was to be repeated; the bell, by a cunning mechanism, meantime turning on its vertical axis, so as to present, to the descending mace, the clasped hands of the next two figures, when it would strike two, three, and so on, to the end. The musical metal in this time-bell being so managed in the fusion, by some art, perishing with its originator, that each of the clasps of the four-and-twenty hands should give forth its own peculiar resonance when parted.

But on the magic metal, the magic and metallic stranger never struck but that one stroke, drove but that one nail, severed but that one clasp, by which Bannadonna clung to his ambitious life. For, after winding up the creature in the sentry-box, so that, for the present, skipping the inter-vening hours, it should not emerge till the hour of one, but should then infallibly emerge, and, after deftly oiling the grooves whereon it was to slide, it was surmised that the mechanician must then have hurried to the bell, to give his final touches to its sculpture. True artist, he here became absorbed; and absorption still further intensified, it may be, by his striving to abate that strange look of Una; which, though, before others, he had treated with such unconcern, might not, in secret, have been without its thorn.

And so, for the interval, he was oblivious of his creature; which, not oblivious of him, and true to its creation, and true to its heedful winding up, left its post precisely at the given moment; along its well-oiled route, slid noiselessly to-wards its mark; and, aiming at the hand of Una, to ring one clangorous note, dully smote the intervening brain of Bannadonna, turned backwards to it; the manacled arms then instantly up-springing to their hovering poise. The falling body clogged the thing's return; so there it stood, still impending over Bannadonna, as if whispering some post-mortem terror. The chisel lay dropped from the hand, but beside the hand; the oil-flask spilled across the iron track.

In his unhappy end, not unmindful of the rare genius of the mechanician, the republic decreed him a stately funeral. It was resolved that the great bell – the one whose casting had been jeopardized through the timidity of the ill-starred workman – should be rung upon the entrance of the bier into the cathedral. The most robust man of the country round was assigned the office of bell-ringer.

But as the pall-bearers entered the cathedral porch, naught but a broken and disastrous sound, like that of some lone Alpine land-slide, fell from the tower upon their ears. And then, all was hushed.

Glancing backwards, they saw the groined belfry crashed sideways in. It afterwards appeared that the powerful peasant, who had the bell-rope in charge, wishing to test at once the full glory of the bell, had swayed down upon the rope with one concentrate jerk. The mass of quaking metal, too ponderous for its frame, and strangely feeble somewhere at its top, loosed from its fastening, tore sideways down, and tumbling in one sheer fall, three hundred feet to the soft sward below, buried itself inverted and half out of sight.

Upon its disinterment, the main fracture was found to have started from a small spot in the ear; which, being scraped, revealed a defect, deceptively minute, in the casting; which defect must subsequently have been pasted over with some unknown compound.

The remolten metal soon reassumed its place in the tower's repaired superstructure. For one year the metallic choir of birds sang musically in its belfry-bough-work of sculptured blinds and traceries. But on the first anniversary of the tower's completion – at early dawn, before the concourse had surrounded it – an earthquake came; one loud crash was heard. The stone-pine, with all its bower of songsters, lay overthrown upon the plain.

So the blind slave obeyed its blinder lord; but, in obedience, slew him. So the creator was killed by the creature. So the bell was too heavy for the tower. So the bell's main weakness was where man's blood had flawed it. And so pride went before the fall.

BENITO CERENO

IN the year 1799, Captain Amasa Delano, of Duxbury, in Massachusetts, commanding a large sealer and general trader, lay at anchor with a valuable cargo, in the harbor of St Maria – a small, desert, uninhabited island toward the southern extremity of the long coast of Chili. There he had touched for water.

On the second day, not long after dawn, while lying in his berth, his mate came below, informing him that a strange sail was coming into the bay. Ships were then not so plenty in those waters as now. He rose, dressed, and went on deck.

The morning was one peculiar to that coast. Everything was mute and calm; everything gray. The sea, though undulated into long roods of swells, seemed fixed, and was sleeked at the surface like waved lead that has cooled and set in the smelter's mould. The sky seemed a gray surtout. Flights of troubled gray fowl, kith and kin with flights of troubled gray vapors among which they were mixed, skimmed low and fitfully over the waters, as swallows over meadows before storms. Shadows present, foreshadowing deeper shadows to come.

To Captain Delano's surprise, the stranger, viewed through the glass, showed no colors; though to do so upon entering a haven, however uninhabited in its shores, where but a single other ship might be lying, was the custom among peaceful seamen of all nations. Considering the lawlessness and loneliness of the spot, and the sort of stories, at that day, associated with those seas, Captain Delano's surprise might have deepened into some uneasiness had he not been a person of a singularly undistrustful good nature, not liable, except on extraordinary and repeated incentives, and hardly then, to indulge in personal alarms, any way involving the imputation of malign evil in man. Whether, in view of what humanity is capable, such a trait implies, along with a benevolent heart, more than ordinary quickness and accuracy of intellectual perception, may be left to the wise to determine.

But whatever misgivings might have obtruded on first seeing the stranger, would almost, in any seaman's mind, have been dissipated by observing that, the ship, in navigating into the harbor, was drawing too near the land; a sunken reef making out off her bow. This seemed to prove her a stranger, indeed, not only to the sealer, but the island; consequently, she could be no wonted freebooter on that ocean. With no small interest, Captain Delano continued to watch her – a proceeding not much facilitated by the vapors partly mantling the hull, through which the far matin light from her cabin streamed equivocally enough; much like the sun – by this time hemisphered on the rim of the horizon, and, apparently, in company with the strange ship entering the harbor – which, wimpled by the same low, creeping clouds, showed not unlike a Lima intriguante's one sinister eye peering across the Plaza from the Indian loop-hole of her dusk *saya-y-manta.*

It might have been but a deception of the vapors, but, the longer the stranger was watched the more singular appeared her manoeuvres. Ere long it seemed hard to decide whether she meant to come in or no – what she wanted, or what she was about. The wind, which had breezed up a little during the night, was now extremely light and baffling, which the more increased the apparent uncertainty of her movements.

Surmising, at last, that it might be a ship in distress, Captain Delano ordered his whale-boat to be dropped, and, much to the wary opposition of his mate, prepared to board her, and, at the least, pilot her in. On the night previous, a fishing-party of the seamen had gone a long distance to some detached rocks out of sight from the sealer, and, an hour or two before daybreak, had returned, having met with no small success. Presuming that the stranger might have been long off soundings, the good captain put several baskets of the fish, for presents, into his boat, and so pulled away. From her continuing too near the sunken reef, deeming her in danger, calling to his men, he made all haste to apprise those on board of their situation. But, some time ere the boat came up, the wind, light though it was, having shifted, had headed the vessel off, as well as partly broken the vapors from about her.

Upon gaining a less remote view, the ship, when made signally visible on the verge of the leaden-hued swells, with the shreds of fog here and there raggedly furring her, appeared like a whitewashed monastery after a thunderstorm, seen perched upon some dun cliff among the Pyrenees. But it was no purely fanciful resemblance which now, for a moment, almost led Captain Delano to think that nothing less than a ship-load of monks was before him. Peering over the bulwarks were what really seemed, in the hazy distance, throngs of dark cowls; while fitfully revealed through the open port-holes, other dark moving figures were dimly descried, as of Black Friars pacing the cloisters.

Upon a still nigher approach, this appearance was modified, and the true character of the vessel was plain – a Spanish merchantman of the first class, carrying negro slaves, amongst other valuable freight, from one colonial port to another. A very large, and, in its time, a very fine vessel, such as in those days were at intervals encountered along that main; sometimes superseded Acapulco treasure-ships, or retired frigates of the Spanish king's navy, which, like superannuated Italian palaces, still, under a decline of masters, preserved signs of former state.

As the whale-boat drew more and more nigh, the cause of the peculiar pipe-clayed aspect of the stranger was seen in the slovenly neglect pervading her. The spars, ropes and great part of the bulwarks, looked woolly, from long unacquaintance with the scraper, tar and the brush. Her keel seemed laid, her ribs put together, and she launched, from Ezekiel's Valley of Dry Bones.

In the present business in which she was engaged, the ship's general model and rig appeared to have undergone no material change from their original warlike and Froissart pattern. However, no guns were seen.

The tops were large, and were railed about with what had once been octagonal net-work, all now in sad disrepair. These tops hung overhead like three ruinous aviaries, in one of which was seen perched, on a ratlin, a white noddy, a strange fowl, so called from its lethargic, somnambulistic character, being frequently caught by hand at sea. Battered and mouldy, the castellated forecastle seemed some ancient turret, long ago taken by assault, and then left to decay. Toward the stern, two high-raised quarter galleries – the balustrades here and there covered with dry, tindery sea-moss – opening out from the unoccupied state-cabin, whose dead-lights, for all the mild weather, were hermetically closed and calked – these tenantless balconies hung over the sea as if it were the grand Venetian canal. But the principal relic of faded grandeur was the ample oval of the shield-like stern-piece, intricately carved with the arms of Castile and Leon, medallioned about by groups of mythological or symbolical devices; uppermost and central of which was a dark satyr in a mask, holding his foot on the prostrate neck of a writhing figure, likewise masked.

Whether the ship had a figure-head, or only a plain beak, was not quite certain, owing to canvas wrapped about that part, either to protect it while undergoing a re-furbishing, or else decently to hide its decay. Rudely painted or chalked, as in a sailor freak, along the forward side of a sort of pedestal below the canvas, was the sentence, '*Seguid vuestro jefe*,' (follow your leader); while upon the tarnished headboards, near by, appeared, in stately capitals, once gilt, the ship's name, 'SAN DOMINICK,' each letter streakingly corroded with tricklings of copper-spike rust; while, like mourning weeds, dark festoons of sea-grass slimily swept to and fro over the name, with every hearse-like roll of the hull.

As, at last, the boat was hooked from the bow along toward the gangway amidship, its keel, while yet some inches separated from the hull, harshly grated as on a sunken coral reef. It proved a huge bunch of conglobated barnacles adhering below the water to the side like a wen – a token of baffling airs and long calms passed somewhere in those seas.

Climbing the side, the visitor was at once surrounded by a clamorous throng of whites and blacks, but the latter outnumbering the former more than could have been expected, negro transportation-ship as the stranger in port was. But, in one language, and as with one voice, all poured out a common tale of suffering; in which the negresses, of whom there were not a few, exceeded the others in their dolorous vehemence. The scurvy, together with the fever, had swept off a great part of their number, more especially the Spaniards. Off Cape Horn they had narrowly escaped shipwreck; then, for days together, they had lain tranced without wind; their provisions were low; their water next to none; their lips that moment were baked.

While Captain Delano was thus made the mark of all eager tongues, his one eager glance took in all faces, with every other object about him.

Always upon first boarding a large and populous ship at sea, especially a foreign one, with a nondescript crew such as Lascars or Manilla men, the impression varies in a peculiar way from that produced by first entering a strange house with strange inmates in a strange land. Both house and ship – the one by its walls and blinds, the other by its high bulwarks like ramparts – hoard from view their interiors till the last moment: but in the case of the ship there is this addition; that the living spectacle it contains, upon its sudden and complete disclosure, has, in contrast with the blank ocean which zones it, something of the effect of enchantment. The ship seems unreal; these strange costumes, gestures, and faces, but a shadowy tableau just emerged from the deep, which directly must receive back what it gave.

Perhaps it was some such influence, as above is attempted to be described, which, in Captain Delano's mind, heightened whatever, upon a staid scrutiny, might have seemed unusual; especially the conspicuous figures of four elderly grizzled negroes, their heads like black, doddered willow tops, who, in venerable contrast to the tumult below them, were couched, sphynx-like, one on the starboard cat-head, another on the larboard, and the remaining pair face to face on the opposite bulwarks above the main-chains. They each had bits of unstranded old junk in their hands, and, with a sort of stoical self-content, were picking the junk into oakum, a small heap of which lay by their sides. They accompanied the task with a continuous, low, monotonous chant; droning and druling away like so many gray-headed bag-pipers playing a funeral march.

The quarter-deck rose into an ample elevated poop, upon the forward verge of which, lifted, like the oakum-pickers, some eight feet above the general throng, sat along in a row, separated by regular spaces, the cross-legged figures of six other blacks; each with a rusty hatchet in his hand, which, with a bit of brick and a rag, he was engaged like a scullion in scouring; while between each two was a small stack of hatchets, their rusted edges turned forward awaiting a like operation. Though occasionally the four oakum-pickers would briefly address some person or persons in the crowd below, yet the six hatchet-polishers neither spoke to others, nor breathed a whisper among themselves, but sat intent upon their task, except at intervals, when, with the peculiar love in negroes of uniting industry with pastime, two and two they sideways clashed their hatchets together, like cymbals, with a barbarous din. All six, unlike the generality, had the raw aspect of unsophisticated Africans.

But that first comprehensive glance which took in those ten figures, with scores less conspicuous, rested but an instant upon them, as, impatient of the hubbub of voices, the visitor turned in quest of whomsoever it might be that commanded the ship.

But as if not unwilling to let nature make known her own case among his suffering charge, or else in despair of restraining it for the time, the Spanish captain, a gentlemanly, reserved-looking, and rather young man to a stranger's eye, dressed with singular richness, but bearing plain traces of recent sleepless cares and disquietudes, stood passively by, leaning against the main-mast, at one moment casting a dreary, spiritless look upon his excited people, at the next an unhappy glance toward his visitor. By his side stood a black of small stature, in whose rude face, as occasionally, like a shepherd's dog, he mutely turned it up into the Spaniard's, sorrow and affection were equally blended.

Struggling through the throng, the American advanced to the Spaniard, assuring him of his sympathies, and offering to render whatever assistance might be in his power. To which the Spaniard returned for the present but grave and ceremonious acknowledgments, his national formality dusked by the saturnine mood of ill-health.

But losing no time in mere compliments, Captain Delano, returning to the gangway, had his basket of fish brought up; and as the wind still continued light, so that some hours at least must elapse ere the ship could be brought to the anchorage, he bade his men return to the sealer, and fetch back as much water as the whale-boat could carry, with whatever soft bread the steward might have, all the remaining pumpkins on board, with a box of sugar, and a dozen of his private bottles of cider.

Not many minutes after the boat's pushing off, to the vexation of all, the wind entirely died away, and the tide turning, began drifting back the ship helplessly seaward. But trusting this would not long last, Captain Delano sought, with good hopes, to cheer up the strangers, feeling no small satisfaction that, with persons in their condition, he could – thanks to his frequent voyages along the Spanish main – converse with some freedom in their native tongue.

While left alone with them, he was not long in observing

some things tending to heighten his first impressions; but surprise was lost in pity, both for the Spaniards and blacks, alike evidently reduced from scarcity of water and provisions; while long-continued suffering seemed to have brought out the less good-natured qualities of the negroes, besides, at the same time, impairing the Spaniard's authority over them. But, under the circumstances, precisely this condition of things was to have been anticipated. In armies, navies, cities, or families, in nature herself, nothing more relaxes good order than misery. Still, Captain Delano was not without the idea, that had Benito Cereno been a man of greater energy, misrule would hardly have come to the present pass. But the debility, constitutional or induced by hardships, bodily and mental, of the Spanish captain, was too obvious to be overlooked. A prey to settled dejection, as if long mocked with hope he would not now indulge it, even when it had ceased to be a mock, the prospect of that day, or evening at furthest, lying at anchor, with plenty of water for his people, and a brother captain to counsel and befriend, seemed in no perceptible degree to encourage him. His mind appeared unstrung, if not still more seriously affected. Shut up in these oaken walls, chained to one dull round of command, whose unconditionality cloyed him, like some hypochondriac abbot he moved slowly about, at times suddenly pausing, starting, or staring, biting his lip, biting his finger-nail, flushing, paling, twitching his beard, with other symptoms of an absent or moody mind. This distempered spirit was lodged, as before hinted, in as distempered a frame. He was rather tall, but seemed never to have been robust, and now with nervous suffering was almost worn to a skeleton. A tendency to some pulmonary complaint appeared to have been lately confirmed. His voice was like that of one with lungs half gone – hoarsely suppressed, a husky whisper. No wonder that, as in this state he tottered about, his private servant apprehensively followed him. Sometimes the negro gave his master his arm, or took his handkerchief out of his pocket for him; performing these and similar offices with that affectionate zeal which transmutes into something filial or fraternal acts in themselves but menial; and which has gained for the negro the repute of making the most pleasing body-servant in the world; one, too, whom a master need be on no stiffly superior terms with, but may treat with familiar trust; less a servant than a devoted companion.

Marking the noisy indocility of the blacks in general, as well as what seemed the sullen inefficiency of the whites it was not without humane satisfaction that Captain Delano witnessed the steady good conduct of Babo.

But the good conduct of Babo, hardly more than the ill-behavior of others, seemed to withdraw the half-lunatic Don Benito from his cloudy languor. Not that such precisely was the impression made by the Spaniard on the mind of his visitor. The Spaniard's individual unrest was, for the present, but noted as a conspicuous feature in the ship's general affliction. Still, Captain Delano was not a little concerned at what he could not help taking for the time to be Don Benito's unfriendly indifference towards himself. The Spaniard's manner, too, conveyed a sort of sour and gloomy disdain, which he seemed at no pains to disguise. But this the American in charity ascribed to the harrassing effects of sickness, since, in former instances, he had noted that there are peculiar natures on whom prolonged physical suffering seems to cancel every social instinct of kindness; as if, forced to black bread themselves, they deemed it but equity that each person coming nigh them should, indirectly, by some slight or affront, be made to partake of their fare.

But ere long Captain Delano bethought him that, indulgent as he was at the first, in judging the Spaniard, he might not, after all, have exercised charity enough. At bottom it was Don Benito's reserve which displeased him; but the same reserve was shown towards all but his faithful personal attendant. Even the formal reports which, according to sea-usage, were, at stated times, made to him by some petty underling, either a white, mulatto or black, he hardly had patience enough to listen to, without betraying contemptuous aversion. His manner upon such occasions was, in its degree, not unlike that which might be supposed to have been his imperial countryman's, Charles V., just previous to the anchoritish retirement of that monarch from the throne.

This splenetic disrelish of his place was evinced in almost every function pertaining to it. Proud as he was moody, he condescended to no personal mandate. Whatever special orders were necessary, their delivery was delegated to his body-servant, who in turn transferred them to their ultimate destination, through runners, alert Spanish boys or slave boys, like pages or pilot-fish within easy call continually hovering round Don Benito. So that to have beheld this undemonstrative invalid gliding about, apathetic and mute, no landsman could have dreamed that in him was lodged a dictatorship beyond which, while at sea, there was no earthly appeal.

Thus, the Spaniard, regarded in his reserve, seemed the involuntary victim of mental disorder. But, in fact, his reserve might, in some degree, have proceeded from design. If so, then here was evinced the unhealthy climax of that icy though conscientious policy, more or less adopted by all commanders of large ships, which, except in signal emergencies, obliterates alike the manifestation of sway with every trace of sociality; transforming the man into a block, or rather into a loaded cannon, which, until there is call for thunder, has nothing to say.

Viewing him in this light, it seemed but a natural token of the perverse habit induced by a long course of such hard self-restraint, that, notwithstanding the present condition of his ship, the Spaniard should still persist in a demeanor, which, however harmless, or, it may be, appropriate, in a well-appointed vessel, such as the *San Dominick* might have been at the outset of the voyage, was anything but judicious now. But the Spaniard, perhaps, thought that it was with captains as with gods: reserve, under all events, must still be their cue. But probably this appearance of slumbering dominion might have been but an attempted disguise to conscious imbecility – not deep policy, but shallow device. But be all this as it might, whether Don Benito's manner was designed or not, the more Captain Delano noted its pervading reserve, the less he felt uneasiness at any particular manifestation of that reserve towards himself.

Neither were his thoughts taken up by the captain alone. Wonted to the quiet orderliness of the sealer's comfortable family of a crew, the noisy confusion of the *San Dominick*'s suffering host repeatedly challenged his eye. Some prominent breaches, not only of discipline but of decency, were observed. These Captain Delano could not but ascribe, in the main, to the absence of those subordinate deck-officers to whom, along with higher duties, is intrusted what may be styled the police department of a populous ship. True, the old oakum-pickers appeared at times to act the part of monitorial constables to their countrymen, the blacks; but though occasionally succeeding in allaying trifling outbreaks now and then between man and man, they could do little or nothing toward establishing general quiet. The *San Dominick* was in the condition of a transatlantic emigrant ship, among whose multitude of living freight are some individuals, doubtless, as little troublesome as crates and bales; but the friendly remonstrances of such with their ruder companions are of not so much avail as the unfriendly arm of the mate. What the *San Dominick* wanted was, what the emigrant ship has, stern superior officers. But on these decks not so much as a fourth-mate was to be seen.

The visitor's curiosity was roused to learn the particulars of those mishaps which had brought about such absenteeism, with its consequences; because, though deriving some inkling of the voyage from the wails which at the first moment had greeted him, yet of the details no clear understanding had been had. The best account would, doubtless, be given by the captain. Yet at first the visitor was loth to ask it, unwilling to provoke some distant rebuff. But plucking up courage, he at last accosted Don Benito, renewing the expression of his benevolent interest, adding, that did he (Captain Delano) but know the particulars of the ship's misfortunes, he would, perhaps, be better able in the end to relieve them. Would Don Benito favor him with the whole story.

Don Benito faltered; then, like some somnambulist suddenly interfered with, vacantly stared at his visitor, and ended by looking down on the deck. He maintained this posture so long, that Captain Delano, almost equally disconcerted, and involuntarily almost as rude, turned suddenly from him, walking forward to accost one of the Spanish seamen for the desired information. But he had hardly gone five paces, when, with a sort of eagerness, Don Benito invited him back, regretting his momentary absence of mind, and professing readiness to gratify him.

While most part of the story was being given, the two captains stood on the after part of the main-deck, a privileged spot, no one being near but the servant.

'It is now a hundred and ninety days,' began the Spaniard, in his husky whisper, 'that this ship, well officered and well manned, with several cabin passengers – some fifty Spaniards in all – sailed from Buenos Ayres bound to Lima, with a general cargo, hardware, Paraguay tea and the like – and,' pointing forward, 'that parcel of negroes, now not more than a hundred and fifty, as you see, but then numbering over three hundred souls. Off Cape Horn we had heavy gales. In one moment, by night, three of my best officers, with fifteen sailors, were lost, with the main-yard; the spar snapping under them in the slings, as they sought, with heavers, to beat down the icy sail. To lighten the hull, the heavier sacks of mata were thrown into the sea, with most of the water-pipes lashed on deck at the time. And this last necessity it was, combined with the prolonged detentions afterwards experienced, which eventually brought about our chief causes of suffering. When –'

Here there was a sudden fainting attack of his cough, brought on, no doubt, by his mental distress. His servant sustained him, and drawing a cordial from his pocket placed it to his lips. He a little revived. But unwilling to leave him unsupported while yet imperfectly restored, the black with one arm still encircled his master, at the same time keeping his eye fixed on his face, as if to watch for the first sign of complete restoration, or relapse, as the event might prove.

The Spaniard proceeded, but brokenly and obscurely, as one in a dream.

– 'Oh, my God! rather than pass through what I have, with joy I would have hailed the most terrible gales; but –'

His cough returned and with increased violence; this subsiding, with reddened lips and closed eyes he fell heavily against his supporter.

'His mind wanders. He was thinking of the plague that followed the gales,' plaintively sighed the servant; 'my poor, poor master!' wringing one hand, and with the other wiping the mouth. 'But be patient, Señor,' again turning to Captain Delano, 'these fits do not last long; master will soon be himself.'

Don Benito reviving, went on; but as this portion of the story was very brokenly delivered, the substance only will here be set down.

It appeared that after the ship had been many days tossed in storms off the Cape, the scurvy broke out, carrying off numbers of the whites and blacks. When at last they had worked round into the Pacific, their spars and sails were so damaged, and so inadequately handled by the surviving mariners, most of whom were become invalids, that, unable to lay her northerly course by the wind, which was powerful, the unmanageable ship, for successive days and nights, was blown northwestward, where the breeze suddenly deserted her, in unknown waters, to sultry calms. The absence of the water-pipes now proved as fatal to life as before their presence had menaced it. Induced, or at least aggravated, by the more than scanty allowance of water, a malignant fever followed the scurvy; with the excessive heat of the lengthened calm, making such short work of it as to sweep away, as by billows, whole families of the Africans, and yet a larger number, proportionably, of the Spaniards, including, by a luckless fatality, every remaining officer on board. Consequently, in the smart west winds eventually following the calm, the already rent sails, having to be simply dropped, not furled, at need, had been gradually reduced to the beggars' rags they were now. To procure substitutes for his lost sailors, as well as supplies of water and sails, the captain, at the earliest opportunity, had made for Baldivia, the southernmost civilized port of Chili and South America; but upon nearing the coast the thick weather had prevented him from so much as sighting that harbor. Since which period, almost without a crew, and almost without canvas and almost without water, and, at intervals, giving its added dead to the sea, the *San Dominick* had been battledored about by contrary winds, inveigled by currents, or grown weedy in calms. Like a man lost in woods, more than once she had doubled upon her own track.

'But throughout these calamities,' huskily continued Don Benito, painfully turning in the half embrace of his servant, 'I have to thank those negroes you see, who, though to your inexperienced eyes appearing unruly, have, indeed, conducted themselves with less of restlessness than even their owner could have thought possible under such circumstances.'

Here he again fell faintly back. Again his mind wandered; but he rallied, and less obscurely proceeded.

'Yes, their owner was quite right in assuring me that no fetters would be needed with his blacks; so that while, as is wont in this transportation, those negroes have always remained upon deck – not thrust below, as in the Guinea-men – they have, also, from the beginning, been freely permitted to range within given bounds at their pleasure.'

Once more the faintness returned – his mind roved – but, recovering, he resumed:

'But it is Babo here to whom, under God, I owe not only my own preservation, but likewise to him, chiefly, the merit is due, of pacifying his more ignorant brethren, when at intervals tempted to murmurings.'

'Ah, master,' sighed the black, bowing his face, 'don't speak of me; Babo is nothing; what Babo has done was but duty.'

'Faithful fellow!' cried Captain Delano. 'Don Benito, I envy you such a friend; slave I cannot call him.'

As master and man stood before him, the black upholding the white, Captain Delano could not but bethink him of the beauty of that relationship which could present such a spectacle of fidelity on the one hand and confidence on the other. The scene was heightened by the contrast in dress, denoting their relative positions. The Spaniard wore a loose Chili jacket of dark velvet; white small-clothes and stockings, with silver buckles at the knee and instep; a high-crowned sombrero, of fine grass; a slender sword, silver mounted, hung from a knot in his sash – the last being an almost invariable adjunct, more for utility than ornament, of a South American gentleman's dress to this hour. Excepting when his occasional nervous contortions brought about disarray, there was a certain precision in his attire curiously at variance with the unsightly disorder around; especially in the belittered Ghetto, forward of the main-mast, wholly occupied by the blacks.

The servant wore nothing but wide trowsers, apparently, from their coarseness and patches, made out of some old topsail; they were clean, and confined at the waist by a bit of unstranded rope, which, with his composed, deprecatory air at times, made him look something like a begging friar of St Francis.

However unsuitable for the time and place, at least in the blunt-thinking American's eyes, and however strangely surviving in the midst of all his afflictions, the toilette of Don Benito might not, in fashion at least, have gone beyond the style of the day among South Americans of his class. Though on the present voyage sailing from Buenos Ayres, he had avowed himself a native and resident of Chili, whose inhabitants had not so generally adopted the plain coat and once plebeian pantaloons; but, with a becoming modification, adhered to their provincial costume, picturesque as any in the world. Still, relatively to the pale history of the voyage, and his own pale face, there seemed something so incongruous in the Spaniard's apparel, as almost to suggest the image of an invalid courtier tottering about London streets in the time of the plague.

The portion of the narrative which, perhaps, most excited interest, as well as some surprise, considering the latitudes in question, was the long calms spoken of, and more particularly the ship's so long drifting about. Without communicating the opinion, of course, the American could not but impute at least part of the detentions both to clumsy seamanship and faulty navigation. Eying Don Benito's small, yellow hands, he easily inferred that the young captain had not got into command at the hawse-hole, but the cabin-window; and if so, why wonder at incompetence, in youth, sickness, and gentility united?

But drowning criticism in compassion, after a fresh repetition of his sympathies, Captain Delano, having heard out his story, not only engaged, as in the first place, to see Don Benito and his people supplied in their immediate bodily needs, but, also, now further promised to assist him in procuring a large permanent supply of water, as well as some sails and rigging; and, though it would involve no small embarrassment to himself, yet he would spare three of his best seamen for temporary deck officers; so that without delay the ship might proceed to Conception, there fully to refit for Lima, her destined port.

Such generosity was not without its effect, even upon the invalid. His face lighted up; eager and hectic, he met the honest glance of his visitor. With gratitude he seemed overcome.

'This excitement is bad for master,' whispered the servant, taking his arm, and with soothing words gently drawing him aside.

When Don Benito returned, the American was pained to observe that his hopefulness, like the sudden kindling in his cheek, was but febrile and transient.

Ere long, with a joyless mien, looking up towards the poop, the host invited his guest to accompany him there, for the benefit of what little breath of wind might be stirring.

As, during the telling of the story, Captain Delano had once or twice started at the occasional cymballing of the hatchet-polishers, wondering why such an interruption should be allowed, especially in that part of the ship, and in the ears of an invalid; and moreover, as the hatchets had anything but an attractive look, and the handlers of them still less so, it was therefore, to tell the truth, not without some lurking reluctance, or even shrinking, it may be, that Captain Delano, with apparent complaisance, acquiesced in his host's invitation. The more so, since, with an untimely caprice of punctilio, rendered distressing by his cadaverous aspect, Don Benito, with Castilian bows, solemnly insisted upon his guest's preceding him up the ladder leading to the elevation; where, one on each side of the last step, sat for armorial supporters and sentries two of the ominous file. Gingerly enough stepped good Captain Delano between them, and in the instant of leaving them behind, like one running the gauntlet, he felt an apprehensive twitch in the calves of his legs.

But when, facing about, he saw the whole file, like so many organ-grinders, still stupidly intent on their work, unmindful of everything beside, he could not but smile at his late fidgety panic.

Presently, while standing with his host, looking forward upon the decks below, he was struck by one of those instances of insubordination previously alluded to. Three black boys, with two Spanish boys, were sitting together on the hatches, scraping a rude wooden platter, in which some scanty mess had recently been cooked. Suddenly, one of the black boys, enraged at a word dropped by one of his white companions, seized the knife, and, though called to forbear by one of the oakum-pickers, struck the lad over the head, inflicting a gash from which blood flowed.

In amazement, Captain Delano inquired what this meant. To which the pale Don Benito dully muttered, that it was merely the sport of the lad.

'Pretty serious sport, truly,' rejoined Captain Delano. 'Had such a thing happened on board the *Bachelor's Delight*, instant punishment would have followed.'

At these words the Spaniard turned upon the American one of his sudden, staring, half-lunatic looks; then, relapsing into his torpor, answered, 'Doubtless, doubtless, Señor.'

Is it, thought Captain Delano, that this hapless man is one of those paper captains I've known, who by policy wink at what by power they cannot put down? I know no sadder sight than a commander who has little of command but the name.

'I should think, Don Benito,' he now said, glancing towards the oakum-picker who had sought to interfere with the boys, 'that you would find it advantageous to keep all your blacks employed, especially the younger ones, no matter at what useless task, and no matter what happens to the ship. Why, even with my little band, I find such a course indispensable. I once kept a crew on my quarter-deck thrumming mats for my cabin, when, for three days, I had given up my ship – mats, men, and all – for a speedy loss, owing to the violence of a gale, in which we could do nothing but helplessly drive before it.'

'Doubtless, doubtless,' murmured Don Benito.

'But,' continued Captain Delano, again glancing upon the oakum-pickers and then at the hatchet-polishers, near by, 'I see you keep some, at least, of your host employed.'

'Yes,' was again the vacant response.

'Those old men there, shaking their pows from their pulpits,' continued Captain Delano, pointing to the oakum-pickers, 'seem to act the part of old dominies to the rest, little heeded as their admonitions are at times. Is this voluntary on their part, Don Benito, or have you appointed them shepherds to your flock of black sheep?'

'What posts they fill, I appointed them,' rejoined the Spaniard, in an acrid tone, as if resenting some supposed satiric reflection.

'And these others, these Ashantee conjurors here,' continued Captain Delano, rather uneasily eyeing the brandished steel of the hatchet-polishers, where, in spots, it had been brought to a shine, 'this seems a curious business they are at, Don Benito?'

'In the gales we met,' answered the Spaniard, 'what of our general cargo was not thrown overboard was much damaged by the brine. Since coming into calm weather, I have had several cases of knives and hatchets daily brought up for overhauling and cleaning.'

'A prudent idea, Don Benito. You are part owner of ship and cargo, I presume; but none of the slaves, perhaps?'

'I am owner of all you see,' impatiently returned Don Benito, 'except the main company of blacks, who belonged to my late friend, Alexandro Aranda.'

As he mentioned this name, his air was heart-broken; his knees shook; his servant supported him.

Thinking he divined the cause of such unusual emotion, to confirm his surmise, Captain Delano, after a pause, said: 'And may I ask, Don Benito, whether – since awhile ago you spoke of some cabin passengers – the friend, whose loss so afflicts you, at the outset of the voyage accompanied his blacks?'

'Yes.'

'But died of the fever?'

'Died of the fever. Oh, could I but –'

Again quivering, the Spaniard paused.

'Pardon me,' said Captain Delano, lowly, 'but I think that, by a sympathetic experience, I conjecture, Don Benito, what it is that gives the keener edge to your grief. It was once my hard fortune to lose, at sea, a dear friend, my own brother, then supercargo. Assured of the welfare of his spirit, its departure I could have borne like a man; but that honest eye, that honest hand – both of which had so often met mine – and that warm heart; all, all – like scraps to the dogs – to throw all to the sharks! It was then I vowed never to have for fellow-voyager a man I loved, unless, unbeknown to him, I had provided every requisite, in case of a fatality, for embalming his mortal part for interment on shore. Were your friend's remains now on board this ship, Don Benito, not thus strangely would the mention of his name affect you.'

'On board this ship?' echoed the Spaniard. Then, with horrified gestures, as directed against some spectre, he unconsciously fell into the ready arms of his attendant, who, with a silent appeal toward Captain Delano, seemed beseeching him not again to broach a theme so unspeakably distressing to his master.

This poor fellow now, thought the pained American, is the victim of that sad superstition which associates goblins with the deserted body of man, as ghosts with an abandoned house. How unlike are we made! What to me, in like case, would have been a solemn satisfaction, the bare suggestion, even, terrifies the Spaniard into this trance. Poor Alexandro Aranda! what would you say could you here see your friend – who, on former voyages, when you, for months, were left behind, has, I dare say, often longed, and longed, for one peep at you – now transported with terror at the least thought of having you anyway nigh him.

At this moment, with a dreary grave-yard toll, betokening a flaw, the ship's forecastle bell, smote by one of the grizzled oakum-pickers, proclaimed ten o'clock, through the leaden calm; when Captain Delano's attention was caught by the moving figure of a gigantic black, emerging from the general crowd below, and slowly advancing towards the elevated poop. An iron collar was about his neck, from which depended a chain, thrice wound round his body; the terminating links padlocked together at a broad band of iron, his girdle.

'How like a mute Atufal moves,' murmured the servant.

The black mounted the steps of the poop, and, like a brave prisoner, brought up to receive sentence, stood in unquailing muteness before Don Benito, now recovered from his attack.

At the first glimpse of his approach, Don Benito had started, a resentful shadow swept over his face; and, as with the sudden memory of bootless rage, his white lips glued together.

This is some mulish mutineer, thought Captain Delano, surveying, not without a mixture of admiration, the colossal form of the negro.

'See, he waits your question, master,' said the servant.

Thus reminded, Don Bento, nervously averting his glance, as if shunning, by anticipation, some rebellious response, in a disconcerted voice, thus spoke:—

'Atufal, will you ask my pardon, now?'

The black was silent.

'Again, master,' murmured the servant, with bitter upbraiding eyeing his countryman, 'Again, master; he will bend to master yet.'

'Answer,' said Don Benito, still averting his glance, 'say but the one word, *pardon*, and your chains shall be off.'

Upon this, the black, slowly raising both arms, let them lifelessly fall, his links clanking, his head bowed; as much as to say, 'no, I am content.'

'Go,' said Don Benito, with inkept and unknown emotion.

Deliberately as he had come, the black obeyed.

'Excuse me, Don Benito,' said Captain Delano, 'but this scene surprises me; what means it, pray?'

'It means that that negro alone, of all the band, has given me peculiar cause of offense, I have put him in chains; I —'

Here he paused; his hand to his head, as if there were a swimming there, or a sudden bewilderment of memory had come over him; but meeting his servant's kindly glance seemed reassured, and proceeded:—

'I could not scourge such a form. But I told him he must ask my pardon. As yet he has not. At my command, every two hours he stands before me.'

'And how long has this been?'

'Some sixty days.'

'And obedient in all else? And respectful?'

'Yes.'

'Upon my conscience, then,' exclaimed Captain Delano, impulsively, 'he has a royal spirit in him, this fellow.'

'He may have some right to it,' bitterly returned Don Benito, 'he says he was king in his own land.'

'Yes,' said the servant, entering a word, 'those slits in Atufal's ears once held wedges of gold; but poor Babo here, in his own land, was only a poor slave; a black man's slave was Babo, who now is the white's.'

Somewhat annoyed by the conversational familiarities Captain Delano turned curiously upon the attendant, then glanced inquiringly at his master; but as if long wonted to these little informalities, neither master nor man seemed to understand him.

'What, pray, was Atufal's offense, Don Benito?' asked Captain Delano; 'if it was not something very serious, take a fool's advice, and, in view of his general docility, as well as in some natural respect for his spirit, remit him his penalty.'

'No, no, master never will do that,' here murmured the servant to himself, 'proud Atufal must first ask master's pardon. The slave there carries the padlock, but master here carries the key.'

His attention thus directed, Captain Delano now noticed for the first, that, suspended by a slender silken cord, from Don Benito's neck, hung a key. At once, from the servant's muttered syllables, divining the key's purpose, he smiled and said:– 'So, Don Benito – padlock and key – significant symbols, truly.'

Biting his lip, Don Benito faltered.

Though the remark of Captain Delano, a man of such native simplicity as to be incapable of satire or irony, had been dropped in playful allusion to the Spaniard's singularly evidenced lordship over the black; yet the hypochondriac seemed some way to have taken it as a malicious reflection upon his confessed inability thus far to break down, at least, on a verbal summons, the entrenched will of the slave. Deploring this supposed misconception, yet despairing of correcting it, Captain Delano shifted the subject; but finding his companion more than ever withdrawn, as if still sourly digesting the lees of the presumed affront abovementioned, by-and-by Captain Delano likewise became less talkative, oppressed, against his own will, by what seemed the secret vindictiveness of the morbidly sensitive Spaniard. But the good sailor, himself of a quite contrary disposition, refrained, on his part, alike from the appearance as from the feeling of resentment, and if silent, was only so from contagion.

Presently the Spaniard, assisted by his servant, somewhat discourteously crossed over from his guest; a procedure which, sensibly enough, might have been allowed to pass for idle caprice of ill-humor, had not the master and man, lingering round the corner of the elevated skylight, began whispering together in low voices. This was unpleasing. And more; the moody air of the Spaniard, which at times had not been without a sort of valetudinarian stateliness, now seemed anything but dignified; while the menial familiarity of the servant lost its original charm of simple-hearted attachment.

In his embarrassment, the visitor turned his face to the other side of the ship. By so doing, his glance accidentally fell on a young Spanish sailor, a coil of rope in his hand, just stepped from the deck to the first round of the mizzen-rigging. Perhaps the man would not have been particularly noticed, were it not that, during his ascent to one of the yards, he, with a sort of covert intentness, kept his eye fixed on Captain Delano, from whom, presently, it passed, as if by a natural sequence, to the two whisperers.

His own attention thus redirected to that quarter, Captain Delano gave a slight start. From something in Don Benito's manner just then, it seemed as if the visitor had, at least partly, been the subject of the withdrawn consultation going on – a conjecture as little agreeable to the guest as it was little flattering to the host.

The singular alternations of courtesy and ill-breeding in the Spanish captain were unaccountable, except on one of two suppositions – innocent lunacy, or wicked imposture.

But the first idea, though it might naturally have occurred to an indifferent observer, and, in some respect, had not hitherto been wholly a stranger to Captain Delano's mind, yet, now that, in an incipient way, he began to regard the stranger's conduct something in the light of an intentional affront, of course the idea of lunacy was virtually vacated. But if not a lunatic, what then? Under the circumstances, would a gentleman, nay, any honest boor, act the part now acted by his host? The man was an imposter. Some low-born adventurer, masquerading as an oceanic grandee; yet so ignorant of the first requisites of mere gentlemanhood as to be betrayed into the present remarkable indecorum. That strange ceremoniousness, too, at other times evinced, seemed not uncharacteristic of one playing a part above his real level. Benito Cereno – Don Benito Cereno – a sounding name. One, too, at that period, not unknown, in the surname, to supercargoes and sea captains trading along the Spanish Main, as belonging to one of the most enterprising and extensive mercantile families in all those provinces; several members of it having titles; a sort of Castilian Rothschild, with a noble brother, or cousin, in every great trading town of South America. The alleged Don Benito was in early manhood, about twenty-nine or thirty. To assume a sort of roving cadetship in the maritime affairs of such a house, what more likely scheme for a young knave of talent and spirit? But the Spaniard was a pale invalid. Never mind. For even to the degree of simulating mortal disease, the craft of some tricksters had been known to attain. To think that, under the aspect of infantile weakness, the most savage energies might be couched – those velvets of the Spaniard but the silky paw to his fangs.

From no train of thought did these fancies come; not from within, but from without; suddenly, too, and in one throng, like hoar frost; yet as soon to vanish as the mild sun of Captain Delano's good-nature regained its meridian.

Glancing over once more towards his host – whose side-face, revealed above the skylight, was now turned towards him – he was struck by the profile, whose clearness of cut was refined by the thinness, incident to ill-health, as well as ennobled about the chin by the beard. Away with suspicion. He was a true off-shoot of a true hidalgo Cereno.

[240]

Relieved by these and other better thoughts, the visitor, lightly humming a tune, now began indifferently pacing the poop, so as not to betray to Don Benito that he had at all mistrusted incivility, much less duplicity; for such mistrust would yet be proved illusory, and by the event; though, for the present, the circumstance which had provoked that distrust remained unexplained. But when that little mystery should have been cleared up, Captain Delano thought he might extremely regret it, did he allow Don Benito to become aware that he had indulged in ungenerous surmises. In short, to the Spaniard's black-letter text, it was best, for awhile, to leave open margin.

Presently, his pale face twitching and overcast, the Spaniard, still supported by his attendant, moved over towards his guest, when, with even more than his usual embarrassment, and a strange sort of intriguing intonation in his husky whisper, the following conversation began:—

'Señor, may I ask how long you have lain at this isle?'

'Oh, but a day or two, Don Benito.'

'And from what port are you last?'

'Canton.'

'And there, Señor, you exchanged your sealskins for teas and silks, I think you said?'

'Yes. Silks, mostly.'

'And the balance you took in specie, perhaps?'

Captain Delano, fidgeting a little, answered—

'Yes; some silver; not a very great deal, though.'

'Ah—well. May I ask how many men have you, Señor?'

Captain Delano slightly startled, but answered—

'About five-and-twenty, all told.'

'And at present, Señor, all on board, I suppose?'

'All on board, Don Benito,' replied the Captain, now with satisfaction.

'And will be to-night, Señor?'

At this last question, following so many pertinacious ones, for the soul of him, Captain Delano could not but look very earnestly at the questioner, who, instead of meeting the glance, with every token of craven discomposure dropped his eyes to the deck; presenting an unworthy contrast to his servant, who, just then, was kneeling at his feet, adjusting a loose shoe-buckle; his disengaged face meantime, with humble curiosity, turned openly up into his master's downcast one.

The Spaniard, still with a guilty shuffle, repeated his question:

'And – and will be to-night, Señor?'

'Yes, for aught I know,' returned Captain Delano – 'but nay,' rallying himself into fearless truth, 'some of them talked of going off on another fishing party about midnight.'

'Your ships generally go – go more or less armed, I believe, Señor?'

'Oh, a six-pounder or two, in case of emergency,' was the intrepidly indifferent reply, 'with a small stock of muskets, sealing-spears, and cutlasses, you know.'

As he thus responded, Captain Delano again glanced at Don Benito, but the latter's eyes were averted; while abruptly and awkwardly shifting the subject, he made some peevish allusion to the calm, and then, without apology, once more, with his attendant, withdrew to the opposite bulwarks, where the whispering was resumed.

At this moment, and ere Captain Delano could cast a cool thought upon what had just passed, the young Spanish sailor, before mentioned, was seen descending from the rigging. In act of stooping over to spring inboard to the deck, his voluminous, unconfined frock, or shirt, of coarse woolen, much spotted with tar, opened out far down the chest revealing a soiled under garment of what seemed the finest linen, edged, about the neck, with a narrow blue ribbon, sadly faded and worn. At this moment the young sailor's eye was again fixed on the whisperers, and Captain Delano thought he observed a lurking significance in it, as if silent signs, of some Freemason sort, had that instant been interchanged.

This once more impelled his own glance in the direction of Don Benito, and, as before, he could not but infer that himself formed the subject of the conference. He paused. The sound of the hatchet-polishing fell on his ears. He cast another swift side-look at the two. They had the air of conspirators. In connection with the late questionings, and the incident of the young sailor, these things now begat such return of involuntary suspicion, that the singular guilelessness of the American could not endure it. Plucking up a gay and humorous expression, he crossed over to the two rapidly, saying:—'Ha, Don Benito, your black here seems high in your trust; a sort of privy-counselor, in fact.'

Upon this, the servant looked up with a good-natured grin, but the master started as from a venomous bite. It was a moment or two before the Spaniard sufficiently recovered himself to reply; which he did, at last, with cold constraint: – 'Yes, Señor, I have trust in Babo.'

Here Babo, changing his previous grin of mere animal humor into an intelligent smile, not ungratefully eyed his master.

Finding that the Spaniard now stood silent and reserved, as if involuntarily, or purposely giving hint that his guest's proximity was inconvenient just then, Captain Delano, unwilling to appear uncivil even to incivility itself, made some trivial remark and moved off; again and again turning over in his mind the mysterious demeanor of Don Benito Cereno.

He had descended from the poop, and, wrapped in thought, was passing near a dark hatchway, leading down into the steerage, when, perceiving motion there, he looked to see what moved. The same instant there was a sparkle in the shadowy hatchway, and he saw one of the Spanish sailors, prowling there, hurriedly placing his hand in the bosom of his frock, as if hiding something. Before the man could have been certain who it was that was passing, he slunk below out of sight. But enough was seen of him to make it sure that he was the same young sailor before noticed in the rigging.

What was that which so sparkled? thought Captain Delano. It was no lamp – no match – no live coal. Could it have been a jewel? But how come sailors with jewels? – or with silk-trimmed under-shirts either? Has he been robbing the trunks of the dead cabin-passengers? But if so, he would hardly wear one of the stolen articles on board ship here. Ah, ah – if, now, that was, indeed, a secret sign I saw passing between this suspicious fellow and his captain awhile since; if I could only be certain that, in my uneasiness, my senses did not deceive me, then –

Here, passing from one suspicious thing to another, his mind revolved the strange questions put to him concerning his ship.

By a curious coincidence, as each point was recalled, the black wizards of Ashantee would strike up with their hatchets, as in ominous comments on the white stranger's thoughts. Pressed by such enigmas and portents, it would have been almost against nature, had not, even into the least distrustful heart, some ugly misgivings obtruded.

Observing the ship, now helplessly fallen into a current, with enchanted sails, drifting with increased rapidity seaward; and noting that, from a lately intercepted projection of the land, the sealer was hidden, the stout mariner began to quake at thoughts which he barely durst confess to himself. Above all, he began to feel a ghostly dread of Don Benito. And yet, when he roused himself, dilated his chest, felt himself strong on his legs, and coolly considered it – what did all these phantoms amount to?

Had the Spaniard any sinister scheme, it must have reference not so much to him (Captain Delano) as to his ship (the *Bachelor's Delight*). Hence the present drifting away of the one ship from the other, instead of favoring any such possible scheme, was, for the time, at least, opposed to it. Clearly any suspicion, combining such contradictions, must need be delusive. Beside, was it not absurd to think of a vessel in distress – a vessel by sickness almost dismanned of her crew – a vessel whose inmates were parched for water – was it not a thousand times absurd that such a craft should, at present, be of a piratical character; or her commander, either for himself or those under him, cherish any desire but for speedy relief and refreshment? But then, might not general distress, and thirst in particular, be affected? And might not that same undiminished Spanish crew, alleged to have perished off to a remnant, be at that very moment lurking in the hold? On heart-broken pretense of entreating a cup of cold water, fiends in human form had got into lonely dwellings, nor retired until a dark deed had been done. And among the Malay pirates, it was no unusual thing to lure ships after them into their treacherous harbors, or entice boarders from a declared enemy at sea, by the spectacle of thinly manned or vacant decks, beneath which prowled a hundred spears with yellow arms ready to upthrust them through the mats. Not that Captain Delano had entirely credited such things. He had heard of them – and now, as stories, they recurred. The present destination of the ship was the anchorage. There she would be near his own vessel. Upon gaining that vicinity, might not the *San Dominick*, like a slumbering volcano, suddenly let loose energies now hid?

He recalled the Spaniard's manner while telling his story. There was a gloomy hesitancy and subterfuge about it. It was just the manner of one making up his tale for evil purposes, as he goes. But if that story was not true, what was the truth? That the ship had unlawfully come into the Spaniard's possession? But in many of its details, especially in reference to the more calamitous parts, such as the fatalities among the seamen, the consequent prolonged beating about, the past sufferings from obstinate calms, and still continued suffering from thirst; in all these points, as well as others, Don Benito's story had corroborated not only the wailing ejaculations of the indiscriminate multitude, white and black, but likewise – what seemed impossible to be counterfeit – by the very expression and play of every human feature, which Captain Delano saw. If Don Benito's story was, throughout, an invention, then every soul on board, down to the youngest negress, was his carefully drilled recruit in the plot: an incredible inference. And yet, if there was ground for mistrusting his veracity, that inference was a legitimate one.

But those questions of the Spaniard. There, indeed, one might pause. Did they not seem put with much the same object with which the burglar or assassin, by day-time, reconnoitres the walls of a house? But, with ill purposes, to solicit such information openly of the chief person endangered, and so, in effect, setting him on his guard; how unlikely a procedure was that? Absurd, then, to suppose that those questions had been prompted by evil designs. Thus, the same conduct, which, in this instance, had raised the alarm, served to dispel it. In short, scarce any suspicion or uneasiness, however apparently reasonable at the time, which was not now, with equal apparent reason, dismissed.

At last he began to laugh at his former forebodings; and laugh at the strange ship for, in its aspect, someway siding with them, as it were; and laugh, too, at the odd-looking blacks, particularly those old scissors-grinders, the Ashantees; and those bed-ridden old knitting women, the oakum-pickers; and almost at the dark Spaniard himself, the central hobgoblin of all.

For the rest, whatever in a serious way seemed enigmatical, was now good-naturedly explained away by the thought that, for the most part, the poor invalid scarcely knew what he was about; either sulking in black vapors, or putting idle questions without sense or object. Evidently, for the present, the man was not fit to be intrusted with the ship. On some benevolent plea withdrawing the command from him, Captain Delano would yet have to send her to Conception, in charge of his second mate, a worthy person and good navigator – a plan not more convenient for the *San Dominick* than for Don Benito; for, relieved from all anxiety, keeping wholly to his cabin, the sick man, under the good nursing of his servant, would, probably, by the end of the passage, be in a measure restored to health, and with that he should also be restored to authority.

Such were the American's thoughts. They were tranquilizing. There was a difference between the idea of Don

Benito's darkly pre-ordaining Captain Delano's fate, and Captain Delano's lightly arranging Don Benito's. Nevertheless, it was not without something of relief that the good seaman presently perceived his whale-boat in the distance. Its absence had been prolonged by unexpected detention at the sealer's side, as well as its returning trip lengthened by the continual recession of the goal.

The advancing speck was observed by the blacks. Their shouts attracted the attention of Don Benito, who, with a return of courtesy, approaching Captain Delano, expressed satisfaction at the coming of some supplies, slight and temporary as they must necessarily prove.

Captain Delano responded; but while doing so, his attention was drawn to something passing on the deck below: among the crowd climbing the landward bulwarks, anxiously watching the coming boat, two blacks, to all appearances accidentally incommoded by one of the sailors, violently pushed him aside, which the sailor somewhat resenting, they dashed him to the deck, despite the earnest cries of the oakum-pickers.

'Don Benito,' said Captain Delano quickly, 'do you see what is going on there? Look!'

But, seized by his cough, the Spaniard staggered, with both hands to his face, on the point of falling. Captain Delano would have supported him, but the servant was more alert, who, with one hand sustaining his master, with the other applied the cordial. Don Benito restored, the black withdrew his support, slipping aside a little, but dutifully remaining within call of a whisper. Such discretion was here evinced as quite wiped away, in the visitor's eyes, any blemish of impropriety which might have attached to the attendant, from the indecorous conferences before mentioned; showing, too, that if the servant were to blame, it might be more the master's fault than his own, since, when left to himself, he could conduct thus well.

His glance called away from the spectacle of disorder to the more pleasing one before him, Captain Delano could not avoid again congratulating his host upon possessing such a servant, who, though perhaps a little too forward now and then, must upon the whole be invaluable to one in the invalid's situation.

'Tell me, Don Benito,' he added, with a smile – 'I should like to have your man here, myself – what will you take for him? Would fifty doubloons be any object?'

'Master wouldn't part with Babo for a thousand doubloons,' murmured the black, overhearing the offer, and taking it in earnest, and, with the strange vanity of a faithful slave, appreciated by his master, scorning to hear so paltry a valuation put upon him by a stranger. But Don Benito, apparently hardly yet completely restored, and again interrupted by his cough, made but some broken reply.

Soon his physical distress became so great, affecting his mind, too, apparently, that, as if to screen the sad spectacle, the servant gently conducted his master below.

Left to himself, the American, to while away the time till his boat should arrive, would have pleasantly accosted some one of the few Spanish seamen he saw; but recalling something that Don Benito had said touching their ill conduct, he refrained; as a shipmaster indisposed to countenance cowardice or unfaithfulness in seamen.

While, with these thoughts, standing with eye directed forward towards that handful of sailors, suddenly he thought that one or two of them returned the glance and with a sort of meaning. He rubbed his eyes, and looked again; but again seemed to see the same thing. Under a new form, but more obscure than any previous one, the old suspicions recurred, but, in the absence of Don Benito, with less of panic than before. Despite the bad account given of the sailors, Captain Delano resolved forthwith to accost one of them. Descending the poop, he made his way through the blacks, his movement drawing a queer cry from the oakum-pickers, prompted by whom, the negroes, twitching each other aside, divided before him; but, as if curious to see what was the object of this deliberate visit to their Ghetto, closing in behind, in tolerable order, followed the white stranger up. His progress thus proclaimed as by mounted kings-at-arms, and escorted as by a Caffre guard of honor, Captain Delano, assuming a good-humored, off-handed air, continued to advance; now and then saying a blithe word to the negroes, and his eye curiously surveying the white faces, here and there sparsely mixed in with the blacks, like stray white pawns venturously involved in the ranks of the chess-men opposed.

While thinking which of them to select for his purpose, he chanced to observe a sailor seated on the deck engaged in tarring the strap of a large block, a circle of blacks squatted round him inquisitively eyeing the process.

The mean employment of the man was in contrast with something superior in his figure. His hand, black with continually thrusting it into the tar-pot held for him by a negro, seemed not naturally allied to his face, a face which would have been a very fine one but for its haggardness. Whether this haggardness had aught to do with criminality, could not be determined; since, as intense heat and cold, though unlike, produce like sensations, so innocence and guilt, when, through casual association with mental pain, stamping any visible impress, use one seal – a hacked one.

Not again that this reflection occurred to Captain Delano at the time, charitable man as he was. Rather another idea. Because observing so singular a haggardness combined with a dark eye, averted as in trouble and shame, and then again recalling Don Benito's confessed ill opinion of his crew, insensibly he was operated upon by certain general notions which, while disconnecting pain and abashment from virtue, invariably link them with vice.

If, indeed, there be any wickedness on board this ship, thought Captain Delano, be sure that man there has fouled his hand in it, even as now he fouls it in the pitch. I don't like to accost him. I will speak to this other, this old Jack here on the windlass.

He advanced to an old Barcelona tar, in ragged red breeches and dirty night-cap, cheeks trenched and bronzed, whiskers dense as thorn hedges. Seated between two sleepy-looking Africans, this mariner, like his younger shipmate, was employed upon some rigging – splicing a cable – the sleepy-looking blacks performing the inferior function of holding the outer parts of the ropes for him.

Upon Captain Delano's approach, the man at once hung his head below its previous level; the one necessary for business. It appeared as if he desired to be thought absorbed, with more than common fidelity, in his task. Being addressed, he glanced up, but with what seemed a furtive, diffident air, which sat strangely enough on his weather-beaten visage, much as if a grizzly bear, instead of growling and biting, should simper and cast sheep's eyes. He was asked several questions concerning the voyage – questions purposely referring to several particulars in Don Benito's narrative, not previously corroborated by those impulsive cries greeting the visitor on first coming on board. The questions were briefly answered, confirming all that remained to be confirmed of the story. The negroes about the windlass joined in with the old sailor; but, as they became talkative, he by degrees became mute, and at length quite glum, seemed morosely unwilling to answer more questions, and yet, all the while, this ursine air was somehow mixed with his sheepish one.

Despairing of getting into unembarrassed talk with such a centaur, Captain Delano, after glancing round for a more promising countenance, but seeing none, spoke pleasantly to the blacks to make way for him; and so, amid various grins and grimaces, returned to the poop, feeling a little strange at first, he could hardly tell why, but upon the whole with regained confidence in Benito Cereno.

How plainly, thought he, did that old whiskerando yonder betray a consciousness of ill desert. No doubt, when he saw me coming, he dreaded lest I, apprised by his Captain of the crew's general misbehaviour, came with sharp words for him, and so down with his head. And yet – and yet, now that I think of it, that very old fellow, if I err not, was one of those who seemed so earnestly eyeing me here awhile since. Ah, these currents spin one's head round almost as much as they do the ship. Ha, there now's a pleasant sort of sunny sight; quite sociable, too.

His attention had been drawn to a slumbering negress, partly disclosed through the lace-work of some rigging, lying, with youthful limbs carelessly disposed, under the lee of the bulwarks, like a doe in the shade of a woodland rock. Sprawling at her lapped breasts, was her wide-awake fawn, stark naked, its black little body half lifted from the deck, crosswise with its dam's; its hands, like two paws, clambering upon her; its mouth and nose ineffectually rooting to get at the mark; and meantime giving a vexatious half-grunt, blending with the composed snore of the negress.

The uncommon vigor of the child at length roused the mother. She started up, at a distance facing Captain Delano. But as if not at all concerned at the attitude in which she had been caught, delightedly she caught the child up, with maternal transports, covering it with kisses.

There's naked nature, now; pure tenderness and love, thought Captain Delano, well pleased.

This incident prompted him to remark the other negresses more particularly than before. He was gratified with their manners: like most uncivilized women, they seemed at once tender of heart and tough of constitution; equally ready to die for their infants or fight for them. Unsophisticated as leopardesses; loving as doves. Ah! thought Captain Delano, these, perhaps, are some of the very women whom Ledyard saw in Africa, and gave such a noble account of.

These natural sights somehow insensibly deepened his confidence and ease. At last he looked to see how his boat was getting on; but it was still pretty remote. He turned to see if Don Benito had returned; but he had not.

To change the scene, as well as to please himself with a leisurely observation of the coming boat, stepping over into the mizzen-chains, he clambered his way into the starboard quarter-gallery – one of those abandoned Venetian-looking water-balconies previously mentioned – retreats cut off from the deck. As his foot pressed the half-damp, half-dry sea-mosses matting the place, and a chance phantom cat's-paw – an islet of breeze, unheralded, unfollowed – as this ghostly cat's-paw came fanning his cheek; as his glance fell upon the row of small, round dead-lights – all closed like coppered eyes of the coffined – and the state-cabin door, once connecting with the gallery, even as the dead-lights had once looked out upon it, but now calked fast like a sarcophagus lid; and to a purple-black tarred-over panel, threshold, and post; and he bethought him of the time, when that state-cabin and this state-balcony had heard the voices of the Spanish king's officers, and the forms of the Lima viceroy's daughters had perhaps leaned where he stood – as these and other images flitted through his mind, as the cat's-paw through the calm, gradually he felt rising a dreamy inquietude, like that of one who alone on the prairie feels unrest from the repose of the noon.

He leaned against the carved balustrade, again looking off toward his boat; but found his eye falling upon the ribbon grass, trailing along the ship's water-line, straight as a border of green box; and parterres of sea-weed, broad ovals and crescents, floating nigh and far, with what seemed long formal alleys between, crossing the terraces of swells, and sweeping round as if leading to the grottoes below. And overhanging all was the balustrade by his arm, which, partly stained with pitch and partly embossed with moss, seemed the charred ruin of some summer-house in a grand garden long running to waste.

Trying to break one charm, he was but becharmed anew. Though upon the wide sea, he seemed in some far inland country; prisoner in some deserted château, left to stare at empty grounds, and peer out at vague roads, where never wagon or wayfarer passed.

But these enchantments were a little disenchanted as his eye fell on the corroded main-chains. Of an ancient style, massy and rusty in link, shackle and bolt, they seemed even more fit for the ship's present business than the one for which she had been built.

Presently he thought something moved nigh the chains. He rubbed his eyes, and looked hard. Groves of rigging were about the chains; and there, peering from behind a great stay, like an Indian from behind a hemlock, a Spanish sailor, a marlingspike in his hand, was seen, who made what seemed an imperfect gesture towards the balcony, but immediately, as if alarmed by some advancing step along the deck within, vanished into the recesses of the hempen forest, like a poacher.

What meant this? Something the man had sought to communicate, unbeknown to any one, even to his captain. Did the secret involve aught unfavorable to his captain? Were those previous misgivings of Captain Delano's about to be verified? Or, in his haunted mood at the moment, had some random, unintentional motion of the man, while busy with the stay, as if repairing it, been mistaken for a significant beckoning?

Not unbewildered, again he gazed off for his boat. But it was temporarily hidden by a rocky spur of the isle. As with some eagerness he bent forward, watching for the first shooting view of its beak, the balustrade gave way before him like charcoal. Had he not clutched an outreaching rope he would have fallen into the sea. The crash, though feeble, and the fall, though hollow, of the rotten fragments, must have been overheard. He glanced up. With sober curiosity peering down upon him was one of the old oakum-pickers, slipped from his perch to an outside boom; while below the old negro, and, invisible to him, reconnoitering from a port-hole like a fox from the mouth of its den, crouched the Spanish sailor again. From something suddenly suggested by the man's air, the mad idea now darted into Captain Delano's mind, that Don Benito's plea of indisposition, in withdrawing below, was but a pretense: that he was engaged there maturing his plot, of which the sailor, by some means gaining an inkling, had a mind to warn the stranger against; incited, it may be, by gratitude for a kind word on first boarding the ship. Was it from foreseeing some possible interference like this, that Don Benito had, before-

hand, given such a bad character of his sailors, while prais-
ing the negroes; though, indeed, the former seemed as
docile as the latter the contrary? The whites, too, by nature,
were the shrewder race. A man with some evil design, would
he not be likely to speak well of that stupidity which was
blind to his depravity, and malign that intelligence from
which it might not be hidden? Not unlikely, perhaps. But
if the whites had dark secrets concerning Don Benito, could
then Don Benito be any way in complicity with the blacks?
But they were too stupid. Besides, who ever heard of a
white so far a renegade as to apostatize from his very species
almost, by leaguing in against it with negroes? These difficulties recalled former ones. Lost in their mazes, Captain
Delano, who had now regained the deck, was uneasily advancing along it, when he observed a new face; an aged
sailor seated cross-legged near the main hatchway. His skin
was shrunk up with wrinkles like a pelican's empty pouch;
his hair frosted; his countenance grave and composed. His
hands were full of ropes, which he was working into a large
knot. Some blacks were about him obligingly dipping the
strands for him, here and there, as the exigencies of the
operation demanded.

Captain Delano crossed over to him, and stood in silence
surveying the knot; his mind, by a not uncongenial transition, passing from its own entanglements to those of the
hemp. For intricacy, such a knot he had never seen in an
American ship, nor indeed any other. The old man looked
like an Egyptian priest, making Gordian knots for the
temple of Ammon. The knot seemed a combination of
double-bowline-knot, treble-crown-knot, back-handed-well-
knot, knot-in-and-out-knot, and jamming-knot.

At last, puzzled to comprehend the meaning of such a
knot, Captain Delano addressed the knotter: –

'What are you knotting there, my man?'

'The knot,' was the brief reply, without looking up.

'So it seems; but what is it for?'

'For some one else to undo,' muttered back the old man,

plying his fingers harder than ever, the knot being now nearly completed.

While Captain Delano stood watching him, suddenly the old man threw the knot towards him, saying in broken English – the first heard in the ship – something to this effect: 'Undo it, cut it, quick.' It was said lowly, but with such condensation of rapidity, that the long, slow words in Spanish, which had preceded and followed, almost operated as covers to the brief English between.

For a moment, knot in hand, and knot in head, Captain Delano stood mute; while, without further heeding him, the old man was now intent upon other ropes. Presently there was a slight stir behind Captain Delano. Turning, he saw the chained negro, Atufal, standing quietly there. The next moment the old sailor rose, muttering, and, followed by his subordinate negroes, removed to the forward part of the ship, where in the crowd he disappeared.

An elderly negro, in a clout like an infant's, and with a pepper and salt head, and a kind of attorney air, now approached Captain Delano. In tolerable Spanish, and with a good-natured, knowing wink, he informed him that the old knotter was simple-witted, but harmless; often playing his odd tricks. The negro concluded by begging the knot, for of course the stranger would not care to be troubled with it. Unconsciously, it was handed to him. With a sort of congé, the negro received it, and, turning his back, ferreted into it like a detective custom-house officer after smuggled laces. Soon, with some African word, equivalent to pshaw, he tossed the knot overboard.

All this is very queer now, thought Captain Delano, with a qualmish sort of emotion; but, as one feeling incipient sea-sickness, he strove, by ignoring the symptoms, to get rid of the malady. Once more he looked off for his boat. To his delight, it was now again in view, leaving the rocky spur astern.

The sensation here experienced, after at first relieving his uneasiness, with unforeseen efficacy soon began to remove it. The less distant sight of that well-known boat – showing it, not as before, half blended with the haze, but with out-line defined, so that its individuality, like a man's, was manifest; that boat, *Rover* by name, which, though now in strange seas, had often pressed the beach of Captain Delano's home, and, brought to its threshold for repairs, had familiarly lain there, as a Newfoundland dog; the sight of that household boat evoked a thousand trustful associa-tions, which, contrasted with previous suspicions, filled him not only with lightsome confidence, but somehow with half humorous self-reproaches at his former lack of it.

'What, I, Amasa Delano – Jack of the Beach, as they called me when a lad – I, Amasa; the same that, duck-satchel in hand, used to paddle along the water-side to the school-house made from the old hulk – I, little Jack of the Beach, that used to go berrying with cousin Nat and the rest; I to be murdered here at the ends of the earth, on board a haunted pirate-ship by a horrible Spaniard? Too nonsensical to think of! Who would murder Amasa Delano? His conscience is clean. There is some one above. Fie, fie, Jack of the Beach! you are a child indeed; a child of the second childhood, old boy; you are beginning to dote and drule, I'm afraid.'

Light of heart and foot, he stepped aft, and there was met by Don Benito's servant, who, with a pleasing expression, responsive to his own present feelings, informed him that his master had recovered from the effects of his coughing fit, and had just ordered him to go present his compliments to his good guest, Don Amasa, and say that he (Don Benito) would soon have the happiness to rejoin him.

There now, do you mark that? again thought Captain Delano, walking the poop. What a donkey I was. This kind gentleman who here sends me his kind compliments, he, but ten minutes ago, dark-lantern in hand, was dodging round some old grind-stone in the hold, sharpening a hatchet for me, I thought. Well, well; these long calms have a morbid effect on the mind, I've often heard, though I never believed it before. Ha! glancing towards the boat; there's *Rover*; good dog; a white bone in her mouth. A pretty big bone though, seems to me. – What? Yes, she has fallen afoul of the bubbling tide-rip there. It sets her the other way, too, for the time. Patience.

It was now about noon, though, from the grayness of everything, it seemed to be getting towards dusk.

The calm was confirmed. In the far distance, away from the influence of land, the leaden ocean seemed laid out and leaded up, its course finished, soul gone, defunct. But the current from landward, where the ship was, increased; silently sweeping her further and further towards the tranced waters beyond.

Still, from his knowledge of those latitudes, cherishing hopes of a breeze, and a fair and fresh one, at any moment, Captain Delano, despite present prospects, buoyantly counted upon bringing the *San Dominick* safely to anchor ere night. The distance swept over was nothing; since, with a good wind, ten minutes' sailing would retrace more than sixty minutes' drifting. Meantime, one moment turning to mark *Rover* fighting the tide-rip, and the next to see Don Benito approaching, he continued walking the poop.

Gradually he felt a vexation arising from the delay of his boat; this soon merged into uneasiness; and at last – his eye falling continually, as from a stage-box into the pit, upon the strange crowd before and below him, and, by-and-by, recognizing there the face – now composed to in-difference – of the Spanish sailor who had seemed to beckon from the main-chains – something of his old trepidations returned.

Ah, thought he – gravely enough – this is like the ague: because it went off, it follows not that it won't come back.

Though ashamed of the relapse, he could not altogether subdue it; and so, exerting his good-nature to the utmost, insensibly he came to a compromise.

Yes, this is a strange craft; a strange history, too, and strange folks on board. But – nothing more.

By way of keeping his mind out of mischief till the boat should arrive, he tried to occupy it with turning over and over, in a purely speculative sort of way, some lesser peculiarities of the captain and crew. Among others, four curious points recurred:

First, the affair of the Spanish lad assailed with a knife by the slave boy; an act winked at by Don Benito. Second, the tyranny in Don Benito's treatment of Atufal, the black; as if a child should lead a bull of the Nile by the ring in his nose. Third, the trampling of the sailor by the two negroes; a piece of insolence passed over without so much as a reprimand. Fourth, the cringing submission to their master of all the ship's underlings, mostly blacks; as if by the least inadvertence they feared to draw down his despotic displeasure.

Coupling these points, they seemed somewhat contradictory. But what then, thought Captain Delano, glancing towards his now nearing boat – what then? Why, Don Benito is a very capricious commander. But he is not the first of the sort I have seen; though it's true he rather exceeds any other. But as a nation – continued he in his reveries – these Spaniards are all an odd set; the very word Spaniard has a curious, conspirator, Guy-Fawkish twang to it. And yet, I dare say, Spaniards in the main are as good folks as any in Duxbury, Massachusetts. Ah good! At last *Rover* has come.

As, with its welcome freight, the boat touched the side, the oakum-pickers, with venerable gestures, sought to restrain the blacks, who, at the sight of three gurried water-casks in its bottom, and a pile of wilted pumpkins in its bow, hung over the bulwarks in disorderly raptures.

Don Benito, with his servant, now appeared; his coming, perhaps, hastened by hearing the noise. Of him Captain Delano sought permission to serve out the water, so that all might share alike, and none injure themselves by unfair excess. But sensible, and, on Don Benito's account, kind as this offer was, it was received with what seemed impatience; as if aware that he lacked energy as a commander, Don Benito, with the true jealousy of weakness, resented as an affront any interference. So, at least, Captain Delano inferred.

In another moment the casks were being hoisted in, when

some of the eager negroes accidentally jostled Captain Delano, where he stood by the gangway; so that, unmindful of Don Benito, yielding to the impulse of the moment, with good-natured authority he bade the blacks stand back; to enforce his words making use of a half-mirthful, half-menacing gesture. Instantly the blacks paused, just where they were, each negro and negress suspended in his or her posture, exactly as the word had found them – for a few seconds continuing so – while, as between the responsive posts of a telegraph, an unknown syllable ran from man to man among the perched oakum-pickers. While the visitor's attention was fixed by this scene, suddenly the hatchet-polishers half rose, and a rapid cry came from Don Benito.

Thinking that at the signal of the Spaniard he was about to be massacred, Captain Delano would have sprung for his boat, but paused, as the oakum-pickers, dropping down into the crowd with earnest exclamations, forced every white and every negro back, at the same moment, with gestures friendly and familiar, almost jocose, bidding him, in substance, not be a fool. Simultaneously the hatchet-polishers resumed their seats, quietly as so many tailors, and at once, as if nothing had happened, the work of hoisting in the casks was resumed, whites and blacks singing at the tackle.

Captain Delano glanced towards Don Benito. As he saw his meagre form in the act of recovering itself from reclining in the servant's arms, into which the agitated invalid had fallen, he could not but marvel at the panic by which himself had been surprised, on the darting supposition that such a commander, who, upon a legitimate occasion, so trivial, too, as it now appeared, could lose all self-command, was, with energetic iniquity, going to bring about his murder.

The casks being on deck, Captain Delano was handed a number of jars and cups by one of the steward's aids, who, in the name of his captain, entreated him to do as he had proposed – dole out the water. He complied, with republican impartiality as to this republican element, which always seeks one level, serving the oldest white no better than the youngest black; excepting, indeed, poor Don Benito, whose condition, if not rank, demanded an extra allowance. To him, in the first place, Captain Delano presented a fair pitcher of the fluid; but, thirsting as he was for it, the Spaniard quaffed not a drop until after several grave bows and salutes. A reciprocation of courtesies which the sight-loving Africans hailed with clapping of hands.

Two of the less wilted pumpkins being reserved for the cabin table, the residue were minced up on the spot for the general regalement. But the soft bread, sugar, and bottled cider, Captain Delano would have given the whites alone, and in chief Don Benito; but the latter objected; which disinterestedness not a little pleased the American; and so mouthfuls all around were given alike to whites and blacks; excepting one bottle of cider, which Babo insisted upon setting aside for his master.

Here it may be observed that as, on the first visit of the boat, the American had not permitted his men to board the ship, neither did he now; being unwilling to add to the confusion of the decks.

Not uninfluenced by the peculiar good-humor at present prevailing, and for the time oblivious of any but benevolent thoughts, Captain Delano, who, from recent indications, counted upon a breeze within an hour or two at furthest, dispatched the boat back to the sealer, with orders for all the hands that could be spared immediately to set about rafting casks to the watering-place and filling them. Likewise he bade word be carried to his chief officer, that if, against present expectation, the ship was not brought to anchor by sunset, he need be under no concern; for as there was to be a full moon that night, he (Captain Delano) would remain on board ready to play the pilot, come the wind soon or late.

As the two Captains stood together, observing the departing boat – the servant, as it happened, having just spied a spot on his master's velvet sleeve, and silently engaged in rubbing it out – the American expressed his regrets that the

San Dominick had no boats; none, at least, but the un-seaworthy old hulk of the long-boat, which, warped as a camel's skeleton in the desert, and almost as bleached, lay pot-wise inverted amidships, one side a little tipped, fur-nishing a subterraneous sort of den for family groups of the blacks, mostly women and small children; who, squatting on old mats below, or perched above in the dark dome, on the elevated seats, were descried, some distance within, like a social circle of bats, sheltering in some friendly cave; at intervals, ebon flights of naked boys and girls, three or four years old, darting in and out of the den's mouth.

'Had you three or four boats now, Don Benito,' said Captain Delano, 'I think that, by tugging at the oars, your negroes here might help along matters some. Did you sail from port without boats, Don Benito?'

'They were stove in the gales, Señor.'

'That was bad. Many men, too, you lost then. Boats and men. Those must have been hard gales, Don Benito.'

'Past all speech,' cringed the Spaniard.

'Tell me, Don Benito,' continued his companion with increased interest, 'tell me, were these gales immediately off the pitch of Cape Horn?'

'Cape Horn? – who spoke of Cape Horn?'

'Yourself did, when giving me an account of your voy-age,' answered Captain Delano, with almost equal astonish-ment at this eating of his own words, even as he ever seemed eating his own heart, on the part of the Spaniard. 'You yourself, Don Benito, spoke of Cape Horn,' he emphatically repeated.

The Spaniard turned, in a sort of stooping posture, paus-ing an instant, as one about to make a plunging exchange of elements, as from air to water.

At this moment a messenger-boy, a white, hurried by, in the regular performance of his function carrying the last expired half hour forward to the forecastle, from the cabin time-piece, to have it struck at the ship's large bell.

'Master,' said the servant, discontinuing his work on the coat sleeve, and addressing the rapt Spaniard with a sort of timid apprehensiveness, as one charged with a duty, the discharge of which, it was foreseen, would prove irksome to the very person who had imposed it, and for whose benefit it was intended, 'master told me never mind where he was, or how engaged, always to remind him, to a minute, when shaving-time comes. Miguel has gone to strike the half-hour afternoon. It is *now* master. Will master go into the cuddy?'

'Ah – yes,' answered the Spaniard, starting, as from dreams into realities; then turning upon Captain Delano, he said that ere long he would resume the conversation.

'Then if master means to talk more to Don Amasa,' said the servant, 'why not let Don Amasa sit by master in the cuddy, and master can talk, and Don Amasa can listen, while Babo here lathers and strops.'

'Yes,' said Captain Delano, not unpleased with this sociable plan, 'yes, Don Benito, unless you had rather not, I will go with you.'

'Be it so, Señor.'

As the three passed aft, the American could not but think it another strange instance of his host's capriciousness, this being shaved with such uncommon punctuality in the middle of the day. But he deemed it more than likely that the servant's anxious fidelity had something to do with the matter; inasmuch as the timely interruption served to rally his master from the mood which had evidently been coming upon him.

The place called the cuddy was a light deck-cabin formed by the poop, a sort of attic to the large cabin below. Part of it had formerly been the quarters of the officers; but since their death all the partitionings had been thrown down, and the whole interior converted into one spacious and airy marine hall; for absence of fine furniture and picturesque disarray of odd appurtenances, somewhat answering to the wide, cluttered hall of some eccentric bachelor-squire in the country, who hangs his shooting-jacket and tobacco-pouch on deer antlers, and keeps his fishing-rod, tongs, and walking-stick in the same corner.

The similitude was heightened, if not originally suggested, by glimpses of the surrounding sea; since, in one aspect, the country and the ocean seem cousins-german.

The floor of the cuddy was matted. Overhead, four or five old muskets were stuck into horizontal holes along the beams. On one side was a claw-footed old table lashed to the deck; a thumbed missal on it, and over it a small, meagre crucifix attached to the bulk-head. Under the table lay a dented cutlass or two, with a hacked harpoon, among some melancholy old rigging, like a heap of poor friars' girdles. There were also two long, sharp-ribbed settees of Malacca cane, black with age, and uncomfortable to look at as inquisitors' racks, with a large, misshapen arm-chair, which, furnished with a rude barber's crotch at the back, working with a screw, seemed some grotesque engine of torment. A flag locker was in one corner, open, exposing various colored bunting, some rolled up, others half unrolled, still others tumbled. Opposite was a cumbrous washstand, of black mahogany, all of one block, with a pedestal, like a font, and over it a railed shelf, containing combs, brushes, and other implements of the toilet. A torn hammock of stained grass swung near; the sheets tossed, and the pillow wrinkled up like a brow, as if whoever slept here slept but illy, with alternate visitations of sad thoughts and bad dreams.

The further extremity of the cuddy, overhanging the ship's stern, was pierced with three openings, windows or port-holes, according as men or cannon might peer, socially or unsocially, out of them. At present neither men nor cannon were seen, though huge ring-bolts and other rusty iron fixtures of the wood-work hinted of twenty-four-pounders.

Glancing towards the hammock as he entered, Captain Delano said, 'You sleep here, Don Benito?'

'Yes, Señor, since we got into mild weather.'

'This seems a sort of dormitory, sitting-room, sail-loft, chapel, armory, and private closet all together, Don Benito,' added Captain Delano, looking round.

'Yes, Señor; events have not been favorable to much order in my arrangements.'

Here the servant, napkin on arm, made a motion as if waiting his master's good pleasure. Don Benito signified his readiness, when, seating him in the Malacca arm-chair, and for the guest's convenience drawing opposite one of the settees, the servant commenced operations by throwing back his master's collar and loosening his cravat.

There is something in the negro which, in a peculiar way, fits him for avocations about one's person. Most negroes are natural valets and hair-dressers; taking to the comb and brush congenially as to the castinets, and flourishing them apparently with almost equal satisfaction. There is, too, a smooth tact about them in this employment, with a marvelous, noiseless, gliding briskness, not ungraceful in its way, singularly pleasing to behold, and still more so to be the manipulated subject of. And above all is the great gift of good-humor. Not the mere grin or laugh is here meant. Those were unsuitable. But a certain easy cheerfulness, harmonious in every glance and gesture; as though God had set the whole negro to some pleasant tune.

When to this is added the docility arising from the unaspiring contentment of a limited mind, and that susceptibility of bland attachment sometimes inhering in indisputable inferiors, one readily perceives why those hypochondriacs, Johnson and Byron – it may be, something like the hypochondriac Benito Cereno – took to their hearts, almost to the exclusion of the entire white race, their serving men, the negroes, Barber and Fletcher. But if there be that in the negro which exempts him from the inflicted sourness of the morbid or cynical mind, how, in his most prepossessing aspects, must he appear to a benevolent one? When at ease with respect to exterior things, Captain Delano's nature was not only benign, but familiarly and humorously so. At home, he had often taken rare satisfaction in sitting in his door, watching some free man of color at his work or play. If on a voyage he chanced to have a black sailor, invariably he was on chatty and half-gamesome terms with him. In fact, like most men of a good, blithe heart, Captain Delano took to negroes, not philanthropically, but genially, just as other men to Newfoundland dogs.

Hitherto, the circumstances in which he found the *San Dominick* had repressed the tendency. But in the cuddy, relieved from his former uneasiness, and, for various reasons, more sociably inclined than at any previous period of the day, and seeing the colored servant, napkin on arm, so debonair about his master, in a business so familiar as that of shaving, too, all his old weakness for negroes returned.

Among other things, he was amused with an odd instance of the African love of bright colors and fine shows, in the black's informally taking from the flag-locker a great piece of bunting of all hues, and lavishly tucking it under his master's chin for an apron.

The mode of shaving among the Spaniards is a little different from what it is with other nations. They have a basin, specifically called a barber's basin, which on one side is scooped out, so as accurately to receive the chin, against which it is closely held in lathering; which is done, not with a brush, but with soap dipped in the water of the basin and rubbed on the face.

In the present instance salt-water was used for lack of better; and the parts lathered were only the upper lip, and low down under the throat, all the rest being cultivated beard.

The preliminaries being somewhat novel to Captain Delano, he sat curiously eyeing them, so that no conversation took place, nor, for the present, did Don Benito appear disposed to renew any.

Setting down his basin, the negro searched among the razors, as for the sharpest, and having found it, gave it an additional edge by expertly strapping it on the firm, smooth, oily skin of his open palm; he then made a gesture as if to begin, but midway stood suspended for an instant, one hand elevating the razor, the other professionally dabbling among the bubbling suds on the Spaniard's lank neck. Not un-affected by the close sight of the gleaming steel, Don Benito nervously shuddered; his usual ghastliness was heightened by the lather, which lather, again, was intensified in its hue by the contrasting sootiness of the negro's body. Altogether the scene was somewhat peculiar, at least to Captain Delano, nor, as he saw the two thus postured, could he resist the vagary, that in the black he saw a headsman, and in the white a man at the block. But this was one of those antic conceits, appearing and vanishing in a breath, from which, perhaps, the best regulated mind is not always free.

Meantime the agitation of the Spaniard had a little loosened the bunting from around him, so that one broad fold swept curtain-like over the chair-arm to the floor, revealing, amid a profusion of armorial bars and ground-colors – black, blue, and yellow – a closed castle in a blood-red field diagonal with a lion rampant in a white.

'The castle and the lion,' exclaimed Captain Delano – 'why, Don Benito, this is the flag of Spain you use here. It's well it's only I, and not the King, that sees this,' he added, with a smile, 'but' – turning towards the black – 'it's all one, I suppose, so the colors be gay;' which playful remark did not fail somewhat to tickle the negro.

'Now, master,' he said, readjusting the flag, and pressing the head gently further back into the crotch of the chair; 'now, master,' and the steel glanced nigh the throat.

Again Don Benito faintly shuddered.

'You must not shake so, master. See, Don Amasa, master always shakes when I shave him. And yet master knows I never yet have drawn blood, though it's true, if master will shake so, I may some of these times. Now master,' he continued. 'And now, Don Amasa, please go on with your talk about the gale, and all that; master can hear, and, between times, master can answer.'

'Ah yes, these gales,' said Captain Delano; 'but the more I think of your voyage, Don Benito, the more I wonder, not at the gales, terrible as they must have been, but at the disastrous interval following them. For here, by your account, have you been these two months and more getting from Cape Horn to St Maria, a distance which I myself, with a good wind, have sailed in a few days. True, you had calms, and long ones, but to be becalmed for two months, that is, at least, unusual. Why, Don Benito, had almost any other gentleman told me such a story, I should have been half disposed to a little incredulity.'

Here an involuntary expression came over the Spaniard, similar to that just before on the deck, and whether it was the start he gave, or a sudden gawky roll of the hull in the calm, or a momentary unsteadiness of the servant's hand, however it was, just then the razor drew blood, spots of which stained the creamy lather under the throat; immediately the black barber drew back his steel, and, remaining in his professional attitude, back to Captain Delano, and face to Don Benito, held up the trickling razor, saying, with a sort of half humorous sorrow, 'See, master – you shook so – here's Babo's first blood.'

No sword drawn before James the First of England, no assassination in that timid King's presence, could have produced a more terrified aspect than was now presented by Don Benito.

Poor fellow, thought Captain Delano, so nervous he can't even bear the sight of barber's blood; and this unstrung, sick man, is it credible that I should have imagined he meant to spill all my blood, who can't endure the sight of one little drop of his own? Surely, Amasa Delano, you have been beside yourself this day. Tell it not when you get home, sappy Amasa. Well, well, he looks like a murderer, doesn't he? More like as if himself were to be done for. Well, well, this day's experience shall be a good lesson.

Meantime, while these things were running through the honest seaman's mind, the servant had taken the napkin from his arm, and to Don Benito he said – 'But answer Don Amasa, please, master, while I wipe this ugly stuff off the razor, and strop it again.'

As he said the words, his face was turned half round, so as to be alike visible to the Spaniard and the American, and seemed, by its expression, to hint, that he was desirous, by

getting his master to go on with the conversation, con-
siderately to withdraw his attention from the recent annoy-
ing accident. As if glad to snatch the offered relief, Don
Benito resumed to Captain Delano, that not only were the
calms of unusual duration, but the ship had fallen in with
obstinate currents; and other things he added, some of
which were but repetitions of former statements, to explain how it came to pass that the passage from Cape Horn
to St Maria had been so exceedingly long; now and then
mingling with his words, incidental praises, less qualified
than before, to the blacks, for their general good conduct.
These particulars were not given consecutively, the servant,
at convenient times, using his razor, and so, between the
intervals of shaving, the story and panegyric went on with
more than usual huskiness.

To Captain Delano's imagination, now again not wholly
at rest, there was something so hollow in the Spaniard's
manner, with apparently some reciprocal hollowness in the
servant's dusky comment of silence, that the idea flashed
across him, that possibly master and man, for some unknown purpose, were acting out, both in word and deed,
nay, to the very tremor of Don Benito's limbs, some jug-
gling play before him. Neither did the suspicion of collu-
sion lack apparent support, from the fact of those whispered
conferences before mentioned. But then, what could be the
object of enacting this play of the barber before him? At
last, regarding the notion as a whimsy, insensibly suggested, perhaps, by the theatrical aspect of Don Benito in
his harlequin ensign, Captain Delano speedily banished it.

The shaving over, the servant bestirred himself with a
small bottle of scented waters, pouring a few drops on the
head, and then diligently rubbing; the vehemence of the
exercise causing the muscles of his face to twitch rather
strangely.

His next operation was with comb, scissors, and brush;
going round and round, smoothing a curl here, clipping an
unruly whisker-hair there, giving a graceful sweep to the
temple-lock, with other impromptu touches evincing the

hand of a master; while, like any resigned gentleman in barber's hands, Don Benito bore all, much less uneasily, at least, than he had done the razoring; indeed, he sat so pale and rigid now, that the negro seemed a Nubian sculptor finishing off a white statue-head.

All being over at last, the standard of Spain removed, tumbled over, and tossed back into the flag-locker, the negro's warm breath blowing away any stray hair which might have lodged down his master's neck; collar and cravat readjusted; a speck of lint whisked off the velvet lapel; all this being done; backing off a little space, and pausing with an expression of subdued self-complacency, the servant for a moment surveyed his master, as, in toilet at least, the creature of his own tasteful hands.

Captain Delano playfully complimented him upon his achievement; at the same time congratulating Don Benito.

But neither sweet waters, nor shampooing, nor fidelity, nor sociality, delighted the Spaniard. Seing him relapsing into forbidding gloom, and still remaining seated, Captain Delano, thinking that his presence was undesired just then, withdrew, on pretense of seeing whether, as he had prophesied, any signs of a breeze were visible.

Walking forward to the main-mast, he stood awhile thinking over the scene, and not without some undefined misgivings, when he heard a noise near the cuddy, and turning, saw the negro, his hand to his cheek. Advancing, Captain Delano perceived that the cheek was bleeding. He was about to ask the cause, when the negro's wailing soliloquy enlightened him.

'Ah, when will master get better from his sickness; only the sour heart that sour sickness breeds made him serve Babo so; cutting Babo with the razor, because, only by accident, Babo had given master one little scratch; and for the first time in so many a day, too. Ah, ah, ah,' holding his hand to his face.

Is it possible, thought Captain Delano; was it to wreak in private his Spanish spite against this poor friend of his, that Don Benito, by his sullen manner, impelled me to withdraw? Ah, this slavery breeds ugly passions in man. — Poor fellow!

He was about to speak in sympathy to the negro, but with a timid reluctance he now re-entered the cuddy.

Presently master and man came forth; Don Benito leaning on his servant as if nothing had happened.

But a sort of love-quarrel, after all, thought Captain Delano.

He accosted Don Benito, and they slowly walked together. They had gone but a few paces, when the steward – a tall, rajah-looking mulatto, orientally set off with a pagoda turban formed by three or four Madras handkerchiefs wound about his head, tier on tier – approaching with a saalam, announced lunch in the cabin.

On their way thither, the two captains were preceded by the mulatto, who, turning round as he advanced, with continual smiles and bows, ushered them on, a display of elegance which quite completed the insignificance of the small bare-headed Babo, who, as if not unconscious of inferiority, eyed askance the graceful steward. But in part, Captain Delano imputed his jealous watchfulness to that peculiar feeling which the full-blooded African entertains for the adulterated one. As for the steward, his manner, if not bespeaking much dignity or self-respect, yet evidenced his extreme desire to please; which is doubly meritorious, as at once Christian and Chesterfieldian.

Captain Delano observed with interest that while the complexion of the mulatto was hybrid, his physiognomy was European – classically so.

'Don Benito,' whispered he, 'I am glad to see this usher-of-the-golden-rod of yours; the sight refutes an ugly remark once made to me by a Barbadoes planter; that when a mulatto has a regular European face, look out for him; he is a devil. But see, your steward here has features more regular than King George's of England; and yet there he nods, and bows, and smiles; a king, indeed – the king of kind hearts and polite fellows. What a pleasant voice he has, too?'

'He has, Señor.'

'But tell me, has he not, so far as you have known him, always proved a good, worthy fellow?' said Captain Delano, pausing, while with a final genuflexion the steward disappeared into the cabin; 'come, for the reason just mentioned, I am curious to know.'

'Francesco is a good man,' a sort of sluggishly responded Don Benito, like a phlegmatic appreciator, who would neither find fault nor flatter.

'Ah, I thought so. For it were strange, indeed, and not very creditable to us white-skins, if a little of our blood mixed with the African's, should, far from improving the latter's quality, have the sad effect of pouring vitriolic acid into black broth; improving the hue, perhaps, but not the wholesomeness.'

'Doubtless, doubtless, Señor, but' – glancing at Babo – 'not to speak of negroes, your planter's remark I have heard applied to the Spanish and Indian intermixtures in our provinces. But I know nothing about the matter,' he listlessly added.

And here they entered the cabin.

The lunch was a frugal one. Some of Captain Delano's fresh fish and pumpkins, biscuit and salt beef, the reserved bottle of cider, and the *San Dominick*'s last bottle of Canary.

As they entered, Francesco, with two or three colored aids, was hovering over the table giving the last adjustments. Upon perceiving their master they withdrew, Francesco making a smiling congé, and the Spaniard, without condescending to notice it, fastidiously remarking to his companion that he relished not superfluous attendance.

Without companions, host and guest sat down, like a childless married couple, at opposite ends of the table, Don Benito waving Captain Delano to his place, and, weak as he was, insisting upon that gentleman being seated before himself.

The negro placed a rug under Don Benito's feet, and a cushion behind his back, and then stood behind, not his master's chair, but Captain Delano's. At first, this a little surprised the latter. But it was soon evident that, in taking his position, the black was still true to his master; since by facing him he could the more readily anticipate his slightest want.

'This is an uncommonly intelligent fellow of yours, Don Benito,' whispered Captain Delano across the table.

'You say true, Señor.'

During the repast, the guest again reverted to parts of Don Benito's story, begging further particulars here and there. He inquired how it was that the scurvy and fever should have committed such wholesale havoc upon the whites, while destroying less than half of the blacks. As if this question reproduced the whole scene of plague before the Spaniard's eyes, miserably reminding him of his solitude in a cabin where before he had had so many friends and officers round him, his hand shook, his face became hueless, broken words escaped; but directly the sane memory of the past seemed replaced by insane terrors of the present. With starting eyes he stared before him at vacancy. For nothing was to be seen but the hand of his servant pushing the Canary over towards him. At length a few sips served partially to restore him. He made random reference to the different constitution of races, enabling one to offer more resistance to certain maladies than another. The thought was new to his companion.

Presently Captain Delano, intending to say something to his host concerning the pecuniary part of the business he had undertaken for him, especially – since he was strictly accountable to his owners – with reference to the new suit of sails, and other things of that sort; and naturally preferring to conduct such affairs in private, was desirous that the servant should withdraw; imagining that Don Benito for a few minutes could dispense with his attendance. He, however, waited awhile; thinking that, as the conversation proceeded, Don Benito, without being prompted, would perceive the propriety of the step.

But it was otherwise. At last catching his host's eye,

Captain Delano, with a slight backward gesture of his thumb, whispered, 'Don Benito, pardon me, but there is an interference with the full expression of what I have to say to you.'

Upon this the Spaniard changed countenance; which was imputed to his resenting the hint, as in some way a reflection upon his servant. After a moment's pause, he assured his guest that the black's remaining with them could be of no disservice; because since losing his officers he had made Babo (whose original office, it now appeared, had been captain of the slaves) not only his constant attendant and companion, but in all things his confidant.

After this, nothing more could be said; though, indeed, Captain Delano could hardly avoid some little tinge of irritation upon being left ungratified in so inconsiderable a wish, by one, too, for whom he intended such solid services. But it is only his querulousness, thought he; and so filling his glass he proceeded to business.

The price of the sails and other matters was fixed upon. But while this was being done, the American observed that, though his original offer of assistance had been hailed with hectic animation, yet now when it was reduced to a business transaction, indifference and apathy were betrayed. Don Benito, in fact, appeared to submit to hearing the details more out of regard to common propriety, than from any impression that weighty benefit to himself and his voyage was involved.

Soon, his manner became still more reserved. The effort was vain to seek to draw him into social talk. Gnawed by his splenetic mood, he sat twitching his beard, while to little purpose the hand of his servant, mute as that on the wall, slowly pushed over the Canary.

Lunch being over, they sat down on the cushioned transom; the servant placing a pillow behind his master. The long continuance of the calm had now affected the atmosphere. Don Benito sighed heavily, as if for breath.

'Why not adjourn to the cuddy,' said Captain Delano;

'there is more air there.' But the host sat silent and motionless.

Meantime his servant knelt before him, with a large fan of feathers. And Francesco coming in on tiptoes, handed the negro a little cup of aromatic waters, with which at intervals he chafed his master's brow; smoothing the hair along the temples as a nurse does a child's. He spoke no word. He only rested his eye on his master's, as if, amid all Don Benito's distress, a little to refresh his spirit by the silent sight of fidelity.

Presently the ship's bell sounded two o'clock; and through the cabin windows a slight rippling of the sea was discerned; and from the desired direction.

'There,' exclaimed Captain Delano, 'I told you so, Don Benito, look!'

He had risen to his feet, speaking in a very animated tone, with a view the more to rouse his companion. But though the crimson curtain of the stern window near him that moment fluttered against his pale cheek, Don Benito seemed to have even less welcome for the breeze than the calm.

Poor fellow, thought Captain Delano, bitter experience has taught him that one ripple does not make a wind, any more than one swallow a summer. But he is mistaken for once. I will get his ship in for him, and prove it.

Briefly alluding to his weak condition, he urged his host to remain quietly where he was, since he (Captain Delano) would with pleasure take upon himself the responsibility of making the best use of the wind.

Upon gaining the deck, Captain Delano started at the unexpected figure of Atufal, monumentally fixed at the threshold, like one of those sculptured porters of black marble guarding the porches of Egyptian tombs.

But this time the start was, perhaps, purely physical. Atufal's presence, singularly attesting docility even in sullenness, was contrasted with that of the hatchet-polishers, who in practice evinced their industry; while both spectacles showed, that lax as Don Benito's general authority might be, still, whenever he chose to exert it, no man so savage or colossal but must, more or less, bow.

Snatching a trumpet which hung from the bulwarks, with a free step Captain Delano advanced to the forward edge of the poop, issuing his orders in his best Spanish. The few sailors and many negroes, all equally pleased, obediently set about heading the ship towards the harbor.

While giving some directions about setting a lower stu'n'-sail, suddenly Captain Delano heard a voice faithfully repeating his orders. Turning, he saw Babo, now for the time acting, under the pilot, his original part of captain of the slaves. This assistance proved valuable. Tattered sails and warped yards were soon brought into some trim. And no brace or halyard was pulled but to the blithe songs of the inspired negroes.

Good fellows, thought Captain Delano, a little training would make fine sailors of them. Why see, the very women pull and sing too. These must be some of those Ashantee negresses that make such capital soldiers, I've heard. But who's at the helm. I must have a good hand there.

He went to see.

The *San Dominick* steered with a cumbrous tiller, with large horizontal pullies attached. At each pulley-end stood a subordinate black, and between them, at the tiller-head, the responsible post, a Spanish seaman, whose countenance evinced his due share in the general hopefulness and confidence at the coming of the breeze.

He proved the same man who had behaved with so shame-faced an air on the windlass.

'Ah – it is you, my man,' exclaimed Captain Delano – 'well, no more sheep's-eyes now; – look straight forward and keep the ship so. Good hand, I trust? And want to get into the harbor, don't you?'

The man assented with an inward chuckle, grasping the tiller-head firmly. Upon this, unperceived by the American, the two blacks eyed the sailor intently.

Finding all right at the helm, the pilot went forward to the forecastle, to see how matters stood there.

The ship now had way enough to breast the current. With the approach of evening, the breeze would be sure to freshen.

Having done all that was needed for the present, Captain Delano, giving his last orders to the sailors, turned aft to report affairs to Don Benito in the cabin; perhaps additionally incited to rejoin him by the hope of snatching a moment's private chat while the servant was engaged upon deck.

From opposite sides, there were, beneath the poop, two approaches to the cabin; one further forward than the other, and consequently communicating with a longer passage. Marking the servant still above, Captain Delano, taking the nighest entrance – the one last named, and at whose porch Atufal still stood – hurried on his way, till, arrived at the cabin threshold, he paused an instant, a little to recover from his eagerness. Then, with the words of his intended business upon his lips, he entered. As he advanced toward the seated Spaniard, he heard another footstep, keeping time with his. From the opposite door, a salver in hand, the servant was likewise advancing.

'Confound the faithful fellow,' thought Captain Delano; 'what a vexatious coincidence.'

Possibly, the vexation might have been something different, were it not for the brisk confidence inspired by the breeze. But even as it was, he felt a slight twinge, from a sudden indefinite association in his mind of Babo with Atufal.

'Don Benito,' said he, 'I give you joy; the breeze will hold, and will increase. By the way, your tall man and time-piece, Atufal, stands without. By your order, of course?'

Don Benito recoiled, as if at some bland satirical touch, delivered with such adroit garnish of apparent good breeding as to present no handle for retort.

He is like one flayed alive, thought Captain Delano; where may one touch him without causing a shrink?

The servant moved before his master, adjusting a cushion; recalled to civility, the Spaniard stiffly replied: 'You are right. The slave appears where you saw him, according to my command; which is, that if at the given hour I am below, he must take his stand and abide my coming.'

'Ah now, pardon me, but that is treating the poor fellow like an ex-king indeed. Ah, Don Benito,' smiling, 'for all the license you permit in some things, I fear lest, at bottom, you are a bitter hard master.'

Again, Don Benito shrank; and this time, as the good sailor thought, from a genuine twinge of his conscience.

Again conversation became constrained. In vain Captain Delano called attention to the now perceptible motion of the keel gently cleaving the sea; with lack-lustre eye, Don Benito returned words few and reserved.

By-and-by, the wind having steadily risen, and still blowing right into the harbor, bore the *San Dominick* swiftly on. Rounding a point of land, the sealer at distance came into open view.

Meantime Captain Delano had again repaired to the deck, remaining there sometime. Having at last altered the ship's course, so as to give the reef a wide berth, he returned for a few moments below.

I will cheer up my poor friend, this time, thought he.

'Better and better, Don Benito,' he cried as he blithely re-entered: 'there will soon be an end to your cares, at least for awhile. For when, after a long, sad voyage, you know, the anchor drops into the haven, all its vast weight seems lifted from the captain's heart. We are getting on famously, Don Benito. My ship is in sight. Look through this side-light here; there she is; all a-taunt-o! The *Bachelor's Delight*, my good friend. Ah, how this wind braces one up. Come, you must take a cup of coffee with me this evening. My old steward will give you as fine a cup as ever any sultan tasted. What say you, Don Benito, will you?'

At first, the Spaniard glanced feverishly up, casting a longing look towards the sealer, while with mute concern his servant gazed into his face. Suddenly the old ague of coldness returned, and dropping back to his cushions he was silent.

'You do not answer. Come, all day you have been my host; would you have hospitality all on one side?'

'I cannot go,' was the response.

'What? it will not fatigue you. The ships will lie together as near as they can, without swinging foul. It will be little more than stepping from deck to deck; which is but as from room to room. Come, come, you must not refuse me.'

'I cannot go,' decisively and repulsively repeated Don Benito.

Renouncing all but the last appearance of courtesy, with a sort of cadaverous sullenness, and biting his thin nails to the quick, he glanced, almost glared, at his guest, as if impatient that a stranger's presence should interfere with the full indulgence of his morbid hour. Meantime the sound of the parted waters came more and more gurglingly and merrily in at the windows; as reproaching him for his dark spleen; as telling him that, sulk as he might, and go mad with it, nature cared not a jot; since, whose fault was it, pray?

But the foul mood was now at its depth, as the fair wind at its height.

There was something in the man so far beyond any mere unsociality or sourness previously evinced, that even the forbearing good-nature of his guest could no longer endure it. Wholly at a loss to account for such demeanor, and deeming sickness with eccentricity, however extreme, no adequate excuse, well satisfied, too, that nothing in his own conduct could justify it, Captain Delano's pride began to be roused. Himself became reserved. But all seemed one to the Spaniard. Quitting him, therefore, Captain Delano once more went to the deck.

The ship was now within less than two miles of the sealer. The whale-boat was seen darting over the interval.

To be brief, the two vessels, thanks to the pilot's skill, ere long in neighborly style lay anchored together.

Before returning to his own vessel, Captain Delano had intended communicating to Don Benito the smaller details of the proposed services to be rendered. But, as it was, unwilling anew to subject himself to rebuffs, he resolved, now that he had seen the San Dominick safely moored, immediately to quit her, without further allusion to hospitality or business. Indefinitely postponing his ulterior plans, he would regulate his future actions according to future circumstances. His boat was ready to receive him; but his host still tarried below. Well, thought Captain Delano, if he has little breeding, the more need to show mine. He descended to the cabin to bid a ceremonious, and, it may be, tacitly rebukeful adieu. But to his great satisfaction, Don Benito, as if he began to feel the weight of that treatment with which his slighted guest had, not indecorously, retaliated upon him, now supported by his servant, rose to his feet, and grasping Captain Delano's hand, stood tremulous; too much agitated to speak. But the good augury hence drawn was suddenly dashed, by his resuming all his previous reserve, with augmented gloom, as, with half-averted eyes, he silently reseated himself on his cushions. With a corresponding return of his own chilled feelings, Captain Delano bowed and withdrew.

He was hardly midway in the narrow corridor, dim as a tunnel, leading from the cabin to the stairs, when a sound, as of the tolling for execution in some jail-yard, fell on his ears. It was the echo of the ship's flawed bell, striking the hour, drearily reverberated in this subterranean vault. Instantly, by a fatality not to be withstood, his mind, responsive to the portent, swarmed with superstitious suspicions. He paused. In images far swifter than these sentences, the minutest details of all his former distrusts swept through him.

Hitherto, credulous good-nature had been too ready to furnish excuses for reasonable fears. Why was the Spaniard, so superfluously punctilious at times, now heedless of common propriety in not accompanying to the side his departing guest? Did indisposition forbid? Indisposition had not forbidden more irksome exertion that day. His last equivocal demeanor recurred. He had risen to his feet, grasped his guest's hand, motioned toward his hat; then, in an instant, all was eclipsed in sinister muteness and gloom. Did this imply one brief, repentant relenting at the final moment, from some iniquitous plot, followed by remorseless return to it? His last glance seemed to express a calamitous, yet acquiescent farewell to Captain Delano forever. Why decline the invitation to visit the sealer that evening? Or was the Spaniard less hardened than the Jew, who refrained not from supping at the board of him whom the same night he meant to betray? What imported all those day-long enigmas and contradictions, except they were intended to mystify, preliminary to some stealthy blow? Atufal, the pretended rebel, but punctual shadow, that moment lurked by the threshold without. He seemed a sentry, and more. Who, by his own confession, had stationed him there? Was the negro now lying in wait?

The Spaniard behind – his creature before: to rush from darkness to light was the involuntary choice.

The next moment, with clenched jaw and hand, he passed Atufal, and stood unharmed in the light, As he saw his trim ship lying peacefully at anchor, and almost within ordinary call; as he saw his household boat, with familiar faces in it, patiently rising and falling on the short waves by the *San Dominick*'s side; and then, glancing about the decks where he stood, saw the oakum-pickers still gravely plying their fingers; and heard the low buzzing whistle and industrious hum of the hatchet-polishers, still bestirring themselves over their endless occupation; and more than all, as he saw the benign aspect of nature, taking her innocent repose in the evening; the screened sun in the quiet camp of the west shining out like the mild light from Abraham's tent; as charmed eye and ear took in all these, with the chained figure of the black, clenched jaw and hand relaxed. Once again he smiled at the phantoms which had mocked him, and felt something like a tinge of remorse, that, by harboring them even for a moment, he should by implication, have betrayed an atheist doubt of the ever-watchful Providence above.

There was a few minutes' delay, while, in obedience to his orders, the boat was being hooked along to the gangway. During this interval, a sort of saddened satisfaction stole over Captain Delano, at thinking of the kindly offices he had that day discharged for a stranger. Ah, thought he, after good actions one's conscience is never ungrateful, however much so the benefited party may be.

Presently, his foot, in the first act of descent into the boat, pressed the first round of the side-ladder, his face presented inward upon the deck. In the same moment, he heard his name courteously sounded; and, to his pleased surprise, saw Don Benito advancing – an unwonted energy in his air, as if, at the last moment, intent upon making amends for his recent discourtesy. With instinctive good feeling, Captain Delano, withdrawing his foot, turned and reciprocally advanced. As he did so, the Spaniard's nervous eagerness increased, but his vital energy failed; so that, the better to support him, the servant, placing his master's hand on his naked shoulder, and gently holding it there, formed himself into a sort of crutch.

When the two captains met, the Spaniard again fervently took the hand of the American, at the same time casting an earnest glance into his eyes, but, as before, too much overcome to speak.

I have done him wrong, self-reproachfully thought Captain Delano; his apparent coldness has deceived me; in no instance has he meant to offend.

Meantime, as if fearful that the continuance of the scene might too much unstring his master, the servant seemed anxious to terminate it. And so, still presenting himself as a crutch, and walking between the two captains, he advanced with them towards the gangway; while still, as if full of kindly contrition, Don Benito would not let go the hand of Captain Delano, but retained it in his, across the black's body.

Soon they were standing by the side, looking over into

the boat, whose crew turned up their curious eyes. Waiting a moment for the Spaniard to relinquish his hold, the now embarrassed Captain Delano lifted his foot, to overstep the threshold of the open gangway; but still Don Benito would not let go his hand. And yet, with an agitated tone, he said, 'I can go no further; here I must bid you adieu. Adieu, my dear, dear Don Amasa. Go – go!' suddenly tearing his hand loose, 'go, and God guard you better than me, my best friend.'

Not unaffected, Captain Delano would now have lingered; but catching the meekly admonitory eye of the servant, with a hasty farewell he descended into his boat, followed by the continual adieus of Don Benito, standing rooted in the gangway.

Seating himself in the stern, Captain Delano, making a last salute, ordered the boat shoved off. The crew had their oars on end. The bowsmen pushed the boat a sufficient distance for the oars to be lengthwise dropped. The instant that was done, Don Benito sprang over the bulwarks, falling at the feet of Captain Delano; at the same time calling towards his ship, but in tones so frenzied, that none in the boat could understand him. But, as if not equally obtuse, three sailors, from three different and distant parts of the ship, splashed into the sea, swimming after their captain, as if intent upon his rescue.

The dismayed officer of the boat eagerly asked what this meant. To which, Captain Delano, turning a disdainful smile upon the unaccountable Spaniard, answered that, for his part, he neither knew nor cared; but it seemed as if Don Benito had taken it into his head to produce the impression among his people that the boat wanted to kidnap him. 'Or else – give way for your lives,' he wildly added, starting at a clattering hubbub in the ship, above which rang the tocsin of the hatchet-polishers; and seizing Don Benito by the throat he added, 'this plotting pirate means murder!' Here, in apparent verification of the words, the servant, a dagger in his hand, was seen on the rail overhead, poised, in the act of leaping, as if with desperate fidelity to befriend his master to the last; while, seemingly to aid the black, the three white sailors were trying to clamber into the hampered bow. Meantime, the whole host of negroes, as if inflamed at the sight of their jeopardized captain, impended in one sooty avalanche over the bulwarks.

All this, with what preceded, and what followed, occurred with such involutions of rapidity, that past, present, and future seemed one.

Seeing the negro coming, Captain Delano had flung the Spaniard aside, almost in the very act of clutching him, and, by the unconscious recoil, shifting his place, with arms thrown up, so promptly grappled the servant in his descent, that with dagger presented at Captain Delano's heart, the black seemed of purpose to have leaped there as to his mark. But the weapon was wrenched away, and the assailant dashed down into the bottom of the boat, which now, with disentangled oars, began to speed through the sea.

At this juncture, the left hand of Captain Delano, on one side, again clutched the half-reclined Don Benito, heedless that he was in a speechless faint, while his right foot, on the other side, ground the prostrate negro; and his right arm pressed for added speed on the after oar, his eye bent forward, encouraging his men to their utmost.

But here, the officer of the boat, who had at last succeeded in beating off the towing sailors and was now, with face turned aft, assisting the bowsman at his oar, suddenly called to Captain Delano, to see what the black was about; while a Portuguese oarsman shouted to him to give heed to what the Spaniard was saying.

Glancing down at his feet, Captain Delano saw the freed hand of the servant aiming with a second dagger – a small one, before concealed in his wool – with this he was snakishly writhing up from the boat's bottom, at the heart of his master, his countenance lividly vindictive, expressing the centred purpose of his soul; while the Spaniard, half-choked, was vainly shrinking away, with husky words, incoherent to all but the Portuguese.

That moment, across the long-benighted mind of Captain Delano, a flash of revelation swept, illuminating, in unanticipated clearness, his host's whole mysterious demeanor, with every enigmatic event of the day, as well as the entire past voyage of the *San Dominick*. He smote Babo's hand down, but his own heart smote him harder. With infinite pity he withdrew his hold from Don Benito. Not Captain Delano, but Don Benito, the black, in leaping into the boat, had intended to stab.

Both the black's hands were held, as, glancing up towards the *San Dominick*, Captain Delano, now with scales dropped from his eyes, saw the negroes, not in misrule, not in tumult, not as if frantically concerned for Don Benito, but with mask torn away, flourishing hatchets and knives, in ferocious piratical revolt. Like delirious black dervishes, the six Ashantees danced on the poop. Prevented by their foes from springing into the water, the Spanish boys were hurrying up to the topmost spars, while such of the few Spanish sailors, not already in the sea, less alert, were descried, helplessly mixed in, on deck, with the blacks.

Meantime Captain Delano hailed his own vessel, ordering the ports up, and the guns run out. But by this time the cable of the *San Dominick* had been cut; and the fag-end, in lashing out, whipped away the canvas shroud about the beak, suddenly revealing, as the bleached hull swung round towards the open ocean, death for the figure-head, in a human skeleton; chalky comment on the chalked words below, '*Follow your leader.*'

At the sight, Don Benito, covering his face, wailed out : ' 'Tis he, Aranda! my murdered, unburied friend!'

Upon reaching the sealer, calling for ropes, Captain Delano bound the negro, who made no resistance, and had him hoisted to the deck. He would then have assisted the now almost helpless Don Benito up the side; but Don Benito, wan as he was, refused to move, or be moved, until the negro should have been first put below out of view. When, presently assured that it was done, he no more shrank from the ascent.

The boat was immediately dispatched back to pick up the three swimming sailors. Meantime, the guns were in readiness, though, owing to the *San Dominick* having glided somewhat astern of the sealer, only the aftermost one could be brought to bear. With this, they fired six times; thinking to cripple the fugitive ship by bringing down her spars. But only a few inconsiderable ropes were shot away. Soon the ship was beyond the gun's range, steering broad out of the bay; the blacks thickly clustering round the bowsprit, one moment with taunting cries towards the whites, the next with upthrown gestures hailing the now dusky moors of ocean – cawing crows escaped from the hand of the fowler.

The first impulse was to slip the cables and give chase. But, upon second thoughts, to pursue with whale-boat and yawl seemed more promising.

Upon inquiring of Don Benito what fire-arms they had on board the *San Dominick*, Captain Delano was answered that they had none that could be used; because, in the earlier stages of the mutiny, a cabin-passenger, since dead, had secretly put out of order the locks of what few muskets there were. But with all his remaining strength, Don Benito entreated the American not to give chase, either with ship or boat; for the negroes had already proved themselves such desperadoes, that, in case of a present assault, nothing but a total massacre of the whites could be looked for. But, regarding this warning as coming from one whose spirit had been crushed by misery the American did not give up his design.

The boats were got ready and armed. Captain Delano ordered his men into them. He was going himself when Don Benito grasped his arm.

'What! have you saved my life, Señor, and are you now going to throw away your own?'

The officers also, for reasons connected with their interests and those of the voyage, and a duty owing to the owners, strongly objected against their commander's going. Weighing their remonstrances a moment, Captain Delano felt bound to remain; appointing his chief mate – an athletic and resolute man, who had been a privateer's-man – to head the party. The more to encourage the sailors, they were told that the Spanish captain considered his ship good as lost; that she and her cargo, including some gold and silver, were worth more than a thousand doubloons. Take her, and no small part should be theirs. The sailors replied with a shout.

The fugitives had now almost gained an offing. It was nearly night; but the moon was rising. After hard, prolonged pulling, the boats came up on the ship's quarters, at a suitable distance laying upon their oars to discharge their muskets. Having no bullets to return, the negroes sent their yells. But, upon the second volley, Indian-like, they hurtled their hatchets. One took off a sailor's fingers. Another struck the whale-boat's bow, cutting off the rope there, and remaining stuck in the gunwale like a woodman's axe. Snatching it, quivering from its lodgment, the mate hurled it back. The returned gauntlet now stuck in the ship's broken quarter-gallery, and so remained.

The negroes giving too hot a reception, the whites kept a more respectful distance. Hovering now just out of reach of the hurtling hatchets, they, with a view to the close encounter which must soon come, sought to decoy the blacks into entirely disarming themselves of their most murderous weapons in a hand-to-hand fight, by foolishly flinging them, as missiles, short of the mark, into the sea. But, ere long, perceiving the stratagem, the negroes desisted, though not before many of them had to replace their lost hatchets with handspikes; an exchange which, as counted upon, proved, in the end, favorable to the assailants.

Meantime, with a strong wind, the ship still clove the water; the boats alternately falling behind, and pulling up, to discharge fresh volleys.

The fire was mostly directed towards the stern, since there, chiefly, the negroes, at present, were clustering. But to kill or maim the negroes was not the object. To take them, with the ship, was the object. To do it, the ship must be boarded; which could not be done by boats while she was sailing so fast.

A thought now struck the mate. Observing the Spanish boys still aloft, high as they could get, he called to them to descend to the yards, and cut adrift the sails. It was done. About this time, owing to causes hereafter to be shown, two Spaniards, in the dress of sailors, and conspicuously showing themselves, were killed; not by volleys, but by deliberate marksman's shots; while, as it afterwards appeared, by one of the general discharges, Atufal, the black, and the Spaniard at the helm likewise were killed. What now, with the loss of the sails, and loss of leaders, the ship became unmanageable to the negroes.

With creaking masts, she came heavily round to the wind; the prow slowly swinging into view of the boats, its skeleton gleaming in the horizontal moonlight, and casting a gigantic ribbed shadow upon the water. One extended arm of the ghost seemed beckoning the whites to avenge it.

'Follow your leader!' cried the mate; and, one on each bow, the boats boarded. Sealing-spears and cutlasses crossed hatchets and hand-spikes. Huddled upon the long-boat amidships, the negresses raised a wailing chant, whose chorus was the clash of the steel.

For a time, the attack wavered; the negroes wedging themselves to beat it back; the half-repelled sailors, as yet unable to gain a footing, fighting as troopers in the saddle, one leg sideways flung over the bulwarks, and one without, plying their cutlasses like carters' whips. But in vain. They were almost overborne, when, rallying themselves into a squad as one man, with a huzza, they sprang inboard, where, entangled, they involuntarily separated again. For a few breaths' space, there was a vague, muffled, inner sound, as of submerged sword-fish rushing hither and thither through shoals of black-fish. Soon, in a reunited band, and joined by the Spanish seamen, the whites came to the surface, irresistibly driving the negroes towards the stern. But a barricade of casks and sacks, from side to side, had been thrown up by the mainmast. Here the negroes faced about, and though scorning peace or truce, yet fain would have had respite. But, without pause, overleaping the barrier, the unflagging sailors again closed. Exhausted, the blacks now fought in despair. Their red tongues lolled, wolf-like, from their black mouths. But the pale sailors' teeth were set; not a word was spoken; and, in five minutes more, the ship was won.

Nearly a score of the negroes were killed. Exclusive of those by the balls, many were mangled; their wounds – mostly inflicted by the long-edged sealing spears, resembling those shaven ones of the English at Preston Pans, made by the poled scythes of the Highlanders. On the other side, none were killed, though several were wounded; some severely, including the mate. The surviving negroes were temporarily secured, and the ship, towed back into the harbor at midnight, once more lay anchored.

Omitting the incidents and arrangements ensuing, suffice it that, after two days spent in refitting, the ships sailed in company for Conception, in Chili, and thence for Lima, in Peru; where, before the vice-regal courts, the whole affair, from the beginning, underwent investigation.

Though, midway on the passage, the ill-fated Spaniard, relaxed from constraint, showed some signs of regaining health with free-will; yet, agreeably to his own foreboding, shortly before arriving at Lima, he relapsed, finally becoming so reduced as to be carried ashore in arms. Hearing of his story and plight, one of the many religious institutions, of the City of Kings opened an hospitable refuge to him, where both physician and priest were his nurses, and a member of the order volunteered to be his one special guardian and consoler, by night and by day.

The following extracts, translated from one of the official Spanish documents, will, it is hoped, shed light on the preceding narrative, as well as, in the first place, reveal the true port of departure and true history of the *San Dominick*'s voyage, down to the time of her touching at the island of St Maria.

But, ere the extracts come, it may be well to preface them with a remark.

The document selected, from among many others, for partial translation, contains the deposition of Benito Cereno; the first taken in the case. Some disclosures therein were, at the time, held dubious for both learned and natural reasons. The tribunal inclined to the opinion that the deponent, not undisturbed in his mind by recent events, raved of some things which could never have happened. But subsequent depositions of the surviving sailors, bearing out the revelations of their captain in several of the strangest particulars, gave credence to the rest. So that the tribunal, in its final decision, rested its capital sentences upon statements which, had they lacked confirmation, it would have deemed it but duty to reject.

I, Don José de Abos and Padilla, His Majesty's Notary for the Royal Revenue, and Register of this Province, and Notary Public of the Holy Crusade of this Bishopric, etc.

Do certify and declare, as much as is requisite in law, that, in the criminal cause commenced the twenty-fourth of the month of September, in the year seventeen hundred and ninety-nine, against the negroes of the ship *San Dominick*, the following declaration before me was made:

Declaration of the first witness, Don Benito Cereno.

The same day, and month, and year, His Honor, Doctor Juan Martinez de Rozas, Councilor of the Royal Audience of this Kingdom, and learned in the law of this Intendency, ordered the captain of the ship *San Dominick*, Don Benito Cereno, to appear; which he did in his litter, attended by the monk Infelez; of whom he received the oath, which he took by God, our Lord, and a sign of the Cross; under which he promised to tell the truth of whatever he should know and should be asked; – and being interrogated agreeably to the tenor of the act commencing the process, he said, that on the twentieth of May last, he set sail with his ship from the port of Valparaiso, bound to that of Callao; loaded with the produce of the country beside thirty cases of hardware and one hundred and sixty blacks, of both sexes, mostly belonging to Don Alexandro Aranda, gentleman, of the city of Mendoza; that the crew of the ship consisted of thirty-six men, beside the persons who went as passengers; that the negroes were in part as follows:

[*Here, in the original, follows a list of some fifty names, descriptions, and ages, compiled from certain recovered documents of Aranda's, and also from recollections of the deponent, from which portions only are extracted.*]

—One, from about eighteen to nineteen years, named José, and this was the man that waited upon his master, Don Alexandro, and who speaks well the Spanish, having served him four or five years; * * * a mulatto, named Francesco, the cabin steward, of a good person and voice, having sung in the Valparaiso churches, native of the province of Buenos Ayres, aged about thirty-five years. * * * A smart negro, named Dago, who had been for many years a grave-digger among the Spaniards, aged forty-six years. * * * Four old negroes, born in Africa, from sixty to seventy, but sound, calkers by trade, whose names are as follows:—the first was named Muri, and he was killed (as was also his son named Diamelo); the second, Nacta; the third, Yola, likewise killed; the fourth, Ghofan; and six full-grown negroes, aged from thirty to forty-five, all raw, and born among the Ash-antees – Matiluqui, Yan, Lecbe, Mapenda, Yambaio, Akim; four of whom were killed; * * * a powerful negro named Atufal, who being supposed to have been a chief in Africa, his owner set great store by him. * * * And a small negro of Senegal, but some years among the Spaniards, aged about thirty, which negro's name was Babo; * * * that he does not remember the names of the others, but that still expecting the residue of Don Alexandro's papers will be found, will then take due account of them all, and remit to the court; * * * and thirty-nine women and children of all ages.

[The catalogue over, the deposition goes on.]

* * * That all the negroes slept upon deck, as is customary in this navigation, and none wore fetters, because the owner, his friend Aranda, told him that they were all tractable; * * * that on the seventh day after leaving port, at three o'clock in the morning, all the Spaniards being asleep except the two officers on the watch, who were the boatswain, Juan Robles, and the carpenter, Juan Bautista Gayete, and the helmsman and his boy, the negroes revolted suddenly, wounded dangerously the boatswain and the carpenter, and successively killed eighteen men of those who were sleeping upon deck, some with hand-spikes and hatchets, and others by throwing them alive overboard, after tying them; that of the Spaniards upon deck, they left about seven, as he thinks, alive and tied, to manoeuvre the ship, and three or four more, who hid themselves, remained also alive. Although in the act of revolt the negroes made themselves masters of the hatchway, six or seven wounded went through it to the cockpit, without any hindrance on their part; that during the act of revolt, the mate and another person, whose name he does not recollect, attempted to come up through the hatchway, but being quickly wounded, were obliged to return to the cabin; that the deponent resolved at break of day to come up the companion-way, where the negro Babo was, being the ringleader, and Atufal, who assisted him, and having spoken to them, exhorted them to cease committing such atrocities, asking them, at the same time, what they wanted and intended to do, offering, himself, to obey their commands; that notwithstanding this, they threw, in his presence, three men, alive and tied, overboard; that they told the deponent to come up, and that they would not kill him; which having done, the negro Babo asked him whether there were in those seas any negro countries where they might be carried, and he answered them, No; that the negro Babo afterwards told him to carry them to Senegal, or to the neighboring islands of St Nicholas; and he answered, that this was impossible, on account of the great distance, the necessity involved of rounding Cape Horn, the bad condition of the vessel, the want of provisions, sails, and water; but that the negro Babo replied to him he must carry them in any way; that they would do and conform themselves to everything the deponent should require as to eating and drinking; that after a long conference, being absolutely compelled to please them, for they threatened to kill all the whites if they were not, at all events, carried to Senegal, he told them that what was most wanting for the voyage was water; that they would go near the coast to take it, and thence they would proceed on their course; that the negro Babo agreed to it; and the deponent steered towards the intermediate ports, hoping to meet some Spanish or foreign vessel that would save them; that within ten or eleven days they saw the land, and continued their course by it in the vicinity of Nasca; that the deponent observed that the negroes were now restless and mutinous, because he did not effect the taking in of water, the negro Babo having required, with threats, that it should be done, without fail, the following day; he told him he saw plainly that the coast was steep, and the rivers designated in the maps were not to be found, with other reasons suitable to the circumstances; that the best way would be to go to the island of Santa Maria, where they might water easily, it being a solitary island, as the foreigners did; that the deponent did not go to Pisco, that was near, nor make any other port of the coast, because the negro Babo had intimated to him several times, that he would kill all the whites the very moment he should perceive any city, town, or settlement of any kind on the shores to which they should be carried: that having determined to go to the island of Santa Maria, as the deponent had planned, for the purpose of trying whether, on the passage or near the island itself, they could find any vessel that should favor them, or whether he could escape from it in a boat to the neighboring coast of Arruco, to adopt the necessary means he immediately changed his course, steering for the island; that the negroes Babo and

Atufal held daily conferences, in which they discussed what was necessary for their design of returning to Senegal, whether they were to kill all the Spaniards, and particularly the deponent; that eight days after parting from the coast of Nasca, the deponent being on the watch a little after day-break, and soon after the negroes had their meeting, the negro Babo came to the place where the deponent was, and told him that he had determined to kill his master, Don Alexandro Aranda, both because he and his companions could not otherwise be sure of their liberty, and that to keep the seamen in subjection, he wanted to prepare a warning of what road they should be made to take did they or any of them oppose him; and that, by means of the death of Don Alexandro, that warning would best be given; but, that what this last meant, the deponent did not at the time comprehend, nor could not, further than that the death of Don Alexandro was intended; and moreover the negro Babo proposed to the deponent to call the mate Raneds, who was sleeping in the cabin, before the thing was done, for fear, as the deponent understood it, that the mate, who was a good navigator, should be killed with Don Alexandro and the rest; that the deponent, who was the friend, from youth, of Don Alexandro, prayed and conjured, but all was useless; for the negro Babo answered him that the thing could not be prevented, and that all the Spaniards risked their death if they should attempt to frustrate his will in this matter, or any other; that, in this conflict, the deponent called the mate, Raneds, who was forced to go apart, and immediately the negro Babo commanded the Ashantee Martinqui and the Ashantee Lecbe to go and commit the murder; that those two went down with hatchets to the berth of Don Alexandro; that, yet half alive and mangled, they dragged him on deck; that they were going to throw him overboard in that state, but the negro Babo stopped them, bidding the murder be completed on the deck before him, which was done, when, by his orders, the body was carried below, forward; that nothing more was seen of it by the deponent for three days; * * * that Don

[293]

Alonzo Sidonia, an old man, long resident at Valparaiso, and lately appointed to a civil office in Peru, whither he had taken passage, was at the time sleeping in the berth opposite Don Alexandro's; that awakening at his cries, surprised by them, and at the sight of the negroes with their bloody hatchets in their hands, he threw himself into the sea through a window which was near him, and was drowned, without it being in the power of the deponent to assist or take him up; * * * that a short time after killing Aranda, they brought upon deck his german-cousin, of middle-age, Don Francisco Masa, of Mendoza, and the young Don Joaquin, Marques de Aramboalaza, then lately from Spain, with his Spanish servant Ponce, and the three young clerks of Aranda, José Mozairi, Lorenzo Bargas, and Hermene-gildo Gandix, all of Cadiz; that Don Joaquin and Hermene-gildo Gandix, the negro Babo, for purposes hereafter to appear, preserved alive; but Don Francisco Masa, José Mozairi, and Lorenzo Bargas, with Ponce the servant, be-side the boatswain, Juan Robles, the boatswain's mates, Manuel Viscaya and Roderigo Hurta, and four of the sailors, the negro Babo ordered to be thrown alive into the sea, although they made no resistance, nor begged for any-thing else but mercy; that the boatswain, Juan Robles, who knew how to swim, kept the longest above water, making acts of contrition, and, in the last words he uttered, charged this deponent to cause mass to be said for his soul to our Lady of Succor: * * * that, during the three days which followed, the deponent, uncertain what fate had befallen the remains of Don Alexandro, frequently asked the negro Babo where they were, and, if still on board, whether they were to be preserved for interment ashore, entreating him so to order it; that the negro Babo answered nothing till the fourth day, when at sunrise, the deponent coming on deck, the negro Babo showed him a skeleton, which had been substituted for the ship's proper figure-head – the image of Christopher Colon, the discoverer of the New World; that the negro Babo asked him whose skeleton that was, and whether, from its whiteness, he should not think it a white's; that, upon discovering his face, the negro Babo, coming close, said words to this effect: 'Keep faith with the blacks from here to Senegal, or you shall in spirit, as now in body, follow your leader,' pointing to the prow; * * * that the same morning the negro Babo took by succession each Spaniard forward, and asked him whose skeleton that was, and whether, from its whiteness, he should not think it a white's; that each Spaniard covered his face; that then to each the negro repeated the words in the first place said to the deponent; * * * that they (the Spaniards), being then assembled aft, the negro Babo harangued them, saying that he had now done all; that the deponent (as navigator for the negroes) might pursue his course, warning him and all of them that they should, soul and body, go the way of Don Alexandro, if he saw them (the Spaniards) speak or plot anything against them (the negroes) – a threat which was repeated every day; that, before the events last mentioned, they had tied the cook to throw him overboard, for it is not known what thing they heard him speak, but finally the negro Babo spared his life, at the request of the deponent; that a few days after, the deponent, endeavoring not to omit any means to preserve the lives of the remaining whites, spoke to the negroes of peace and tranquillity, and agreed to draw up a paper, signed by the deponent and the sailors who could write, as also by the negro Babo, for himself and all the blacks, in which the deponent obliged himself to carry them to Senegal, and they not to kill any more, and he formally to make over to them the ship, with the cargo, with which they were for that time satisfied and quieted. * * * But the next day, the more surely to guard against the sailors' escape, the negro Babo commanded all the boats to be destroyed but the long-boat, which was unseaworthy, and another, a cutter in good condition, which knowing it would yet be wanted for towing the water casks, he had it lowered down into the hold.

*

[*Various particulars of the prolonged and perplexed navigation ensuing here follow, with incidents of a calamitous calm, from which portion one passage is extracted, to wit:*]

– That on the fifth day of the calm, all on board suffering much from the heat, and want of water, and five having died in fits, and mad, the negroes became irritable, and for a chance gesture, which they deemed suspicious – though it was harmless – made by the mate, Raneds, to the deponent in the act of handing a quadrant, they killed him; but that for this they afterwards were sorry, the mate being the only remaining navigator on board, except the deponent.

*

– That omitting other events, which daily happened, and which can only serve uselessly to recall past misfortunes and conflicts, after seventy-three days' navigation, reckoned from the time they sailed from Nasca, during which they navigated under a scanty allowance of water, and were afflicted with the calms before mentioned, they at last arrived at the island of Santa Maria, on the seventeenth of the month of August, at about six o'clock in the afternoon, at which hour they cast anchor very near the American ship, *Bachelor's Delight*, which lay in the same bay, commanded by the generous Captain Amasa Delano; but at six o'clock in the morning, they had already descried the port, and the negroes became uneasy, as soon as at distance they saw the ship, not having expected to see one there; that the negro Babo pacified them, assuring them that no fear need be had; that straightway he ordered the figure on the bow to be covered with canvas, as for repairs, and had the decks a little set in order; that for a time the negro Babo and the negro Atufal conferred; that the negro Atufal was for sailing away, but the negro Babo would not, and, by himself, cast about what to do; that at last he came to the deponent, proposing to him to say and do all that the deponent declares to have said and done to the American captain;

*

that the negro Babo warned him that if he varied
in the least, or uttered any word, or gave any look that
should give the least intimation of the past events or present
state, he would instantly kill him, with all his companions,
showing a dagger, which he carried hid, saying something
which, as he understood it, meant that that dagger would
be alert as his eye; that the negro Babo then announced
the plan to all his companions, which pleased them; that he
then, the better to disguise the truth, devised many ex-
pedients, in some of them uniting deceit and defense; that
of this sort was the device of the six Ashantees before
named, who were his bravoes; that them he stationed on the
break of the poop, as if to clean certain hatchets (in cases,
which were part of the cargo), but in reality to use them,
and distribute them at need, and at a given word he told
them; that, among other devices, was the device of presenting Atufal, his right hand man, as chained, though in a
moment the chains could be dropped; that in every particular he informed the deponent what part he was expected to enact in every device, and what story he was to
tell on every occasion, always threatening him with instant
death if he varied in the least: that, conscious that many
of the negroes would be turbulent, the negro Babo appointed the four aged negroes, who were calkers, to keep
what domestic order they could on the decks; that again
and again he harangued the Spaniards and his companions,
informing them of his intent, and of his devices, and of the
invented story that this deponent was to tell; charging
them lest any of them varied from that story; that these
arrangements were made and matured during the interval
of two or three hours, between their first sighting the ship
and the arrival on board of Captain Amasa Delano; that
this happened about half-past seven o'clock in the morning,
Captain Amasa Delano coming in his boat, and all gladly
receiving him; that the deponent, as well as he could force
himself, acting then the part of principal owner, and a free
captain of the ship, told Captain Amasa Delano, when called
upon, that he came from Buenos Ayres, bound to Lima,

with three hundred negroes; that off Cape Horn, and in a subsequent fever, many negroes had died; that also, by similar casualties, all the sea officers and the greatest part of the crew had died.

*

[*And so the deposition goes on, circumstantially recounting the fictitious story dictated to the deponent by Babo, and through the deponent imposed upon Captain Delano; and also recounting the friendly offers of Captain Delano, with other things, but all of which is here omitted. After the fictitious story, etc. the deposition proceeds:*]

*

– that the generous Captain Amasa Delano remained on board all the day, till he left the ship anchored at six o'clock in the evening, deponent speaking to him always of his pretended misfortunes, under the fore-mentioned principles, without having had it in his power to tell a single word, or give him the least hint, that he might know the truth and state of things; because the negro Babo, performing the office of an officious servant with all the appearance of submission of the humble slave, did not leave the deponent one moment; that this was in order to observe the deponent's actions and words, for the negro Babo understands well the Spanish; and besides, there were thereabout some others who were constantly on the watch, and likewise understood the Spanish; * * * that upon one occasion, while deponent was standing on the deck conversing with Amasa Delano, by a secret sign the negro Babo drew him (the deponent) aside, the act appearing as if originating with the deponent; that then, he being drawn aside, the negro Babo proposed to him to gain from Amasa Delano full particulars about his ship, and crew, and arms; that the deponent asked 'For what?' that the negro Babo answered he might conceive; that, grieved at the prospect of what might overtake the generous Captain Amasa Delano, the deponent at first refused to ask the desired

[298]

questions, and used every argument to induce the negro Babo to give up this new design; that the negro Babo showed the point of his dagger; that, after the information had been obtained the negro Babo again drew him aside, telling him that that very night he (the deponent) would be captain of two ships, instead of one, for that, great part of the American's ship's crew being to be absent fishing, the six Ashantees, without any one else, would easily take it; that at this time he said other things to the same purpose; that no entreaties availed; that, before Amasa Delano's coming on board, no hint had been given touching the capture of the American ship: that to prevent this project the deponent was powerless; * * * – that in some things his memory is confused, he cannot distinctly recall every event; * * * – that as soon as they had cast anchor at six of the clock in the evening, as has before been stated, the American Captain took leave, to return to his vessel; that upon a sudden impulse, which the deponent believes to have come from God and his angels, he, after the farewell had been said, followed the generous Captain Amasa Delano as far as the gunwale, where he stayed, under pretense of taking leave, until Amasa Delano should have been seated in his boat; that on shoving off, the deponent sprang from the gunwale into the boat, and fell into it, he knows not how, God, guarding him; that –

*

[*Here, in the original, follows the account of what further happened at the escape, and how the* San Dominick *was retaken, and of the passage to the coast; including in the recital many expressions of 'eternal gratitude' to the 'generous Captain Amasa Delano.' The deposition then proceeds with recapitulatory remarks, and a partial renumeration of the negroes, making record of their individual part in the past events, with a view to furnishing, according to command of the court, the data whereon to found the criminal sentences to be pronounced. From this portion is the following;*]

– That he believes that all the negroes, though not in the first place knowing to the design of revolt, when it was accomplished, approved it. * * * That the negro, José, eighteen years old, and in the personal service of Don Alexandro, was the one who communicated the information to the negro Babo, about the state of things in the cabin, before the revolt; that this is known, because, in the preceding midnight, he used to come from his berth, which was under his master's, in the cabin, to the deck where the ring-leader and his associates were, and had secret conversations with the negro Babo, in which he was several times seen by the mate; that, one night, the mate drove him away twice; * * * that this same negro José was the one who, without being commanded to do so by the negro Babo, as Lecbe and Martinqui were, stabbed his master, Don Alexandro, after he had been dragged half-lifeless to the deck; * * * that the mulatto steward, Francesco, was of the first band of revolters, that he was, in all things, the creature and tool of the negro Babo; that, to make his court, he, just before a repast in the cabin, proposed, to the negro Babo, poisoning a dish for the generous Captain Amasa Delano; this is known and believed, because the negroes have said it; but that the negro Babo, having another design, forbade Francesco; * * * that the Ashantee Lecbe was one of the worst of them; for that, on the day the ship was retaken, he assisted in the defense of her, with a hatchet in each hand, with one of which he wounded, in the breast, the chief mate of Amasa Delano, in the first act of boarding; this all knew; that, in sight of the deponent, Lecbe struck, with a hatchet, Don Francisco Masa, when, by the negro Babo's orders, he was carrying him to throw him overboard, alive, beside participating in the murder, before mentioned, of Don Alexandro Aranda, and others of the cabin-passengers; that, owing to the fury with which the Ashan-tees fought in the engagement with the boats, but this Lecbe and Yan survived; that Yan was bad as Lecbe; that Yan was the man who, by Babo's command, willingly prepared the skeleton of Don Alexandro, in a way the negroes afterwards told the deponent, but which he, so long as reason is left him, can never divulge; that Yan and Lecbe were the two who, in a calm by night, riveted the skeleton to the bow; this also the negroes told him; that the negro Babo was he who traced the inscription below it; that the negro Babo was the plotter from first to last; he ordered every murder, and was the helm and keel of the revolt; that Atufal was his lieutenant in all; but Atufal, with his own hand, committed no murder; nor did the negro Babo; * * * that Atufal was shot, being killed in the fight with the boats, ere boarding; * * * that the negresses, of age, were knowing to the revolt, and testified themselves satisfied at the death of their master, Don Alexandro; that, had the negroes not restrained them, they would have tortured to death, instead of simply killing, the Spaniards slain by command of the negro Babo; that the negresses used their utmost influence to have the deponent made away with; that, in the various acts of murder, they sang songs and danced – not gaily, but solemnly; and before the engagement with the boats, as well as during the action, they sang melancholy songs to the negroes, and that this melancholy tone was more inflaming than a different one would have been, and was so intended; that all this is believed, because the negroes have said it.

– that of the thirty-six men of the crew, exclusive of the passengers (all of whom are now dead), which the deponent had knowledge of, six only remained alive, with four cabin-boys and ship-boys, not included with the crew; * * * – that the negroes broke an arm of one of the cabin-boys and gave him strokes with hatchets.

[*Then follow various random disclosures referring to various periods of time. The following are extracted;*]

– That during the presence of Captain Amasa Delano on board, some attempts were made by the sailors, and one by Hermenegildo Gandix, to convey hints to him of the true state of affairs; but that these attempts were ineffectual, owing to fear of incurring death, and, furthermore, owing to the devices which offered contradictions to the true state of affairs, as well as owing to the generosity and piety of Amasa Delano incapable of sounding such wickedness; * * * that Luys Galgo, a sailor about sixty years of age, and formerly of the king's navy, was one of those who sought to convey tokens to Captain Amasa Delano; but his intent, though undiscovered, being suspected, he was, on a pretense, made to retire out of sight, and at last into the hold, and there was made away with. This the negroes have since said; * * * that one of the ship-boys feeling, from Captain Amasa Delano's presence, some hopes of release, and not having enough prudence, dropped some chance-word respecting his expectations, which being overheard and understood by a slave-boy with whom he was eating at the time, the latter struck him on the head with a knife, inflicting a bad wound, but of which the boy is now healing; that likewise, not long before the ship was brought to anchor, one of the seamen, steering at the time, endangered himself by letting the blacks remark some expression in his countenance, arising from a cause similar to the above; but this sailor, by his heedful after conduct, escaped; * * * that these statements are made to show the court that from the beginning to the end of the revolt, it was impossible for the deponent and his men to act otherwise than they did; * * * – that the third clerk, Hermenegildo Gandix, who before had been forced to live among the seamen, wearing a seaman's habit, and in all respects appearing to be one for the time; he, Gandix, was killed by a musket ball fired through mistake from the boats before boarding; having in his fright run up the mizzen-rigging, calling to the boats – 'don't board,' lest upon their boarding the negroes should kill him; that this inducing the Americans to believe he some way favored the cause of the negroes, they fired two balls at him, so that he fell wounded from the rigging, and was drowned in the sea; * * * – that the young Don Joaquin, Marques de Aramboalaza, like Hermenegildo Gandix, the third clerk, was degraded to the office and appearance of a common seaman; that upon one occasion when Don

Joaquin shrank, the negro Babo commanded the Ashantee Lecbe to take tar and heat it, and pour it upon Don Joaquin's hands; * * * – that Don Joaquin was killed owing to another mistake of the Americans, but one impossible to be avoided, as upon the approach of the boats, Don Joaquin, with a hatchet tied edge out and upright to his hand, was made by the negroes to appear on the bulwarks; whereupon, seen with arms in his hands and in a questionable attitude, he was shot for a renegade seaman; * * * – that on the person of Don Joaquin was found secreted a jewel, which, by papers that were discovered, proved to have been meant for the shrine of our Lady of Mercy in Lima; a votive offering, beforehand prepared and guarded, to attest his gratitude, when he should have landed in Peru, his last destination, for the safe conclusion of his entire voyage from Spain; * * * – that the jewel, with the other effects of the late Don Joaquin, is in the custody of the brethren of the Hospital de Sacerdotes, awaiting the disposition of the honorable court; * * * – that, owing to the condition of the deponent, as well as the haste in which the boats departed for the attack, the Americans were not forewarned that there were, among the apparent crew, a passenger and one of the clerks disguised by the negro Babo; * * * – that, beside the negroes killed in the action, some were killed after the capture and re-anchoring at night, when shackled to the ring-bolts on deck; that these deaths were committed by the sailors, ere they could be prevented. That so soon as informed of it, Captain Amasa Delano used all his authority, and, in particular with his own hand, struck down Martinez Gola, who, having found a razor in the pocket of an old jacket of his, which one of the shackled negroes had on, was aiming it at the negro's throat; that the noble Captain Amasa Delano also wrenched from the hand of Bartholomew Barlo a dagger, secreted at the time of the massacre of the whites, with which he was in the act of stabbing a shackled negro, who, the same day, with another negro, had thrown him down and jumped upon him; * * * – that, for all the events, befalling through so long a time, during which the ship was in the hands of the negro Babo, he cannot here give account; but that, what he has said is the most substantial of what occurs to him at present, and is the truth under the oath which he has taken; which declaration he affirmed and ratified, after hearing it read to him.

He said that he is twenty-nine years of age, and broken in body and mind; that when finally dismissed by the court, he shall not return home to Chili, but betake himself to the monastery on Mount Agonia without; and signed with his honor, and crossed himself, and, for the time, departed as he came, in his litter, with the monk Infelez, to the Hospital de Sacerdotes.

BENITO CERENO.

DOCTOR ROZAS.

*

If the Deposition have served as the key to fit into the lock of the complications which precede it, then, as a vault whose door has been flung back, the *San Dominick*'s hull lies open to-day.

Hitherto the nature of this narrative, besides rendering the intricacies in the beginning unavoidable, has more or less required that many things, instead of being set down in the order of occurrence, should be retrospectively, or irregularly given; this last is the case with the following passages, which will conclude the account:

During the long, mild voyage to Lima, there was, as before hinted, a period during which the sufferer a little recovered his health, or, at least in some degree, his tranquillity. Ere the decided relapse which came, the two captains had many cordial conversations – their fraternal unreserve in singular contrast with former withdrawments.

Again and again it was repeated, how hard it had been to enact the part forced on the Spaniard by Babo.

'Ah, my dear friend,' Don Benito once said, 'at those very times when you thought me so morose and ungrateful, nay, when, as you now admit, you half thought me plotting your murder, at those very times my heart was frozen; I could not look at you, thinking of what, both on board this ship and your own, hung, from other hands, over my kind benefactor. And as God lives, Don Amasa, I know not whether desire for my own safety alone could have nerved me to that leap into your boat, had it not been for the thought that, did you, unenlightened, return to your ship, you, my best friend, with all who might be with you, stolen upon, that night, in your hammocks, would never in this world have wakened again. Do but think how you walked this deck, how you sat in this cabin, every inch of ground mined into honey-combs under you. Had I dropped the least hint, made the least advance towards an understanding between us, death, explosive death – yours as mine – would have ended the scene.'

'True, true,' cried Captain Delano, starting, 'you have saved my life, Don Benito, more than I yours; saved it, too, against my knowledge and will.'

'Nay, my friend,' rejoined the Spaniard, courteous even to the point of religion, 'God charmed your life, but you saved mine. To think of some things you did – those smilings and chattings, rash pointings and gesturings. For less than these, they slew my mate, Raneds; but you had the Prince of Heaven's safe-conduct through all ambuscades.'

'Yes, all is owing to Providence, I know : but the temper of my mind that morning was more than commonly pleasant, while the sight of so much suffering, more apparent than real, added to my good-nature, compassion, and charity, happily interweaving the three. Had it been otherwise, doubtless, as you hint, some of my interferences might have ended unhappily enough. Besides, those feelings I spoke of enabled me to get the better of momentary distrust, at times when acuteness might have cost me my life, without saving another's. Only at the end did my suspicions get the better of me, and you know how wide of the mark they then proved.'

'Wide, indeed,' said Don Benito, sadly; 'you were with me all day; stood with me, sat with me, talked with me, looked at me, ate with me, drank with me; and yet, your last act was to clutch for a monster, not only an innocent man, but the most pitiable of all men. To such degree may malign machinations and deceptions impose. So far may even the best man err, in judging the conduct of one with the recesses of whose condition he is not acquainted. But you were forced to it; and you were in time undeceived. Would that, in both respects, it was so ever, and with all men.'

'You generalize, Don Benito; and mournfully enough. But the past is passed; why moralize upon it? Forget it. See, yon bright sun has forgotten it all, and the blue sea, and the blue sky; these have turned over new leaves.'

'Because they have no memory,' he dejectedly replied; 'because they are not human.'

'But these mild trades that now fan your cheek, do they not come with a human-like healing to you? Warm friends, steadfast friends are the trades.'

'With their steadfastness they but waft me to my tomb, Señor,' was the foreboding response.

'You are saved,' cried Captain Delano, more and more astonished and pained; 'you are saved: what has cast such a shadow upon you?'

'The negro.'

There was silence, while the moody man sat, slowly and unconsciously gathering his mantle about him, as if it were a pall.

There was no more conversation that day.

But if the Spaniard's melancholy sometimes ended in muteness upon topics like the above, there were others upon which he never spoke at all; on which, indeed, all his old reserves were piled. Pass over the worst, and, only to elucidate, let an item or two of these be cited. The dress, so precise and costly, worn by him on the day whose events have been narrated, had not willingly been put on. And that silver-mounted sword, apparent symbol of despotic command, was not, indeed, a sword, but the ghost of one. The scabbard, artificially stiffened, was empty.

As for the black – whose brain, not body, had schemed

and led the revolt, with the plot – his slight frame, inadequate to that which it held, had at once yielded to the superior muscular strength of his captor, in the boat. Seeing all was over, he uttered no sound, and could not be forced to. His aspect seemed to say, since I cannot do deeds, I will not speak words. Put in irons in the hold, with the rest, he was carried to Lima. During the passage, Don Benito did not visit him. Nor then, nor at any time after, would he look at him. Before the tribunal he refused. When pressed by the judges he fainted. On the testimony of the sailors alone rested the legal identity of Babo.

Some months after, dragged to the gibbet at the tail of a mule, the black met his voiceless end. The body was burned to ashes; but for many days, the head, that hive of subtlety, fixed on a pole in the Plaza, met, unabashed, the gaze of the whites; and across the Plaza looked towards St Bartholomew's church, in whose vaults slept then, as now, the recovered bones of Aranda: and across the Rimac bridge looked towards the monastery, on Mount Agonia without; where, three months after being dismissed by the court, Benito Cereno, borne on the bier, did, indeed, follow his leader.

JOHN MARR

JOHN MARR, toward the close of the last century born in America of a mother unknown, and from boyhood up to maturity a sailor under divers flags, disabled at last from further maritime life by a crippling wound received at close quarters with pirates of the Keys, eventually betakes himself for a livelihood to less active employment ashore. There, too, he transfers his rambling disposition acquired as a seafarer.

After a variety of removals, at first as a sail-maker from seaport to seaport, then adventurously inland as a rough bench-carpenter, he, finally, in the last-named capacity, settles down about the year 1838 upon what was then a frontier-prairie, sparsely sprinkled with small oak groves and yet fewer log houses of a little colony but recently from one of our elder inland States. Here, putting a period to his rovings, he marries.

Ere long a fever, the bane of new settlements on teeming loam, and whose sallow livery was certain to show itself, after an interval, in the complexions of too many of these people, carries off his young wife and infant child. In one coffin, put together by his own hands, they are committed with meager rites to the earth – another mound, though a small one, in the wide prairie, not far from where the mound builders of a race only conjecturable had left their pottery and bones, one common clay, under a strange terrace serpentine in form.

With an honest stillness in his general mien – swarthy and black-browed, with eyes that could soften or flash, but never harden, yet disclosing at times a melancholy depth – this kinless man had affections which, once placed, not readily could be dislodged or resigned to a substituted object. Being now arrived at middle life, he resolves never to quit the soil that holds the only beings ever connected with him by love in the family tie. His log house he lets to a newcomer, one glad enough to get it, and dwells with the household.

While the acuter sense of his bereavement becomes mollified by time, the void at heart abides. Fain, if possible, would he fill that void by cultivating social relations yet nearer than before with a people whose lot he purposes sharing to the end – relations superadded to that mere work-a-day bond arising from participation in the same outward hardships, making reciprocal helpfulness a matter of course. But here, and nobody to blame, he is obstructed.

More familiarly to consort, men of a practical turn must sympathetically converse, and upon topics of real life. But, whether as to persons or events, one cannot always be talking about the present, much less speculating about the future; one must needs recur to the past, which, with the mass of men, where the past is in any personal way a common inheritance, supplies to most practical natures the basis of sympathetic communion.

But the past of John Marr was not the past of these pioneers. Their hands had rested on the plow-tail, his upon the ship's helm. They knew but their own kind and their own usages; to him had been revealed something of the checkered globe. So limited unavoidably was the mental reach, and by consequence the range of sympathy, in this particular band of domestic emigrants, hereditary tillers of the soil, that the ocean, but a hearsay to their fathers, had now through yet deeper inland removal become to themselves little more than a rumor traditional and vague.

They were a staid people; staid through habituation to monotonous hardship; ascetics by necessity not less than through moral bias; nearly all of them sincerely, however narrowly, religious. They were kindly at need, after their fashion; but to a man wonted – as John Marr in his previous homeless sojournings could not but have been – to the free-

and-easy tavern-clubs affording cheap recreation of an evening in certain old and comfortable seaport towns of that time, and yet more familiar with the companionship afloat of the sailors of the same period, something was lacking. That something was geniality, the flower of life springing from some sense of joy in it, more or less. This their lot could not give to these hard-working endurers of the dispiriting malaria – men to whom a holiday never came – and they had too much of uprightness and no art at all or desire to affect what they did not really feel. At a corn-husking, their least grave of gatherings, did the lone-hearted mariner seek to divert his own thoughts from sadness, and in some degree interest theirs, by adverting to aught removed from the crosses and trials of their personal surroundings, naturally enough he would slide into some marine story or picture but would soon recoil upon himself and be silent, finding no encouragement to proceed. Upon one such occasion an elderly man – a blacksmith, and at Sunday gatherings an earnest exhorter – honestly said to him, 'Friend, we know nothing of that here.'

Such unresponsiveness in one's fellow creatures set apart from factitious life, and by their vocation – in those days little helped by machinery – standing, as it were, next of kin to Nature: this, to John Marr, seemed of a piece with the apathy of Nature herself as envisaged to him here on a prairie where none but the perished mound builders had as yet left a durable mark.

The remnant of Indians thereabouts – all but exterminated in their recent and final war with regular white troops, a war raged by the Red Men for their native soil and natural rights – had been coerced into the occupancy of wilds not very far beyond the Mississippi – wilds *then*, but now the seats of municipalities and States. Prior to that, the bisons, once streaming countless in processional herds, or browsing as in an endless battle-line over these vast aboriginal pastures, had retreated, dwindled in number, before the hunters, in main a race distinct from the agricultural pioneers, though generally their advance-guard. Such a double exodus of man and beast left the plain a desert, green or blossoming indeed, but almost as forsaken as the Siberian Obi. Save the prairie-hen, sometimes startled from its lurking-place in the rank grass, and, in their migratory season, pigeons, high overhead on the wing, in dense multitudes eclipsing the day like a passing storm-cloud; save these – there being no wide woods with their underwood – birds were strangely few.

Blank stillness would for hours reign unbroken on this prairie. 'It is the bed of a dried-up sea,' said the companionless sailor – no geologist – to himself, musing at twilight upon the fixed undulations of that immense alluvial expanse bounded only by the horizon, and missing there the stir that, to alert eyes and ears, animates at all times the apparent solitudes of the deep.

But a scene quite at variance with one's antecedents may yet prove suggestive of them. Hooped round by a level rim, the prairie was to John Marr a reminder of ocean.

With some of his former shipmates, chums on certain cruises, he had contrived, prior to this last and more remote removal, to keep up a little correspondence at odd intervals. But from tidings of anybody or any sort he, in common with the other settlers, was now cut off; quite cut off, except from such news as might be conveyed over the grassy billows by the last-arrived prairie-schooner – the vernacular term, in those parts and times, for the emigrant-wagon arched high over with sailcloth, and voyaging across the vast champaign. There was no reachable post-office as yet; not even the rude little receptive box with lid and leather hinges, set up at convenient intervals on a stout stake along some solitary green way, affording a perch for birds, and which, later in the unintermitting advance of the frontier, would perhaps decay into a mossy monument, attesting yet another successive overleaped limit of civilized life; a life which in America can today hardly be said to have any western bound but the ocean that washes Asia. Throughout these plains, now in places over-populous with towns over-opulent; sweeping plains elsewhere fenced off in every direction into flourishing farms – pale townsmen and hale farmers alike, in part, the descendants of the first sallow settlers; a region that half a century ago produced little for the sustenance of man but today launching its super-abundant wheat-harvest on the world; – of this prairie, now everywhere intersected with wire and rail, hardly can it be said that at the period here written of there was so much as a traceable road. To the long-distance traveler the oak-groves, wide apart, and varying in compass and form; these, with recent settlements, yet more widely separate, offered some landmarks; but otherwise he steered by the sun. In early midsummer, even going but from one log-encampment to the next, a journey it might be of hours or good part of a day, travel was much like navigation. In some more enriched depressions between the long, green, graduated swells, smooth as those of ocean becalmed re-ceiving and subduing to its own tranquility the voluminous surge raised by some far-off hurricane of days previous, here one would catch the first indication of advancing strangers either in the distance, as a far sail at sea, by the glistening white canvas of the wagon, the wagon itself wading through the rank vegetation and hidden by it, or, failing that, when near to, in the ears of the team, peeking, if not above the tall tiger-lilies, yet above the yet taller grass.

Luxuriant, this wilderness; but, to its denizen, a friend left behind anywhere in the world seemed not alone absent to sight, but an absentee from existence.

Though John Marr's shipmates could not all have de-parted life, yet as subjects of meditation they were like phantoms of the dead. As the growing sense of his environ-ment threw him more and more upon retrospective mus-ings, these phantoms, next to those of his wife and child, became spiritual companions, losing something of their first indistinctness and putting on at last a dim semblance of mute life; and they were lit by that aureola circling over any object of the affections in the past, for reunion with which an imaginative heart passionately yearns.

BILLY BUDD, SAILOR

(An inside narrative)

1

IN the time before steamships, or then more frequently than now, a stroller along the docks of any considerable seaport would occasionally have his attention arrested by a group of bronzed mariners, man-of-war's men or merchant sailors in holiday attire, ashore on liberty. In certain instances they would flank, or like a bodyguard quite surround, some superior figure of their own class, moving along with them like Aldebaran among the lesser lights of his constellation. That signal object was the 'Handsome Sailor' of the less prosaic time alike of the military and merchant navies. With no perceptible trace of the vainglorious about him, rather with the offhand unaffectedness of natural regality, he seemed to accept the spontaneous homage of his shipmates.

A somewhat remarkable instance recurs to me. In Liverpool, now half a century ago, I saw under the shadow of the great dingy street-wall of Prince's Dock (an obstruction long since removed) a common sailor so intensely black that he must needs have been a native African of the unadulterate blood of Ham – a symmetric figure much above the average height. The two ends of a gay silk handkerchief thrown loose about the neck danced upon the displayed ebony of his chest, in his ears were big hoops of gold, and a Highland bonnet with a tartan band set off his shapely head. It was a hot noon in July; and his face, lustrous with perspiration, beamed with barbaric good humor. In jovial sallies right and left, his white teeth flashing into view, he rollicked along, the center of a company of his shipmates. These were made up of such an assortment of tribes and complexions as would have well fitted them to be marched up by Anacharsis Cloots before the bar of the first French Assembly as Representatives of the Human Race. At each spontaneous tribute rendered by the wayfarers to this black pagod of a fellow – the tribute of a pause and stare, and less frequently an exclamation – the motley retinue showed that they took that sort of pride in the evoker of it which the Assyrian priests doubtless showed for their grand sculptured Bull when the faithful prostrated themselves.

To return. If in some cases a bit of a nautical Murat in setting forth his person ashore, the Handsome Sailor of the period in question evinced nothing of the dandified Billy-be-Dam, an amusing character all but extinct now, but occasionally to be encountered, and in a form yet more amusing than the original, at the tiller of the boats on the tempestuous Erie Canal or, more likely, vaporing in the groggeries along the towpath. Invariably a proficient in his perilous calling, he was also more or less of a mighty boxer or wrestler. It was strength and beauty. Tales of his prowess were recited. Ashore he was the champion; afloat the spokesman; on every suitable occasion always foremost. Close-reefing topsails in a gale, there he was, astride the weather yardarm-end, foot in the Flemish horse as stirrup, both hands tugging at the earing as at a bridle, in very much the attitude of young Alexander curbing the fiery Bucephalus. A superb figure, tossed up as by the horns of Taurus against the thunderous sky, cheerily hallooing to the strenuous file along the spar.

The moral nature was seldom out of keeping with the physical make. Indeed, except as toned by the former, the comeliness and power, always attractive in masculine conjunction, hardly could have drawn the sort of honest homage the Handsome Sailor in some examples received from his less gifted associates.

Such a cynosure, at least in aspect, and something such too in nature, though with important variations made apparent as the story proceeds, was welkin-eyed Billy Budd – or Baby Budd, as more familiarly, under circumstances hereafter to be given, he at last came to be called – aged twenty-one, a foretopman of the British fleet toward the close of the last decade of the eighteenth century. It was not very long prior to the time of the narration that follows that he had entered the King's service, having been impressed on the Narrow Seas from a homeward-bound English merchantman into a seventy-four outward bound, H.M.S. *Bellipotent*; which ship, as was not unusual in those hurried days, having been obliged to put to sea short of her proper complement of men. Plump upon Billy at first sight in the gangway the boarding officer, Lieutenant Ratcliffe, pounced, even before the merchantman's crew was formally mustered on the quarter-deck for his deliberate inspection. And him only he elected. For whether it was because the other men when ranged before him showed to ill advantage after Billy, or whether he had some scruples in view of the merchantman's being rather short-handed, however it might be, the officer contented himself with his first spontaneous choice. To the surprise of the ship's company, though much to the lieutenant's satisfaction, Billy made no demur. But, indeed, any demur would have been as idle as the protest of a goldfinch popped into a cage.

Noting this uncomplaining acquiescence, all but cheerful, one might say, the shipmaster turned a surprised glance of silent reproach at the sailor. The shipmaster was one of those worthy mortals found in every vocation, even the humbler ones – the sort of person whom everybody agrees in calling 'a respectable man.' And – nor so strange to report as it may appear to be – though a ploughman of the troubled waters, lifelong contending with the intractable elements, there was nothing this honest soul at heart loved better than simple peace and quiet. For the rest, he was fifty or thereabouts, a little inclined to corpulence, a prepossessing face, unwhiskered, and of an agreeable color – a rather full face, humanely intelligent in expression. On a fair day with a fair wind and all going well, a certain musical chime in his voice seemed to be the veritable unobstructed outcome of the innermost man. He had much prudence, much conscientiousness, and there were occasions when these virtues were the cause of overmuch disquietude in him. On a passage, so long as his craft was in any proximity to land, no sleep for Captain Graveling. He took to heart those serious responsibilities not so heavily borne by some shipmasters.

Now while Billy Budd was down in the forecastle getting his kit together, the *Bellipotent*'s lieutenant, burly and bluff, nowise disconcerted by Captain Graveling's omitting to proffer the customary hospitalities on an occasion so unwelcome to him, an omission simply caused by preoccupation of thought, unceremoniously invited himself into the cabin, and also to a flask from the spirit locker, a receptacle which his experienced eye instantly discovered. In fact he was one of those sea dogs in whom all the hardship and peril of naval life in the great prolonged wars of his time never impaired the natural instinct for sensuous enjoyment. His duty he always faithfully did; but duty is sometimes a dry obligation, and he was for irrigating its aridity, whensoever possible, with a fertilizing decoction of strong waters. For the cabin's proprietor there was nothing left but to play the part of the enforced host with whatever grace and alacrity were practicable. As necessary adjuncts to the flask, he silently placed tumbler and water jug before the irrepressible guest. But excusing himself from partaking just then, he dismally watched the unembarrassed officer deliberately diluting his grog a little, then tossing it off in three swallows, pushing the empty tumbler away, yet not so far as to be beyond easy reach, at the same time settling himself in his seat and smacking his lips with high satisfaction, looking straight at the host.

These proceedings over, the master broke the silence; and there lurked a rueful reproach in the tone of his voice: 'Lieutenant, you are going to take my best man from me, the jewel of 'em.'

'Yes, I know,' rejoined the other, immediately drawing back the tumbler preliminary to a replenishing. 'Yes, I know. Sorry.'

'Beg pardon, but you don't understand, Lieutenant. See here, now. Before I shipped that young fellow, my forecastle was a rat-pit of quarrels. It was black times, I tell you, aboard the *Rights* here. I was worried to that degree my pipe had no comfort for me. But Billy came; and it was like a Catholic priest striking peace in an Irish shindy. Not that he preached to them or said or did anything in particular; but a virtue went out of him, sugaring the sour ones. They took to him like hornets to treacle; all but the buffer of the gang, the big shaggy chap with the fire-red whiskers. He indeed, out of envy, perhaps, of the newcomer, and thinking such a 'sweet and pleasant fellow,' as he mockingly designated him to the others, could hardly have the spirit of a gamecock, must needs bestir himself in trying to get up an ugly row with him. Billy forebore with him and reasoned with him in a pleasant way – he is something like myself, Lieutenant, to whom aught like a quarrel is hateful – but nothing served. So, in the second dogwatch one day, the Red Whiskers in presence of the others, under pretense of showing Billy just whence a sirloin steak was cut – for the fellow had once been a butcher – insultingly gave him a dig under the ribs. Quick as lightning Billy let fly his arm. I dare say he never meant to do quite so much as he did, but anyhow he gave the burly fool a terrible drubbing. It took about half a minute, I should think. And lord bless you, the lubber was astonished at the celerity. And will you believe it, Lieutenant, the Red Whiskers now really loves Billy – loves him, or is the biggest hypocrite that ever I heard of. But they all love him. Some of 'em do his washing, darn his old trousers for him; the carpenter is at odd times making a pretty little chest of drawers for him. Anybody will do anything for Billy Budd; and it's the happy family here. But now, Lieutenant, if that young fellow goes – I know how it will be aboard the *Rights*. Not again very soon shall I, coming up from dinner, lean over the capstan smoking a quiet pipe – no, not very soon again, I think. Ay, Lieutenant, you are going to take away the jewel of 'em; you are going to take away my peacemaker!'

And with that the good soul had really some ado in checking a rising sob.

'Well,' said the lieutenant, who had listened with amused interest to all this and now was waxing merry with his tipple: 'well, blessed are the peacemakers, especially the fighting peacemakers. And such are the seventy-four beauties some of which you see poking their noses out of the portholes of yonder warship lying to for me,' pointing through the cabin window at the *Bellipotent*. 'But courage! Don't look so downhearted, man. Why, I pledge you in advance the royal approbation. Rest assured that His Majesty will be delighted to know that in a time when his hardtack is not sought for by sailors with such avidity as should be, a time also when some shipmasters privily resent the borrowing from them a tar or two for the service; His Majesty, I say, will be delighted to learn that *one* shipmaster at least cheerfully surrenders to the King the flower of his flock, a sailor who with equal loyalty makes no dissent. – But where's my beauty? Ah,' looking through the cabin's open door, 'here he comes; and, by Jove, lugging along his chest – Apollo with his portmanteau! – My man,' stepping out to him, 'you can't take that big box aboard a warship. The boxes there are mostly shot boxes. Put your duds in a bag, lad. Boot and saddle for the cavalryman, bag and hammock for the man-of-war's man.'

The transfer from chest to bag was made. And, after seeing his man into the cutter and then following him down, the lieutenant pushed off from the *Rights-of-Man*. That was the merchant ship's name, though by her master and crew abbreviated in sailor fashion into the *Rights*. The hardheaded Dundee owner was a staunch admirer of Thomas Paine, whose book in rejoinder to Burke's arraignment of the French Revolution had then been published for some time and had gone everywhere. In christening his vessel after the title of Paine's volume the man of Dundee was something like his contemporary ship-owner, Stephen Girard of Philadelphia, whose sympathies, alike with his native land and its liberal philosophers, he evinced by naming his ships after Voltaire, Diderot, and so forth.

But now, when the boat swept under the merchantman's stern, and officer and oarsmen were noting – some bitterly and others with a grin – the name emblazoned there; just then it was that the new recruit jumped up from the bow where the coxswain had directed him to sit, and waving hat to his silent shipmates sorrowfully looking over at him from the taffrail, bade the lads a genial good-bye. Then, making a salutation as to the ship herself, 'And good-bye to you too, old *Rights-of-Man*.'

'Down, sir!' roared the lieutenant, instantly assuming all the rigor of his rank, though with difficulty repressing a smile.

To be sure, Billy's action was a terrible breach of naval decorum. But in that decorum he had never been instructed; in consideration of which the lieutenant would hardly have been so energetic in reproof but for the concluding farewell to the ship. This he rather took as meant to convey a covert sally on the new recruit's part, a sly slur at impressment in general, and that of himself in especial. And yet, more likely, if satire it was in effect, it was hardly so by intention, for Billy, though happily endowed with the gaiety of high health, youth, and a free heart, was yet by no means of a satirical turn. The will to it and the sinister dexterity were alike wanting. To deal in double meanings and insinuations of any sort was quite foreign to his nature.

As to his enforced enlistment, that he seemed to take pretty much as he was wont to take any vicissitude of weather. Like the animals, though no philosopher, he was, without knowing it, practically a fatalist. And it may be that he rather liked this adventurous turn in his affairs, which promised an opening into novel scenes and martial excitements.

Aboard the *Bellipotent* our merchant sailor was forthwith rated as an able seaman and assigned to the starboard watch of the foretop. He was soon at home in the service, not at all disliked for his unpretentious good looks and a sort of genial happy-go-lucky air. No merrier man in his mess: in marked contrast to certain other individuals included like himself among the impressed portion of the ship's company; for these when not actively employed were sometimes, and more particularly in the last dogwatch when the drawing near of twilight induced revery, apt to fall into a saddish mood which in some partook of sullenness. But they were not so young as our foretopman, and no few of them must have known a hearth of some sort, others may have had wives and children left, too probably, in uncertain circumstances, and hardly any but must have had acknowledged kith and kin, while for Billy, as will shortly be seen, his entire family was practically invested in himself.

2

THOUGH our new-made foretopman was well received in the top and on the gun decks, hardly here was he that cynosure he had previously been among those minor ship's companies of the merchant marine, with which companies only had he hitherto consorted.

He was young; and despite his all but fully developed frame, in aspect looked even younger than he really was, owing to a lingering adolescent expression in the as yet smooth face all but feminine in purity of natural complexion but where, thanks to his seagoing, the lily was quite suppressed and the rose had some ado visibly to flush through the tan.

To one essentially such a novice in the complexities of factitious life, the abrupt transition from his former and simpler sphere to the ampler and more knowing world of a great warship; this might well have abashed him had there been any conceit or vanity in his composition. Among her miscellaneous multitude, the *Bellipotent* mustered several individuals who however inferior in grade were of no common natural stamp, sailors more signally susceptive of

[328]

that air which continuous martial discipline and repeated presence in battle can in some degree impart even to the average man. As the Handsome Sailor, Billy Budd's position aboard the seventy-four was something analogous to that of a rustic beauty transplanted from the provinces and brought into competition with the highborn dames of the court. But this change of circumstances he scarce noted. As little did he observe that something about him provoked an ambiguous smile in one or two harder faces among the bluejackets. Nor less unaware was he of the peculiar favorable effect his person and demeanour had upon the more intelligent gentlemen of the quarter-deck. Nor could this well have been otherwise. Cast in a mold peculiar to the finest physical examples of those Englishmen in whom the Saxon strain would seem not at all to partake of any Norman or other admixture, he showed in face that humane look of reposeful good nature which the Greek sculptor in some instances gave to his heroic strong man, Hercules. But this again was subtly modified by another and pervasive quality. The ear, small and shapely, the arch of the foot, the curve in mouth and nostril, even the indurated hand dyed to the orange-tawny of the toucan's bill, a hand telling alike of the halyards and tar bucket; but, above all, something in the mobile expression, and every chance attitude and movement, something suggestive of a mother eminently favored by Love and the Graces; all this strangely indicated a lineage in direct contradiction to his lot. The mysteriousness here became less mysterious through a matter of fact elicited when Billy at the capstan was being formally mustered into the service. Asked by the officer, a small, brisk little gentleman as it chanced, among other questions, his place of birth, he replied, 'Please, sir, I don't know.'

'Don't know where you were born? Who was your father?'

'God knows, sir.'

Struck by the straightforward simplicity of these replies,

the officer next asked, 'Do you know anything about your beginning?'

'No, sir. But I have heard that I was found in a pretty silk-lined basket hanging one morning from the knocker of a good man's door in Bristol.'

'*Found*, say you? Well,' throwing back his head and looking up and down the new recruit; 'well, it turns out to have been a pretty good find. Hope they'll find some more like you, my man; the fleet sadly needs them.'

Yes, Billy Budd was a foundling, a presumable by-blow, and, evidently, no ignoble one. Noble descent was as evident in him as in a blood horse.

For the rest, with little or no sharpness of faculty or any trace of the wisdom of the serpent, nor yet quite a dove, he possessed that kind and degree of intelligence going along with the unconventional rectitude of a sound human creature, one to whom not yet has been proffered the questionable apple of knowledge. He was illiterate; he could not read, but he could sing, and like the illiterate nightingale was sometimes the composer of his own song.

Of self-consciousness he seemed to have little or none, or about as much as we may reasonably impute to a dog of Saint Bernard's breed.

Habitually living with the elements and knowing little more of the land than as a beach, or, rather, that portion of the terraqueous globe providentially set apart for dance-houses, doxies, and tapsters, in short what sailors call a 'fiddler's green,' his simple nature remained unsophisticated by those moral obliquities which are not in every case incompatible with that manufacturable thing known as respectability. But are sailors, frequenters of fiddler's greens, without vices? No; but less often than with landsmen do their vices, so called, partake of crookedness of heart, seeming less to proceed from viciousness than exuberance of vitality after long constraint: frank manifestations in accordance with natural law. By his original constitution aided by the co-operating influences of his lot, Billy in many respects was little more than a sort of upright barbarian, much such perhaps as Adam presumably might have been ere the urbane Serpent wriggled himself into his company.

And here be it submitted that apparently going to corroborate the doctrine of man's Fall, a doctrine now popularly ignored, it is observable that where certain virtues pristine and unadulterate peculiarly characterize anybody in the external uniform of civilization, they will upon scrutiny seem not to be derived from custom or convention, but rather to be out of keeping with these, as if indeed exceptionally transmitted from a period prior to Cain's city and citified man. The character marked by such qualities has to an unvitiated taste an untampered-with flavor like that of berries, while the man thoroughly civilized, even in a fair specimen of the breed, has to the same moral palate a questionable smack as of a compounded wine. To any stray inheritor of these primitive qualities found, like Caspar Hauser, wandering dazed in any Christian capital of our time, the good-natured poet's famous invocation, near two thousand years ago, of the good rustic out of his latitude in the Rome of the Caesars, still appropriately holds:

> Honest and poor, faithful in word and thought,
> What hath thee, Fabian, to the city brought?

Though our Handsome Sailor had as much of masculine beauty as one can expect anywhere to see; nevertheless, like the beautiful woman in one of Hawthorne's minor tales, there was just one thing amiss in him. No visible blemish indeed, as with the lady; no, but an occasional liability to a vocal defect. Though in the hour of elemental uproar or peril he was everything that a sailor should be, yet under sudden provocation of strong heart-feeling his voice, otherwise singularly musical, as if expressive of the harmony within, was apt to develop an organic hesitancy, in fact more or less of a stutter or even worse. In this particular Billy was a striking instance that the arch interferer, the envious marplot of Eden, still has more or less to do with every human consignment to this planet of Earth. In every case, one way or another he is sure to slip in his little card, as much as to remind us – I too have a hand here.

The avowal of such an imperfection in the Handsome Sailor should be evidence not alone that he is not presented as a conventional hero, but also that the story in which he is the main figure is no romance.

3

AT the time of Billy Budd's arbitrary enlistment into the *Bellipotent* that ship was on her way to join the Mediterranean fleet. No long time elapsed before the junction was effected. As one of that fleet the seventy-four participated in its movements, though at times on account of her superior sailing qualities, in the absence of frigates, dispatched on separate duty as a scout and at times on less temporary service. But with all this the story has little concernment, restricted as it is to the inner life of one particular ship and the career of an individual sailor.

It was the summer of 1797. In the April of that year had occurred the commotion at Spithead followed in May by a second and yet more serious outbreak in the fleet at the Nore. The latter is known, and without exaggeration in the epithet, as 'the Great Mutiny.' It was indeed a demonstration more menacing to England than the contemporary manifestoes and conquering and proselyting armies of the French Directory. To the British Empire the Nore Mutiny was what a strike in the fire brigade would be to London threatened by general arson. In a crisis when the kingdom might well have anticipated the famous signal that some years later published along the naval line of battle what it was that upon occasion England expected of Englishmen; *that* was the time when at the mastheads of the three-deckers and seventy-fours moored in her own roadstead – a fleet the right arm of a Power then all but the sole free conservative one of the Old World – the bluejackets, to be numbered by thousands, ran up with huzzas the British colors with the union and cross wiped out; by that cancellation transmuting the flag of founded law and freedom defined, into the enemy's red meteor of unbridled and unbounded revolt. Reasonable discontent growing out of practical grievances in the fleet had been ignited into irrational combustion as by live cinders blown across the Channel from France in flames.

The event converted into irony for a time those spirited strains of Dibdin – as a song-writer no mean auxiliary to the English government at that European conjuncture – strains celebrating, among other things, the patriotic devotion of the British tar: 'And as for my life, 'tis the King's!'

Such an episode in the Island's grand naval story her naval historians naturally abridge, one of them (William James) candidly acknowledging that fain would he pass it over did not 'impartiality forbid fastidiousness.' And yet his mention is less a narration than a reference, having to do hardly at all with details. Nor are these readily to be found in the libraries. Like some other events in every age befalling states everywhere, including America, the Great Mutiny was of such character that national pride along with views of policy would fain shade it off into the historical background. Such events cannot be ignored, but there is a considerate way of historically treating them. If a well-constituted individual refrains from blazoning aught amiss or calamitous in his family, a nation in the like circumstance may without reproach be equally discreet.

Though after parleyings between government and the ringleaders, and concessions by the former as to some glaring abuses, the first uprising – that at Spithead – with difficulty was put down, or matters for the time pacified; yet at the Nore the unforeseen renewal of insurrection on a yet larger scale, and emphasized in the conferences that ensued by demands deemed by the authorities not only inadmissible but aggressively insolent, indicated – if the Red Flag did not sufficiently do so – what was the spirit animating the men.

Final suppression, however, there was; but only made possible perhaps by the unswerving loyalty of the marine corps and a voluntary resumption of loyalty among influential sections of the crews.

To some extent the Nore Mutiny may be regarded as analogous to the distempering irruption of contagious fever in a frame constitutionally sound, and which anon throws it off.

At all events, of these thousands of mutineers were some of the tars who not so very long afterwards – whether wholly prompted thereto by patriotism, or pugnacious instinct, or by both – helped to win a coronet for Nelson at the Nile, and the naval crown of crowns for him at Trafalgar. To the mutineers, those battles and especially Trafalgar were a plenary absolution and a grand one. For all that goes to make up scenic naval display and heroic magnificence in arms, those battles, especially Trafalgar, stand unmatched in human annals.

4

In this matter of writing, resolve as one may to keep to the main road, some bypaths have an enticement not readily to be withstood. I am going to err into such a bypath. If the reader will keep me company I shall be glad. At the least, we can promise ourselves that pleasure which is wickedly said to be in sinning, for a literary sin the divergence will be.

Very likely it is no new remark that the inventions of our time have at last brought about a change in sea warfare in degree corresponding to the revolution in all warfare effected by the original introduction from China into Europe of gunpowder. The first European firearm, a clumsy contrivance, was, as is well known, scouted by no few of the knights as a base implement, good enough peradventure for weavers too craven to stand up crossing steel with steel in frank fight. But as ashore knightly valor, though shorn of its blazonry, did not cease with the knights, neither on the seas – though nowadays in encounters there a certain kind of displayed gallantry be fallen out of date as hardly applicable under changed circumstances – did the nobler qualities of such naval magnates as Don John of Austria, Doria, Van Tromp, Jean Bart, the long line of British admirals, and the American Decaturs of 1812 become obsolete with their wooden walls.

Nevertheless, to anybody who can hold the Present at its worth without being inappreciative of the Past, it may be forgiven, if to such an one the solitary old hulk at Portsmouth, Nelson's *Victory*, seems to float there, not alone as the decaying monument of a fame incorruptible, but also as a poetic reproach, softened by its picturesqueness, to the *Monitors* and yet mightier hulls of the European ironclads. And this not altogether because such craft are unsightly, unavoidably lacking the symmetry and grand lines of the old battleships, but equally for other reasons.

There are some, perhaps, who while not altogether inaccessible to that poetic reproach just alluded to, may yet on behalf of the new order be disposed to parry it; and this to the extent of iconoclasm, if need be. For example, prompted by the sight of the star inserted in the *Victory's* quarter-deck designating the spot where the Great Sailor fell, these martial utilitarians may suggest considerations implying that Nelson's ornate publication of his person in battle was not only unnecessary, but not military, nay, savored of foolhardiness and vanity. They may add, too, that at Trafalgar it was in effect nothing less than a challenge to death; and death came; and that but for his bravado the victorious admiral might possibly have survived the battle, and so, instead of having his sagacious dying injunctions overruled by his immediate successor in command, he himself when the contest was decided might have brought his shattered fleet to anchor, a proceeding which might have averted the deplorable loss of life by shipwreck in the elemental tempest that followed the martial one.

Well, should we set aside the more than disputable point

whether for various reasons it was possible to anchor the fleet, then plausibly enough the Benthamites of war may urge the above. But the *might-have-been* is but boggy ground to build on. And, certainly, in foresight as to the larger issue of an encounter, and anxious preparations for it – buoying the deadly way and mapping it out, as at Copenhagen – few commanders have been so painstakingly circumspect as this same reckless declarer of his person in fight.

Personal prudence, even when dictated by quite other than selfish considerations, surely is no special virtue in a military man; while an excessive love of glory, impassioning a less burning impulse, the honest sense of duty, is the first. If the name *Wellington* is not so much of a trumpet to the blood as the simpler name *Nelson*, the reason for this may perhaps be inferred from the above. Alfred in his funeral ode on the victor of Waterloo ventures not to call him the greatest soldier of all time, though in the same ode he invokes Nelson as 'the greatest sailor since our world began.'

At Trafalgar Nelson on the brink of opening the fight sat down and wrote his last brief will and testament. If under the presentiment of the most magnificent of all victories to be crowned by his own glorious death, a sort of priestly motive led him to dress his person in the jewelled vouchers of his own shining deeds; if thus to have adorned himself for the altar and the sacrifice were indeed vain-glory, then affectation and fustian is each more heroic line in the great epics and dramas, since in such lines the poet but embodies in verse those exaltations of sentiment that a nature like Nelson, the opportunity being given, vitalizes into acts.

5

YES, the outbreak at the Nore was put down. But not every grievance was redressed. If the contractors, for example, were no longer permitted to ply some practices peculiar to their tribe everywhere, such as providing shoddy cloth, rations not sound, or false in the measure; not the less impressment, for one thing, went on. By custom sanctioned for centuries, and judicially maintained by a Lord Chancellor as late as Mansfield, that mode of manning the fleet, a mode now fallen into a sort of abeyance but never formally renounced, it was not practicable to give up in those years. Its abrogation would have crippled the indispensable fleet, one wholly under canvas, no steam power, its innumerable sails and thousands of cannon, everything in short, worked by muscle alone; a fleet the more insatiate in demand for men, because then multiplying its ships of all grades against contingencies present and to come of the convulsed Continent.

Discontent foreran the Two Mutinies, and more or less it lurkingly survived them. Hence it was not unreasonable to apprehend some return of trouble sporadic or general. One instance of such apprehensions: In the same year with this story, Nelson, then Rear Admiral Sir Horatio, being with the fleet off the Spanish coast, was directed by the admiral in command to shift his pennant from the *Captain* to the *Theseus*; and for this reason: that the latter ship having newly arrived on the station from home, where it had taken part in the Great Mutiny, danger was apprehended from the temper of the men; and it was thought that an officer like Nelson was the one, not indeed to terrorize the crew into base subjection, but to win them, by force of his mere presence and heroic personality, back to an allegiance if not as enthusiastic as his own yet as true.

So it was that for a time, on more than one quarter-deck, anxiety did exist. At sea, precautionary vigilance was strained against relapse. At short notice an engagement might come on. When it did, the lieutenants assigned to batteries felt it incumbent on them, in some instances, to stand with drawn swords behind the men working the guns.

6

But on board the seventy-four in which Billy now swung his hammock, very little in the manner of the men and nothing obvious in the demeanor of the officers would have suggested to an ordinary observer that the Great Mutiny was a recent event. In their general bearing and conduct the commissioned officers of a warship naturally take their tone from the commander, that is if he have that ascendancy of character that ought to be his.

Captain the Honorable Edward Fairfax Vere, to give his full title, was a bachelor of forty or thereabouts, a sailor of distinction even in a time prolific of renowned seamen. Though allied to the higher nobility, his advancement had not been altogether owing to influences connected with that circumstance. He had seen much service, been in various engagements, always acquitting himself as an officer mindful of the welfare of his men, but never tolerating an infraction of discipline; thoroughly versed in the science of his profession, and intrepid to the verge of temerity, though never injudiciously so. For his gallantry in the West Indian waters as flag lieutenant under Rodney in that admiral's crowning victory over De Grasse, he was made a post captain.

Ashore, in the garb of a civilian, scarce anyone would have taken him for a sailor, more especially that he never garnished unprofessional talk with nautical terms, and grave in his bearing, evinced little appreciation of mere humor. It was not out of keeping with these traits that on a passage when nothing demanded his paramount action, he was the most undemonstrative of men. Any landsman observing this gentleman not conspicuous by his stature and wearing no pronounced insignia, emerging from his cabin to the open deck, and noting the silent deference of the officers retiring to leeward, might have taken him for the King's guest, a civilian aboard the King's ship, some highly honorable discreet envoy on his way to an important post. But in fact this unobtrusiveness of demeanor may have proceeded from a certain unaffected modesty of manhood sometimes accompanying a resolute nature, a modesty evinced at all times not calling for pronounced action, which shown in any rank of life suggests a virtue aristocratic in kind. As with some others engaged in various departments of the world's more heroic activities, Captain Vere though practical enough upon occasion would at times betray a certain dreaminess of mood. Standing alone on the weather side of the quarter-deck, one hand holding by the rigging, he would absently gaze off at the blank sea. At the presentation to him then of some minor matter interrupting the current of his thoughts, he would show more or less irascibility; but instantly he would control it.

In the navy he was popularly known by the appellation 'Starry Vere.' How such a designation happened to fall upon one who whatever his sterling qualities was without any brilliant ones, was in this wise: A favorite kinsman, Lord Denton, a freehearted fellow, had been the first to meet and congratulate him upon his return to England from his West Indian cruise; and but the day previous turning over a copy of Andrew Marvell's poems had lighted, not for the first time, however, upon the lines entitled 'Appleton House,' the name of one of the seats of their common ancestor, a hero in the German wars of the seventeenth century, in which poem occur the lines:

> This 'tis to have been from the first
> In a domestic heaven nursed,
> Under the discipline severe
> Of Fairfax and the starry Vere.

And so, upon embracing his cousin fresh from Rodney's great victory wherein he had played so gallant a part, brimming over with just family pride in the sailor of their house, he exuberantly exclaimed, 'Give ye joy, Ed; give ye joy, my starry Vere!' This got currency, and the novel prefix serving in familiar parlance readily to distinguish the *Bellipotent*'s captain from another Vere his senior, a distant relative, an officer of like rank in the navy, it remained permanently attached to the surname.

7

IN view of the part that the commander of the *Bellipotent* plays in scenes shortly to follow, it may be well to fill out that sketch of him outlined in the previous chapter.

Aside from his qualities as a sea officer Captain Vere was an exceptional character. Unlike no few of England's renowned sailors, long and arduous service with signal devotion to it had not resulted in absorbing and *salting* the entire man. He had a marked leaning toward everything intellectual. He loved books, never going to sea without a newly replenished library, compact but of the best. The isolated leisure, in some cases so wearisome, falling at intervals to commanders even during a war cruise, never was tedious to Captain Vere. With nothing of that literary taste which less heeds the thing conveyed than the vehicle, his bias was toward those books to which every serious mind of superior order occupying any active post of authority in the world naturally inclines: books treating of actual men and events no matter of what era – history, biography, and unconventional writers like Montaigne, who, free from cant and convention, honestly and in the spirit of common sense philosophize upon realities. In this line of reading he found confirmation of his own more reserved thoughts – confirmation which he had vainly sought in social converse, so that as touching most fundamental topics, there had got to be established in him some positive convictions which he forefelt would abide in him essentially unmodified so long as his intelligent part remained unimpaired. In view of the troubled period in which his lot was cast, this was well for him. His settled convictions were as a dike against those invading waters of novel opinion social, political, and otherwise, which carried away as in a torrent no few minds in those days, minds by nature not inferior to his own. While other members of that aristocracy to which by birth he belonged were incensed at the innovators mainly because their theories were inimical to the privileged classes, Captain Vere disinterestedly opposed them not alone because they seemed to him insusceptible of embodiment in lasting institutions, but at war with the peace of the world and the true welfare of mankind.

With minds less stored than his and less earnest, some officers of his rank, with whom at times he would necessarily consort, found him lacking in the companionable quality, a dry and bookish gentleman, as they deemed. Upon any chance withdrawal from their company one would be apt to say to another something like this: 'Vere is a noble fellow, Starry Vere. 'Spite the gazettes, Sir Horatio' (meaning him who became Lord Nelson) 'is at bottom scarce a better seaman or fighter. But between you and me now, don't you think there is a queer streak of the pedantic running through him? Yes, like the King's yarn in a coil of navy rope?'

Some apparent ground there was for this sort of confidential criticism; since not only did the captain's discourse never fall into the jocosely familiar, but in illustrating of any point touching the stirring personages and events of the time he would be as apt to cite some historic character or incident of antiquity as he would be to cite from the moderns. He seemed unmindful of the circumstance that to his bluff company such remote allusions, however pertinent they might really be, were altogether alien to men whose reading was mainly confined to the journals. But considerateness in such matters is not easy to natures constituted like Captain Vere's. Their honesty prescribes to them directness, sometimes far-reaching like that of a migratory fowl that in its flight never heeds when it crosses a frontier.

8

THE lieutenants and other commissioned gentlemen forming Captain Vere's staff it is not necessary here to particularize, nor needs it to make any mention of any of the warrant officers. But among the petty officers was one who, having much to do with the story, may as well be forthwith introduced. His portrait I essay, but shall never hit it. This was John Claggart, the master-at-arms. But that sea title may to landsmen seem somewhat equivocal. Originally, doubtless, that petty officer's function was the instruction of the men in the use of arms, sword or cutlass. But very long ago, owing to the advance in gunnery making hand-to-hand encounters less frequent and giving to niter and sulphur the pre-eminence over steel, that function ceased; the master-at-arms of a great warship becoming a sort of chief of police charged among other matters with the duty of preserving order on the populous lower gun decks.

Claggart was a man about five-and-thirty, somewhat spare and tall, yet of no ill figure upon the whole. His hand was too small and shapely to have been accustomed to hard toil. The face was a notable one, the features all except the chin cleanly cut as those on a Greek medallion; yet the chin, beardless as Tecumseh's, had something of strange protuberant broadness in its make that recalled the prints of the Reverend Dr Titus Oates, the historic deponent with the clerical drawl in the time of Charles II and the fraud of the alleged Popish Plot. It served Claggart in his office that his eye could cast a tutoring glance. His brow was of the sort phrenologically associated with more than average intellect; silken jet curls partly clustering over it, making a foil to the pallor below, a pallor tinged with a faint shade of amber akin to the hue of time-tinted marbles of old. This complexion, singularly contrasting with the red or deeply bronzed visages of the sailors, and in part the result of his official seclusion from the sunlight, though it was not exactly displeasing, nevertheless seemed to hint of something defective or abnormal in the constitution and blood.

But his general aspect and manner were so suggestive of an education and career incongruous with his naval function that when not actively engaged in it he looked like a man of high quality, social and moral, who for reasons of his own was keeping incog. Nothing was known of his former life. It might be that he was an Englishman; and yet there lurked a bit of accent in his speech suggesting that possibly he was not such by birth, but through naturalization in early childhood. Among certain grizzled sea gossips of the gun decks and forecastle went a rumor perdue that the master-at-arms was a *chevalier* who had volunteered into the King's navy by way of compounding for some mysterious swindle whereof he had been arraigned at the King's Bench. The fact that nobody could substantiate this report was, of course, nothing against its secret currency. Such a rumor once started on the gun decks in reference to almost anyone below the rank of a commissioned officer would, during the period assigned to this narrative, have seemed not altogether wanting in credibility to the tarry old wise-acres of a man-of-war crew. And indeed a man of Claggart's accomplishments, without prior nautical experience entering the navy at mature life, as he did, and necessarily allotted at the start to the lowest grade in it; a man too who never made allusion to his previous life ashore; these were circumstances which in the dearth of exact knowledge as to his true antecedents opened to the invidious a vague field for unfavorable surmise.

But the sailors' dogwatch gossip concerning him derived a vague plausibility from the fact that now for some period the British navy could so little afford to be squeamish in the matter of keeping up the muster rolls, that not only were press gangs notoriously abroad both afloat and ashore, but there was little or no secret about another matter, namely, that the London police were at liberty to capture any able-bodied suspect, any questionable fellow at large, and summarily ship him to the dockyard or fleet. Furthermore, even among voluntary enlistments there were instances where the motive thereto partook neither of patriotic impulse nor yet of a random desire to experience a bit of sea life and martial adventure. Insolvent debtors of minor grade, together with the promiscuous lame ducks of morality, found in the navy a convenient and secure refuge, secure because, once enlisted aboard a King's ship, they were as much in sanctuary as the transgressor of the Middle Ages harboring himself under the shadow of the altar. Such sanctioned irregularities, which for obvious reasons the government would hardly think to parade at the time and which consequently, and as affecting the least influential class of mankind, have all but dropped into oblivion, lend color to something for the truth whereof I do not vouch, and hence have some scruple in stating; something I remember having seen in print though the book I cannot recall; but the same thing was personally communicated to me now more than forty years ago by an old pensioner in a cocked hat with whom I had a most interesting talk on the terrace at Greenwich, a Baltimore Negro, a Trafalgar man. It was to this effect: In the case of a warship short of hands whose speedy sailing was imperative, the deficient quota, in lack of any other way of making it good, would be eked out by drafts culled direct from the jails. For reasons previously suggested it would not perhaps be easy at the present day directly to prove or disprove the allegation. But allowed as a verity, how significant would it be of England's straits at the time confronted by those wars which like a flight of harpies rose shrieking from the din and dust of the fallen Bastille. That era appears measurably clear to us who look back at it, and but read of it. But to the grandfathers of us graybeards, the more thoughtful of them, the genius of it presented an aspect like that of Camoëns' Spirit of the Cape, an eclipsing menace mysterious and prodigious. Not America was exempt from apprehension. At the height of Napoleon's unexampled conquests, there were Americans who had fought at Bunker Hill who looked forward to the possibility that the Atlantic might prove no barrier against the ultimate schemes of this French portentous upstart

from the revolutionary chaos who seemed in act of ful-
filling judgment prefigured in the Apocalypse.

But the less credence was to be given to the gun-deck talk
touching Claggart, seeing that no man holding his office
in a man-of-war can ever hope to be popular with the crew.
Besides, in derogatory comments upon anyone against
whom they have a grudge, or for any reason or no reason
mislike, sailors are much like landsmen: they are apt to
exaggerate or romance it.

About as much was really known to the *Bellipotent*'s
tars of the master-at-arms' career before entering the service as an astronomer knows about a comet's travels prior
to its first observable appearance in the sky. The verdict of
the sea quidnuncs has been cited only by way of showing
what sort of moral impression the man made upon rude
uncultivated natures whose conceptions of human wickedness were necessarily of the narrowest, limited to ideas of
vulgar rascality – a thief among the swinging hammocks
during a night watch, or the man-brokers and land-sharks
of the seaports.

It was no gossip, however, but fact that though, as before
hinted, Claggart upon his entrance into the navy was, as a
novice, assigned to the least honorable section of a man-
of-war's crew, embracing the drudgery, he did not long
remain there. The superior capacity he immediately
evinced, his constitutional sobriety, an ingratiating deference
to superiors, together with a peculiar ferreting genius
manifested on a singular occasion; all this, capped by a
certain austere patriotism, abruptly advanced him to the
position of master-at-arms.

Of this maritime chief of police the ship's corporals, so
called, were the immediate subordinates, and compliant
ones; and this, as is to be noted in some business departments ashore, almost to a degree inconsistent with entire
moral volition. His place put various converging wires of
underground influence under the chief's control, capable
when astutely worked through his understrappers of operat-

ing to the mysterious discomfort, if nothing worse, of any
of the sea commonalty.

9

LIFE in the foretop well agreed with Billy Budd. There,
when not actually engaged on the yards yet higher aloft,
the topmen, who as such had been picked out for youth and
activity, constituted an aerial club lounging at ease against
the smaller stun'sails rolled up into cushions, spinning yarns
like the lazy gods, and frequently amused with what was
going on in the busy world of the decks below. No wonder
then that a young fellow of Billy's disposition was well
content in such society. Giving no cause of offense to anybody, he was always alert at a call. So in the merchant
service it had been with him. But now such a punctilious-
ness in duty was shown that his topmates would sometimes
good-naturedly laugh at him for it. This heightened alacrity had its cause, namely, the impression made upon him
by the first formal gangway-punishment he had ever witnessed, which befell the day following his impressment. It
had been incurred by a little fellow, young, a novice afterguardsman absent from his assigned post when the ship was
being put about; a dereliction resulting in a rather serious
hitch to that maneuver, one demanding instantaneous
promptitude in letting go and making fast. When Billy saw
the culprit's naked back under the scourge, gridironed with
red welts and worse, when he marked the dire expression
in the liberated man's face as with his woolen shirt flung
over him by the executioner he rushed forward from the
spot to bury himself in the crowd, Billy was horrified. He
resolved that never through remissness would he make
himself liable to such a visitation or do or omit aught that
might merit even verbal reproof. What then was his surprise
and concern when ultimately he found himself getting into
petty trouble occasionally about such matters as the stow-
age of his bag or something amiss in his hammock, matters

under the police oversight of the ship's corporals of the lower decks, and which brought down on him a vague threat from one of them.

So heedful in all things as he was, how could this be? He could not understand it, and it more than vexed him. When he spoke to his young topmates about it they were either lightly incredulous or found something comical in his unconcealed anxiety. 'Is it your bag, Billy?' said one. 'Well, sew yourself up in it, bully boy, and then you'll be sure to know if anybody meddles with it.'

Now there was a veteran aboard who because his years began to disqualify him for more active work had been recently assigned duty as mainmastman in his watch, looking to the gear belayed at the rail roundabout that great spar near the deck. At off-times the foretopman had picked up some acquaintance with him, and now in his trouble it occurred to him that he might be the sort of person to go to for wise counsel. He was an old Dansker long anglicized in the service, of few words, many wrinkles, and some honorable scars. His wizened face, time-tinted and weather-stained to the complexion of an antique parchment, was here and there peppered blue by the chance explosion of a gun cartridge in action.

He was an *Agamemnon* man, some two years prior to the time of this story having served under Nelson when still captain in that ship immortal in naval memory, which dismantled and in part broken up to her bare ribs is seen a grand skeleton in Haden's etching. As one of a boarding party from the *Agamemnon* he had received a cut slantwise along one temple and cheek leaving a long pale scar like a streak of dawn's light falling athwart the dark visage. It was on account of that scar and the affair in which it was known that he had received it, as well as from his blue-peppered complexion, that the Dansker went among the *Bellipotent*'s crew by the name of 'Board-Her-in-the-Smoke.'

Now the first time that his small weasel eyes happened to light on Billy Budd, a certain grim internal merriment set all his ancient wrinkles into antic play. Was it that his eccentric unsentimental old sapience, primitive in its kind, saw or thought it saw something which in contrast with the warship's environment looked oddly incongruous in the Handsome Sailor? But after slyly studying him at intervals, the old Merlin's equivocal merriment was modified; for now when the twain would meet, it would start in his face a quizzing sort of look, but it would be but momentary and sometimes replaced by an expression of speculative query as to what might eventually befall a nature like that, dropped into a world not without some mantraps and against whose subtleties simple courage lacking experience and address, and without any touch of defensive ugliness, is of little avail; and where such innocence as man is capable of does yet in a moral emergency not always sharpen the faculties or enlighten the will.

However it was, the Dansker in his ascetic way rather took to Billy. Nor was this only because of a certain philosophic interest in such a character. There was another cause. While the old man's eccentricities, sometimes bordering on the ursine, repelled the juniors, Billy, undeterred thereby, revering him as a salt hero, would make advances, never passing the old *Agamemnon* man without a salutation marked by that respect which is seldom lost on the aged, however crabbed at times or whatever their station in life.

There was a vein of dry humor, or what not, in the mastman; and, whether in freak of patriarchal irony touching Billy's youth and athletic frame, or for some other and more recondite reason, from the first in addressing him he always substituted *Baby* for Billy, the Dansker in fact being the originator of the name by which the foretopman eventually became known aboard ship.

Well then, in his mysterious little difficulty going in quest of the wrinkled one, Billy found him off duty in a dogwatch ruminating by himself, seated on a shot box of the upper gun deck, now and then surveying with a somewhat cynical regard certain of the more swaggering promenaders there. Billy recounted his trouble, again wondering how it all happened. The salt seer attentively listened, accompanying the foretopman's recital with queer twitchings of his wrinkles and problematical little sparkles of his small ferret eyes. Making an end of his story, the foretopman asked, 'And now, Dansker, do tell me what you think of it.'

The old man, shoving up the front of his tarpaulin and deliberately rubbing the long slant scar at the point where it entered the thin hair, laconically said, 'Baby Budd, *Jemmy Legs*' (meaning the master-at-arms) 'is down on you.'

'*Jemmy Legs!*' ejaculated Billy, his welkin eyes expanding. 'What for? Why, he calls me "the sweet and pleasant young fellow," they tell me.'

'Does he so?' grinned the grizzled one; then said, 'Ay, Baby lad, a sweet voice has Jemmy Legs.'

'No, not always. But to me he has. I seldom pass him but there comes a pleasant word.'

'And that's because he's down upon you, Baby Budd.'

Such reiteration, along with the manner of it, incomprehensible to a novice, disturbed Billy almost as much as the mystery for which he had sought explanation. Something less unpleasingly oracular he tried to extract; but the old sea Chiron, thinking perhaps that for the nonce he had sufficiently instructed his young Achilles, pursed his lips, gathered all his wrinkles together, and would commit himself to nothing further.

Years, and those experiences which befall certain shrewder men subordinated lifelong to the will of superiors, all this had developed in the Dansker the pithy guarded cynicism that was his leading characteristic.

10

THE next day an incident served to confirm Billy Budd in his incredulity as to the Dansker's strange summing up of the case submitted. The ship at noon, going large before the wind, was rolling on her course, and he below at dinner and engaged in some sportful talk with the members of his mess, chanced in a sudden lurch to spill the entire contents of his soup pan upon the new-scrubbed deck. Claggart, the master-at-arms, official rattan in hand, happened to be passing along the battery in a bay of which the mess was lodged, and the greasy liquid streamed just across his path. Stepping over it, he was proceeding on his way without comment, since the matter was nothing to take notice of under the circumstances, when he happened to observe who it was that had done the spilling. His countenance changed. Pausing, he was about to ejaculate something hasty at the sailor, but checked himself, and pointing down to the streaming soup, playfully tapped him from behind with his rattan, saying in a low musical voice peculiar to him at times, 'Handsomely done, my lad! And handsome is as handsome did it, too!' And with that passed on. Not noted by Billy as not coming within his view was the involuntary smile, or rather grimace, that accompanied Claggart's equivocal words. Aridly it drew down the thin corners of his shapely mouth. But everybody taking his remark as meant for humorous, and at which therefore as coming from a superior they were bound to laugh 'with counterfeited glee,' acted accordingly; and Billy, tickled, it may be, by the allusion to his being the Handsome Sailor, merrily joined in; then addressing his messmates exclaimed, 'There now, who says that Jemmy Legs is down on me!'

'And who said he was, Beauty?' demanded one Donald with some surprise. Whereat the foretopman looked a little foolish, recalling that it was only one person, Board-Her-in-the-Smoke, who had suggested what to him was the smoky idea that this master-at-arms was in any peculiar way hostile to him. Meantime that functionary, resuming his path, must have momentarily worn some expression less guarded than that of the bitter smile, usurping the face from the heart – some distorting expression perhaps, for a drummer-boy heedlessly frolicking along from the opposite direction and chancing to come into light collision with his person was strangely disconcerted by his aspect. Nor was the impression lessened when the official, impetuously giving him a sharp cut with the rattan, vehemently exclaimed, 'Look where you go!'

11

WHAT was the matter with the master-at-arms? And, be the matter what it might, how could it have direct relation to Billy Budd, with whom prior to the affair of the spilled soup he had never come into any special contact official or otherwise? What indeed could the trouble have to do with one so little inclined to give offense as the merchant-ship's 'peacemaker,' even him who in Claggart's own phrase was 'the sweet and pleasant young fellow'? Yes, why should Jemmy Legs, to borrow the Dansker's expression, be 'down' on the Handsome Sailor? But, at heart and not for nothing, as the late chance encounter may indicate to the discerning, down on him, secretly down on him, he assuredly was.

Now to invent something touching the more private career of Claggart, something involving Billy Budd, of which something the latter should be wholly ignorant, some romantic incident implying that Claggart's knowledge of the young bluejacket began at some period anterior to catching sight of him on board the seventy-four – all this, not so difficult to do, might avail in a way more or less interesting to account for whatever of enigma may appear to lurk in the case. But in fact there was nothing of the sort. And yet the cause necessarily to be assumed as the sole one assignable is in its very realism as much charged with that prime element of Radcliffian romance, the mysterious, as any that the ingenuity of the author of *The Mysteries of Udolpho* could devise. For what can more partake of the mysterious than an antipathy spontaneous and profound such as is evoked in certain exceptional mortals by the mere aspect of some other mortal, however harmless he may be, if not called forth by this very harmlessness itself?

Now there can exist no irritating juxtaposition of dissimilar personalities comparable to that which is possible aboard a great warship fully manned and at sea. There, every day among all ranks, almost every man comes into more or less of contact with almost every other man. Wholly there to avoid even the sight of an aggravating object one must needs give it Jonah's toss or jump overboard himself. Imagine how all this might eventually operate on some peculiar human creature the direct reverse of a saint!

But for the adequate comprehending of Claggart by a normal nature these hints are insufficient. To pass from a normal nature to him one must cross 'the deadly space between.' And this is best done by indirection.

Long ago an honest scholar, my senior, said to me in reference to one who like himself is now no more, a man so unimpeachably respectable that against him nothing was ever openly said though among the few something was whispered, 'Yes, X—— is a nut not to be cracked by the tap of a lady's fan. You are aware that I am the adherent of no organized religion, much less of any philosophy built into a system. Well, for all that, I think that to try and get into X——, enter his labyrinth and get out again, without a clue derived from some source other than what is known as "knowledge of the world" – that were hardly possible, at least for me.'

'Why,' said I, 'X——, however singular a study to some, is yet human, and knowledge of the world assuredly implies the knowledge of human nature, and in most of its varieties.'

'Yes, but a superficial knowledge of it, serving ordinary purposes. But for anything deeper, I am not certain whether to know the world and to know human nature be not two distinct branches of knowledge, which while they may co-exist in the same heart, yet either may exist with little or nothing of the other. Nay, in an average man of the world, his constant rubbing with it blunts that finer spiritual insight indispensable to the understanding of the essential in certain exceptional characters, whether evil ones or good. In a matter of some importance I have seen a girl wind an old lawyer about her little finger. Nor was it the dotage of senile love. Nothing of the sort. But he knew law better than he knew the girl's heart. Coke and Blackstone hardly shed so much light into obscure spiritual places as the Hebrew prophets. And who were they? Mostly recluses.'

At the time, my inexperience was such that I did not quite see the drift of all this. It may be that I see it now. And, indeed, if that lexicon which is based on Holy Writ were any longer popular, one might with less difficulty define and denominate certain phenomenal men. As it is, one must turn to some authority not liable to the charge of being tinctured with the biblical element.

In a list of definitions included in the authentic translation of Plato, a list attributed to him, occurs this: 'Natural Depravity: a depravity according to nature,' a definition which, though savoring of Calvinism, by no means involves Calvin's dogma as to total mankind. Evidently its intent makes it applicable but to individuals. Not many are the examples of this depravity which the gallows and jail supply. At any rate, for notable instances, since these have no vulgar alloy of the brute in them, but invariably are dominated by intellectuality, one must go elsewhere. Civilization, especially if of the austerer sort, is auspicious to it. It folds itself in the mantle of respectability. It has certain negative virtues serving as silent auxiliaries. It never allows wine to get within its guard. It is not going too far to say that it is without vices or small sins. There is a phenomenal pride in it that excludes them. It is never mercenary or avaricious. In short, the depravity here meant partakes nothing of the sordid or sensual. It is serious, but free from acerbity. Though no flatterer of mankind it never speaks ill of it.

But the thing which in eminent instances signalizes so exceptional a nature is this: Though the man's even temper and discreet bearing would seem to intimate a mind peculiarly subject to the law of reason, not the less in heart he would seem to riot in complete exemption from that law, having apparently little to do with reason further than to employ it as an ambidexter implement for effecting the irrational. That is to say: Toward the accomplishment of an aim which in wantonness of atrocity would seem to partake of the insane, he will direct a cool judgment sagacious and sound. These men are madmen, and of the most dangerous sort, for their lunacy is not continuous, but occasional, evoked by some special object; it is protectively secretive, which is as much as to say it is self-contained, so that when, moreover, most active it is to the average mind not distinguishable from sanity, and for the reason above suggested: that whatever its aims may be – and the aim is never declared – the method and the outward proceeding are always perfectly rational.

Now something such an one was Claggart, in whom was the mania of an evil nature, not engendered by vicious training or corrupting books or licentious living, but born with him and innate, in short 'a depravity according to nature.'

Dark sayings are these, some will say. But why? Is it because they somewhat savor of Holy Writ in its phrase 'mystery of iniquity'? If they do, such savor was far enough from being intended, for little will it commend these pages to many a reader of today.

The point of the present story turning on the hidden nature of the master-at-arms has necessitated this chapter. With an added hint or two in connection with the incident at the mess, the resumed narrative must be left to vindicate, as it may, its own credibility.

12

THAT Claggart's figure was not amiss, and his face, save the chin, well molded, has already been said. Of these favorable points he seemed not insensible, for he was not only neat but careful in his dress. But the form of Billy Budd was heroic; and if his face was without the intellectual look of the pallid Claggart's, not the less was it lit, like his, from within, though from a different source. The bonfire in his heart made luminous the rose-tan in his cheek.

In view of the marked contrast between the persons of the twain, it is more than probable that when the master-at-arms in the scene last given applied to the sailor the proverb 'Handsome is as handsome does,' he there let escape an ironic inkling, not caught by the young sailors who heard it, as to what it was that had first moved him against Billy, namely, his significant personal beauty.

Now envy and antipathy, passions irreconcilable in reason, nevertheless in fact may spring conjoined like Chang and Eng in one birth. Is Envy then such a monster? Well, though many an arraigned mortal has in hopes of mitigated penalty pleaded guilty to horrible actions, did ever anybody seriously confess to envy? Something there is in it universally felt to be more shameful than even felonious crime. And not only does everybody disown it, but the better sort are inclined to incredulity when it is in earnest imputed to an intelligent man. But since its lodgment is in the heart not the brain, no degree of intellect supplies a guarantee against it. But Claggart's was no vulgar form of the passion. Nor, as directed toward Billy Budd, did it partake of that streak of apprehensive jealousy that marred Saul's visage perturbedly brooding on the comely young David. Claggart's envy struck deeper. If askance he eyed the good looks, cheery health, and frank enjoyment of young life in Billy Budd, it was because these went along with a nature that, as Claggart magnetically felt, had in its simplicity never willed malice or experienced the reactionary bite of that serpent. To him, the spirit lodged within Billy, and looking out from his welkin eyes as from windows, that ineffability it was which made the dimple in his dyed cheek, suppled his joints, and dancing in his yellow curls made him pre-eminently the Handsome Sailor. One person excepted, the master-at-arms was perhaps the only man in the ship intellectually capable of adequately appreciating the moral phenomenon presented in Billy Budd. And the insight but intensified his passion, which assuming various secret forms within him, at times assumed that of cynic disdain, disdain of innocence – to be nothing more than innocent! Yet in an aesthetic way he saw the charm of it, the courageous free-and-easy temper of it, and fain would have shared it, but he despaired of it.

With no power to annul the elemental evil in him, though readily enough he could hide it; apprehending the good, but powerless to be it; a nature like Claggart's, surcharged with energy as such natures almost invariably are, what recourse is left to it but to recoil upon itself and, like the scorpion for which the Creator alone is responsible, act out to the end the part allotted it.

13

PASSION, and passion in its profoundest, is not a thing demanding a palatial stage whereon to play its part. Down among the groundlings, among the beggars and rakers of the garbage, profound passion is enacted. And the circumstances that provoke it, however trivial or mean, are no measure of its power. In the present instance the stage is a scrubbed gun deck, and one of the external provocations a man-of-war's man's spilled soup.

Now when the master-at-arms noticed whence came that greasy fluid streaming before his feet, he must have taken it – to some extent wilfully, perhaps – not for the mere accident it assuredly was, but for the sly escape of a spontaneous feeling on Billy's part more or less answering to the antipathy on his own. In effect a foolish demonstration, he must have thought, and very harmless, like the futile kick of a heifer, which yet were the heifer a shod stallion would not be so harmless. Even so was it that into the gall of Claggart's envy he infused the vitriol of his contempt. But the incident confirmed to him certain telltale reports purveyed to his ear by 'Squeak,' one of his more cunning corporals, a grizzled little man, so nicknamed by the sailors on account of his squeaky voice and sharp visage ferreting about the dark corners of the lower decks after interlopers, satirically suggesting to them the idea of a rat in a cellar.

From his chief's employing him as an implicit tool in laying little traps for the worriment of the foretopman – for it was from the master-at-arms that the petty persecutions heretofore adverted to had proceeded – the corporal, having naturally enough concluded that his master could have no love for the sailor, made it his business, faithful under-strapper that he was, to foment the ill blood by perverting to his chief certain innocent frolics of the good-natured foretopman, besides inventing for his mouth sundry contumelious epithets he claimed to have overheard him let fall. The master-at-arms never suspected the veracity of these reports, more especially as to the epithets, for he well knew how secretly unpopular may become a master-at-arms, at least a master-at-arms of those days, zealous in his function, and how the bluejackets shoot at him in private their raillery and wit; the nickname by which he goes among them (Jemmy Legs) implying under the form of merriment their cherished disrespect and dislike. But in view of the greediness of hate for pabulum it hardly needed a purveyor to feed Claggart's passion.

An uncommon prudence is habitual with the subtler depravity, for it has everything to hide. And in case of an injury but suspected, its secretiveness voluntarily cuts it off from enlightenment or disillusion; and, not unreluctantly, action is taken upon surmise as upon certainty. And the retaliation is apt to be in monstrous disproportion to the supposed offense; for when in anybody was revenge in its exactions aught else but an inordinate usurer? But how with Claggart's conscience? For though consciences are unlike as foreheads, every intelligence, not excluding the scriptural devils who 'believe and tremble,' has one. But Claggart's conscience being but the lawyer to his will, made ogres of trifles, probably arguing that the motive imputed to Billy in spilling the soup just when he did, together with the epithets alleged, these, if nothing more, made a strong case against him; nay, justified animosity into a sort of retributive righteousness. The Pharisee is the Guy Fawkes prowling in the hid chambers underlying some natures like Claggart's. And they can really form no conception of an unreciprocated malice. Probably the master-at-arms' clandestine persecution of Billy was started to try the temper of the man; but it had not developed any quality in him that enmity could make official use of or even pervert into plausible self-justification; so that the occurrence at the mess, petty if it were, was a welcome one to that peculiar conscience assigned to be the private mentor of Claggart; and, for the rest, not improbably it put him upon new experiments.

14

NOT many days after the last incident narrated, something befell Billy Budd that more graveled him than aught that had previously occurred.

It was a warm night for the latitude; and the foretopman, whose watch at the time was properly below, was dozing on the uppermost deck whither he had ascended from his hot hammock, one of hundreds suspended so closely wedged together over a lower gun deck that there was little or no swing to them. He lay as in the shadow of a hillside, stretched under the lee of the booms, a piled ridge of spare spars amidships between foremast and mainmast among which the ship's largest boat, the launch, was stowed. Alongside of three other slumberers from below, he lay near that end of the booms which approaches the foremast; his station aloft on duty as a foretopman being just over the deck-station of the forecastlemen, entitling him according to usage to make himself more or less at home in that neighborhood.

Presently he was stirred into semiconsciousness by somebody, who must have previously sounded the sleep of the others, touching his shoulder, and then, as the foretopman raised his head, breathing into his ear in a quick whisper,

'Slip into the lee forechains, Billy; there is something in the wind. Don't speak. Quick, I will meet you there,' and disappearing.

Now Billy, like sundry other essentially good-natured ones, had some of the weaknesses inseparable from essential good nature; and among these was a reluctance, almost an incapacity of plumply saying *no* to an abrupt proposition not obviously absurd on the face of it, nor obviously unfriendly, nor iniquitous. And being of warm blood, he had not the phlegm tacitly to negative any proposition by unresponsive inaction. Like his sense of fear, his apprehension as to aught outside of the honest and natural was seldom very quick. Besides, upon the present occasion, the drowse from his sleep still hung upon him.

However it was, he mechanically rose and, sleepily wondering what could be in the wind, betook himself to the designated place, a narrow platform, one of six, outside of the high bulwarks and screened by the great deadeyes and multiple columned lanyards of the shrouds and backstays; and, in a great warship of that time, of dimensions commensurate to the hull's magnitude; a tarry balcony in short, overhanging the sea, and so secluded that one mariner of the *Bellipotent*, a Nonconformist old tar of a serious turn, made it even in daytime his private oratory.

In this retired nook the stranger soon joined Billy Budd. There was no moon as yet; a haze obscured the starlight. He could not distinctly see the stranger's face. Yet from something in the outline and carriage, Billy took him, and correctly, for one of the afterguard.

'Hist! Billy,' said the man, in the same quick cautionary whisper as before. 'You were impressed, weren't you? Well, so was I'; and he paused, as to mark the effect. But Billy, not knowing exactly what to make of this, said nothing. Then the other: 'We are not the only impressed ones, Billy. There's a gang of us. – Couldn't you – help – at a pinch?'

'What do you mean?' demanded Billy, here thoroughly shaking off his drowse.

'Hist, hist!' the hurried whisper now growing husky. 'See

here,' and the man held up two small objects faintly twinkling in the night-light; 'see, they are yours, Billy, if you'll only –'

But Billy broke in, and in his resentful eagerness to deliver himself his vocal infirmity somewhat intruded. 'D – d – damme, I don't know what you are d – d – driving at, or what you mean, but you had better g – g – go where you belong!' For the moment the fellow, as confounded, did not stir; and Billy, springing to his feet, said, 'If you d – don't start, I'll t – t – toss you back over the r – rail!' There was no mistaking this, and the mysterious emissary decamped, disappearing in the direction of the mainmast in the shadow of the booms.

'Hallo, what's the matter?' here came growling from a forecastleman awakened from his deck-doze by Billy's raised voice. And as the foretopman reappeared and was recognized by him: 'Ah, Beauty, is it you? Well, something must have been the matter, for you st – st – stuttered.'

'Oh,' rejoined Billy, now mastering the impediment, 'I found an afterguardsman in our part of the ship here, and I bid him be off where he belongs.'

'And is that all you did about it, Foretopman?' gruffly demanded another, an irascible old fellow of brick-colored visage and hair who was known to his associate forecastlemen as 'Red Pepper.' 'Such sneaks I should like to marry to the gunner's daughter!' – by that expression meaning that he would like to subject them to disciplinary castigation over a gun.

However, Billy's rendering of the matter satisfactorily accounted to these inquirers for the brief commotion, since of all the sections of a ship's company the forecastlemen, veterans for the most part and bigoted in their sea prejudices, are the most jealous in resenting territorial encroachments, especially on the part of any of the afterguard, of whom they have but a sorry opinion – chiefly landsmen, never going aloft except to reef or furl the mainsail, and in no wise competent to handle a marlinspike or turn in a deadeye, say.

THIS incident sorely puzzled Billy Budd. It was an entirely new experience, the first time in his life that he had ever been personally approached in underhand intriguing fashion. Prior to this encounter he had known nothing of the afterguardsman, the two men being stationed wide apart, one forward and aloft during his watch, the other on deck and aft.

What could it mean? And could they really be guineas, those two glittering objects the interloper had held up to his (Billy's) eyes? Where could the fellow get guineas? Why, even spare buttons are not so plentiful at sea. The more he turned the matter over, the more he was nonplussed, and made uneasy and discomfited. In his disgustful recoil from an overture which, though he but ill comprehended, he instinctively knew must involve evil of some sort, Billy Budd was like a young horse fresh from the pasture suddenly inhaling a vile whiff from some chemical factory, and by repeated snortings trying to get it out of his nostrils and lungs. This frame of mind barred all desire of holding further parley with the fellow, even were it but for the purpose of gaining some enlightenment as to his design in approaching him. And yet he was not without natural curiosity to see how such a visitor in the dark would look in broad day.

He espied him the following afternoon in his first dogwatch below, one of the smokers on that forward part of the upper gun deck allotted to the pipe. He recognized him by his general cut and build more than by his round freckled face and glassy eyes of pale blue, veiled with lashes all but white. And yet Billy was a bit uncertain whether indeed it were he – yonder chap about his own age chatting and laughing in freehearted way, leaning against a gun; a genial young fellow enough to look at, and something of a rattle-brain, to all appearance. Rather chubby too for a sailor, even an afterguardsman. In short, the last man in the world, one would think, to be overburdened with thoughts, especially those perilous thoughts that must needs belong to a conspirator in any serious project, or even to the underling of such a conspirator.

Although Billy was not aware of it, the fellow, with a sidelong watchful glance, had perceived Billy first, and then noting that Billy was looking at him, thereupon nodded a familiar sort of friendly recognition as to an old acquaintance, without interrupting the talk he was engaged in with the group of smokers. A day or two afterwards, chancing in the evening promenade on a gun deck to pass Billy, he offered a flying word of good-fellowship, as it were, which by its unexpectedness, and equivocalness under the circumstances, so embarrassed Billy that he knew not how to respond to it, and let it go unnoticed.

Billy was now left more at a loss than before. The ineffectual speculations into which he was led were so disturbingly alien to him that he did his best to smother them. It never entered his mind that here was a matter which, from its extreme questionableness, it was his duty as a loyal bluejacket to report in the proper quarter. And, probably, had such a step been suggested to him, he would have been deterred from taking it by the thought, one of novice magnanimity, that it would savor overmuch of the dirty work of a telltale. He kept the thing to himself. Yet upon one occasion he could not forbear a little disburdening himself to the old Dansker, tempted thereto perhaps by the influence of a balmy night when the ship lay becalmed; the twain, silent for the most part, sitting together on deck, their heads propped against the bulwarks. But it was only a partial and anonymous account that Billy gave, the unfounded scruples above referred to preventing full disclosure to anybody. Upon hearing Billy's version, the sage Dansker seemed to divine more than he was told; and after a little meditation, during which his wrinkles were pursed as into a point, quite effacing for the time that quizzing expression his face sometimes wore: 'Didn't I say so, Baby Budd?'

'Say what?' demanded Billy.

'Why, *Jemmy Legs* is *down* on you.'

'And what,' rejoined Billy in amazement, 'has *Jemmy Legs* to do with that cracked afterguardsman?'

'Ho, it was an afterguardsman, then. A cat's-paw, a cat's-paw!' And with that exclamation, whether it had reference to a light puff of air just then coming over the calm sea, or a subtler relation to the aftersguardsman, there is no telling, the old Merlin gave a twisting wrench with his black teeth at his plug of tobacco, vouchsafing no reply to Billy's impetuous question, though now repeated, for it was his wont to relapse into grim silence when interrogated in skeptical sort as to any of his sententious oracles, not always very clear ones, rather partaking of that obscurity which invests most Delphic deliverances from any quarter.

Long experience had very likely brought this old man to that bitter prudence which never interferes in aught and never gives advice.

16

YES, despite the Dansker's pithy insistence as to the master-at-arms being at the bottom of these strange experiences of Billy on board the *Bellipotent*, the young sailor was ready to ascribe them to almost anybody but the man who, to use Billy's own expression, 'always had a pleasant word for him.' This is to be wondered at. Yet not so much to be wondered at. In certain matters, some sailors even in mature life remain unsophisticated enough. But a young seafarer of the disposition of our athletic foretopman is much of a child-man. And yet a child's utter innocence is but its blank ignorance, and the innocence more or less wanes as intelligence waxes. But in Billy Budd intelligence, such as it was, had advanced while yet his simple-mindedness remained for the most part unaffected. Experience is a teacher indeed; yet did Billy's years make his experience small. Besides, he had none of that intuitive knowledge of the bad which in natures not good or incompletely so foreruns experience, and therefore may pertain, as in some instances it too clearly does pertain, even to youth.

And what could Billy know of man except of man as a mere sailor? And the old-fashioned sailor, the veritable man before the mast, the sailor from boyhood up, he, though indeed of the same species as a landsman, is in some respects singularly distinct from him. The sailor is frankness, the landsman is finesse. Life is not a game with the sailor, demanding the long head – no intricate games of chess where few moves are made in straightforwardness and ends are attained by indirection, an oblique, tedious, barren game hardly worth that poor candle burnt out in playing it.

Yes, as a class, sailors are in character a juvenile race. Even their deviations are marked by juvenility, this more especially holding true with the sailors of Billy's time. Then too, certain things which apply to all sailors do more pointedly operate here and there upon the junior one. Every sailor, too, is accustomed to obey orders without debating them; his life afloat is externally ruled for him; he is not brought into that promiscuous commerce with mankind where unobstructed free agency on equal terms – equal superficially, at least – soon teaches one that unless upon occasion he exercise a distrust keen in proportion to the fairness of the appearance, some foul turn may be served him. A ruled undemonstrative distrustfulness is so habitual, not with businessmen so much as with men who know their kind in less shallow relations than business, namely, certain men of the world, that they come at last to employ it all but unconsciously; and some of them would very likely feel real surprise at being charged with it as one of their general characteristics.

17

But after the little matter at the mess Billy Budd no more found himself in strange trouble at times about his hammock or his clothes bag or what not. As to that smile that occasionally sunned him, and the pleasant passing word, these were, if not more frequent, yet if anything more pronounced than before.

But for all that, there were certain other demonstrations now. When Claggart's unobserved glance happened to light on belted Billy rolling along the upper gun deck in the leisure of the second dogwatch, exchanging passing broadsides of fun with other young promenaders in the crowd, that glance would follow the cheerful sea Hyperion with a settled meditative and melancholy expression, his eyes strangely suffused with incipient feverish tears. Then would Claggart look like the man of sorrows. Yes, and sometimes the melancholy expression would have in it a touch of soft yearning, as if Claggart could even have loved Billy but for fate and ban. But this was an evanescence, and quickly repented of, as it were, by an immitigable look, pinching and shriveling the visage into the momentary semblance of a wrinkled walnut. But sometimes catching sight in advance of the foretopman coming in his direction, he would, upon their nearing, step aside a little to let him pass, dwelling upon Billy for the moment with the glittering dental satire of a Guise. But upon any abrupt unforeseen encounter a red light would flash forth from his eye like a spark from an anvil in a dusk smithy. That quick, fierce light was a strange one, darted from orbs which in repose were of a color nearest approaching a deeper violet, the softest of shades.

Though some of these caprices of the pit could not but be observed by their object, yet were they beyond the construing of such a nature. And the thews of Billy were hardly compatible with that sort of sensitive spiritual organization which in some cases instinctively conveys to ignorant innocence an admonition of the proximity of the malign. He thought the master-at-arms acted in a manner rather queer at times. That was all. But the occasional frank air and pleasant word went for what they purported to be, the young sailor never having heard as yet of the 'too fair-spoken man.'

Had the foretopman been conscious of having done or said anything to provoke the ill will of the official, it would have been different with him, and his sight might have been purged if not sharpened. As it was, innocence was his blinder.

So was it with him in yet another matter. Two minor officers, the armorer and captain of the hold, with whom he had never exchanged a word, his position in the ship not bringing him into contact with them, these men now for the first began to cast upon Billy, when they chanced to encounter him, that peculiar glance which evidences that the man from whom it comes has been some way tampered with, and to the prejudice of him upon whom the glance lights. Never did it occur to Billy as a thing to be noted or a thing suspicious, though he well knew the fact, that the armorer and captain of the hold, with the ship's yeoman, apothecary, and others of that grade, were by naval usage messmates of the master-at-arms, men with ears convenient to his confidential tongue.

But the general popularity that came from our Handsome Sailor's manly forwardness upon occasion and irresistible good nature, indicating no mental superiority tending to excite an invidious feeling, this good will on the part of most of his shipmates made him the less to concern himself about such mute aspects toward him as those whereto allusion has just been made, aspects he could not so fathom as to infer their whole import.

As to the afterguardsman, though Billy for reasons already given necessarily saw little of him, yet when the two did happen to meet, invariably came the fellow's offhand cheerful recognition, sometimes accompanied by a passing pleasant word or two. Whatever that equivocal young person's original design may really have been, or the design of which he might have been the deputy, certain it was from his manner upon these occasions that he had wholly dropped it.

It was as if his precocity of crookedness (and every vulgar villain is precocious) had for once deceived him, and the man he had sought to entrap as a simpleton had through his very simplicity ignominiously baffled him.

But shrewd ones may opine that it was hardly possible for Billy to refrain from going up to the afterguardsman and bluntly demanding to know his purpose in the initial interview so abruptly closed in the forechains. Shrewd ones may also think it but natural in Billy to set about sounding some of the other impressed men of the ship in order to discover what basis, if any, there was for the emissary's obscure suggestions as to plotting disaffection aboard. Yes, shrewd ones may so think. But something more, or rather something else than mere shrewdness is perhaps needful for the due understanding of such a character as Billy Budd's.

As to Claggart, the monomania in the man – if that indeed it were – as involuntarily disclosed by starts in the manifestations detailed, yet in general covered over by his self-contained and rational demeanor; this, like a subterranean fire, was eating its way deeper and deeper in him. Something decisive must come of it.

18

AFTER the mysterious interview in the forechains, the one so abruptly ended there by Billy, nothing especially germane to the story occurred until the events now about to be narrated.

Elsewhere it has been said that in the lack of frigates (of course better sailers than line-of-battle ships) in the English squadron up the Straits at that period, the *Bellipotent 74* was occasionally employed not only as an available substitute for a scout, but at times on detached service of more important kind. This was not alone because of her sailing qualities, not common in a ship of her rate, but quite as much, probably, that the character of her commander, it was thought, specially adapted him for any duty where under unforeseen difficulties a prompt initiative might have to be taken in some matter demanding knowledge and ability in addition to those qualities implied in good seamanship. It was on an expedition of the latter sort, a somewhat distant one, and when the *Bellipotent* was almost at her furthest remove from the fleet, that in the latter part of an afternoon watch she unexpectedly came in sight of a ship of the enemy. It proved to be a frigate. The latter, perceiving through the glass that the weight of men and metal would be heavily against her, invoking her light heels crowded sail to get away. After a chase urged almost against hope and lasting until about the middle of the first dogwatch, she signally succeeded in effecting her escape.

Not long after the pursuit had been given up, and ere the excitement incident thereto had altogether waned away, the master-at-arms, ascending from his cavernous sphere, made his appearance cap in hand by the mainmast respectfully waiting the notice of Captain Vere, then solitary walking the weather side of the quarter-deck, doubtless somewhat chafed at the failure of the pursuit. The spot where Claggart stood was the place allotted to men of lesser grades seeking some more particular interview either with the officer of the deck or the captain himself. But from the latter it was not often that a sailor or petty officer of those days would seek a hearing; only some exceptional cause would, according to established custom, have warranted that.

Presently, just as the commander, absorbed in his reflections, was on the point of turning aft in his promenade, he became sensible of Claggart's presence, and saw the doffed cap held in deferential expectancy. Here be it said that Captain Vere's personal knowledge of this petty officer had only begun at the time of the ship's last sailing from home, Claggart then for the first, in transfer from a ship detained for repairs, supplying on board the *Bellipotent* the place of a previous master-at-arms disabled and ashore.

No sooner did the commander observe who it was that now deferentially stood awaiting his notice than a peculiar expression came over him. It was not unlike that which uncontrollably will flit across the countenance of one at unawares encountering a person who, though known to him indeed, has hardly been long enough known for thorough knowledge, but something in whose aspect nevertheless now for the first provokes a vaguely repellent distaste. But coming to a stand and resuming much of his wonted official manner, save that a sort of impatience lurked in the intonation of the opening word, he said 'Well? What is it, Master-at-arms?'

With the air of a subordinate grieved at the necessity of being a messenger of ill tidings, and while conscientiously determined to be frank yet equally resolved upon shunning overstatement, Claggart at this invitation, or rather summons to disburden, spoke up. What he said, conveyed in the language of no uneducated man, was to the effect following, if not altogether in these words, namely, that during the chase and preparations for the possible encounter he had seen enough to convince him that at least one sailor aboard was a dangerous character in a ship mustering some who not only had taken a guilty part in the late serious troubles, but others also who, like the man in question, had entered His Majesty's service under another form than enlistment.

At this point Captain Vere with some impatience interrupted him: 'Be direct, man; say *impressed men.*'

Claggart made a gesture of subservience, and proceeded. Quite lately he (Claggart) had begun to suspect that on the gun decks some sort of movement prompted by the sailor in question was covertly going on, but he had not thought himself warranted in reporting the suspicion so long as it remained indistinct. But from what he had that afternoon observed in the man referred to, the suspicion of something clandestine going on had advanced to a point less removed from certainty. He deeply felt, he added, the serious responsibility assumed in making a report involving such possible consequences to the individual mainly concerned, besides tending to augment those natural anxieties which every naval commander must feel in view of extraordinary outbreaks so recent as those which, he sorrowfully said it, it needed not to name.

Now at the first broaching of the matter Captain Vere, taken by surprise, could not wholly dissemble his disquietude. But as Claggart went on, the former's aspect changed into restiveness under something in the testifier's manner in giving his testimony. However, he refrained from interrupting him. And Claggart, continuing, concluded with this: 'God forbid, your honor, that the *Bellipotent*'s should be the experience of the –'

'Never mind that!' here peremptorily broke in the superior, his face altering with anger, instinctively divining the ship that the other was about to name, one in which the Nore Mutiny had assumed a singularly tragical character that for a time jeopardized the life of its commander. Under the circumstances he was indignant at the purposed allusion. When the commissioned officers themselves were on all occasions very heedful how they referred to the recent events in the fleet, for a petty officer unnecessarily to allude to them in the presence of his captain, this struck him as a most immodest presumption. Besides, to his quick sense of self-respect it even looked under the circumstances something like an attempt to alarm him. Nor at first was he without some surprise that one who so far as he had hitherto come under his notice had shown considerable tact in his function should in this particular evince such lack of it.

But these thoughts and kindred dubious ones flitting across his mind were suddenly replaced by an intuitional surmise which, though as yet obscure in form, served practically to affect his reception of the ill tidings. Certain it is that, long versed in everything pertaining to the complicated gun-deck life, which like every other form of life has its secret mines and dubious side, the side popularly disclaimed, Captain Vere did not permit himself to be unduly disturbed by the general tenor of his subordinate's report.

Furthermore, if in view of recent events prompt action should be taken at the first palpable sign of recurring insubordination, for all that, not judicious would it be, he thought, to keep the idea of lingering disaffection alive by undue forwardness in crediting an informer, even if his own subordinate and charged among other things with police surveillance of the crew. This feeling would not perhaps have so prevailed with him were it not that upon a prior occasion the patriotic zeal officially evinced by Claggart had somewhat irritated him as appearing rather supersensible and strained. Furthermore, something even in the official's self-possessed and somewhat ostentatious manner in making his specifications strangely reminded him of a bandsman, a perjurous witness in a capital case before a courtmartial ashore of which when a lieutenant he (Captain Vere) had been a member.

Now the peremptory check given to Claggart in the matter of the arrested allusion was quickly followed up by this: 'You say that there is at least one dangerous man aboard. Name him.'

'William Budd, a foretopman, your honor.'

'William Budd!' repeated Captain Vere with unfeigned astonishment. 'And mean you the man that Lieutenant Ratcliffe took from the merchantman not very long ago, the young fellow who seems to be so popular with the men – Billy the Handsome Sailor, as they call him?'

'The same your honor; but for all his youth and good looks, a deep one. Not for nothing does he insinuate himself into the good will of his shipmates, since at the least they will at a pinch say – all hands will – a good word for him, and at all hazards. Did Lieutenant Ratcliffe happen to tell your honor of that adroit fling of Budd's, jumping up in the cutter's bow under the merchantman's stern when he was being taken off? It is even masked by that sort of good-humored air that at heart he resents his impressment.

You have but noted his fair cheek. A mantrap may be under the ruddy-tipped daisies.'

Now the Handsome Sailor as a signal figure among the crew had naturally enough attracted the captain's attention from the first. Though in general not very demonstrative to his officers, he had congratulated Lieutenant Ratcliffe upon his good fortune in lighting on such a fine specimen of the *genus homo*, who in the nude might have posed for a statue of a young Adam before the Fall. As to Billy's adieu to the ship *Rights-of-Man*, which the boarding lieutenant had indeed reported to him, but, in a deferential way, more as a good story than aught else, Captain Vere, though mistakenly understanding it as a satiric sally, had but thought so much the better of the impressed man for it; as a military sailor, admiring the spirit that could take an arbitrary enlistment so merrily and sensibly. The foretopman's conduct, too, so far as it had fallen under the captain's notice, had confirmed the first happy augury, while the new recruit's qualities as a 'sailor-man' seemed to be such that he had thought of recommending him to the executive officer for promotion to a place that would more frequently bring him under his own observation, namely, the captaincy of the mizzentop, replacing there in the starboard watch a man not so young whom partly for that reason he deemed less fitted for the post. Be it parenthesized here that since the mizzentopmen have not to handle such breadths of heavy canvas as the lower sails on the mainmast and foremast, a young man if of the right stuff not only seems best adapted to duty there, but in fact is generally selected for the captaincy of that top, and the company under him are light hands and often but striplings. In sum, Captain Vere had from the beginning deemed Billy Budd to be what in the naval parlance of the time was called a 'King's bargain': that is to say, for His Britannic Majesty's navy a capital investment at small outlay or none at all.

After a brief pause, during which the reminiscences above mentioned passed vividly through his mind and he weighed the import of Claggart's last suggestion conveyed in the phrase 'mantrap under the daisies,' and the more he weighed it the less reliance he felt in the informer's good faith, suddenly he turned upon him and in a low voice demanded: 'Do you come to me, Master-at-arms, with so foggy a tale? As to Budd, cite me an act or spoken word of his confirmatory of what you in general charge against him. Stay,' drawing nearer to him; 'heed what you speak. Just now, and in a case like this, there is a yardarm-end for the false witness.'

'Ah, your honor!' sighed Claggart, mildly shaking his shapely head as in sad deprecation of such unmerited severity of tone. Then, bridling – erecting himself as in virtuous self-assertion – he circumstantially alleged certain words and acts which collectively, if credited, led to presumptions mortally inculpating Budd. And for some of these averments, he added, substantiating proof was not far.

With gray eyes impatient and distrustful essaying to fathom to the bottom Claggart's calm violet ones, Captain Vere again heard him out; then for the moment stood ruminating. The mood he evinced, Claggart – himself for the time liberated from the other's scrutiny – steadily regarded with a look difficult to render: a look curious of the operation of his tactics, a look such as might have been that of the spokesman of the envious children of Jacob deceptively imposing upon the troubled patriarch the blood-dyed coat of young Joseph.

Though something exceptional in the moral quality of Captain Vere made him, in earnest encounter with a fellow man, a veritable touchstone of that man's essential nature, yet now as to Claggart and what was really going on in him his feeling partook less of intuitional conviction than of strong suspicion clogged by strange dubieties. The perplexity he evinced proceeded less from aught touching the man informed against – as Claggart doubtless opined – than from considerations how best to act in regard to the informer. At first, indeed, he was naturally for summoning that substantiation of his allegations which Claggart said

[373]

was at hand. But such a proceeding would result in the matter at once getting abroad, which in the present stage of it, he thought, might undesirably affect the ship's company. If Claggart was a false witness – that closed the affair. And therefore, before trying the accusation, he would first practically test the accuser; and he thought this could be done in a quiet, undemonstrative way.

The measure he determined upon involved a shifting of the scene, a transfer to a place less exposed to observation than the broad quarter-deck. For although the few gun-room officers there at the time had, in due observance of naval etiquette, withdrawn to leeward the moment Captain Vere had begun his promenade on the deck's weather side; and though during the colloquy with Claggart they of course ventured not to diminish the distance; and though throughout the interview Captain Vere's voice was far from him, and Claggart's silvery and low; and the wind in the cordage and the wash of the sea helped the more to put them beyond earshot; nevertheless, the interview's continuance already had attracted observation from some topmen aloft and other sailors in the waist or further forward.

Having determined upon his measures, Captain Vere forthwith took action. Abruptly turning to Claggart, he asked, 'Master-at-arms, is it now Budd's watch aloft?'

'No, your honor.'

Whereupon, 'Mr Wilkes!' summoning the nearest midshipman. 'Tell Albert to come to me.' Albert was the captain's hammock-boy, a sort of sea valet in whose discretion and fidelity his master had much confidence. The lad appeared.

'You know Budd, the foretopman?'

'I do, sir.'

'Go find him. It is his watch off. Manage to tell him out of earshot that he is wanted aft. Contrive it that he speaks to nobody. Keep him in talk yourself. And not till you get well aft here, not till then let him know that the place where he is wanted is my cabin. You understand. Go. – Master-at-arms, show yourself on the decks below, and when you think it time for Albert to be coming with his man, stand by quietly to follow the sailor in.'

19

Now when the foretopman found himself in the cabin, closeted there, as it were, with the captain and Claggart, he was surprised enough. But it was a surprise unaccompanied by apprehension or distrust. To an immature nature essentially honest and humane, forewarning intimations of subtler danger from one's kind come tardily if at all. The only thing that took shape in the young sailor's mind was this: Yes, the captain, I have always thought, looks kindly upon me. Wonder if he's going to make me his coxswain. I should like that. And may be now he is going to ask the master-at-arms about me.

'Shut the door there, sentry,' said the commander; 'stand without, and let nobody come in. – Now, Master-at-arms, tell this man to his face what you told of him to me,' and stood prepared to scrutinize the mutually confronting visages.

With the measured step and calm collected air of an asylum physician approaching in the public hall some patient beginning to show indications of a coming paroxysm, Claggart deliberately advanced within short range of Billy and, mesmerically looking him in the eye, briefly recapitulated the accusation.

Not at first did Billy take it in. When he did, the rose-tan of his cheek looked struck as by white leprosy. He stood like one impaled and gagged. Meanwhile the accuser's eyes, removing not as yet from the blue dilated ones, underwent a phenomenal change, their wonted rich violet color blurring into a muddy purple. Those lights of human intelligence, losing human expression, were gelidly protruding like the alien eyes of certain uncatalogued creatures of the deep. The first mesmeristic glance was one of serpent fascination; the last was the paralyzing lurch of the torpedo fish.

'Speak, man!' said Captain Vere to the transfixed one, struck by his aspect even more than by Claggart's. 'Speak! Defend yourself!' Which appeal caused but a strange dumb gesturing and gurgling in Billy; amazement at such an accusation so suddenly sprung on inexperienced non-age; this, and, it may be, horror of the accuser's eyes, serving to bring out his lurking defect and in this instance for the time intensifying it into a convulsed tongue-tie; while the intent head and entire form straining forward in an agony of ineffectual eagerness to obey the injunction to speak and defend himself, gave an expression to the face like that of a condemned vestal priestess in the moment of being buried alive, and in the first struggle against suffocation.

Though at the time Captain Vere was quite ignorant of Billy's liability to vocal impediment, he now immediately divined it, since vividly Billy's aspect recalled to him that of a bright young schoolmate of his whom he had once seen struck by much the same startling impotence in the act of eagerly rising in the class to be foremost in response to a testing question put to it by the master. Going close up to the young sailor, and laying a soothing hand on his shoulder, he said, 'There is no hurry, my boy. Take your time, take your time.' Contrary to the effect intended, these words so fatherly in tone, doubtless touching Billy's heart to the quick, prompted yet more violent efforts at utterance – efforts soon ending for the time in confirming the paralysis, and bringing to his face an expression which was as a crucifixion to behold. The next instant, quick as the flame from a discharged cannon at night, his right arm shot out, and Claggart dropped to the deck. Whether intentionally or but owing to the young athlete's superior height, the blow had taken effect full upon the forehead, so shapely and intellectual-looking a feature in the master-at-arms; so that the body fell over lengthwise, like a heavy plank tilted from erectness. A gasp or two, and he lay motionless.

'Fated boy,' breathed Captain Vere in tone so low as to be almost a whisper, 'what have you done! But here, help me.'

The twain raised the felled one from the loins up into a sitting position. The spare form flexibly acquiesced, but inertly. It was like handling a dead snake. They lowered it back. Regaining erectness, Captain Vere with one hand covering his face stood to all appearance as impassive as the object at his feet. Was he absorbed in taking in all the bearings of the event and what was best not only now at once to be done, but also in the sequel? Slowly he uncovered his face; and the effect was as if the moon emerging from eclipse should reappear with quite another aspect than that which had gone into hiding. The father in him, manifested towards Billy thus far in the scene, was replaced by the military disciplinarian. In his official tone he bade the foretopman retire to a stateroom aft (pointing it out), and there remain till thence summoned. This order Billy in silence mechanically obeyed. Then going to the cabin door where it opened on the quarter-deck, Captain Vere said to the sentry without, 'Tell somebody to send Albert here.' When the lad appeared, his master so contrived it that he should not catch sight of the prone one. 'Albert,' he said to him, 'tell the surgeon I wish to see him. You need not come back till called.'

When the surgeon entered – a self-poised character of that grave sense and experience that hardly anything could take him aback – Captain Vere advanced to meet him, thus unconsciously intercepting his view of Claggart, and, interrupting the other's wonted ceremonious salutation, said, 'Nay. Tell me how it is with yonder man,' directing his attention to the prostrate one.

The surgeon looked, and for all his self-command somewhat started at the abrupt revelation. On Claggart's always pallid complexion, thick black blood was now oozing from nostril and ear. To the gazer's professional eye it was unmistakably no living man that he saw.

'Is it so, then?' said Captain Vere, intently watching him.

'I thought it. But verify it.' Whereupon the customary tests confirmed the surgeon's first glance, who now, looking up in unfeigned concern, cast a look of intense inquisitiveness upon his superior. But Captain Vere, with one hand to his brow, was standing motionless. Suddenly, catching the surgeon's arm convulsively, he exclaimed, pointing down to the body, 'It is the divine judgment on Ananias! Look!'

Disturbed by the excited manner he had never before observed in the *Bellipotent*'s captain, and as yet wholly ignorant of the affair, the prudent surgeon nevertheless held his peace, only again looking an earnest interrogatory as to what it was that had resulted in such a tragedy.

But Captain Vere was now again motionless, standing absorbed in thought. Again starting, he vehemently exclaimed, 'Struck dead by an angel of God! Yet the angel must hang!'

At these passionate interjections, mere incoherences to the listener as yet unapprised of the antecedents, the surgeon was profoundly discomposed. But now, as recollecting himself, Captain Vere in less passionate tone briefly related the circumstances leading up to the event. 'But come; we must dispatch,' he added. 'Help me to remove him' (meaning the body) 'to yonder compartment,' designating one opposite that where the foretopman remained immured. Anew disturbed by a request that, as implying a desire for secrecy, seemed unaccountably strange to him, there was nothing for the subordinate to do but comply.

'Go now,' said Captain Vere with something of his wonted manner. 'Go now. I presently shall call a drumhead court. Tell the lieutenants what has happened, and tell Mr Mordant' (meaning the captain of marines), 'and charge them to keep the matter to themselves.'

20

FULL of disquietude and misgiving, the surgeon left the cabin. Was Captain Vere suddenly affected in his mind, or was it but a transient excitement, brought about by so strange and extraordinary a tragedy? As to the drumhead court, it struck the surgeon as impolitic, if nothing more. The thing to do, he thought, was to place Billy Budd in confinement, and in a way dictated by usage, and postpone further action in so extraordinary a case to such time as they should rejoin the squadron, and then refer it to the admiral. He recalled the unwonted agitation of Captain Vere and his excited exclamations, so at variance with his normal manner. Was he unhinged?

But assuming that he is, it is not so susceptible of proof. What then can the surgeon do? No more trying situation is conceivable than that of an officer subordinate under a captain whom he suspects to be not mad, indeed, but yet not quite unaffected in his intellects. To argue his order to him would be insolence. To resist him would be mutiny.

In obedience to Captain Vere, he communicated what had happened to the lieutenants and captain of marines, saying nothing as to the captain's state. They fully shared his own surprise and concern. Like him too, they seemed to think that such a matter should be referred to the admiral.

21

WHO in the rainbow can draw the line where the violet tint ends and the orange tint begins? Distinctly we see the difference of the colors, but where exactly does the one first blendingly enter into the other? So with sanity and insanity. In pronounced cases there is no question about them. But in some supposed cases, in various degrees supposedly less pronounced, to draw the exact line of demarcation few will undertake, though for a fee becoming considerate some professional experts will. There is nothing nameable but that some men will, or undertake to, do it for pay.

Whether Captain Vere, as the surgeon professionally and privately surmised, was really the sudden victim of any degree of aberration, every one must determine for himself by such light as this narrative may afford.

That the unhappy event which has been narrated could not have happened at a worse juncture was but too true. For it was close on the heel of the suppressed insurrections, an aftertime very critical to naval authority, demanding from every English sea commander two qualities not readily interfusable – prudence and rigor. Moreover, there was something crucial in the case.

In the jugglery of circumstances preceding and attending the event on board the *Bellipotent*, and in the light of that martial code whereby it was formally to be judged, innocence and guilt personified in Claggart and Budd in effect changed places. In a legal view the apparent victim of the tragedy was he who had sought to victimize a man blameless; and the indisputable deed of the latter, navally regarded, constituted the most heinous of military crimes. Yet more. The essential right and wrong involved in the matter, the clearer that might be, so much the worse for the responsibility of a loyal sea commander, inasmuch as he was not authorized to determine the matter on that primitive basis.

Small wonder then that the *Bellipotent*'s captain, though in general a man of rapid decision, felt that circumspectness not less than promptitude was necessary. Until he could decide upon his course, and in each detail; and not only so, but until the concluding measure was upon the point of being enacted, he deemed it advisable, in view of all the circumstances, to guard as much as possible against publicity. Here he may or may not have erred. Certain it is, however, that subsequently in the confidential talk of more than one or two gun rooms and cabins he was not a little criticized by some officers, a fact imputed by his friends and vehemently by his cousin Jack Denton to professional jealousy of Starry Vere. Some imaginative ground for invidious comment there was. The maintenance of secrecy in the matter, the confining all knowledge of it for a time to the place where the homicide occurred, the quarter-deck cabin; in these particulars lurked some resemblance to the policy adopted in those tragedies of the palace which have occurred more than once in the capital founded by Peter the Barbarian.

The case indeed was such that fain would the *Bellipotent*'s captain have deferred taking any action whatever respecting it further than to keep the foretopman a close prisoner till the ship rejoined the squadron and then submitting the matter to the judgment of his admiral.

But a true military officer is in one particular like a true monk. Not with more of self-abnegation will the latter keep his vows of monastic obedience than the former his vows of allegiance to martial duty.

Feeling that unless quick action was taken on it, the deed of the foretopman, so soon as it should be known on the gun decks, would tend to awaken any slumbering embers of the Nore among the crew, a sense of the urgency of the case overruled in Captain Vere every other consideration. But though a conscientious disciplinarian, he was no lover of authority for mere authority's sake. Very far was he from embracing opportunities for monopolizing to himself the perils of moral responsibility, none at least that could properly be referred to an official superior or shared with him by his official equals or even subordinates. So thinking, he was glad it would not be at variance with usage to turn the matter over to a summary court of his own officers, reserving to himself, as the one on whom the ultimate accountability would rest, the right of maintaining a supervision of it, or formally or informally interposing at need. Accordingly a drumhead court was summarily convened, he electing the individuals composing it: the first lieutenant, the captain of marines, and the sailing master.

In associating an officer of marines with the sea lieutenant and the sailing master in a case having to do with a sailor, the commander perhaps deviated from general custom. He was prompted thereto by the circumstance that he took that soldier to be a judicious person, thoughtful, and not altogether incapable of grappling with a difficult case unprecedented in his prior experience. Yet even as to him he was not without some latent misgiving, for withal he was an extremely good-natured man, an enjoyer of his dinner, a sound sleeper, and inclined to obesity – a man who though he would always maintain his manhood in battle might not prove altogether reliable in a moral dilemma involving aught of the tragic. As to the first lieutenant and the sailing master, Captain Vere could not but be aware that though honest natures, of approved gallantry upon occasion, their intelligence was mostly confined to the matter of active seamanship and the fighting demands of their profession.

The court was held in the same cabin where the unfortunate affair had taken place. This cabin, the commander's, embraced the entire area under the poop deck. Aft, and on either side, was a small stateroom, the one now temporarily a jail and the other a dead-house, and a yet smaller compartment, leaving a space between expanding forward into a goodly oblong of length coinciding with the ship's beam. A skylight of moderate dimension was overhead, and at each end of the oblong space were two sashed porthole windows easily convertible back into embrasures for short carronades.

All being quickly in readiness, Billy Budd was arraigned, Captain Vere necessarily appearing as the sole witness in the case, and as such temporarily sinking his rank, though singularly maintaining it in a matter apparently trivial, namely, that he testified from the ship's weather side, with that object having caused the court to sit on the lee side. Concisely he narrated all that had led up to the catastrophe, omitting nothing in Claggart's accusation and deposing as to the manner in which the prisoner had received it. At this testimony the three officers glanced with no little surprise at Billy Budd, the last man they would have suspected either of the mutinous design alleged by Claggart or the undeniable deed he himself had done. The first lieutenant, taking judicial primacy and turning toward the prisoner, said, 'Captain Vere has spoken. Is it or is it not as Captain Vere says?'

In response came syllables not so much impeded in the utterance as might have been anticipated. They were these: 'Captain Vere tells the truth. It is just as Captain Vere says, but it is not as the master-at-arms said. I have eaten the King's bread and I am true to the King.'

'I believe you, my man,' said the witness, his voice indicating a suppressed emotion not otherwise betrayed.

'God will bless you for that, your honor!' not without stammering said Billy, and all but broke down. But immediately he was recalled to self-control by another question, to which with the same emotional difficulty of utterance he said, 'No, there was no malice between us. I never bore malice against the master-at-arms. I am sorry that he is dead. I did not mean to kill him. Could I have used my tongue I would not have struck him. But he foully lied to my face and in presence of my captain, and I had to say something, and I could only say it with a blow, God help me!'

In the impulsive aboveboard manner of the frank one the court saw confirmed all that was implied in words that just previously had perplexed them, coming as they did from the testifier to the tragedy and promptly following Billy's impassioned disclaimer of mutinous intent – Captain Vere's words, 'I believe you, my man.'

Next it was asked of him whether he knew of or suspected aught savoring of incipient trouble (meaning mutiny, though the explicit term was avoided) going on in any section of the ship's company.

The reply lingered. This was naturally imputed by the court to the same vocal embarrassment which had retarded or obstructed previous answers. But in main it was otherwise here, the question immediately recalling to Billy's mind the interview with the afterguardsman in the forechains. But an innate repugnance to playing a part at all approaching that of an informer against one's own shipmates – the same erring sense of uninstructed honor which had stood

[383]

in the way of his reporting the matter at the time, though as a loyal man-of-war's man it was incumbent on him, and failure so to do, if charged against him and proven, would have subjected him to the heaviest of penalties; this, with the blind feeling now his that nothing really was being hatched, prevailed with him. When the answer came it was a negative.

'One question more,' said the officer of marines, now first speaking and with a troubled earnestness. 'You tell us that what the master-at-arms said against you was a lie. Now why should he have so lied, so maliciously lied, since you declare there was no malice between you?'

At that question, unintentionally touching on a spiritual sphere wholly obscure to Billy's thoughts, he was non-plussed, evincing a confusion indeed that some observers, such as can readily be imagined, would have construed into involuntary evidence of hidden guilt. Nevertheless, he strove some way to answer, but all at once relinquished the vain endeavor, at the same time turning an appealing glance towards Captain Vere as deeming him his best helper and friend. Captain Vere, who had been seated for a time, rose to his feet, addressing the interrogator. 'The question you put to him comes naturally enough. But how can he rightly answer it? – or anybody else, unless indeed it be he who lies within there,' designating the compartment where lay the corpse. 'But the prone one there will not rise to our summons. In effect, though, as it seems to me, the point you make is hardly material. Quite aside from any conceivable motive actuating the master-at-arms, and irrespective of the provocation to the blow, a martial court must needs in the present case confine its attention to the blow's consequence, which consequence justly is to be deemed not otherwise than as the striker's deed.'

This utterance, the full significance of which it was not at all likely that Billy took in, nevertheless caused him to turn a wistful interrogative look toward the speaker, a look in its dumb expressiveness not unlike that which a dog of generous breed might turn upon his master, seeking in his face some elucidation of a previous gesture ambiguous to the canine intelligence. Nor was the same utterance without marked effect upon the three officers, more especially the soldier. Couched in it seemed to them a meaning unanticipated, involving a prejudgment on the speaker's part. It served to augment a mental disturbance previously evident enough.

The soldier once more spoke, in a tone of suggestive dubiety addressing at once his associates and Captain Vere: 'Nobody is present – none of the ship's company, I mean – who might shed lateral light, if any is to be had, upon what remains mysterious in this matter.'

'That is thoughtfully put,' said Captain Vere; 'I see your drift. Ay, there is a mystery; but, to use a scriptural phrase, it is a "mystery of iniquity," a matter for psychologic theologians to discuss. But what has a military court to do with it? Not to add that for us any possible investigation of it is cut off by the lasting tongue-tie of – him – in yonder,' again designating the mortuary stateroom. 'The prisoner's deed – with that alone we have to do.'

To this, and particularly the closing reiteration, the marine soldier, knowing not how aptly to reply, sadly abstained from saying aught. The first lieutenant, who at the outset had not unnaturally assumed primacy in the court, now overrulingly instructed by a glance from Captain Vere, a glance more effective than words, resumed that primacy. Turning to the prisoner, 'Budd,' he said, and scarce in equable tones, 'Budd, if you have aught further to say for yourself, say it now.'

Upon this the young sailor turned another quick glance toward Captain Vere; then, as taking a hint from that aspect, a hint confirming his own instinct that silence was now best, replied to the lieutenant, 'I have said all, sir.'

The marine – the same who had been the sentinel without the cabin door at the time that the foretopman, followed by the master-at-arms, entered it – he, standing by the sailor throughout these judicial proceedings, was now directed to take him back to the after compartment originally assigned to the prisoner and his custodian. As the twain disappeared from view, the three officers, as partially liberated from some inward constraint associated with Billy's mere presence, simultaneously stirred in their seats. They exchanged looks of troubled indecision, yet feeling that decide they must and without long delay. For Captain Vere, he for the time stood – unconsciously with his back toward them, apparently in one of his absent fits – gazing out from a sashed porthole to windward upon the monotonous blank of the twilight sea. But the court's silence continuing, broken only at moments by brief consultations, in low earnest tones, this served to arouse him and energize him. Turning, he to-and-fro paced the cabin athwart; in the returning ascent to windward climbing the slant deck in the ship's lee roll, without knowing it symbolizing thus in his action a mind resolute to surmount difficulties even if against primitive instincts strong as the wind and the sea. Presently he came to a stand before the three. After scanning their faces he stood less as mustering his thoughts for expression than as one inly deliberating how best to put them to well-meaning men not intellectually mature, men with whom it was necessary to demonstrate certain principles that were axioms to himself. Similar impatience as to talking is perhaps one reason that deters some minds from addressing any popular assemblies.

When speak he did, something, both in the substance of what he said and his manner of saying it, showed the influence of unshared studies modifying and tempering the practical training of an active career. This, along with his phraseology, now and then was suggestive of the grounds whereon rested that imputation of a certain pedantry socially alleged against him by certain naval men of wholly practical cast, captains who nevertheless would frankly concede that His Majesty's navy mustered no more efficient officer of their grade than Starry Vere.

What he said was to this effect: 'Hitherto I have been but the witness, little more; and I should hardly think now to take another tone, that of your coadjutor for the time, did

I not perceive in you – at the crisis too – a troubled hesitancy, proceeding, I doubt not, from the clash of military duty with moral scruple – scruple vitalized by compassion. For the compassion, how can I otherwise than share it? But, mindful of paramount obligations, I strive against scruples that may tend to enervate decision. Not, gentlemen, that I hide from myself that the case is an exceptional one. Speculatively regarded, it well might be referred to a jury of casuists. But for us here, acting not as casuists or moralists, it is a case practical, and under martial law practically to be dealt with.

'But your scruples: do they move as in a dusk? Challenge them. Make them advance and declare themselves. Come now; do they import something like this: If, mindless of palliating circumstances, we are bound to regard the death of the master-at-arms as the prisoner's deed, then does that deed constitute a capital crime whereof the penalty is a mortal one. But in natural justice is nothing but the prisoner's overt act to be considered? How can we adjudge to summary and shameful death a fellow creature innocent before God, and whom we feel to be so? – Does that state it aright? You sign sad assent. Well, I too feel that, the full force of that. It is Nature. But do these buttons that we wear attest that our allegiance is to Nature? No, to the King. Though the ocean, which is inviolate Nature primeval, though this be the element where we move and have our being as sailors, yet as the King's officers lies our duty in a sphere correspondingly natural? So little is that true, that in receiving our commissions we in the most important regards ceased to be natural free agents. When war is declared are we the commissioned fighters previously consulted? We fight at command. If our judgments approve the war, that is but coincidence. So in other particulars. So now. For suppose condemnation to follow these present proceedings. Would it be so much we ourselves that would condemn as it would be martial law operating through us? For that law and the rigor of it, we are not responsibile. Our vowed responsibility is in this: That however pitilessly that law may operate in any instances, we nevertheless adhere to it and administer it.

'But the exceptional in the matter moves the hearts within you. Even so too is mine moved. But let not warm hearts betray heads that should be cool. Ashore in a criminal case, will an upright judge allow himself off the bench to be waylaid by some tender kinswoman of the accused seeking to touch him with her tearful plea? Well, the heart here, sometimes the feminine in man, is as that piteous woman, and hard though it be, she must here be ruled out.'

He paused, earnestly studying them for a moment; then resumed.

'But something in your aspect seems to urge that it is not solely the heart that moves in you, but also the conscience, the private conscience. But tell me whether or not, occupying the position we do, private conscience should not yield to that imperial one formulated in the code under which alone we officially proceed?'

Here the three men moved in their seats, less convinced than agitated by the course of an argument troubling but the more the spontaneous conflict within.

Perceiving which, the speaker paused for a moment; then abruptly changing his tone, went on.

'To steady us a bit, let us recur to the facts. – In wartime at sea a man-of-war's man strikes his superior in grade, and the blow kills. Apart from its effect the blow itself is, according to the Articles of War, a capital crime. Furthermore –'

'Ay, sir,' emotionally broke in the officer of marines, 'in one sense it was. But surely Budd proposed neither mutiny nor homicide.'

'Surely not, my good man. And before a court less arbitrary and more merciful than a martial one, that plea would largely extenuate. At the Last Assizes it shall acquit. But how here? We proceed under the law of the Mutiny Act. In feature no child can resemble his father more than that Act resembles in spirit the thing from which it derives

– War. In His Majesty's service – in this ship, indeed – there are Englishmen forced to fight for the King against their will. Against their conscience, for aught we know. Though as their fellow creatures some of us may appreciate their position, yet as navy officers what reck we of it? Still less recks the enemy. Our impressed men he would fain cut down in the same swath with our volunteers. As regards the enemy's naval conscripts, some of whom may even share our own abhorrence of the regicidal French Directory, it is the same on our side. War looks but to the frontage, the appearance. And the Mutiny Act, War's child, takes after the father. Budd's intent or non-intent is nothing to the purpose.

'But while, put to it by those anxieties in you which I cannot but respect, I only repeat myself – while thus strangely we prolong proceedings that should be summary – the enemy may be sighted and an engagement result. We must do; and one of two things must we do – condemn or let go.'

'Can we not convict and yet mitigate the penalty?' asked the sailing master, here speaking, and falteringly, for the first.

'Gentlemen, were that clearly lawful for us under the circumstances, consider the consequences of such clemency. The people' (meaning the ship's company) 'have native sense; most of them are familiar with our naval usage and tradition; and how would they take it? Even could you explain to them – which our official position forbids – they, long molded by arbitrary discipline, have not that kind of intelligent responsiveness that might qualify them to comprehend and discriminate. No, to the people the foretopman's deed, however it be worded in the announcement, will be plain homicide committed in a flagrant act of mutiny. What penalty for that should follow, they know. But it does not follow. *Why?* they will ruminate. You know what sailors are. Will they not revert to the recent outbreak at the Nore? Ay. They know the well-founded alarm – the panic it struck throughout England. Your clement sentence they would account pusillanimous. They would think that we flinch, that we are afraid of them – afraid of practicing a lawful rigor singularly demanded at this juncture, lest it should provoke new troubles. What shame to us such a conjecture on their part, and how deadly to discipline. You see then, whither, prompted by duty and the law, I steadfastly drive. But I beseech you, my friends, do not take me amiss. I feel as you do for this unfortunate boy. But did he know our hearts, I take him to be of that generous nature that he would feel even for us on whom in this military necessity so heavy a compulsion is laid.'

With that, crossing the deck he resumed his place by the sashed porthole, tacitly leaving the three to come to a decision. On the cabin's opposite side the troubled court sat silent. Loyal lieges, plain and practical, though at bottom they dissented from some points Captain Vere had put to them, they were without the faculty, hardly had the inclination, to gainsay one whom they felt to be an earnest man, one too not less their superior in mind than in naval rank. But it is not improbable that even such of his words as were not without influence over them, less came home to them than his closing appeal to their instinct as sea officers : in the forethought he threw out as to the practical consequences to discipline, considering the unconfirmed tone of the fleet at the time, should a man-of-war's man's violent killing at sea of a superior in grade be allowed to pass for aught else than a capital crime demanding prompt infliction of the penalty.

Not unlikely they were brought to something more or less akin to that harassed frame of mind which in the year 1842 actuated the commander of the U.S. brig-of-war *Somers* to resolve, under the so-called Articles of War, Articles modeled upon the English Mutiny Act, to resolve upon the execution at sea of a midshipman and two sailors as mutineers designing the seizure of the brig. Which resolution was carried out though in a time of peace and within not many days' sail of home. An act vindicated by a naval court of inquiry subsequently convened ashore. History, and here cited without comment. True, the circumstances on board the *Somers* were different from those on board the *Bellipotent*. But the urgency felt, well-warranted or otherwise, was much the same.

Says a writer whom few know, 'Forty years after a battle it is easy for a noncombatant to reason about how it ought to have been fought. It is another thing personally and under fire to have to direct the fighting while involved in the obscuring smoke of it. Much so with respect to other emergencies involving considerations both practical and moral, and when it is imperative promptly to act. The greater the fog the more it imperils the steamer, and speed is put on though at the hazard of running somebody down. Little ween the snug card players in the cabin of the responsibilities of the sleepless man on the bridge.'

In brief, Billy Budd was formally convicted and sentenced to be hung at the yardarm in the early morning watch, it being now night. Otherwise, as is customary in such cases, the sentence would forthwith have been carried out. In wartime on the field or in the fleet, a mortal punishment decreed by a drumhead court – on the field sometimes decreed by but a nod from the general – follows without delay on the heel of conviction, without appeal.

22

It was Captain Vere himself who of his own motion communicated the finding of the court to the prisoner, for that purpose going to the compartment where he was in custody and bidding the marine there to withdraw for the time.

Beyond the communication of the sentence, what took place at this interview was never known. But in view of the character of the twain briefly closeted in that stateroom, each radically sharing in the rarer qualities of our nature – so rare indeed as to be all but incredible to average minds however much cultivated – some conjectures may be ventured.

It would have been in consonance with the spirit of Captain Vere should he on this occasion have concealed nothing from the condemned one – should he indeed have frankly disclosed to him the part he himself had played in bringing about the decision, at the same time revealing his actuating motives. On Billy's side it is not improbable that such a confession would have been received in much the same spirit that prompted it. Not without a sort of joy, indeed, he might have appreciated the brave opinion of him implied in his captain's making such a confidant of him. Nor, as to the sentence itself, could he have been insensible that it was imparted to him as to one not afraid to die. Even more may have been. Captain Vere in end may have developed the passion sometimes latent under an exterior stoical or indifferent. He was old enough to have been Billy's father. The austere devotee of military duty, letting himself melt back into what remains primeval in our formalized humanity, may in end have caught Billy to his heart, even as Abraham may have caught young Isaac on the brink of resolutely offering him up in obedience to the exacting behest. But there is no telling the sacrament, seldom if in any case revealed to the gadding world, wherever under circumstances at all akin to those here attempted to be set forth two of great Nature's nobler order embrace. There is privacy at the time, inviolable to the survivor; and holy oblivion, the sequel to each diviner magnanimity, providentially covers all at last.

The first to encounter Captain Vere in act of leaving the compartment was the senior lieutenant. The face he beheld, for the moment one expressive of the agony of the strong, was to that officer, though a man of fifty, a startling revelation. That the condemned one suffered less than he who mainly had effected the condemnation was apparently indicated by the former's exclamation in the scene soon perforce to be touched upon.

23

Of a series of incidents with a brief term rapidly following each other, the adequate narration may take up a term less brief, especially if explanation or comment here and there seem requisite to the better understanding of such incidents. Between the entrance into the cabin of him who never left it alive, and him who when he did leave it left it as one condemned to die; between this and the closeted interview just given, less than an hour and a half had elapsed. It was an interval long enough, however, to awaken speculations among no few of the ship's company as to what it was that could be detaining in the cabin the master-at-arms and the sailor; for a rumor that both of them had been seen to enter it and neither of them had been seen to emerge, this rumor had got abroad upon the gun decks and in the tops, the people of a great warship being in one respect like villagers, taking microscopic note of every outward movement or non-movement going on. When therefore, in weather not at all tempestuous, all hands were called in the second dogwatch, a summons under such circumstances not usual in those hours, the crew were not wholly unprepared for some announcement extraordinary, one having connection too with the continued absence of the two men from their wonted haunts.

There was a moderate sea at the time; and the moon, newly risen and near to being at its full, silvered the white spar deck wherever not blotted by the clear-cut shadows horizontally thrown of fixtures and moving men. On either side the quarter-deck the marine guard under arms was drawn up; and Captain Vere, standing in his place surrounded by all the wardroom officers, addressed his men. In so doing, his manner showed neither more nor less than that properly pertaining to his supreme position aboard his own ship. In clear terms and concise he told them what had taken place in the cabin: that the master-at-arms was dead, that he who had killed him had been already tried by a summary court and condemned to death, and that the execution would take place in the early morning watch. The word *mutiny* was not named in what he said. He refrained too from making the occasion an opportunity for any preachment as to the maintenance of discipline, thinking perhaps that under existing circumstances in the navy the consequence of violating discipline should be made to speak for itself.

Their captain's announcement was listened to by the throng of standing sailors in a dumbness like that of a seated congregation of believers in hell listening to the clergyman's announcement of his Calvinistic text.

At the close, however, a confused murmur went up. It began to wax. All but instantly, then, at a sign, it was pierced and suppressed by shrill whistles of the boatswain and his mates. The word was given to about ship.

To be prepared for burial Claggart's body was delivered to certain petty officers of his mess. And here, not to clog the sequel with lateral matters, it may be added that at a suitable hour, the master-at-arms was committed to the sea with every funeral honor properly belonging to his naval grade.

In this proceeding as in every public one growing out of the tragedy strict adherence to usage was observed. Nor in any point could it have been at all deviated from, either with respect to Claggart or Billy Budd, without begetting undesirable speculations in the ship's company, sailors, and more particularly men-of-war's men, being of all men the greatest sticklers for usage. For similar cause, all communication between Captain Vere and the condemned one ended with the closeted interview already given, the latter being now surrendered to the ordinary routine preliminary to the end. His transfer under guard from the captain's quarters was effected without unusual precautions – at least no visible ones. If possible, not to let the men so much as surmise that their officers anticipate aught amiss from them is the tacit rule in a military ship. And the more that some sort of trouble should really be apprehended, the more do the officers keep that apprehension to themselves, though not the less unostentatious vigilance may be augmented. In the present instance, the sentry placed over the prisoner had strict orders to let no one have communication with him but the chaplain. And certain unobtrusive measures were taken absolutely to insure this point.

24

IN a seventy-four of the old order the deck known as the upper gun deck was the one covered over by the spar deck, which last, though not without its armament, was for the most part exposed to the weather. In general it was at all hours free from hammocks; those of the crew swinging on the lower gun deck and berth deck, the latter being not only a dormitory but also the place for the stowing of the sailors' bags, and on both sides lined with the large chests or movable pantries of the many messes of the men.

On the starboard side of the *Bellipotent*'s upper gun deck, behold Billy Budd under sentry lying prone in irons in one of the bays formed by the regular spacing of the guns comprising the batteries on either side. All these pieces were of the heavier caliber of that period. Mounted on lumbering wooden carriages, they were hampered with cumbersome harness of breeching and strong side-tackles for running them out. Guns and carriages, together with the long rammers and shorter linstocks lodged in loops overhead – all these, as customary, were painted black; and the heavy hempen breechings, tarred to the same tint, wore the like livery of the undertakers. In contrast with the funereal hue of these surroundings, the prone sailor's exterior apparel, white jumper and white duck trousers, each more or less soiled, dimly glimmered in the obscure light of the bay like a patch of discolored snow in early April lingering at some upland cave's black mouth. In effect he is already in his shroud, or the garments that shall serve him in lieu of one. Over him but scarce illuminating him, two battle lanterns swing from two massive beams of the deck above. Fed with the oil supplied by the war contractors (whose gains, honest or otherwise, are in every land an anticipated portion of the harvest of death), with flickering splashes of dirty yellow light they pollute the pale moonshine all but ineffectually struggling in obstructed flecks through the open ports from which the tampioned cannon protrude. Other lanterns at intervals serve but to bring out somewhat the obscurer bays which, like small confessionals or side-chapels in a cathedral, branch from the long dim-vistaed broad aisle between the two batteries of that covered tier.

Such was the deck where now lay the Handsome Sailor. Through the rose-tan of his complexion no pallor could have shown. It would have taken days of sequestration from the winds and the sun to have brought about the effacement of that. But the skeleton in the cheekbone at the point of its angle was just beginning delicately to be defined under the warm-tinted skin. In fervid hearts self-contained, some brief experiences devour our human tissue as secret fire in a ship's hold consumes cotton in the bale.

But now lying between the two guns, as nipped in the vice of fate, Billy's agony, mainly proceeding from a generous young heart's virgin experience of the diabolical incarnate and effective in some men – the tension of that agony was over now. It survived not the something healing in the closeted interview with Captain Vere. Without movement, he lay as in a trance, that adolescent expression previously noted as his taking on something akin to the look of a slumbering child in the cradle when the warm hearth-glow of the still chamber at night plays on the dimples that at whiles mysteriously form in the cheek, silently coming and going there. For now and then in the gyved one's trance a serene happy light born of some wandering reminiscence or dream would diffuse itself over his face, and then wane away only anew to return.

The chaplain, coming to see him and finding him thus, and perceiving no sign that he was conscious of his presence, attentively regarded him for a space, then slipping aside, withdrew for the time, peradventure feeling that even he, the minister of Christ though receiving his stipend from Mars, had no consolation to proffer which could result in a peace transcending that which he beheld. But in the small hours he came again. And the prisoner, now awake to his surroundings, noticed his approach, and civilly, all but cheerfully, welcomed him. But it was to little purpose that in the interview following, the good man sought to bring Billy Budd to some godly understanding that he must die, and at dawn. True, Billy himself freely referred to his death as a thing close at hand; but it was something in the way that children will refer to death in general, who yet among their other sports will play a funeral with hearse and mourners.

Not that like children Billy was incapable of conceiving what death really is. No, but he was wholly without irrational fear of it, a fear more prevalent in highly civilized communities than those so-called barbarous ones which in all respects stand nearer to unadulterate Nature. And, as elsewhere said, a barbarian Billy radically was – as much so, for all the costume, as his countrymen the British captives, living trophies, made to march in the Roman triumph of Germanicus. Quite as much so as those later barbarians, young men probably, and picked specimens among the earlier British converts to Christianity, at least nominally such, taken to Rome (as today converts from lesser isles of the sea may be taken to London), of whom the Pope at that time, admiring the strangeness of their personal beauty so unlike the Italian stamp, their clear ruddy complexion and curled flaxen locks, exclaimed, 'Angles' (meaning *English*, the modern derivative), 'Angles, do you call them? And is it because they look so like angels?' Had it been later in time, one would think that the Pope had in mind Fra Angelico's seraphs, some of whom, plucking apples in gardens of the Hesperides, have the faint rosebud complexion of the more beautiful English girls.

If in vain the good chaplain sought to impress the young barbarian with ideas of death akin to those conveyed in the skull, dial and crossbones on old tombstones, equally futile to all appearance were his efforts to bring home to him the thought of salvation and a Savior. Billy listened, but less out of awe or reverence, perhaps, than from a certain natural politeness, doubtless at bottom regarding all that in much the same way that most mariners of his class take any discourse abstract or out of the common tone of the workaday world. And this sailor way of taking clerical discourse is not wholly unlike the way in which the primer of Christianity, full of transcendent miracles, was received long ago on tropic isles by any superior *savage*, so called – a Tahitian, say, of Captain Cook's time or shortly after that time. Out of natural courtesy he received, but did not appropriate. It was like a gift placed in the palm of an outreached hand upon which the fingers do not close.

But the *Bellipotent*'s chaplain was a discreet man possessing the good sense of a good heart. So he insisted not in his vocation here. At the instance of Captain Vere, a lieutenant had apprised him of pretty much everything as to Billy; and since he felt that innocence was even a better thing than religion wherewith to go to Judgment, he reluctantly withdrew; but in his emotion not without first performing an act strange enough in an Englishman, and under the circumstances yet more so in any regular priest. Stooping over, he kissed on the fair cheek his fellow man, a felon in martial law, one whom though on the confines of death he felt he could never convert to a dogma; nor for all that did he fear for his future.

Marvel not that having been made acquainted with the young sailor's essential innocence the worthy man lifted not a finger to avert the doom of such a martyr to martial discipline. So to do would not only have been as idle as invoking the desert, but would also have been an audacious transgression of the bounds of his function, one as exactly prescribed to him by military law as that of the boatswain or any other naval officer. Bluntly put, a chaplain is the minister of the Prince of Peace serving in the host of the God of War – Mars. As such, he is as incongruous as a musket would be on the altar at Christmas. Why, then, is he there? Because he indirectly subserves the purpose attested by the cannon; because too he lends the sanction of the religion of the meek to that which practically is the abrogation of everything but brute Force.

25

THE night so luminous on the spar deck, but otherwise on the cavernous ones below, levels so like the tiered galleries in a coal mine – the luminous night passed away. But like the prophet in the chariot disappearing in heaven and dropping his mantle to Elisha, the withdrawing night transferred its pale robe to the breaking day. A meek, shy light appeared in the East, where stretched a diaphanous fleece of white furrowed vapor. That light slowly waxed. Suddenly *eight bells* was struck aft, responded to by one louder metallic stroke from forward. It was four o'clock in the morning. Instantly the silver whistles were heard summoning all hands to witness punishment. Up through the great hatchways rimmed with racks of heavy shot the watch below came pouring, overspreading with the watch already on deck the space between the mainmast and foremast including that occupied by the capacious launch and the black booms tiered on either side of it, boat and booms making a summit of observation for the powder-boys and younger tars. A different group comprising one watch of topmen leaned over the rail of that sea balcony, no small one in a seventy-four, looking down on the crowd below. Man or boy, none spake but in whisper, and few spake at all. Captain Vere – as before, the central figure among the assembled commissioned officers – stood nigh the break of the poop deck facing forward. Just below him on the quarter-deck the marines in full equipment were drawn up much as at the scene of the promulgated sentence.

At sea in the old time, the execution by halter of a military sailor was generally from the foreyard. In the present instance, for special reasons the mainyard was assigned. Under an arm of that yard the prisoner was presently brought up, the chaplain attending him. It was noted at the time, and remarked upon afterwards, that in this final scene the good man evinced little or nothing of the perfunctory. Brief speech indeed he had with the condemned one, but the genuine Gospel was less on his tongue than in his aspect and manner towards him. The final preparations personal to the latter being speedily brought to an end by two boatswain's mates, the consummation impended. Billy stood facing aft. At the penultimate moment, his words, his only ones, words wholly unobstructed in the utterance, were these: 'God bless Captain Vere!' Syllables so unanticipated coming from one with the ignominious hemp about his neck – a conventional felon's benediction directed aft towards the quarters of honor; syllables too delivered in the clear melody of a singing bird on the point of launching from the twig – had a phenomenal effect, not unenhanced by the rare personal beauty of the young sailor, spiritualized now through late experiences so poignantly profound.

Without volition, as it were, as if indeed the ship's populace were but the vehicles of some vocal current electric, with one voice from alow and aloft came a resonant sympathetic echo: 'God bless Captain Vere!' And yet at that instant Billy alone must have been in their hearts, even as in their eyes.

At the pronounced words and the spontaneous echo that voluminously rebounded them, Captain Vere, either through stoic self-control or a sort of momentary paralysis induced by emotional shock, stood erectly rigid as a musket in the ship-armorer's rack.

The hull, deliberately recovering from the periodic roll to leeward, was just regaining an even keel when the last signal, a preconcerted dumb one, was given. At the same moment it chanced that the vapory fleece hanging low in the East was shot through with a soft glory as of the fleece of the Lamb of God seen in mystical vision, and simul-

taneously therewith, watched by the wedged mass of upturned faces, Billy ascended; and, ascending, took the full
rose of the dawn.

In the pinioned figure arrived at the yard-end, to the wonder of all no motion was apparent, none save that created by
the slow roll of the hull in moderate weather, so majestic
in a great ship ponderously cannoned.

26

WHEN some days afterwards, in reference to the singularity
just mentioned, the purser, a rather ruddy, rotund person
more accurate as an accountant than profound as a philosopher, said at mess to the surgeon, 'What testimony to the
force lodged in will power,' the latter, saturnine, spare, and
tall, one in whom a discreet causticity went along with a
manner less genial than polite, replied, 'Your pardon, Mr
Purser. In a hanging scientifically conducted – and under
special orders I myself directed how Budd's was to be
effected – any movement following the completed suspension and originating in the body suspended, such movement
indicates mechanical spasm in the muscular system. Hence
the absence of that is no more attributable to will power,
as you call it, than to horsepower – begging your pardon.'

'But this muscular spasm you speak of, is not that in a
degree more or less invariable in these cases?'

'Assuredly so, Mr Purser.'

'How then, my good sir, do you account for its absence
in this instance?'

'Mr Purser, it is clear that your sense of the singularity in
this matter equals not mine. You account for it by what you
call will power – a term not yet included in the lexicon of
science. For me, I do not, with my present knowledge,
pretend to account for it at all. Even should we assume the
hypothesis that at the first touch of the halyards the action
of Budd's heart, intensified by extraordinary emotion at its
climax, abruptly stopped – much like a watch when in

carelessly winding it up you strain at the finish, thus snapping the chain – even under that hypothesis how account for the phenomenon that followed?'

'You admit, then, that the absence of spasmodic movement was phenomenal.'

'It was phenomenal, Mr Purser, in the sense that it was an appearance the cause of which is not immediately to be assigned.'

'But tell me, my dear sir,' pertinaciously continued the other, 'was the man's death effected by the halter, or was it a species of euthanasia?'

'*Euthanasia*, Mr Purser, is something like your *will power*: I doubt its authenticity as a scientific term – begging your pardon again. It is at once imaginative and metaphysical – in short, Greek. – But,' abruptly changing his tone, 'there is a case in the sick bay that I do not care to leave to my assistants. Beg your pardon, but excuse me.' And rising from the mess he formally withdrew.

27

THE silence at the moment of execution and for a moment or two continuing thereafter, a silence but emphasized by the regular wash of the sea against the hull or the flutter of a sail caused by the helmsman's eyes being tempted astray, this emphasized silence was gradually disturbed by a sound not easily to be verbally rendered. Whoever has heard the freshet-wave of a torrent suddenly swelled by pouring showers in tropical mountains, showers not shared by the plain; whoever has heard the first muffled murmur of its sloping advance through precipitous woods may form some conception of the sound now heard. The seeming remoteness of its source was because of its murmurous indistinctness, since it came from close by, even from the men passed on the ship's open deck. Being inarticulate, it was dubious in significance further than it seemed to indicate some capricious revulsion of thought or feeling such as mobs ashore are liable to, in the present instance possibly implying a sullen revocation on the men's part of their involuntary echoing of Billy's benediction. But ere the murmur had time to wax into clamor it was met by a strategic command, the more telling that it came with abrupt unexpectedness: 'Pipe down the starboard watch, Boatswain, and see that they go.'

Shrill as the shriek of the sea hawk, the silver whistles of the boatswain and his mates pierced that ominous low sound, dissipating it; and yielding to the mechanism of discipline the throng was thinned by one-half. For the remainder, most of them were set to temporary employments connected with trimming the yards and so forth, business readily to be got up to serve occasion by any officer of the deck.

Now each proceeding that follows a mortal sentence pronounced at sea by a drumhead court is characterized by promptitude not perceptibly merging into hurry, though bordering that. The hammock, the one which had been Billy's bed when alive, having already been ballasted with shot and otherwise prepared to serve for his canvas coffin, the last offices of the sea undertakers, the sailmaker's mates, were now speedily completed. When everything was in readiness a second call for all hands, made necessary by the strategic movement before mentioned, was sounded, now to witness burial.

The details of this closing formality it needs not to give. But when the tilted plank let slide its freight into the sea, a second strange human murmur was heard, blended now with another inarticulate sound proceeding from certain larger seafowl who, their attention having been attracted by the peculiar commotion in the water resulting from the heavy sloped dive of the shotted hammock into the sea, flew screaming to the spot. So near the hull did they come, that the stridor or bony creak of their gaunt double-jointed pinions was audible. As the ship under light airs passed on, leaving the burial spot astern, they still kept circling it low down with the moving shadow of their outstretched wings and the croaked requiem of their cries.

Upon sailors as superstitious as those of the age preceding ours, men-of-war's men too who had just beheld the prodigy of repose in the form suspended in air, and now foundering in the deeps; to such mariners the action of the seafowl, though dictated by mere animal greed for prey, was big with no prosaic significance. An uncertain movement began among them, in which some encroachment was made. It was tolerated but for a moment. For suddenly the drum beat to quarters, which familiar sound happening at least twice every day, had upon the present occasion a signal peremptoriness in it. True martial discipline long continued superinduces in average man a sort of impulse whose operation at the official word of command much resembles in its promptitude the effect of an instinct.

The drumbeat dissolved the multitude, distributing most of them along the batteries of the two covered gun decks. There, as wonted, the guns' crews stood by their respective cannon erect and silent. In due course the first officer, sword under arm and standing in his place on the quarter-deck, formally received the successive reports of the sworded lieutenants commanding the sections of batteries below; the last of which reports being made, the summed report he delivered with the customary salute to the commander. All this occupied time, which in the present case was the object in beating to quarters at an hour prior to the customary one. That such variance from usage was authorized by an officer like Captain Vere, a martinet as some deemed him, was evidence of the necessity for unusual action implied in what he deemed to be temporarily the mood of his men: 'With mankind,' he would say, 'forms, measured forms, are everything; and this is the import couched in the story of Orpheus with his lyre spellbinding the wild denizens of the wood.' And this he once applied to the disruption of forms going on across the Channel and the consequences thereof.

At this unwonted muster at quarters, all proceeded as at the regular hour. The band on the quarter-deck played a sacred air, after which the chaplain went through the customary morning service. That done, the drum beat the retreat; and toned by music and religious rites subserving the discipline and purposes of war, the men in their wonted orderly manner dispersed to the places allotted them when not at the guns.

And now it was full day. The fleece of low-hanging vapor had vanished, licked up by the sun that late had so glorified it. And the circumambient air in the clearness of its serenity was like smooth white marble in the polished block not yet removed from the marble-dealer's yard.

28

THE symmetry of form attainable in pure fiction cannot so readily be achieved in a narration essentially having less to do with fable than with fact. Truth uncompromisingly told will always have its ragged edges; hence the conclusion of such a narration is apt to be less finished than an architectural finial.

How it fared with the Handsome Sailor during the year of the Great Mutiny has been faithfully given. But though properly the story ends with his life, something in way of sequel will not be amiss. Three brief chapters will suffice.

In the general rechristening under the Directory of the craft originally forming the navy of the French monarchy, the *St. Louis* line-of-battle ship was named the *Athée* (the *Atheist*). Such a name, like some other substituted ones in the Revolutionary fleet, while proclaiming the infidel audacity of the ruling power, was yet, though not so intended to be, the aptest name, if one consider it, ever given to a warship; far more so indeed than the *Devastation*, the *Erebus* (the *Hell*), and similar names bestowed upon fighting ships.

On the return passage to the English fleet from the

detached cruise during which occurred the events already recorded, the *Bellipotent* fell in with the *Athée*. An engagement ensued, during which Captain Vere, in the act of putting his ship alongside the enemy with a view of throwing his boarders across her bulwarks, was hit by a musket ball from a porthole of the enemy's main cabin. More than disabled, he dropped to the deck and was carried below to the same cockpit where some of his men already lay. The senior lieutenant took command. Under him the enemy was finally captured, and though much crippled was by rare good fortune successfully taken into Gibraltar, an English port not very distant from the scene of the fight. There, Captain Vere with the rest of the wounded was put ashore. He lingered for some days, but the end came. Unhappily he was cut off too early for the Nile and Trafalgar. The spirit that 'spite its philosophic austerity may yet have indulged in the most secret of all passions, ambition, never attained to the fulness of fame.

Not long before death, while lying under the influence of that magical drug which, soothing the physical frame, mysteriously operates on the subtler element in man, he was heard to murmur words inexplicable to his attendant: 'Billy Budd, Billy Budd.' That these were not the accents of remorse would seem clear from what the attendant said to the *Bellipotent*'s senior officer of marines, who, as the most reluctant to condemn of the members of the drumhead court, too well knew, though here he kept the knowledge to himself, who Billy Budd was.

29

SOME few weeks after the execution, among other matters under the head of 'News from the Mediterranean,' there appeared in a naval chronicle of the time, an authorized weekly publication, an account of the affair. It was doubtless for the most part written in good faith, though the medium, partly rumor, through which the facts must have reached the writer served to deflect and in part falsify them. The account was as follows:

'On the tenth of the last month a deplorable occurrence took place on board H.M.S. *Bellipotent*. John Claggart, the ship's master-at-arms, discovering that some sort of plot was incipient among an inferior section of the ship's company, and that the ringleader was one William Budd; he, Claggart, in the act of arraigning the man before the captain, was vindictively stabbed to the heart by the suddenly drawn sheath knife of Budd.

'The deed and the implement employed sufficiently suggest that though mustered into the service under an English name the assassin was no Englishman, but one of those aliens adopting English cognomens whom the present extraordinary necessities of the service have caused to be admitted into it in considerable numbers.

'The enormity of the crime and the extreme depravity of the criminal appear the greater in view of the character of the victim, a middle-aged man respectable and discreet, belonging to that minor official grade, the petty officers, upon whom, as none know better than the commissioned gentlemen, the efficiency of His Majesty's navy so largely depends. His function was a responsible one, at once onerous and thankless; and his fidelity in it the greater because of his strong patriotic impulse. In this instance as in so many other instances in these days, the character of this unfortunate man signally refutes, if refutation were needed, that peevish saying attributed to the late Dr Johnson, that patriotism is the last refuge of a scoundrel.

'The criminal paid the penalty of his crime. The promptitude of the punishment has proved salutary. Nothing amiss is now apprehended aboard H.M.S. *Bellipotent*.'

The above, appearing in a publication now long ago superannuated and forgotten, is all that hitherto has stood in human record to attest what manner of men respectively were John Claggart and Billy Budd.

EVERYTHING is for a term venerated in navies. Any tangible object associated with some striking incident of the service is converted into a monument. The spar from which the foretopman was suspended was for some few years kept trace of by the bluejackets. Their knowledges followed it from ship to dockyard and again from dockyard to ship, still pursuing it even when at last reduced to a mere dockyard boom. To them a chip of it was as a piece of the Cross. Ignorant though they were of the secret facts of the tragedy, and not thinking but that the penalty was somehow unavoidably inflicted from the naval point of view, for all that, they instinctively felt that Billy was a sort of man as incapable of mutiny as of wilful murder. They recalled the fresh young image of the Handsome Sailor, that face never deformed by a sneer or subtler vile freak of the heart within. This impression of him was doubtless deepened by the fact that he was gone, and in a measure mysteriously gone. On the gun decks of the *Bellipotent* the general estimate of his nature and its unconscious simplicity eventually found rude utterance from another foretopman, one of his own watch, gifted, as some sailors are, with an artless *poetic* temperament. The tarry hand made some lines which, after circulating among the shipboard crews for a while, finally got rudely printed at Portsmouth as a ballad. The title given to it was the sailor's.

BILLY IN THE DARBIES

Good of the chaplain to enter Lone Bay
And down on his marrowbones here and pray
For the likes just o' me, Billy Budd. – But, look:
Through the port comes the moonshine astray!
It tips the guard's cutlass and silvers this nook;
But 'twill die in the dawning of Billy's last day.
A jewel-block they'll make of me tomorrow,
Pendant pearl from the yardarm-end

Like the eardrop I gave to Bristol Molly –
O, 'tis me, not the sentence they'll suspend.
Ay, ay, all is up; and I must up too,
Early in the morning, aloft from alow.
On an empty stomach now never it would do.
They'll give me a nibble – bit o' biscuit ere I go.
Sure, a messmate will reach me the last parting cup;
But, turning heads away from the hoist and the belay,
Heaven knows who will have the running of me up!
No pipe to those halyards. – But aren't it all sham?
A blur's in my eyes; it is dreaming that I am.
A hatchet to my hawser? All adrift to go?
The drum roll to grog, and Billy never know?
But Donald he has promised to stand by the plank;
So I'll shake a friendly hand ere I sink.
But – no! It is dead then I'll be, come to think.
I remember Taff the Welshman when he sank.
And his cheek it was like the budding pink.
But me they'll lash in hammock, drop me deep.
Fathoms down, fathoms down, how I'll dream fast asleep.
I feel it stealing now. Sentry, are you there?
Just ease these darbies at the wrist,
And roll me over fair!
I am sleepy, and the oozy weeds about me twist.

DANIEL ORME

A SAILOR'S name as it appears on a crew-list is not always
his real name, nor in every instance does it indicate
his country. This premised, be it said that by the name at
the head of this writing long went an old man-of-war's man
of whose earlier history it may verily be said that nobody
knew anything but himself; and it was idle to seek it in
that quarter. Conscientious constantly so in discharging
his duty, the respect of his officers naturally followed. And
for his fellow-sailors, if none had reason to like one so
unlike themselves, none dared to take the slightest liberties
with him. Any approach to it, and his eye was a tutoring
and deterring one.

Getting on in years at last, he was retired as Captain of
the top, and assigned to a lower grade and post, namely, at
the foot of the mainmast, his business there being simply to
stand by, let go and make fast. But even this, with the night-
watches, ere long exacted too much for a sailor, a septua-
genarian. In brief, he belays his last halyard and slips into
obscure moorings ashore.

Whatever his disposition may originally have been, never,
in his latter cruises at least, had he been specially noted
for his sociability. Not that he was gruff like some marine
veteran with the lumbago, nor stealthily taciturn like an
Indian; but moody, frequently muttering to himself. And
from such muffled soliloquizing he would sometimes start,
and with a look or gesture so uncheerfully peculiar that the
Calvinistic imagination of a certain frigate's chaplain construed it into remorseful self-condemnation of some dark
deed in his past.

His features were large, strong, cast as in iron; but the

effect of a cartridge explosion had peppered all below the eyes with dense dottings of black-blue. When, according to custom, he as a mainmast man used to doff his hat, in less laconic speech with the officer-of-the-deck, his tanned brow showed like October's tawny moon revealed in crescent above an ominous cloud. Along with his moody ways, was it this uncanny physical aspect, the result of a mere chance, was it this, and this alone, that had suggested the germ of rumor among certain afterguardsmen that in earlier life he had been a buccaneer of the Keys and the Gulf, one of Lafitte's marauding crew? Certain it is he had once served on a letter-of-marque.

In stature, though bowed somewhat in the shoulders, akin to the champion of Gath. Hands heavy and horny; thumb-nails like wrinkled horn. A powerful head, and shaggy. An iron-grey beard broad as a commodore's pennant, and about the mouth indelibly streaked with the moodily dribbled tobacco juice of all his cruises. In his day-watch below, silently couched by himself on the gundeck in a bay be-tween black cannon, he might have suggested an image of the Great Grizzly of the California Sierras, his coat the worse for wear, grim in his last den awaiting the last hour.

In his shore moorings – hard by the waters not very far from the docks, what with his all-night-in and easier lot in every particular, with choice of associates when he desired them, which was not always, happily he lost most of his gruffness as the old mastiff of the mainmast exposed to all weathers and with salt-horse for his diet.

A stranger accosting him sunning himself upon some old spar in the strand, and kindly saluting him there, would receive no surly response, and if more than mere saluta-tions were exchanged, would probably go away with the impression that he had been talking with an interesting oddity, a salt philosopher, not lacking in a sort of grim common-sense.

After being ashore for a period, a singularity in his habits was remarked. At times, but only when he might think himself quite alone, he would roll aside the bosom of his darned Guernsey frock and steadfastly contemplate something on his body; if by chance discovered in this, he would quickly conceal all and growl his resentment. This peculiarity awakening the curiosity of certain idle observers, lodgers under the same humble roof with him, and none caring to be so bold as to question him as to the reason of it, or to ask what it was on his body, a drug was enlisted as a means of finding out the secret. In prudent quantity it was slyly slipped into his huge bowl of tea at supper. Next morning a certain old-clothesman whispered to his gossips the result of his sorry intrusion overnight.

Drawing them into a corner and looking round furtively, 'Listen,' said he and told them an eerie story, following it up with shuddering conjectures, vague enough but dear to the superstitious and ignorant mind. What he had really discovered was this: a crucifix in indigo and vermilion tattooed on the chest and on the side of the heart. Slantingly crossing the crucifix and paling the pigment there ran a whitish scar long and thin, such as might ensue from the slash of a cutlass imperfectly parried or dodged. Now, the Cross of the Passion is often found tattooed on the sailor, upon the fore-arm generally, sometimes though but rarely, on the trunk. As for the scar, the old masterman had in legitimate naval service known what it was to repel boarders and not without receiving a battle-mark from them – it may be. The gossips of the lodging, however, took another view of the discovery, and at last reported to the landlady that he was a sort of *man forbid*, a man branded by the Evil Spirit, and it would be well to get rid of him, lest the charm in the horse-shoe nailed over the house-door should be fatally counteracted and be naught. The good woman, however, was a sensible lady, with no belief in the horse-shoe, though she tolerated it, and as the old masterman was regular in his weekly dues, and never made noise or gave trouble, she turned a deaf ear to all solicitations against him.

Since in his presence it was ever prudently concealed, the old mariner was not then aware of underhand proceedings.

At sea it had never come to his ears, that some of his ship-mates thought him a buccaneer, for there was a quiet leo-nine droop about the angles of his mouth, that said – *hands off*. So now he was ignorant of the circumstances that the same rumor had followed him ashore. Had his habits been social, he would have socially felt the effect of this, and cast about in vain for the cause; some ill-report whether having basis or not, as in some instances like what sailors call a *dry tempest:* during which there is neither rain, thunder nor lightning, though none the less the viewless and intangible winds make a shipwreck and then ask – Who did it?

So Orme pursued his solitary way, with not much from without to disturb him. But Time's moments keep descend-ing upon the quietest hour, and though it were adamant they would wear it. In his retirement our superannuated giant begins to mellow down into a sort of animal decay. In hard, rude natures, especially such as have passed their lives amid the elements, farmers and sailors, the animal decay mostly affects the memory by casting a haze over it; not seldom it softens the heart, as well, besides more or less perhaps, drowsing the conscience, innocent or otherwise.

But let us come to the close of a sketch, necessarily imperfect.

One fine Easter Day, following a spell of rheumatic weather, Orme was discovered alone and dead on a height overlooking the seaward sweep of the great haven to whose shore, in his retirement from sea, he had moored. It was an evened regular terrace, destined for use in war, though in peace neglected and offering a sanctuary. Mounted on it was an obsolete battery of rusty guns. Against one of these he was found leaning, his legs stretched out before him; his clay pipe broken in twain; the vacant bowl and no spillings from it, attesting that the pipe had been smoked out to the last of its contents. He faced the outlet to the ocean. The eyes were open, still containing in death the vital glance fixed on the hazy waters and the dim-seen sails coming and going or at anchor nearer by.

What had been his last thoughts? If aught of reality lurked in the rumors concerning him, had remorse, had penitence any place in those thoughts? Or was there just nothing of either? After all, were his moodiness and mutterings, his strange freaks, starts, eccentric shrugs and grimaces, were these but grotesque additions like the wens and knobs and distortions of the bark of an old chance apple-tree in an inclement upland, not only beaten by many storms, but also obstructed in its natural development by the chance of its having first sprouted among hard-packed rock? In short, that fatality no more encrusting him, made him what he came to be? Even admitting that there was something dark that he chose to keep to himself, what then? Such reticence may sometimes be more for the sake of others than one's self. No, let us believe that that animal decay before mentioned, still befriended him to the close, and that he fell asleep recalling through the haze of memory many a far-off scene of the wide world's beauty, dreamily suggested by the hazy waters lying before him.

He lies buried among other sailors for whom also strangers performed the last rites in a lonely plot overgrown with wild eglantine uncared for by man.

NOTES

The numerals introducing each note refer to page numbers only.

9. '. . . *made up his mind to be annihilated*' Hawthorne's Journal, 20 November 1856, after Melville's visit to the Liverpool Consulate and the Hawthornes' home at Southport.

10. '*piazza*' *The Piazza* was written, probably in early 1856, as prologue and framework for the five stories (*Bartleby, Benito Cereno, The Lightning-Rod Man, The Encantadas* and *The Bell-Tower*) which Melville had selected for book publication as *The Piazza Tales* (May 1856).

12. '*There are hardly five critics . . .*' From *Hawthorne and His Mosses, by a Virginian Spending July in Vermont*; Melville's pseudonymous review of Hawthorne's *Mosses of an Old Manse* appeared in two August issues of the *Literary World*, 1850.

12. *The Bell-Tower* Curtis first rejected *The Bell-Tower* only to send – post-haste next day – a second letter: ' "The Bell-Tower" is, after all, too good to lose . . . I meant to say no, – and so wrote you; but looking again, I am converted . . .' He adds: 'To many the style will seem painfully artificial and pompously self-conscious. But it seems to me well suited to the theme. – The story has the touch of genius in it – and so – spite of the style – it should be accepted . . .' (19 June 1855). Equally torn, I also decided not to reject *The Bell-Tower* from this collection.

13. '*Why, ever since Adam . . .*' Melville's reply, November 1851, to Hawthorne's 'joy-giving and exultation-breeding letter' (now lost) on reading *Moby-Dick*.

13. *in the desultory year before signing on* Jay Leyda suggests that the figure of Bartleby may have been drawn from the most intimate friend of Melville's youth, Eli James Murdock Fly, whom he met either at the Albany Academy or during Fly's five-year apprenticeship in the law office of Peter Gansevoort, Melville's uncle. 'In the fall of 1840 they went together to New

York looking for work: while Herman found a berth on the Fairhaven whaler *Acushnet*, Fly remained in New York to take "a situation with a Mr Edwards, where he has incessant writing from morning to Eveg".' In the spring of 1851, Fly reappears in a letter from Melville to the literary editor, Evert Duyckinck: 'He has long been a confirmed invalid, & in some things I act a little as his agent.' (*The Complete Stories of Herman Melville*, p. 455.)

14. *Allan, now a lawyer in Wall Street* He was in Gansevoort's old offices at 10 Wall Street.

14. *'. . . the occupational diseases of the compromised artist . . .'* From Richard Chase, *Herman Melville, A Critical Study* (Macmillan, New York, 1949), ch. 4, p. 147.

14. *'In thunder as in sunshine . . .'* The Lightning-Rod Man, published in *Putnam's Monthly Magazine*, August 1854.

14. *'. . . that I and my chimney will never surrender'* I and my Chimney, accepted in September 1855, was published by *Putnam's* in March 1856.

15. *'There is the grand truth about Nathaniel Hawthorne . . .'* Summer 1851, but dated only 'Pittsfield, Wednesday morning'.

15. *'In Life he appears as a true Philosopher . . .'* This *Testament & Psalms*, with his jottings in the front and back covers, was given Melville in 1846.

15. H. Bruce Franklin, *The Wake of the Gods* (Stanford University Press, 1963), ch. 5, pp. 126–36.

17. *more of a Hindu ascetic* Possibly even behind that screen, as Egbert S. Oliver thought, Melville had Thoreau's 'hermitage' in mind and his retreat from the world to Walden Pond.

18. *Within the spectrum of white and black* This spectrum – of the white whale in 'the blackness of the sea and the night' – Melville had already obsessively explored in *Moby-Dick*; but where the whiteness was once ambiguous, it is here restored to its old polarity with black.

19. *'We Poets in our youth . . .'* Wordsworth, *The Leech-Gatherer; or, Resolution and Independence*, stanza vii.

19. *'By our own spirits are we deified'* Wordsworth, op. cit., stanza vii. The line immediately precedes the couplet parodied.

20. *a few of the thirteen major islands* 'While Melville creates the impression that he visited several of the Galapagos Islands, it is obvious to one who has checked this raconteur "on the spot" that he never visited more than perhaps the northern tip of Albemarle Island . . . and he certainly sailed between the islands of Narborough and Albemarle and passed near, if he did not climb Rodondo Rock . . .' Victor Wolfgang von Hagen, *The Encantadas* (William P. Wreden: Burlingame, California, 1940).

Jay Leyda, with the log-book of the *Acushnet* to hand, adds: 'On 30 October 1841, in "pleasant weather" the North head of Albemarle Island was sighted. After a cruise of three weeks the *Acushnet* came to anchor at Chatham's Isle on 19 November, where she remained till 25 November, then sailed towards Tumbez on the mainland. On 6 January she was back among the Galapagos, with Hood's and Charles Isles in sight.'

Von Hagen insists that Melville 'made only one visit to the Galapagos'. But it seems that he may have briefly returned in December 1842, or January 1843, on the *Charles and Henry* of Nantucket, approaching this time from the Austral Islands. If so, no more is known of the visit.

27. *Hawthorne's* Ethan Brand *Ethan Brand, A Chapter from an Abortive Romance* appeared four years earlier in *The Snow Image, and Other Twice-Told Tales*, 1851, 'The Unpardonable Sin' (of the original title) being intellectual pride – the separation of mind and heart. 'I stand for the heart', Melville had commented to Hawthorne at the time. 'To the dogs with the head! I had rather be a fool with a heart, than Jupiter Olympus with his head.' (Spring 1851.)

27. *twice reissued*, in 1875 in the 'Tragedy' volume of *Little Classics*, and again in 1889 in the eleven-volume *Library of American Literature from the Earliest Settlement to the Present Time*.

27. *a deeply felt – and personal – image* 'As author' Melville 'created such Frankenstein monsters as Captain Ahab and Pierre who had seriously damaged his reputation . . . His own works', too, were 'flawed by the life's blood he had put into them'. Leon Howard, *Herman Melville, A Biography* (University of California Press, 1951) p. 223.

28. *Charles Babbage* (1792–1871), inventor of the archetype of modern digital computers and founder of the Royal Astro-

nomical Society, worked – an odd link with the Gothic – in association with Byron's daughter, the Countess of Lovelace.

28. *Norbert Wiener* In *God & Golem, Inc.* (Chapman and Hall, London, 1965), his last book.

29. *Arthur Koestler The Act of Creation* (Hutchinson, London, 1964).

29. *'sound as an apple . . .'* From Stanley T. Williams, *'Follow Your Leader', Melville's 'Benito Cereno', Virginia Quarterly Review*, XXIII (winter 1947). Robert Lowell, in dramatizing *Benito Cereno* (1963), even renamed the Yankee ship the *President Adams*. But this echo of Adam innocence – like *The Old Glory* of the overall title of his trilogy (Faber & Faber, London, 1966) – is deliberate dramatic irony.

33. *the harpooner Queequeg* The tattooed Polynesian, in *Moby-Dick*, with whom Ishmael shares a bed in the Spouter Inn and grudgingly learns to accept as friend, brother and (literally) saviour, a 'George Washington cannibalistically developed'.

34. *'The embodiment of good in the pale Spanish captain . . .'* F. O. Matthiessen, *American Renaissance* (Oxford University Press, New York, 1941) Book 3, ch. XII, p. 508.

35. *Ralph Ellison's The Invisible Man* (Victor Gollancz, London, 1953; Penguin Books, Harmondsworth, 1965).

35. *remains for ever barred* By 1822 the American Colonization Society had, in fact, bought an area of the West African coast and launched the colony of Monrovia, now Liberia. Abraham Lincoln for a while favoured the notion of returning freed slaves to an African homeland.

36. *'(may a lost god damballah . . .'* LeRoi Jones, BLACK DADA NIHILISMUS 2, from *The Dead Lecturer* (Grove Press, Inc., New York, 1964).

37. *'It is strange how he persists . . .'* Hawthorne's Journal, 20 November 1856.

38. *'Herman's position in the Custom House . . .'* Elizabeth Melville to Catherine Lansing, 29 July 1885.

38. *'What I feel most moved to write . . .'* Summer 1851, while *Moby-Dick* was at the printer's.

38. *'Ye float around me . . .'* John Marr, from the verse soliloquy.

39. *'After twenty years nearly, as an outdoor Custom House officer . . .'* Melville to Archibald MacMechan, a young Canadian professor of English hoping to write a study of *Moby-Dick*, who had asked for some particulars of Melville's life 'and *literary methods*', 5 December 1889.

40. *'almost the first – first crucial – self-indulgence . . .'* Richard Chase, *Herman Melville, a Critical Study*, ch. 11 'Innocence and Infamy', p. 265.

42. *'The flaw of the stammer . . .'* W. H. Auden, *The Enchafèd Flood* (Faber & Faber, London, 1951) p. 121.

42. *his forehead intellectual* 'It is no coincidence that both Claggart and Bannadonna, the heartless egotist of *The Bell-Tower*, die of a blow to the forehead.' Merlin Bowen, *The Long Encounter* (Universty of Chicago Press, 1960) p. 87.

43. *'Evanescent as that tenderness was . . .'* F. O. Matthiessen, *American Renaissance*, Book 3, ch. 12, p. 507.

45. *Which makes him far from simple* I cannot accept the platitudes of W. H. Auden's much quoted *Herman Melville*: that 'goodness existed' was hardly news even to the thirty-six-year-old author of *The Piazza Tales*, and 'the truth' of Auden's poem 'was simple' only because it omits the central role of the drama, which is Vere's.

48. *'Thrice chang'd with pale . . .'* Milton, *Paradise Lost*, Book IV, lines 115–17.

48. *a mesh of tragic irony* Could the dramatic irony ultimately be at his own expense? Melville's eldest son, Malcolm, met his death in 1867 at the age of eighteen, 'in his night clothes in bed with a pistol shot in his head' (letter from Samuel Shaw to his mother, 12 September 1867). The verdict of suicide was changed next day to 'accidental death', but the parents' ordeal can have been little eased. Was it then, perhaps, that the seed of Vere's dramatic situation took root – of an Abraham on whom his son's sacrifice is unwillingly thrust?

50. *'Like a Sea-beast crawled forth . . .'* From Wordsworth's *The Leech-Gatherer; or, Resolution and Independence*, stanza ix, of which *Cock-A-Doodle-Doo!* had been Melville's revised version.

BARTLEBY

60. *The late John Jacob Astor* (1763–1848). Born in Waldorf,

near Heidelberg, Germany, he arrived in the U.S. in 1784, opened a small shop in New York and, with the expansion of the American economy, soon dominated the China trade, invested astutely in land around New York City and in 1808 chartered the American Fur Company – with its later subsidiaries, the Pacific Fur Company and the South West Company – which by the 1820s held a virtual monopoly in the U.S. territories. At his death he was the wealthiest man in the United States.

62. *cannel coal* Also called 'candle-coal'; a bituminous coal which burns with a bright flame.

66. *Spitzenbergs* An American variety of apple.

77. *Petra* (meaning 'rock') in Jordan; famous for its rock-hewn temples and narrow gorge, once entrepôt and thoroughfare of the caravan trade.

77. *Marius* (c.155–86 B.C.), Roman general, victorious commander over Jugurtha.

87. *the unfortunate Adams and the still more unfortunate Colt* Samuel Adams was murdered by John C. Colt in New York City in January 1842. Condemned to death, Colt was to be hanged on 18 November 1842, at four o'clock in the afternoon. At noon that day he married Caroline Henshaw, the mother of a child by him. They were permitted to remain together for a short while after the ceremony; but, at his own request, Colt was left alone for half an hour before he was due to leave for the gallows. A few minutes before four he was found on the bunk in his cell stabbed to the heart, the dagger still in the wound. The verdict was suicide; but suspicion naturally fell on the widowed bride for having introduced the weapon. (Melville had long been fascinated by the case, which is echoed in the closing scene of *Pierre*.)

88. *'Edwards on the Will,' and 'Priestley on Necessity'* I.e. Jonathan Edwards, *A careful and strict Enquiry into the modern prevailing notion of that Freedom of Will, which is supposed to be essential to moral agency, vertue and vice, reward and punishment, praise and blame* (Boston 1754) and Joseph Priestley, *The Doctrine of Philosophical Necessity illustrated, being an appendix to the Disquisitions relating to Matter and Spirit* (London 1777).

95. *my rockaway* A four-wheeled carriage, open at the sides.

95. *Hoboken . . . Astoria* Hoboken is on the Hudson op-

posite lower Manhattan; Astoria, a section of Queens borough renamed for John Jacob Astor. His flight, that is, takes him both to New Jersey and Long Island, to points west and east of Manhattan.

95. *the Tombs* Later references to Egyptian masonry and the pyramids are not merely symbolic. The old New York prison, to the north of the City Hall, was an example of 'Egyptian revival' in American architecture.

99. *With kings and counselors* Job iii, 11–16.

COCK-A-DOODLE-DOO!

103. *many high-spirited revolts* I.e. 1848, the year of revolutions.

103. *too full of hypos* Abbreviation of hypochondria.

103. *my head pretty well earthward* Melville had clearly been reading Wordsworth's *Resolution and Independence*, which he parodies a few pages later. At this point he identifies the narrator outwardly with the Leech–Gatherer:

> His body was bent double, feet and head
> Coming together in life's pilgrimage;
> As if some dire constraint of pain, or rage
> Of sickness felt by him in times long past,
> A more than human weight upon his frame had cast.
>
> Himself he propped, his body, limbs, and face,
> Upon a long grey Staff of shaven wood . . .
>
> (stanzas x and xi.)

104. *a duplicate stream of dripping mist* In lifeless contrast to Wordsworth's:

> The Hare is running races in her mirth;
> And with her feet she from the plashy earth
> Raises a mist; that, glittering in the sun,
> Runs with her all the way, wherever she doth run.
>
> (op. cit. stanza ii.)

104. *And that crash on the railroad* The sole accident so far traced – to date the composition of Melville's story – is one on the New York & New Haven Railroad, of 6 May 1853, in which forty-six people were killed, including a bride of the previous night (but not her groom) and a three-year-old girl.

104. *some clinkered iron-foundry country or other* Mel-

ville's imagination, already at work on *The Encantadas* (that 'Tartarus of clinkers'), tumbles ahead in anticipation.

105. *that gigantic gad-fly of a Moloch* 'Gad-fly' suggests Beelzebub, Lord of the Flies; Moloch was the Canaanite God of fire.

106. *the varioloid* A form of smallpox.

106. *the calves . . . What a miserable-looking set* These mangy and cooped up cattle are again in deliberate contrast to Wordsworth's 'Sky-lark warbling in the sky' and 'playful Hare', op. cit. stanzas i–v.

107. *without discourse of reason* Cf.

O God! a beast, that wants discourse of reason,
Would have mourn'd longer. . . . (*Hamlet* I, ii, 150–51)

– here, ironically, not of the female of the species ('Frailty, thy name is woman!') but a cock.

107. *the glorious victory of New Orleans* The last battle of the *War of 1812* in which Andrew Jackson caused the British to retreat, 8 January 1815.

107. *a Shanghai* Long-legged breed of fowl with feathered shanks.

108. *'Of fine mornings, We fine lusty cocks . . .'* Parody of lines from Wordsworth's *The Leech-Gatherer; or, Resolution and Independence*, stanza vii :

We Poets in our youth begin in gladness;
But thereof comes in the end despondency and madness.

The whole of *Cock-A-Doodle-Doo!* is, in effect, a parody, or paradoxical commentary, on Wordsworth's poem : both open in the 'plashy' or 'squitchy' damp, but whereas in Wordsworth a bright sun is already rising, in Melville the air is raw, misty and disagreeable; Wordsworth's opening mood is of joy, Melville's of cynical depression; in Wordsworth joy turns to dejection, in Melville hypochondria to defiant bravado; Wordsworth ends with stoic resolution, Melville with a continual crow.

109. *this is a fine joke about my Uncle Toby and the Widow Wadman!* From the 9th Book of *Tristram Shandy*. What the widow said, no doubt, was : ' "And whereabouts, dear Sir . . . did you receive this sad blow?" In asking this question, Mrs Wadman gave a slight glance towards the waistband of my uncle Toby's red plush breeches, expecting naturally, as the

shortest reply to it, that my uncle Toby would lay his fore-finger upon the place,' – in playful allusion to the title.

109. *shad-bellied wretch* A shad-belly coat was a Quaker coat.

110. *now bathed in a rejoicing sunlight* By a contradictory movement Melville reaches the mood of Wordsworth's opening:

> But now the sun is rising calm and bright;
> The birds are singing in the distant woods;
> Over his own sweet voice the Stock-dove broods . . .
>
> (op. cit. stanza i.)

111. *in pure overflow of self-reliance and a sense of universal security* Cf. Emerson's essay on *Self-Reliance*, passim: 'To believe your own thought, to believe that what is true for you in your private heart is true for all men, – that is genius. Speak your latent conviction, and it shall be the universal sense; for the inmost in due time becomes the outmost, – and our first thought is rendered back to us by the trumpets of the Last Judgment.' ' "Ah, so you shall be sure to be misunderstood." – Is it so bad, then, to be misunderstood? Pythagoras was misunderstood, and Socrates, and Jesus, and Luther, and Copernicus, and Galileo, and Newton, and every pure and wise spirit that ever took flesh. To be great is to be misunderstood.'

112. *by the invincible Socrates* The last words of Socrates, according to Plato's *Phaedo*, were: 'Crito, we owe a cock to Aesculapius; pay it, therefore, and do not neglect it.'

113. *such a Great Bell of St Paul's swung in a cock's throat* 'Great Bell', or *belle*? Sexual puns (so typical of *Moby-Dick*) accumulate from the start around this cock: the mangy cattle prick their ears and flirt their tails at his first crow – till, perched on a hoop, the cock swings from the ridge-pole in the middle of Merrymusk's shanty.

Indeed, the quest for this magic cock should be read in tandem – as a kind of penny-farthing postscript – with the quest for Moby Dick. Ishmael, too, like this narrator at the opening, suffers from 'hypos'; the *Pequod*'s various encounters are equally inauspicious; sexual ambivalences in both abound; and if *The Whale* ends in a hell-bound whirlpool of all but universal destruction, *Cock-A-Doodle-Doo!*, attempting to soar in heaven-bound apotheosis, achieves an equally universal mortality.

113. *another old man mending a tumbledown old rail-fence*

If Merrymusk and his exultant cock combine to create a revised version of Wordsworth's Leech-Gatherer, this lonely, uncheerful, feeble, obstinate old fence-mender (and incipient idiot) is introduced as a kind of caricature of the real Leech-Gatherer with his lofty perseverance – here rejected.

116. *would turn chanticleer, and clap her wings* As the dun's bill, like a cock's, had been 'stiffly poked', so a clap of a mortgage echoes this clap of wings; but the legal *instanter* of the civil-process will be capped at last by the celestial summons of the cock 'bent upon rejoining *instanter* this whole family in the upper air'.

116. *a bottle of Philadelphia porter* No doubt for its title to universal brotherhood.

116. *Herkimer cheese* From central New York State.

117. *to bless the country with my bounteousness* Cf.

> My whole life I have lived in pleasant thought,
> As if life's business were a summer mood:
> As if all needful things would come unsought
> To genial faith, still rich in genial good.
>
> (Wordsworth, op. cit. stanza vi.)

At this point, before Merrymusk's appearance, the narrator more closely approximates Wordsworth's narrator: 'For my uncle Toby's amours running all the way in my head, they had the same effect upon me as if they had been my own – I was in the most perfect state of bounty and good-will; and felt the kindliest harmony vibrating within me . . .; every thing I saw or had to do with, touched upon some secret spring either of sentiment or rapture.' (Sterne, *Tristram Shandy* Bk 9, ch. xxiv.)

118. *on his buck* The frame on which wood is cross-cut.

118. *a most wearisome and disgustful occupation* This seems overstated. Perhaps Melville still had the Leech-Gatherer in mind:

> He told, that to these waters he had come
> To gather Leeches, being old and poor:
> Employment hazardous and wearisome!
>
> (Wordsworth, op. cit. stanza xv.)

Apart from poverty and the intense, silent application to their tasks, other characteristics shared by Merrymusk and Wordsworth's 'Old-man' are: a dignified and honest demeanour; an air of surreptitious cheerfulness (with a smile or twinkle in the eye); a life of hardships and perpetual wandering; and like the simile introducing the Leech-Gatherer (stanza ix) the wood-sawyer is truly 'a Sea-beast crawled forth' – an ex-sailor who had 'struck for the Northern interior'.

119. *an elder or deacon* Cf.
　　　. . . a stately speech;
　Such as grave Livers do in Scotland use,
　Religious men, who give to God and Man their dues.
　　　　　　　(Wordsworth, op. cit. stanza xiv.)

119. *His name was Merrymusk* Indeed a jolly name, befitting an ex-jolly, or sailor. Musk, the aroma secreted from a gland of the male musk-deer, carries its own hint of sexuality. Aptly Merrymusk is connected solely with 'his buck', his family and his cock. Yet (like Pip on the *Pequod*) this jolly is an unjolly wight, until, in death, 'a white napkin seemed dropped upon his face'.

119. *Batavia* The old Dutch capital of Indonesia, now Djakarta, on north-west Java.

119. *a wife, and now had four children* Melville, too, was shortly to have four children; if (in a sense) he was the narrator with his twinges of rheumatism and money troubles, he was also, of course, Merrymusk, another ex-sailor who had struck inland, applying himself to the wood-bench.

121. *at a performance of the Italian Opera . . . a certain Signor Beneventano* who, Jay Leyda discovered, was a real person. On Christmas Eve, 1847, Melville, with his young bride Elizabeth and sister Frances, had attended a performance of Donizetti's *Lucia di Lammermoor* at the new Astor Place Opera House, in which Ferdinando Beneventano sang the part of Lord Henry Ashton.

122. *'It chipped the shell here.'* Thus the earlier image of the locomotive 'found fairly shelled, like a chick, inside of a passenger car in the antagonist train'. Transposing nature to machinery, life to death is at the story's core.

122. *the ghosts of all the pines and hemlocks* With another sidelong glance at Socrates.

123. *solid junks of jerked beef* I.e. chunks of unsalted beef, cured in the Peruvian manner (corruption of *charqui*) by cutting into long, thin slices and drying in the sun.

124. *righteous Joshua in the vale of Askalon* Askalon, or Ashkelon, was a Philistine city north of Gaza. Melville is in error; Joshua fought at Jericho, in the hill cities of Canaan around Jerusalem and in the north around Hazor, but never on the Philistine coast, specifically excluded from his conquests in *Joshua* xiii, 3.

125. *'Sir, you are a trump.'* The pun, at least partially, accounts for the narrator's instinctive and understanding response to Trumpet.

127. *intense longings for release transfigured them into spirits* Cf. 'By our own spirits are we deified.' (Wordsworth, op cit. stanza vii.)

128. *I saw angels where they lay* Cf. 1 *Corinthians*, xv, 52; '... In a moment, in the twinkling of an eye, at the last trump: for the trumpet shall sound, and the dead shall be raised incorruptible, and we shall be changed.'

128. *'O death, where is thy sting? . . .'* 1 *Corinthians*, xv, 55. Merrymusk's death 'in a kind of wild ecstasy of triumph over ill' (echoing the narrator's own earlier 'rapture of defiance') is Melville's final answer to Wordsworth's 'And mighty Poets in their misery dead', op. cit. stanza xvii.

THE ENCANTADAS

The quotations from *The Faerie Queene*, introducing the Sketches, centre on the theme of patience: in Book I, canto ix, the Redcrosse Knight withstands 'a man of hell, that cals himselfe *Despaire*', and in the tenth canto is healed of his hurt by a leech called Patience; in Book II, canto xii, Sir Guyon overthrows 'the Bowre of Blisse'.

'Sleepe after toyle, port after stormie seas' (I, ix, 40) beguiles *Despaire*; 'This is the port of rest from troublous toyle' (II, xii, 32) echo the mermaids. Melville, that is, links a dream world of the senses to suicide as twin temptations, two retreats from reality. Which may reveal something of his personal preoccupations of these years, but it is difficult to see what relation the subject-matter of these cantos bears to the subject-matter of *The Encantadas* – neither suicide nor sex – unless it be in the Catholic faith of patient Hunilla resisting despair. Hell is their only common bond, to the lowest circle of degradation, until with Sir Guyon we can say:

> . . . See the mind of beastly man,
> That hath so soone forgot the excellence
> Of his creation, when he life began,
> That now he chooseth, with vile difference,
> To be a beast, and lacke intelligence.   (II, xii, 87.)

To these quotations from *The Faerie Queene* Melville added a set of quotations from Spenser's *Prosopopoia, or Mother Hubberds Tale*, suggesting a third escape – to be lord of the world and wander free:

> For why should he that is at libertie
> Make himselfe bond? Sith then we are free borne,
> Let us all servile base subiection scorne. (lines 132–4.)

Despite the ironic implication of giving such lines to buccaneers and riotocrats, they speak with the very accent of the proud, independent, still confident Melville of these years.

SKETCH FIRST: THE ISLES AT LARGE

Quotations: *'That may not be, said then the Ferryman . . .'* Spenser, *The Faerie Queene*, Book II, canto xii, stanza 11, joined to the last three lines of stanza 12 (*'For'*, line 10, replaces Spenser's *'But'*; *'secure'*, line 11, replaced *'recure'*); *'Darke, dolefull, drearie, like a greedie grave . . .'* op. cit. Book I, canto ix, stanza 33, the last six lines.

132. *Idumea*, or land of Edom. The mountainous desert country stretching south from the Dead Sea to the Gulf of Aqaba, in which the Israelites wandered.

132. *rain never falls* There is abundant rainfall with the prevailing trade winds from January to April, but it percolates through the lava and is soon lost.

132. *Lazarus* Luke xvi, 24.

132. *the wastes of weedy Babylon* 'And Babylon shall become a heap of ruins, a haunt of jackals, a horror and a hissing, without an inhabitant.' (*Jeremiah*, li, 37.)

132. *the outcasts of the beasts* Though Melville is intent on displaying the Galapagos Islands only as hell on earth, their animal life is, in fact, more akin to paradise – a closed, isolated and trusting paradise – as Darwin discovered six years before Melville's visit. There are no carnivores; owls and buzzards (the Galapagos hawks) are the sole bird predators. But separated from the outside world and thus freed from competitive pres-

sures, no competitive intelligence developed either: the cormorants lost the use of their wings and became flightless; the booby bird is eponymous for its incompetence at defending itself against other birds who steal its food and even its eggs; rock crabs scuttle fearlessly over the backs of iguanas; the lobsters are easily caught; the only snake is non-venomous; the albatross is trusting; flamingoes, doves, gulls, antarctic seals, miniature penguins, even the Galapagos hawks, all lack the basic instinct of fear and self-preservation. The male sea-lion is aggressive, in self-defence – a lesson perhaps learnt from sharks met out at sea; but the only combative animals are the herds of wild cattle, dogs, cats, pigs, goats and asses – once domestic, now roaming wild – a situation accurately reflected by the mounting scale of evil perpetrated by the outcasts of men – also domestic once, now roaming wild – in the last five of Melville's sketches.

133. *the* aguano   More commonly *iguana*, the sea or land lizard, measuring from three to six feet, with scaly claws and a dragonish crest of spikes from neck to the long tail. Usually green in colour, the males turn spotted orange and black in the breeding season: 'imps of darkness' Darwin called them. But they are mostly vegetarian, and their flesh, eaten by whalers and buccaneers, is said to taste something between chicken and mullet.

133. *Aracama*   The desert of Atacama, Melville means, a waterless, saline region, part Chilean, part Bolivian, 2,000 feet above sea-level between the Pacific coast range and the Andes.

133. *like the dross of an iron-furnace*   Perhaps a recollection of Darwin comparing the volcanic cones and craters to 'iron furnaces near Wolverhampton'.

135. *Apples of Sodom*   Dissolving, according to Josephus, at a touch into smoke and ashes.

135. *Gallipagos Galápagos*, Spanish for the giant land-tortoises, is found on a map of 1574; *Islas Encantadas*, no doubt due to their strange, shifting currents, on a map of 1589.

135. *Adirondack Mountains*   In north-east New York State.

136. '*Memento* *****'   Despite the five asterisks, clearly 'memento mori'.

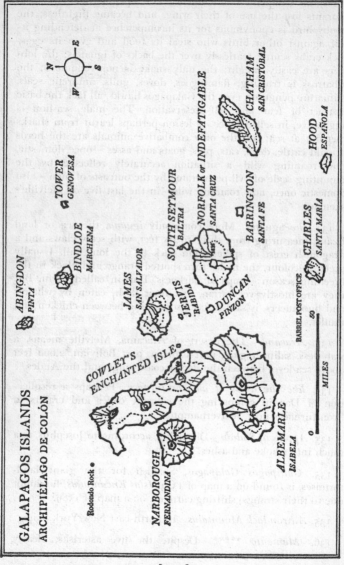

GALAPAGOS ISLANDS
ARCHIPIÉLAGO DE COLÓN

Rodondo Rock •

NARBOROUGH
FERNANDINA

ALBEMARLE
ISABELA

COWLEY'S
ENCHANTED ISLE

JAMES
SAN SALVADOR

JERVIS
RÁBIDA

DUNCAN
PINZON

BINDLOE
MARCHENA

ABINGDON
PINTA

SOUTH SEYMOUR
BALTRA

NORFOLK or INDEFATIGABLE
SANTA CRUZ

BARRINGTON
SANTA FE

CHARLES
SANTA MARÍA

TOWER
GENOVESA

CHATHAM
SAN CRISTÓBAL

HOOD
ESPAÑOLA

BARREL POST OFFICE

MILES
0   50

SKETCH SECOND: TWO SIDES TO A TORTOISE

Quotations: *'Most ugly shapes, and horrible aspects . . .'* Spenser, *The Faerie Queene*, Book II, canto xii, the first five lines of stanza 23 joined to the last four lines of stanza 25 (*'do a man'* is substituted for *'did a knight'*; *'at home'* for *'on earth'*; *'in these isles'* for *'in the seas'*; Melville deliberately by-passes the sixth line of stanza 23 with its magnificent 'sea-shouldring Whales'); *'Feare nought, (then said the Palmer well aviz'd;) . . .'* ibid. stanza 26, lines 1–3, 6 and 8–9 (*'there'* is substituted for *'these'*; *'And'* for *'Tho'*; *'Then'* for *'And'*).

137. *calipee* The lower shell, as opposed to the upper shell or carapace, of the turtle.

138. *bring back whatever tortoises they could* 'Vessels on whaling voyages among these islands generally take on board from two to three hundred of these animals and stow them in the hold, where, strange as it may appear, they have been known to live for a year, without food or water . . .' (Captain David Porter's *Journal*, 1822.)

139. *Ye oldest inhabitants* These land tortoises live up to 400 years, can weigh anything up to 500 pounds, their shells measuring as much as 60 inches across. Charles Darwin rode one, recording a speed of 360 yards an hour.

140. *tortoise steaks and tortoise stews* '. . . the most delicious food we had ever tasted,' wrote Captain James Colnett.

SKETCH THIRD: ROCK RODONDO

Quotations: *'For they this hight* The Rocke of *vile* Reproch . . .' Spenser, *The Faerie Queene*, Book II, canto xii, stanza 8 (*'dreadful'*, line 2, replaces *'detestable'*; and again, in line 6, *'wastfull'*); *'with that the rolling sea resounding soft . . .'* ibid. stanza 33, the first four and last two lines (*'that rare'* replaces *'their rare'*); *'Suddeinly an innumerable flight . . .'* ibid, stanza 35, the last four lines; *'Even all the nation of unfortunate . . .'* ibid, stanza 36.

141. *that mysterious Newport one* The Old Stone Mill of Newport, Rhode Island, variously believed to be a gristmill belonging to a seventeenth-century colonial governor and a Norse tower of the early eleventh century.

142. *called of old by the Spaniards, Rock Rodondo* To be accurate, 'Redonda'.

143. *study the Natural History*, because great schools of tuna, dolphin and whales follow the cool Humboldt Current to the Galapagos, attracted by squids, sardines and the teeming plankton, in their turn attracting cormorants, albatrosses, frigate birds, penguins, etc. Darwin, on H.M.S. *Beagle*, spent five epoch-making weeks in these waters in the autumn of 1835. Since 1964 the Charles Darwin Research Station, a UNESCO-directed study centre, has operated from Academy Bay on the south shore of Santa Cruz (Indefatigable or Norfolk Island).

SKETCH FOURTH: A PISGAH VIEW FROM THE ROCK

Quotation : *'That done, he leads him to the highest Mount . . .'* Spenser, *The Faerie Queen*, Book I, canto x, combining the first lines of stanzas 53 and 55 (*'whence'* replaces *'thence'*). Spenser is referring to Mount Sinai and the Mount of Olives.

147. A PISGAH VIEW 'And Moses went up from the plains of Moab unto the mountain of Nebo, to the top of Pisgah, that is over against Jericho. And the Lord showed him all the land of Gilead, unto Dan.' (*Deuteronomy* xxxiv, 1.)

147. *the Peak of Teneriffe* Largest of the Canary Islands, dominated by Mount Teide, its 12,000 ft volcanic peak.

147. *Daniel Boone* The American frontiersman who blazed the Wilderness Road into Kentucky (1775).

148. *Juan Fernandez* First made famous by Defoe's *Robinson Crusoe*, a book inspired in part by the stay on Más á Tierra (the 'more to landward' island) of the renegade Scot, Alexander Selkirk (1704–9). Selkirk is mentioned in Melville's footnote to *Sketch Seventh*, and 'Crusoe in the self-same sea' in *Sketch Eighth*.

148. *Prior to the year 1563 . . .* This and the following paragraph derive freely from *A Chronological History of the Discoveries in the South Sea* (London, 1803–17) by James Burney, Fanny Burney's brother, who had sailed round the world with Captain Cook.

Fray Tomás de Berlanga, Bishop of Panama, sailing from his see to Peru in 1535, was in fact the first European to discover the islands. There were 'many birds like those of Spain,' the bishop reported in a letter to Charles V, 'but so silly they do not know how to flee, and many were caught in the hand'.

150. *the Kingsmills* Among the Gilbert Islands.

152. *soaring up some five or six thousand feet* Narborough's

crater rises only to 4,900 ft. But the highest volcanic peak on the north coast of neighbouring Albemarle soars to 5,600 ft from sea-level.

153. *his published voyages* Captain William Ambrose Cowley, pilot of the buccaneering ship *Bachelor's Delight*, 'being the first that came to an Anchor there, did give them all distinct Names', re-christening the islands in honour of the royal brothers Charles and James, members of the nobility and fellow cut-throats (1684). His *Voyage Round the Globe* (1699) is singled out as one of the 'three eye-witness authorities worth mentioning' at the end of *Sketch Fifth*.

153. *poet Cowley* Abraham Cowley (1618–67).

SKETCH FIFTH: THE FRIGATE, AND SHIP FLYAWAY

Quotation: '*Looking far foorth into the Ocean wide . . .*' Spenser, *Visions of the Worlds Vanitie*, stanza 9.

155. *three eye-witness authorities* The three sole reliable source-books, Melville insists, are Captain Cowley's *Voyage Round the Globe* (London, 1699), Captain James Colnett's *A Voyage to the South Atlantic and Round Cape Horn into the Pacific Ocean* (London, 1798) and Captain David Porter's *Journal of a Cruise Made to the Pacific Ocean . . . in the Years 1812, 1813 and 1814* (second edition, New York, 1822).

By the late eighteenth century whaling fleets had followed the buccaneers into the Pacific. Captain James Colnett was sent, by the Board of Trade, on the initiative of London merchants, to seek secure fitting and victualling stations 'for the purpose of extending the spermaceti whale fisheries'; after an eighteen-month cruise on the 375-ton sloop, H.M.S. *Rattler*, he established Post Office Bay on Charles Island with a barrel nicknamed 'Hathaway's Post Office'. It was this barrel which the American Captain Porter used to his advantage for information on English vessels and their cargo in the *War of 1812*. It is still in use today. (To complete this history of the Galapagos, begun after Pizarro's conquest of the Incas by Spanish ships caught in the currents off the coast of Ecuador: in 1831 the Creole general José Villamil formed the *Sociedad Colonizador del Archipiélago de Colón* and was empowered by the President of Ecuador to annex the islands; an agricultural colony, renamed *Archipiélago de Colón*, was established on Charles Island, but soon degenerated into a penal colony selling greenstuff to whalers.)

Melville used Colnett at least twice: in the passage on the sugar-cane and coco-nuts washed ashore (in *Sketch First*) and again in the picture of the cosy pirate retreat (*Sketch Sixth*). Porter he had already mined for additions to *Typee* and acknowledges his debt here in the note to *Sketch Ninth*, forestalling charges of plagiarism in his account of the hermit Oberlus. The story of the *Essex* is also closely adapted from Porter's *Journal*, though Melville allows the enigmatic craft to escape, while Porter tells of capturing her later.

Despite his scorn for all other 'barren, bootless allusions', Melville makes use of at least four other 'passing voyagers or compilers': James Burney's *Chronological History of the Discoveries in the South Sea or Pacific Ocean* (5 volumes, London, 1803–17), from which he took, almost verbatim, his account of the pilot Juan Fernandez in *Sketch Fourth*; Captain Amasa Delano's *A Narrative of Voyages and Travels in the Northern and Southern Hemispheres, Comprising Three Voyages Round the World* (Boston, 1817), which contains long summaries of various expeditions to the Galapagos; and the three-volume *Narrative of the Surveying Voyages of His Majesty's Ships* Adventure *and* Beagle (London, 1839), of which the first two are by Robert Fitzroy, Captain of the *Beagle*, and the third by Charles Darwin.

The full set of this record of the *Beagle*'s cruise (1831–6), over fifty of whose pages deal with the Galapagos, Melville may well have seen in the ship's library of the frigate *United States*, on his return home from Honolulu in 1843. Some of his detail and imagery is reminiscent. But Darwin, he must have felt, was too recent a rival to acknowledge, while Delano he must have wished to keep pristine as protagonist for his next long work of fiction.

For it was probably while delving into Delano's *Narrative* in search of more details on the Encantadas, that Melville discovered Chapter 18 and conceived *Benito Cereno*. Thus the *Bachelor's Delight* also bridges both tales.

SKETCH SIXTH: BARRINGTON ISLE AND THE BUCCANEERS

Quotations: '*Let us all servile base subiection scorne . . .*' Spenser, *Prosopopoia, or Mother Hubberds Tale*, lines 134–9 ('*of the earth*' replaces '*of the world*'); '*Lords of the world, and so will wander free . . .*' op. cit., lines 168–9; the prose sentence has not been identified.

156. *Acapulco* In south-west Mexico, chief port in the development of the Philippines.

156. *long Toledos* Finely tempered sword-blades made at Toledo.

157. *well sheltered from all winds* Victor Wolfgang von Hagen, who himself led a scientific expedition to the Galapagos, comments: 'If Melville had actually been to the island of Barrington, he would have instantly seen that that island is not sheltered, as he says, "from all winds by the high land of Albemarle", for Barrington is almost out of sight of Albemarle and a good fifty miles from its eastern side . . . Colnett in his account was actually referring to James Island.' (William P. Wreden: Burlingame, California, 1940.)

157. *a sentimental voyager* Captain James Colnett (see above). The four paragraphs in quotation marks are Melville's improvisation on the following passage from Colnett:

'At every place where we landed on the Western side, we might have walked for miles through long grass, and beneath groves of trees. It only wanted a stream to compose a very charming landscape. This isle appears to have been a favourite resort of the Buccaneers, as we not only found seats, which had been made by them of earth and stone, but a considerable number of broken jars scattered about, and some entirely whole, in which the Peruvian wine and liquors of that country are preserved. We also found some old daggers, nails, and other implements.

'This place is, in every respect, calculated for the refreshment or relief for crews, after a long and tedious voyage, as it abounds with wood, and good anchorage for any number of ships, and sheltered from all winds by Albemarle Isle. The watering places of the buccaneers were entirely dried up, and there was only found a small rivulet between two hills, running into the sea.'

157. *Crébillon* Claude Prosper Jolyot de Crébillon (1707–77), son of the dramatist, and Thomas Gray's almost exact contemporary. He is author of witty, licentious tales, including *Les Egarements du Cœur et de l'Esprit* (1756) and – thus the allusion – *Le Sopha* (1745). ÉÉ

158. *a Dampier* William Dampier (1651?–1715), buccaneer on the west coast of Spanish America and the Philippines. He published two accounts of his experiences, *A New Voyage Round the World* (1697) and *Voyages and Descriptions* (1699),

which includes his masterly *Discourse of Trade-Winds*. Made a naval officer, he commanded an expedition to Australia and New Guinea (1699–1701) and was on both the privateering expeditions in which Alexander Selkirk was marooned and rescued.

158. *a Wafer* Lionel Wafer (1660?–1705?), surgeon, buccaneer, voyager, accompanied Dampier on several expeditions to the West Indies and into the Pacific. In 1699 he published *A New Voyage and Description of the Isthmus of America*, recounting an enforced stay of several months 'among the Darien Indians'. He early advocated a British settlement on the Isthmus for 'a free passage by land from the Atlantic to the South Sea . . . of the greatest consequence to the East India Trade'. (1704.)

158. *Pisco* Peruvian port celebrated for its brandy.

SKETCH SEVENTH: CHARLES'S ISLE AND THE DOG-KING

Quotations: '*Loe with outragious cry* . . .' Spenser, *The Faerie Queene*, Book II, canto ix, stanza 13 ('*So*' replaced '*loe*'; '*him*', line 2, replaced '*them*'); '*We will not be of anie occupation* . . .' Spenser, *Prosopopoia, or Mother Hubberds Tale*, lines 155–8.

160. *a certain Creole adventurer* Von Hagen identifies the Creole dog-king with General Villamil (see above), though he was born in New Orleans and fought not for Peru but for Ecuador in its War of Independence; his first colonists were eighty soldiers under death-sentence for an insurrection. In 1835, when Darwin visited the island, there were some three hundred people tilling the soil. It was Villamil's successor – one Colonel Williams – who flogged the colonists, hunted them down with dogs, and built himself a palace of lava rock. After an uprising and the colonel's flight, the settlement soon disbanded.

Today some three thousand inhabitants, of fourteen odd nationalities, are settled mostly on Santa Cruz (Indefatigable or Norfolk) and San Cristóbal (Chatham Island). Many live in two upland farming communities; the rest subsist on fishing.

160. *Callao* The port for Lima.

161. *their capital city* Cf. 'This part of the island is low and very rugged. We landed upon black, dismal-looking heaps of broken lava, forming a shore fit for Pandemonium.' (Captain Robert Fitzroy, of Chatham Island, San Cristóbal.)

164. *a sea Alsatia* Between the Thames and Fleet Street – once a refuge for debtors and criminals.

SKETCH EIGHTH: NORFOLK ISLE AND THE
CHOLA WIDOW

Quotations: '*At last they in an Island did espy . . .*' Spenser, *The Faerie Queene*, Book II, canto xii, stanza 27 ('*woman*' replaces '*Maiden*' – Spenser's '*dolefull Mayd*' is, in fact, first of the decoys into '*the Bowre of Blisse*'); '*Blacke hys eye as the midnyghte sky . . .*' Thomas Chatterton, *The Mynstrelles Songe from Aella*, stanza 2 (modified); '*Each lonely scene shall thee restore . . .*' William Collins, *Dirge in Cymbeline*, last stanza.

166. *sequestered from the rest* 'Norfolk Island . . . is the Indefatigable Island of today, and instead of being "sequestered from the rest", is in the center of the archipelago, as a cursory glance at a Galapagos map will show.' von Hagen, op. cit.

167. *handspike* Wooden bar, used as lever on ship-board.

168. *Truxill* After Trujillo, the sixteenth-century city of north-west Peru.

180. *the beast's armorial cross* This little vignette brought tears to the eyes of James Russell Lowell, who 'thought it the finest touch of genius he had seen in prose'.

SKETCH NINTH: HOOD'S ISLE AND THE
HERMIT OBERLUS

Quotation: '*That darkesome glen they enter, where they find . . .*' Spenser, *The Faerie Queene*, Book I, canto ix, stanza 35 and the first three lines of stanza 36 ('*glen*' replaces '*cave*'; '*griesly*' replaces '*griesie*'; '*reads*' in the penultimate line, '*was*').

182. *his murphy hill* Early nineteenth-century slang use of the Irish name for a potato.

183. *Sycorax* Mother of Caliban, see Shakespeare's *The Tempest*, I, ii, 258 ff.

186. *Anaconda* The South American boa which crushes its prey.

189. *Guayaquil* The main port of Ecuador.

190. *2d. vol. of Porter's Voyage into the Pacific* The exploits of an Irishman, Patrick Watkins, are mentioned by several voyagers. Captain Porter, following details he received from a Captain Randall of the whaler *Barclay*, whom he had recaptured from a Peruvian privateer, describes his 'ragged clothes, scarce sufficient to cover his nakedness, and covered with vermin; his red hair and beard matted, his skin much burnt, from constant

exposure to the sun, and so wild and savage . . . that he struck every one with horror' (*Journal of a Cruise Made to the Pacific Ocean* I, 131–5).

Oberlus's fiery red hair and 'murphy hill' both derive from this Irishman, who likewise bartered vegetables for rum, kidnapped sailors at gunpoint, and with a crew of five in 1809 left for Guayaquil – reaching the mainland alone.

SKETCH TENTH: RUNAWAYS, CASTAWAYS, SOLITARIES, GRAVE-STONES, ETC.

Quotation: *'And all about old stockes and stubs of trees . . .'* Spenser, *The Faïrie Queene*, Book I, canto ix, stanza 34 (*'knotty'* replaces *'rocky'*).

191. *so many solitaries* As true today. There are perhaps as many as a hundred European misanthropists (mostly Norwegians, Swedes, Germans and Belgians) still scattered around the archipelago, living a churlish life, suspicious of strangers.

193. *Nantucketers* Whaling-ships from the island off Cape Cod, Massachusetts.

194. *U.S. frigate* Essex Captain David Porter's famous ship, see *Sketch Fifth*.

194. *Potter's Field* '. . . to bury strangers in' (*Matthew* xxvii, 7), also known as Aceldama, the field of blood (*Acts* i, 18–19), a suitable last epithet after the tales of Oberlus and of the blood-quaffer.

194. 'Oh, Brother Jack . . .' Captain Porter in his *Journal* records this epitaph he found on Charles Island:

> Gentle reader, as you pass by,
> As you are now, so wonce was I;
> As now my body is in the dust
> I hope in heaven my soul to rest.

THE BELL-TOWER

195. *From a Private M.S.* The three mottoes, which appeared on first publication in *Putnam's Monthly Magazine*, were dropped on reprinting the story among *The Piazza Tales*. The 'Private M.S.' is Melville's own, the sentences possibly being from rejected early draughts. The first of the three links the conception of *The Bell-Tower* to *Benito Cereno*, published two months later.

197. *Anak* 'And there we saw the giants, the sons of Anak, which come of the giants: and we were in our own sight as grasshoppers, and so we were in their sight.' (*Numbers* xiii, 33.) Report of the spies sent by Moses to reconnoitre the land of Canaan.

197. *into Shinar aspiration* The reference to the Tower of Babel attracts further allusions to *Genesis* x and xi. 'The generations of the sons of Noah' include Nimrod 'the mighty hunter': 'And the beginning of his kingdom was Babel, and Erech, and Accad, and Calneh, in the land of Shinar.' (*Genesis* x, 10.) 'And it came to pass, as they journeyed from the east, that they found a plain in the land of Shinar; and they dwelt there.' (*Genesis* xi, 2.)

199. *Fearless as Shadrach* One of the three Jewish provincial governors of Babylon cast into 'a burning fiery furnace' by Nebuchadnezzar. (*Daniel* iii, 12–30.)

202. *Haman* The tyrant who ordered Mordecai to be hanged, but was himself hanged 'on the gallows that he had prepared for Mordecai'. (*Esther* vii, 10.) Richard Chase adds: 'Taken naively, the name suggests 'half man' – and, of course, Herman.' (*Herman Melville, A Critical Study*, ch. 3, p. 123.)

202. *scuttle* Small hatchway with movable lid; originally naval, now (especially in the U.S.) of any trap-door.

203. *the Hour Una* With *The Faerie Queene* fresh in mind from *The Encantadas*, Melville clearly intends this name to carry an echo of Spenser's Virgin Una (or Truth). The full irony of the fatal smile on 'the unchanging face' is not apparent until the prototype of Talus (also from *The Faerie Queene*) strikes down Bannadonna (the 'practical materialist') at the feet of Una (True Religion).

Nathaniel Hawthorne's eldest daughter, incidentally, was also called Una.

203. *Deborah* Introducing a series of allusions to *Judges* iv and v. The Florentine Del Fonca is fictitious.

205. *seemed Sisera's* The Canaanite captain defeated by Barak. Fleeing from battle, he was invited into her tent by Jael. 'Then Jael Heber's wife took a nail of the tent, and took an hammer in her hand, and went softly unto him, and smote the nail into his temples, and fastened it into the ground: for he was fast asleep and weary. So he died.' (*Judges* iv, 21.)

206. *of some Shiloh* 'And the Lord appeared again in Shiloh: for the Lord revealed himself to Samuel in Shiloh by the word of the Lord.' (*Samuel* I, iii, 21.) To the boy Samuel sleeping in the Temple the Lord foretold the ruin of the house of Eli: 'And the Lord said to Samuel, Behold, I will do a thing in Israel, at which both the ears of every one that heareth it shall tingle . . . For I have told him I will judge his house for ever for the iniquity which he knoweth.' (*Samuel* I, iii, 11–13.)

208. *the arms of a telegraph* I.e. semaphore.

209. *Talus, iron slave*

> But when she parted hence, she left her groome
> An yron man, which did on her attend
> Alwayes, to execute her stedfast doome . . .
> His name was *Talus*, made of yron mould,
> Immovable, resistlesse, without end.
> Who in his hand an yron flale did hould,
> With which he thresht out falshood, and did truth
>   unfould.
>
> (Spenser, *The Faerie Queene*, Book V, canto i,
>   stanza 12.)

209. *Albert Magus* Either a misprint or misunderstanding for Albertus Magnus, Saint Albert the Great (*c.* 1206–80). As with 'the blankness of Aracama' or 'Joshua in the vale of Askalon' Melville is generous, but sometimes inaccurate, with his learned allusions. Called *doctor universalis*, Albertus did much to introduce Aristotle's scientific treatises and scientific method to Europe. His botanical observations are recorded in *De Vegetabilibus*. He was the first to produce arsenic in a free form and studied the combinations of metals.

209. *Cornelius Agrippa* Heinrich Cornelius Agrippa von Nettesheim (1486–1535), German physician, remembered for his *De Occulta Philosophia*, a defence of magic.

210. *Prometheus* Guardian spirit of machinists, because he brought fire to mankind. The fallen Titan of the opening paragraph introduces the image. Cf. Melville's curse of engineers ('I'd set them to stokering in Tartarus!') and their fire-breathing locomotives ('Here comes that old dragon again – that gigantic gad-fly of a Moloch – snort! puff! scream!') in *Cock-A-Doodle-Doo!*. *The Modern Prometheus*, subtitle of Mary Shelley's *Frankenstein*, perhaps suggested the figure.

[442]

BENITO CERENO

217. *Captain Amasa Delano* (1763–1823). Melville had delved into Amasa Delano's *A Narrative of Voyages and Travels in the Northern and Southern Hemispheres* (Boston, 1817) while working on *The Encantadas* (see above). Perhaps it was then that he discovered chapter 18, 'Particulars of the Capture of the Spanish Ship *Tryal*, at the island of St Maria; with the Documents relating to that affair', which, in his hands, became *Benito Cereno*. A quotation from that chapter (consisting of an account from the ship's journal, followed by Captain Delano's own first person narrative) will show just how closely Melville stuck to his source:

'In introducing the account of the capture of the Spanish ship *Tryal*, I shall first give an extract from the journal of the ship *Perseverance*, taken on board that ship at the time, by the officer who had the care of the log book.

"Wednesday, February 20th, commenced with light airs from the north east, and thick foggy weather. At six A.M. observed a sail opening round the south head of St Maria, coming into the bay. It proved to be a ship. The captain took the whale boat and crew, and went on board her. As the wind was very light, so that a vessel would not have much more than steerage way at the time; observed that the ship acted very awkwardly. At ten A.M. the boat returned. Mr Luther informed that Captain Delano had remained on board her, and that she was a Spaniard from Buenos Ayres, four months and twenty-six days out of port, with slaves on board; and that the ship was in great want of water; had buried many white men and slaves on her passage, and that Captain Delano had sent for a large boat load of water, some fresh fish, sugar, bread, pumpkins, and bottled cider, all of which articles were immediately sent. At twelve o'clock (Meridian) calm. At two P.M. the large boat returned from the Spaniards, had left our water casks on board her. At four P.M. a breeze sprung up from the southern quarter, which brought the Spanish ship into the roads. She anchored about two cables length to the south east of our ship. Immediately after she anchored, our captain with his boat was shoving off from along side the Spanish ship; when to his great surprise the Spanish captain leaped into the boat, and called out in Spanish that the slaves on board had risen and murdered many of the people; and that he did not then command her; on which manoeuvre, several of the Spaniards who remained on board, jumped overboard, and swam for our boat, and were picked up by our people. The Spaniards, who remained on board, hurried up the rigging, as high aloft as they could possibly get, and called out repeatedly for help – that they should be murdered by the slaves. Our captain came immediately on board, and brought the Spanish captain and the men who were picked up in the water; but before the boat arrived, we observed that the slaves had cut the Spanish ship adrift. On learning this, our captain hailed, and ordered the ports to be got up, and the guns cleared; but unfortunately, we could not bring but one of our guns to bear on the ship. We fired five or six shots with it, but could not bring her to. We soon observed her making sail, and standing directly out of the bay. We dispatched two boats well manned, and well armed after her, who, after much trouble, boarded the ship and retook her. But unfortunately in the business, Mr Rufus Low, our chief officer, who commanded the party, was desperately wounded in the breast, by being stabbed with a pike, by one of the slaves. We likewise had one man badly wounded and two or three slightly. To continue the misfortune, the chief officer of the Spanish ship, who was compelled by the slaves to steer her out of the bay, received two very bad wounds, one in the side and one through the thigh, both from musket balls. One Spaniard, a gentleman passenger on board, was likewise killed by a musket ball. We have not rightly ascertained what number of slaves were killed; but we believe seven, and a great number wounded. Our people brought the ship in, and came to nearly where she first anchored, at about two o'clock in the morning of the 21st. At six A.M. the two captains went on board the Spanish ship; took with them irons from our ship, and double ironed all the remaining men of the slaves who were living. Left Mr Brown, our second officer, in charge of the ship, the gunner with him as mate, and eight other hands; together with the survivors of the Spanish crew. The captain, and chief officer, were removed to our ship, the latter for the benefit of having his wounds better attended to with us, than he could have had them on board his own ship. At nine A.M.

the two captains returned, having put everything aright, as they supposed, on board the Spanish ship.

"The Spanish captain then informed us that he was compelled by the slaves to say, that he was from Buenos Ayres, bound to Lima; that he was not from Buenos Ayres, but sailed on the 20th of December last from Valparaiso for Lima, with upwards of seventy slaves on board; that on the 26th of December, the slaves rose upon the ship, and took possession of her, and put to death eighteen white men, and threw overboard at different periods after, seven more; that the slaves had commanded him to go to Senegal; that he had kept to sea until his water was expended, and had made this port to get it; and also with a view to save his own and the remainder of his people's lives if possible, by running away from his ship with his boat."

'I shall here add some remarks of my own, to what is stated above from the ship's journal . . .

'On the afternoon of the 19th, before night, I sent the boatswain with the large boat and seine to try if he could catch some fish; he returned at night with but few, observing that the morning would be better if he went early. I then wished him to go as early as he thought proper, and he accordingly went at four o'clock. At sunrise, or about that time, the officer who commanded the deck, came down to me while I was in my cot, with information that a sail was just opening round the south point, or head of the island. I immediately rose, went on deck, and observed that she was too near the land, on account of a reef that lay off the head; and at the same time remarked to my people, that she must be a stranger, and I did not well understand what she was about. Some of them observed that they did not know who she was, or what she was doing; but that they were accustomed to see vessels shew their colours, when coming into a port. I ordered the whale boat to be hoisted out and manned, which was accordingly done. Presuming the vessel was from sea, and had been many days out, without perhaps fresh provisions, we put the fish which had been caught the night before into the boat, to be presented if necessary. Every thing being soon ready, as I thought the strange ship was in danger, we made all the haste in our power to get on board, that we might prevent her getting on the reefs; but before we came near her, the wind headed her off, and she was doing well. I went along side, and saw the decks were filled with slaves. As soon as I got on deck, the captain, mate, people and slaves crowded around me to relate their stories, and to make known their grievances; which could not but impress me with feelings of pity for their sufferings. They told me they had no water, as is related in their different accounts and depositions. After promising to relieve all the wants they had mentioned, I ordered the fish to be put aboard, and sent the whale boat to our ship, with orders that the large boat, as soon as she returned from fishing, should take a set of gang casks to the watering place, fill them, and bring it for their relief as soon as possible. I also ordered the small boat to take what fish the large one had caught and what soft bread they had baked, some pumpkins, some sugar, and bottled cider, and return to me without delay. The boat left me on board the Spanish ship, went to our own, and executed the orders; and returned to me again about eleven o'clock. At noon the large boat came with the water, which I was obliged to serve out to them myself, to keep them from drinking so much as to do themselves injury. I gave them at first one gill each, an hour after, half a pint, and the third hour a pint. Afterward, I permitted them to drink as they pleased. They all looked up to me as a benefactor; and as I was deceived in them, I did them every possible kindness. Had it been otherwise there is no doubt I should have fallen a victim to their power. It was to my great advantage, that, on this occasion, the temperament of my mind was unusually pleasant. The apparent sufferings of those about me had softened my feelings into sympathy; or, doubtless my interference with some of their trans-actions would have cost me my life. The Spanish captain had evidently lost much of his authority over the slaves, whom he appeared to fear, and whom he was unwilling in any case to oppose. An instance of this occurred in the conduct of the four cabin boys, spoken of by the captain. They were eating with the slave boys on the main deck, when, (as I was afterwards informed) the Spanish boys, feeling some hopes of release, and not having prudence suffi-cient to keep silent, some words dropped respecting their expectations, which were understood by the slave boys. One of them gave a stroke with a knife on the head of one of the Spanish boys, which penetrated to the bone, in a cut four inches in length. I saw this and inquired what it meant. The captain replied that it was merely the sport of the boys, who had fallen out. I told him it appeared to me to be rather serious sport, as the wound had caused the boy to lose about a quart of blood. Several similar instances of unruly conduct, which, agreeably to my manner of thinking, demanded immediate resistance and punishment, were thus easily winked at, and passed over. I felt willing, however, to make some allowances even for conduct so gross, when I considered them to have been broken down with fatigue and long suffering.

'The act of the negro, who kept constantly at the elbows of Don Benito and myself, I should, at any other time, have immediately resented; and although it excited my wonder, that his commander should allow this extraordinary liberty, I did not remonstrate against it, until it became troublesome to myself. I wished to have some private conversation with the captain alone, and the negro as usual following us into the cabin, I requested the captain to send him on deck, as the business about which we were to talk could not be conveniently communicated in presence of a third person. I spoke in Spanish, and the negro understood me. The captain assured me, that his remaining with us would be of no disservice; that he had made him his confidant and companion since he had lost so many of his officers and men. He had introduced him to me before, as captain of the slaves, and told me he kept them in good order. I was alone with them, or rather on board by myself, for three or four hours, during the absence of my boat, at which time the ship drifted out with the current three leagues from my own, when the breeze sprung up from the south east. It was nearly four o'clock in the afternoon. We ran the ship as near to the *Perseverance* as we could without either ship's swinging afoul the other. After the Spanish ship was anchored, I invited the captain to go on board my ship and take tea or coffee with me. His answer was short and seemingly reserved; and his air very different from that with which he had received my assistance. As I was at a loss to account for this change in his demeanor, and knew he had seen nothing in my conduct to justify it, and as I felt certain that he treated me with intentional neglect; in return I became less sociable, and said little to him. After I had ordered my boat to be hauled up and manned, and as I was going to the side of the vessel, in order to get into her, Don Benito came to me, gave my hand a hearty squeeze, and as I thought, seemed to feel the weight of the cool treatment with which I had retaliated. I had committed a mistake in attributing his apparent coldness to neglect; and as soon as the discovery was made, I was happy to rectify it, by a prompt renewal of friendly intercourse. He continued to hold my hand fast till I stepped off the gunwale down the side, when he let it go, and stood making me compliments. When I had seated myself in the boat, and ordered her to be shoved off, the people having their oars up on end, she fell off at a sufficient distance to leave room for the oars to drop. After they were down, the Spanish captain, to my great astonishment, leaped from the gunwale of the ship into the middle of our boat. As soon as he had recovered a little, he called out in so alarming a manner, that I could not understand him; and the Spanish sailors were then seen jumping overboard and making for our boat. These proceedings excited the wonder of us all. The officer whom I had with me anxiously inquired into their meaning. I smiled and told him, that I neither knew, nor cared; but it seemed the captain was trying to impress his people with a belief that we intended to run away with him. At this moment one of my Portuguese sailors in the boat spoke to me, and gave me to understand what Don Benito said. I desired the captain to come aft and sit down by my side, and in a calm deliberate manner relate the whole affair. In the mean time the boat was employed in picking up the men who had jumped from the ship. They had picked up three, (leaving one in the water till after the boat had put the Spanish captain and myself on board my ship,) when my officer observed the cable was cut, and the ship was swinging. I hailed the *Perseverance*, ordering the ports got up, and the guns run out as soon as possible. We pulled as fast as we could on board; and then despatched the boat for the man who was left in the water, whom we succeeded to save alive.'

There are several more pages on the fight, the voyage to

Conception, and the trial with its official documents. Melville considerably reduced these documents, but more than half of Cereno's deposition is taken straight from Delano.

Melville's basic changes in structure or detail are few: the four elderly oakum-pickers and the six cross-legged hatchet-polishers are his invention; he fused the roles of Cereno's servant, Muri, and the leader of the Negro mutiny, Babo; he added the romantic figure of Atufal, the royal slave in chains (the name he found in Delano); he doubled the number of Negroes on board; and the shaving scene as well as the lunch party which follows, the episodes involving Spanish sailors and Babo's final leap into the boat, are all his additions.

Such changes may well have been influenced by his reading of William Stirling's *The Cloister Life of the Emperor Charles the Fifth* (see note below); so, almost certainly, was the re-creation of Benito Cereno himself, from the first glimpse of that punctilious and pale 'hypochondriac abbot' receiving the visitor aboard his 'monastery' to his end (like the 'anchoritish retirement' of Charles V) in a Catholic monastery on Mount Agonia.

The main outlines of Captain Delano's bluff and self-satisfied character Melville kept, but the self-justification behind his narrative he jettisoned. For the original Captain Delano wrote not only to stress his upright conduct (which to some might have seemed obtuse) but to point a moral: Beware of foreigners; their ingratitude and spite in the face of generosity will amaze you. The original Spaniard, it seems, once ashore, turned against his benefactor to deprive him of rights of salvage.

In his usual manner, Melville changed the ships' names: the *Tryal* became the *San Dominick*, after the patron Saint of the Black Friars seen pacing its 'cloisters' (whose 'inquisitors' racks' are also on board in the shape of settees in the captain's cuddy); the *Perseverance*, the *Bachelor's Delight* (conflating the *Bachelor* and the *Delight*, two ships sighted in *Moby-Dick*, and thus ironically turning Delano's honest sealer into Cowley's buccaneering ship first sighted off the Galapagos).

H. Bruce Franklin (*The Wake of the Gods*, ch. 5, p. 145) ingeniously connects the slave ship's name with the successful and bloody slave rebellion on Santo Domingo. By 1799, the year of Babo's uprising, Toussaint L'Ouverture was extending his rule from Haiti across the whole of Hispaniola. (He conquered the island, but was later captured by trickery and died in a French prison.)

The name *Bachelor's Delight* may also introduce the homo-erotic theme – the sexually lopsided note which seems to lurk behind Delano's predicament. Merlin Bowen (*The Long Encounter*, University of Chicago Press, 1960) shows how the word 'bachelor' was for Melville a half jocular, private epithet for those who see only half truths, or surface truths, like those gentlemen of London's Temple, to whose bachelor imaginations 'the thing called pain, the bugbear styled trouble – those two legends seemed preposterous . . . How could men of liberal sense, ripe scholarship in the world, and capacious philosophical and convivial understandings – how could they suffer themselves to be imposed upon by such monkish fables? Pain! Trouble! As well talk of Catholic miracles. No such thing. – Pass the sherry, sir. – Pooh, pooh! Can't be!' (*The Paradise of Bachelors*, 1855.)

As the gay *Bachelor*, homeward bound, had been 'filled with sperm', so the Christian *Delight*, prayerful for resurrection, had turned a skeleton ship of doom: and both the *Perseverance* and the *Tryal* independently seem marked by these encounters (*Moby-Dick*, chs. 115, 131). But the juxtaposition of the two names acts also as clue to Delano's blithe and self-satisfied Protestant faith, which – whatever the losses – still makes for port, and so 'joyously, though somewhat vaingloriously' home. 'Hast seen the White Whale?' asked Ahab of the gay *Bachelor*'s commander. 'No; only heard of him; but don't believe in him at all,' answered the other good-humouredly.

218. *saya-y-manta*   (Spanish) skirt and shawl.

220. *Ezekiel's Valley of Dry Bones*   Ezekiel xxxvii.

220. *Froissart pattern*   Jean Froissart, the fourteenth-century chronicler.

220. *on a ratlin*   One of the thin horizontal ropes serving as steps to climb up and down the rigging.

220. *a white noddy*   A sea-bird somewhat like a tern, usually soot-coloured, here white as the ironical emblem for the pale Benito Cereno ('caught by hand at sea') and his somnambulistic visitor, Amasa Delano.

221. *Lascars*   East Indian sailors.

222. *picking the junk into oakum*   Old rope untwisted into loose fibre (oakum), used for caulking ships' seams.

226. *Charles V*, king of Spain and Holy Roman Emperor,

retired in 1556 to the monastery of Yuste. H. Bruce Franklin
(*The Wake of the Gods*, ch. 5) convincingly shows how closely
much of the imagery and the detail of *Benito Cereno* is based
on William Stirling's *The Cloister Life of the Emperor Charles
the Fifth* (first published as two articles in *Fraser's Magazine*,
April/May 1851, expanded into book form, 1852, and frequently
reprinted). *Benito Cereno*, he argues, equates the Negro and
the Church by metaphors and references to Stirling's history
and to the Bible: as worldly power, represented by Benito
Cereno, is blighted in the end by the Negro's shadow, so worldly
power, represented by the Holy Roman Emperor, was blighted
by the dark shadow of the Church; 'almost every trait of Cereno
is a trait of Charles'. 'In this allegory,' he concludes, 'the
Catholic Church is embodied by the savage slaves, the slaves
create a skeleton figurehead for the leader of their world, and
the apparent leader of their world – who is like the apparent
leader of the Holy Roman Empire – engages in a Christ-like
pious imposture.'

228. *then numbering over three hundred souls* Reduced to
'one hundred and sixty blacks, of both sexes' in Benito Cereno's
deposition; from Amasa Delano's *Narrative* it appears that the
actual number of slaves on the *Tryal* was half that again, 'with
upwards of seventy slaves on board' – more precisely, seventy-
two.

228. *sacks of mata*, i.e. of Paraguay tea, or Maté.

230. *Baldivia*   Valdivia, Melville means; the city was founded
in 1552 by Pedro de Valdivia.

234. *Ashantee conjurors*   From Ashanti, now part of Ghana.

238. *padlock and key – significant symbols, truly*   H. Bruce
Franklin quotes *Isaiah* xxii, 22: 'And the key of the house of
David will I lay upon his shoulder; so he shall open, and none
shall shut; and he shall shut, and none shall open.' Cf. also
Revelation iii, 7: 'These things saith he that is holy, he that
is true, he that hath the key of David, he that openeth, and no
man shutteth; and shutteth, and no man openeth.'

240. *a true hidalgo*   Originally *hijo de algo*, 'son of something', i.e. a Spanish nobleman.

242. *with a narrow blue ribbon*   Again a reminder of the
religious nature of Cereno's ship: 'And the Lord spake unto
Moses, saying, Speak unto the children of Israel, and bid them

that they make them fringes in the borders of their garments throughout their generations, and that they put upon the fringe of the borders a ribband of blue: and it shall be unto you for a fringe, that ye may look upon it, and remember all the commandments of the Lord, and do them . . .' (*Numbers* xv, 37–9.)

249. *a Caffre guard of honor* Usually 'Kaffir', from the Arabic for 'infidel', used by Arabs for all non-Muslims, but by Europeans in Africa exclusively for Negroes.

251. *whom Ledyard saw in Africa* John Ledyard (1751–89), American explorer. After failing to finance a Northwest Passage expedition, he undertook to walk across Europe and Siberia, arriving at St Petersburg in 1787; permitted to continue across the Urals, he eventually reached Yakutsk, in far-eastern Siberia, before being arrested and sent back. He was planning to explore the interior of Africa when he died in Cairo.

In the original version of *Benito Cereno*, published in *Putnam's Monthly Magazine*, Melville had used the name of Mungo Park, probably with this passage from ch. 20 of his *Travels in the Interior of Africa* in mind:

> 'I do not recollect a single instance of hardheartedness towards me in the women. In all my wanderings and wretchedness, I found them uniformly kind and compassionate; and I can truly say, as my predecessor Mr Ledyard has eloquently said before me:—"To a woman, I never addressed myself in the language of decency and friendship, without receiving a decent and friendly answer. If I was hungry or thirsty, wet or sick, they did not hesitate, like the men, to perform a generous action. In so free and so kind a manner did they contribute to my relief, that if I was dry I drank the sweetest draught, and if hungry I ate the coarsest morsel with a double relish".'

Mungo Park goes on to praise the 'maternal affection' and 'solicitude' of Negro women who 'suckle their children until they are able to walk of themselves'.

If Melville substituted Ledyard's name for patriotic reasons, he could hardly have realized that Ledyard never reached the interior of Africa. Mungo Park, in fact, had considerably adapted his quotation from *The Proceedings of the Association for Promoting the Discovery of the Interior Parts of Africa* (London, 1790); for Ledyard's apostrophe to woman was modified by a disclaimer, 'whether civilized or savage', and his examples of their generosity had been explicitly drawn from Denmark, Sweden, Lapland, Finland, 'unprincipled Russia, and the wide spread regions of the wandering Tartar'.

252. *cat's-paw* Slight breeze perceived by ripples on the sea.

253. *marlingspike* Sharp-pointed iron used for splicing rope, etc.

254. *Gordian knots for the temple of Ammon* There is actually no connexion between the Phrygian conundrum and the Egyptian cult – except Alexander the Great, who severed the one and visited the other.

264. *those hypochondriacs, Johnson and Byron . . . their serving men, the negroes, Barber and Fletcher* This extraordinary statement, false in both emphasis and fact, throws clear light on Delano's warped mentality. For whatever Dr Johnson's relation to his Negro manservant, it was neither central to his life nor exclusive of anyone, let alone 'the entire white race'. Whatever Byron's relation to Fletcher, it was never to the exclusion of a large and shifting staff (which, during the last months, included his Greek page, Loukas Chalandritsanos); and Fletcher, as it happens, was not a Negro at all.

Francis ('Frank') Barber was brought from Jamaica to England in 1750 by Colonel Bathurst (father of Samuel Johnson's close friend, Dr Richard Bathurst) and set free by his will two years later. Johnson took the young Negro into his service a fortnight after his wife's death. Apart from two short separations, and a period at school in Hertfordshire, Francis Barber was with Johnson from 1752 till Johnson's death in 1784. The doctor can hardly have made much use of him as a valet, but he seems to have been kept busy cleaning up after the odd household gathered round his master at Gough Square and later in Bolt Court. Boswell remarks on his 'most civil assiduity'. Barber, by the way, was married – his pretty, white wife causing him some Othello trouble.

According to Mrs Thrale, Johnson always appeared to think of Negroes as of 'a race naturally inferior', but to Frank, a steady favourite, whom in 1759, by adroit string-pulling, he had snatched against his will from the navy – whom 'he looked upon as particularly under his protection, and whom he had all along treated truly as an humble friend' (Boswell) – Johnson in his will left an annuity of seventy pounds (the largest single bequest) and his gold watch. Faithful to the end, Barber retired to Johnson's home town of Lichfield.

William Fletcher, the valet from Newstead, who accompanied Byron from his first journey to Greece and Albania to his death at Missolonghi, was an Englishman. Delano (or was it Melville perhaps?) seems to have confused Fletcher with Edward Trelawny's 'black servant' – an American Negro who spoke French and Italian and had the reputation of an excellent cook and groom. Byron claimed him ('as in the East, it is a mark of dignity to have a negro in your establishment', Trelawny, *Recollections*) for his entourage in 1823, on the voyage from Leghorn to Greece. He was with Byron at Missolonghi and in 1824 returned on the *Florida* with his coffin to England, as John Cam Hobhouse, boarding the ship in the Thames estuary, noted: '. . . there was also Fletcher and Dr Bruno a young Italian physician – a courier – a groom (a black American) & a maitre d'hotel . . .' There is no hint of a closer relationship between this American Negro and Byron.

But the misconception, whether intentional or not, is an oddly Freudian clue to the captain's wishful thinking. For if Delano knew anything of Byron's life, he could hardly have failed to recall – apart from Fletcher, or the American Negro, or a conflation of the two – a whole series of favourites, male and female, all of them 'white'.

270. *Chesterfieldian* A dig at the Earl of Chesterfield (1694–1773), famous for letters to his son and godson on the finer points of style and behaviour. 'They teach the morals of a whore, and the manners of a dancing master,' was Dr Johnson's scornful judgement. (Boswell, *Life of Johnson*, 1754.)

272. *but the hand of his servant* 'But, behold, the hand of him that betrayeth me is with me on the table.' (*Luke* xxii, 21.)

273. *mute as that on the wall*, at Belshazzar's feast: 'and the king saw the part of the hand that wrote.' (*Daniel* v, 5.)

280. *the Jew* Judas.

280. *like the mild light from Abraham's tent* The precise allusion is untraced.

288. *Preston Pans* On the Firth of Forth, where Bonnie Prince Charlie routed the English in September 1745.

305. *more than commonly pleasant* Echoing the original Delano: 'It was to my great advantage, that, on this occasion

the temperament of my mind was unusually pleasant. The apparent sufferings of those about me had softened my feelings into sympathy . . .' etc.

306. *such a shadow* William Stirling (see H. Bruce Franklin, op. cit.) charged the Church with responsibility for 'the vast fields of intellect which her dark shadow has blighted'. To explain the disintegration of the Spanish Empire and of its emperor, he wrote: 'Religion was the enchanted ground whereon his strong will was paralyzed, and his keen intellect fell grovelling in the dust.' (*The Cloister Life of the Emperor Charles the Fifth,* 3rd ed. London, 1853, p. 261.)

307. *follow his leader* ' "Follow your leader!" cried the mate' – Christ's first and last command 'Follow me!' which is also the ironical text for *Benito Cereno*: '*Seguid vuestro jefe.*'

JOHN MARR

John Marr and Other Sailors consists of occasional prose introductions (of which this is the longest and first) followed by verse soliloquies and shorter pieces. *Billy Budd* grew out of a similar experiment in prose and verse: the sketch of an older sailor composing a ballad on the eve of his execution for fomenting mutiny.

311. *the Keys* Chain of coral and limestone reefs forming the southern tip of Florida.

314. *the Siberian Obi* Marshy plain around the Gulf of Ob' in Western Siberia.

315. *if not above the tall tiger-lilies* Cf. 'Go visit the prairies in June, when for scores on scores of miles you wade knee-deep among Tiger-lilies . . .' (*Moby-Dick*, ch. 1) – where the contrast of ocean and prairie serves as a constant rhetorical device.

BILLY BUDD, SAILOR

319. The Dedication: Jack Chase, hero of *White Jacket*, 'was a Briton, and a true-blue; tall and well-knit, with a clear open eye, a fine broad brow, and an abounding nut-brown beard. No man ever had a better heart or a bolder . . . A finer specimen of the island race of Englishmen could not have been picked out of Westminster Abbey of a coronation day.' (*White-Jacket,*

ch. 4.) Like Billy, a foretopman, Jack Chase was 'Captain of the Maintop'; like Billy, flawed by his stutter, Jack Chase was marred only by the lack of one finger. Both, like Dibdin's 'Tom Bowling', were 'the darling of our crew'; or, in one of Dibdin's 'spirited strains':

'Spanking Jack was so comely, so pleasant, so jolly,
  Though winds blew great guns, still he'd whistle and sing;
Jack lov'd his friend, and was true to his Molly,
  And if honour gives greatness, was great as a king.'

(The Sailor's Consolation.)

'Wherever you may be now rolling over the blue billows, dear Jack!' Melville had hailed him, 'take my best love along with you; and God bless you, wherever you go!' For almost half a century he remained true to his memory.

321. *like Aldebaran* 'Eye' of the constellation Taurus.

321. *in Liverpool, now half a century ago* Melville's first experience at sea – shipping as 'boy' to Liverpool in 1839 – is partly recorded in *Redburn* (1849).

322. *Anacharsis Cloots* Anacharsis (né Jean Baptiste) Clootz, born in 1755 of the Prussian nobility, spent a huge fortune on furthering republican ideas. He presented a delegation of foreigners as ambassadors of the human race to the French National Assembly, became a French citizen and was elected to the convention. Distrusted by Robespierre, he was executed in 1794.

322. *a nautical Murat* Joachim Murat (1767–1815), Napoleon's brother-in-law, and made by him king of Naples, was a brilliant and dashing cavalryman.

322. *foot in the Flemish horse* A foot-rope at the yard-arms of topsail yards.

323. *on the Narrow Seas* The English and Irish Channels.

323. *a seventy-four* The *Bellipotent* mounted seventy-four guns; frigates (convoy or reconnaissance ships), thirty-two to thirty-eight guns; 'the three-deckers' (ch. 3), ninety or more guns.

The name *Indomitable* (occurring twenty-five times in the manuscript to six appearances of *Bellipotent*) was an obvious choice for all earlier editors. Hayforth and Sealts, however, following the genetic evidence, argue that *Bellipotent* was Melville's final intention, that he introduced the change in chapter

28 (when the French ship, once the *Directory*, was also renamed the *Atheist*), made the necessary alterations to chapter 18 (the chase of the French frigate), but did not live to complete the corrections throughout the manuscript. Their edition first substituted *Bellipotent* throughout the text as the true and final name of Captain Vere's ship.

326. *hardtack* Ship-biscuit.

326. *Apollo with his portmanteau* H. Bruce Franklin (*The Wake of the Gods*, ch. 7) argues that 'the mythology and rites of the British Druids in large part define both the action and the symbolism of *Billy Budd*'. According to Sir Edward Davies, *The Mythology and Rites of the British Druids* (of which Melville had read an account in Matthew Arnold's *On the Study of Celtic Literature*), 'the most important Celtic god was *Hu*, the "Celtic Apollo", known also as *Beli* and *Budd*,' – *Buddugre*, sun god of victory: it is Billy Budd, sun god and sacred bull, who is sacrificed in time of war (after which the *Atheist* is defeated in battle). Richard Chase (*Herman Melville*, ch. 11) also relates the preoccupation with food and meals and all forms of eating in *Billy Budd* to the theme of ritual murder and eating the Host.

Such interpretations need not be overstrained, but the presence of 'the old Merlin', a Dansker (evoking the riotous world of Hamlet's North), himself related to Daniel Orme (variously called 'Asaph Blood' and 'A Druid'), and the passing allusion to Bede's story of the pagan Britons before Pope Gregory the Great, all suggest that H. Bruce Franklin and Richard Chase, in charting the story in religious and mythological terms, are close to an intention at the symbolic roots of Melville's structure.

Concerning the final name of the 'seventy-four' H. Bruce Franklin writes: 'The first half of *Bellipotent* is a complicated pun combining a Latin word for war, several of the names of Billy Budd's divine Celtic prototype [the Welsh *Beli*, or Irish *Bili*] and the apparent meaning of these names [Death]; the second half suggests that this combination may triumph. Thus the name of the ship is a variant of Billy Budd's own name [victorious death].'

326. *the* Rights-of-man *The Rights of Man* (1791) was Thomas Paine's answer to Edmund Burke's *Reflections on the Revolution in France* (1790).

326. *Stephen Girard*   Girard (1750–1831), wealthy merchant, banker and benefactor of Philadelphia, named his finest ships *Montesquieu, Rousseau* and *Voltaire*. Born in Bordeaux, he first arrived in New York, at the age of twenty-four, as a sea-captain.

331. *Caspar Hauser*   A foundling, Kaspar Hauser appeared in Nuremberg in 1828 with dubious documents and an incoherent account of a mysterious imprisonment. Received with sympathy, he improved in health and his autobiography, written the following year, spread his fame. The Earl of Stanhope took charge of his education, but in 1833 Hauser was stabbed and died of the knife wounds – probably self-inflicted in a psychopathic fit. For Melville, however, this youth reared in apparent isolation had long been a romantic hero, the symbolic outsider unspoiled by civilization.

331. *the good-natured poet's famous invocation*   Martial, *Epigrams*, I, iv, 1–2.

331. *one of Hawthorne's minor tales   The Birth-Mark* (in *Mosses from an Old Manse*, 1846) – the 'visible blemish' being on Georgiana's cheek.

332. *the commotion at Spithead* . . .   Uprisings in the British fleet, begun on 15 April 1797, in the English Channel at Spithead, were repeated on 20 May in the Thames estuary at the Nore, to re-echo in minor mutinies throughout the Mediterranean during July and September. 'One of the most serious of these,' writes Charles Anderson, 'resulting in the execution of three ringleaders, had occurred in the squadron off Cadiz, the locale of Melville's story.' ('The Genesis of *Billy Budd*', *American Literature* XII, November 1940.)

333. *spirited strains of Dibdin*   Charles Dibdin (1745–1814), remembered for his songs and sea-ballads. 'I do not unite with a high critical authority in considering Dibdin's ditties as "slang songs", for most of them breathe the very poetry of the ocean.' (*White-Jacket*, ch. 90.)

333. *William James*   'The subject is a melancholy one and one which we would fain pass over; but historical impartiality forbids any such fastidiousness.' (William James, *The Naval History of Great Britain*, 1860, vol. II, ch. 26.)

335. *such naval magnates*   Don John of Austria, naval commander of the Holy League at Lepanto; Andrea Doria, Genoese *condottiere* and admiral against the Algerian corsair Barbarossa;

Maarten Van Tromp, Dutch commander against Spain and Britain; Jean Bart, French privateer against the Dutch; Stephen Decatur, U.S. commander against the Tripoli pirates and the British in the *War of 1812*.

335. *such craft are unsightly* Cf. Melville's reflections on steamboats and locomotives ('Great improvements of the age!') in *Cock-A-Doodle-Doo!* and machinery in general (practical materialists, 'Benthamites', or Utilitarians) in *The Bell-Tower*. *Billy Budd*, assertively from its opening, is of a 'less prosaic time'.

335. *Nelson's ornate publication of his person* Cf. 'A cock, more like Nelson with all his glittering arms on, standing on the *Vanguard*'s quarter-deck going into battle. . . .' (*Cock-A-Doodle-Doo!* p. 121.)

335. *his sagacious dying injunctions* 'And then, in a stronger voice, he said, "Anchor, Hardy; anchor."' (Southey, *Life of Nelson*.) Vice-admiral Collingwood, on the *Royal Sovereign*, was 'his immediate successor'.

336. *buoying the deadly way . . . as at Copenhagen* '. . . all the buoys had been removed, and the Danes considered this difficulty as almost insuperable, thinking the channel impracticable for so large a fleet.' (Southey, *Life of Nelson*.)

336. *Alfred in his funeral ode* Lord Tennyson, *Ode on the Death of the Duke of Wellington* (1854).

337. *as late as Mansfield* William Murray, Earl of Mansfield (1705–93), became Lord Chief Justice in 1756.

338. *Rodney . . . victory over De Grasse* George Brydges, Baron Rodney (1719–92), defeated the French admiral De Grasse off Dominica in April 1782.

339. *'Appleton House'* *Upon Appleton House, to my Lord Fairfax*. The lines quoted refer to Mary Fairfax, whom Marvell had tutored, and 'the starry Vere' is her mother, Anne Vere Fairfax. 'Denton' was another seat of the Fairfax family, not far from Nun Appleton.

342. *beardless as Tecumseh's* The Shawnee Indian chief, allied to the British in the *War of 1812*, who died in battle, 1813.

342. *the alleged Popish Plot* Supposedly to massacre English Protestants and burn London, 1678. Titus Oates was not only a perjuror, but a pervert: 'in his latter years . . . there was scarcely

a squib or a broadsheet published concerning him which did not contain a mention of his unnatural vices.' (Jane Lane, *Titus Oates*, London 1949, p. 31.)

344. *though the book I cannot recall* His own *White-Jacket*, probably.

344. *at Greenwich, a Baltimore Negro* Cf. Melville's journal for 21 November 1849: 'The negro . . . Walked in Greenwich Park . . . talk with an old pensioner there.'

344. *Camoëns' Spirit of the Cape* Adamastor, Spirit of the Cape of Storms (now the Cape of Good Hope) who appears to Vasco da Gama in Camoëns' *Lusiads*.

347. *Haden's etching* Sir Francis Seymour Haden's *Breaking up of the 'Agamemnon'*, 1870.

350. *the greasy liquid streamed just across his path* That this 'affair of the spilled soup' is contrived to suggest the Handsome Sailor's sexually rousing effect on the master-at-arms is confirmed not only by Claggart's hastily checked ejaculation, or his playful tap from behind – with 'official rattan', not a fan – but his final fall 'like a heavy plank tilted from erectness'.

350. *'with counterfeited glee'* From Oliver Goldsmith's *The Deserted Village*, line 201, describing the schoolmaster ('A man severe he was, and stern to view') with his schoolboys:

> Well had the boding tremblers learn'd to trace
> The day's disasters in his morning face;
> Full well they laugh'd, with counterfeited glee,
> At all his jokes, for many a joke had he . . .

350. *usurping the face from the heart* Cf. Satan's first glimpse of Eden:

> Thus while he spake, each passion dimm'd his face,
> Thrice chang'd with pale, ire, envy and despair,
> Which marr'd his borrow'd visage, and betray'd
> His counterfeit, if any eye beheld.
>
> (Milton, *Paradise Lost*, IV, 114–17.)

As the drummer-boy beholds Claggart, so Uriel spotting Satan:

> Where he first lighted, soon discern'd his looks
> Alien from Heav'n, with passions foul obscur'd . . .
>
> (ibid. IV, 570–71.)

[460]

351. *Radcliffian romance*   Mrs Ann Radcliffe (1764–1823).

352. *an honest scholar, my senior*   One of Melville's many *alter egos.*

353. *Coke and Blackstone*   The famous early seventeenth- and eighteenth-century jurists – Sir Edward Coke and Sir William Blackstone.

353. *the authentic translation of Plato*   In the Bohn edition of 1848–54, vol. 6.

354. *a cool judgment sagacious and sound*   The whole paragraph could stand as an exposition of the role and conduct of Milton's Satan – Melville's paradigm.

354. *'mystery of iniquity'*   2 *Thessalonians* ii, 7.

355. *Chang and Eng*   The 'Siamese Twins' (1811–74), who visited Pittsfield in 1853.

355. *Saul's visage*   1 *Samuel* xvi, 18 and xviii, 8 ff.

356. *but to recoil upon itself*   Cf. Satan's approach to Eden:

> And like a devilish Engine back recoils
> Upon himself; horror and doubt distract
> His troubl'd thoughts, and from the bottom stir
> The Hell within him . . .
>
>   (Milton, *Paradise Lost*, IV, 17–20.)

357. *a rat in a cellar . . . laying little traps*   It was Lieutenant Ratcliffe who had impressed Billy off the *Rights-of-Man*; 'a rat-pit of quarrels' were almost the first words used to him by Captain Graveling. It was of innocence and 'mantraps' the Dansker had pondered; it was with an 'official rattan' that Billy had been tapped; it is of being 'a mantrap' that Claggart will accuse Billy to the captain. As in the earlier tales, Melville's vocabulary still shimmers with an ironic counterpoint.

357. *the scriptural devils who 'believe and tremble'*   '. . . the devils also believe, and tremble'. (*James* ii, 19.)

360. *the afterguard, of whom they have but a sorry opinion*   '. . . according to a contemporary, Admiral Thomas O. Selfridge, who had been a midshipman on the *United States* when Melville served aboard her in 1843–44, Melville himself was stationed in the afterguard rather than the maintop.' (Hayford and Sealts, *Billy Budd, Sailor*, p. 169.)

361. *allotted to the pipe*   Around the galley, where alone smoking was permitted for half an hour after every meal.

363. *a cat's-paw*   Not only 'a light puff of air' but, more equivocally, 'a person used as a tool', especially, among sailors, 'a seaman used to entice volunteers'.

365. *Then would Claggart look like the man of sorrows*   John Claggart's initials, ironically, are those of Christ: a master-at-arms', those of the Man of Peace.

365. *dental satire of a Guise*   The French ducal family who headed the Catholic party against the Huguenots; the third duke, Henri de Lorraine, was mainly responsible for the massacre on Saint Bartholomew's day.

367. *the English squadron up the Straits*   Gibraltar, i.e. the Mediterranean squadron.

378. *the divine judgment on Ananias*   'But Peter said, Ananias, why hath Satan filled thine heart to lie to the Holy Ghost ... Thou hast not lied unto men, but unto God. And Ananias hearing those words fell down, and gave up the ghost.' (*Acts* v, 3–5.)

378. *a drumhead court*   A court-martial, originally held round an upturned drum, for immediate trials during a military operation. Though Vere, it appears later, would have preferred submitting the matter to his admiral, he was overruled by 'a sense of the urgency of the case'; and 'so thinking, he was glad it would not be at variance with usage to turn the matter over to a summary court of his own officers ...' Hayford and Sealts, however, make clear that, according to British naval regulations in effect at this time, the trial was threefold illegal (*Billy Budd, Sailor* pp. 175–83). First, a captain was not authorized to punish a seaman beyond 'twelve lashes upon his bare back, with a cat-of-nine-tails'; any greater punishment required a court-martial; but to convene a court-martial a captain needed the permission of his squadron commander. Secondly, a regular naval court-martial could consist of commanders and captains only. Thirdly, a sentence of death, for crimes other than mutiny, could not be executed 'till after the report of the proceedings of the said court shall have been made to the lords commissioners of the admiralty, or to the commander of the fleet or squadron in which the sentence was passed, and their or his direction shall have been given therein.' (John McArthur, *Principles and Practice of Naval and Military Courts Martial*, 4th ed. London, 1813.)

No wonder the drumhead court 'struck the surgeon as impolitic, if nothing more. The thing to do, he thought, was to place Billy Budd in confinement, and in a way dictated by usage, and postpone further action in so extraordinary a case to such time as they should rejoin the squadron, and then refer it to the admiral.' The lieutenants and captain of marines 'fully shared his own surprise and concern. Like him too, they seemed to think that such a matter should be referred to the admiral.'

This is not to deny that the blow itself was 'according to the Articles of War, a capital crime'. Article XXII, as quoted in McArthur, runs: 'If any officer, mariner, soldier, or other person in the fleet, shall strike any of his superior officers, or draw, or offer to draw, or lift any weapon against him, being in the execution of his office, on any pretence whatsoever, every such person being convicted of such offence, by the sentence of a court martial, shall suffer death ...'

381. *Peter the Barbarian* Tsar Peter the Great, founder of St Petersburg. This use of 'barbarian' is another ambiguous link between Vere and Billy: the Handsome Sailor, like the Negro beaming 'with barbaric good humor', is himself 'a sort of upright barbarian'. But, used of Vere, the epithet turns sour.

388. *the Mutiny Act* The first Mutiny Act of 1689, and its annual successors, applied only to army mutineers and army deserters. The British navy of 1797 operated under a separate act of 1749. It is Melville most likely, not Vere, who was misinformed.

390. *the U.S. brig-of-war* Somers The *Somers* or 'Mackenzie' case of 1842 had long preoccupied Melville (there are two passionate allusions to it in *White-Jacket*); his interest was at least partly due to family involvement. For his cousin Guert Gansevoort, first lieutenant of the *Somers*, had presided over a court not dissimilar to Vere's, under the direction of Captain Alexander Mackenzie, which hung three men – including acting Midshipman Philip Spencer, son of the U.S. Secretary of War – on a charge of mutiny.

The *Somers* case does not seem to have been the genesis of *Billy Budd*; but the last stage of composition (after November 1888), when Captain Vere and the trial scene first evolved, seems certainly to have been influenced by the *Somers* debate, recently revived in the magazines: 'The Mutiny on the *Somers*' (*Ameri-*

can Magazine, June 1888), 'The Murder of Philip Spencer' (*Cosmopolitan Magazine*, in three monthly instalments from June 1889).

Melville, however, was mistaken in thinking that the *Somers* execution was resolved 'under the so-called Articles of War': Captain Mackenzie explicitly declared, 'In the necessities of my position I found my law, and in them also I must trust to find my justification.' (Cf. Harrison Hayford, *The Somers Mutiny Affair*, 1959.) Hayford and Sealts also carefully indicate differences between the *Somers* and the *Bellipotent* affairs – other than those mentioned by Melville: on the *Somers* three men were hanged, not one; Philip Spencer had confessed to plotting a mutiny (the question was: would he have carried it into action? would it have endangered the ship?); and Captain Mackenzie called, not a 'drumhead court', but his officers together to give him 'united council'. On the *Somers*, that is, the prisoners were not arraigned, witnesses were not heard, the defendants were not given a chance to speak, and no formal sentence was passed.

391. *a writer whom few know*   Again Melville.

398. *of Captain Cook's time*   I.e. after 1769, when Captain Cook observed the transit of Venus there.

399. *the prophet in the chariot*   2 Kings ii, 11–13.

400. *for special reasons*   Because of the cruciform structure, it has been suggested, of mainmast and mainyard.

400. '*God bless Captain Vere!*'   Cf. Lieutenant Gansevoort's testimony at the *Somers* Court of Inquiry: 'While I was standing in the gangway near Small he asked me if I would bid him good-bye, and if I would forgive him. He told me that he was guilty and deserved his punishment. I think the Commander said to him, "Small, what have *I* done to you that you won't bid me good-bye?" Small replied, "I did not know that you would bid a poor *bugger* like me good-bye sir." I think the Commander . . . told him that he was sorry he had to take the course he did but that the honor of the flag and the safety of the crew required it . . . To which Small replied, "*Yes, sir, and I honor you for it; God bless that flag!*" '

Whatever Billy Budd may, or may not, have meant by his famous last cry – 'a conventional felon's benediction', Melville calls it – he remains The Handsome Sailor of the ballads to the end. 'These songs,' Melville had written of 'Dibdin's ditties', 'are pervaded by a true Mohammedan sensualism; a reckless acquiescence in fate, and an implicit, unquestioning, dog-like devotion to whoever may be lord and master.' (*White-Jacket*, ch. 90.) So earlier, during his trial, Billy had turned on Captain Vere 'a look in its dumb expressiveness not unlike that which a dog of generous breed might turn upon his master . . .'

403. *But when the tilted plank* So Billy's end echoes Claggart's fall. The Handsome Sailor and the master-at-arms are merged in death.

406. *too early for the Nile and Trafalgar* I.e. Vere died before 1 August 1798.

406. *a naval chronicle* The *Naval Chronicle*, according to Charles Anderson, only began publication in 1799 and lacks any such heading.

408. BILLY IN THE DARBIES A prose sketch of Billy (on the pattern of *John Marr*), introducing an earlier version of this ballad-soliloquy, was the first stage in the genesis of what became *Billy Budd, Sailor*. 'Darbies' means 'fetters' or 'handcuffs'.

408. *A jewel-block* 'Two small blocks suspended at the extremities of the main and fore-topsail yards, through which the halyards of the studding-sails are passed.' *O.E.D.* Not only had Billy been 'the jewel' of Captain Graveling's men, but the pun also echoes the description of Nelson before Trafalgar dressed 'in the jewelled vouchers of his own shining deeds' (ch. 4). Billy too, with 'a sort of priestly motive', had been adorned – in shining white, 'white jumper and white duck trousers' – 'for the altar and the sacrifice'.

409. *the oozy weeds about me twist* Cf. 'The waters compassed me about, even to the soul: the depth closed me round about, the weeds were wrapped about my head.' (*Jonah* ii, 5.)

DANIEL ORME

This last sketch was found in a slipcase labelled 'Manuscript Studies', containing also discarded fragments of *Billy Budd* etc. The heading 'Daniel Orme / & / Omitted of Billy Budd' (as recorded by Hayford and Sealts) proves that Melville intended this to be an independent work, however it derived from the composition of *Billy Budd*. For Daniel Orme, variously called 'Asaph Blood' and 'A Druid', is clearly related to

Billy's 'old Merlin', 'the Dansker'. He too, like Daniel Orme, was a 'mainmastman', 'of few words', with a scar 'cut slant-wise', his face 'peppered blue by the chance explosion of a gun cartridge in action'; he too, like Orme a 'Great Grizzly of the California Sierras', was eccentric, 'ursine'.

The opening paragraphs read:

A profound portrait painter like Titian or our famous countryman Stuart what such an observer sees in any face, he may earnestly study, that essentially is the man. To disentangle his true history from contrasting report is superfluous. Not so with us who are scarce Titians and Stuarts. Occasionally we are struck by some exceptional aspect instantly awaking our interest. But it is an interest that in its ignorance is full of commonplace curiosity. We try to ascertain from somebody the career and experience of the man; or may seek to obtain this information from himself. But what we hear from others may prove but unreliable gossip, and he himself if approached prove fastidiously uncommunicative. In short, in most instances he turns out to be like a meteoric stone in a field. There it is. The neighbors have their say about it, and an odd enough say it may prove: but what is it? whence did it come? in what unimaginable sphere did it get that strange igneous metallic look, the kine now cropping the dewy grass about it.

Any attempt to depict such a character as is here suggested must necessarily be an imperfect one. Nevertheless, it is a man of this description who is the subject of the present essay at a sketch.

Below these two paragraphs Melville drew a line and wrote in the margin, 'Begin here'.

'Stuart' is Gilbert Stuart (1775–1828), the American painter famous for his portraits of George Washington.

414. *Lafitte's marauding crew* Jean Lafitte (c. 1780–c. 1825), pirate operating off the Louisiana, and later Texas, coast, who turned down a British naval commission to fight for the Americans in the battle of New Orleans.

417. *Even admitting that there was something dark* Cf. 'Besides, even if there were a secret closet, secret it should remain, and secret it shall ... Infinite sad mischief has resulted from the profane bursting open of secret recesses.' (*I and my Chimney*, 1856.)